NEITHER HAVE I WINGS

Alice Degan

*This fantasy is dedicated to the memory
of the men and women for whom the
reality was not so easy.*

CONTENTS

Thou shalt not be afraid for any terror by night, / nor for the arrow
    that flieth by day;
For the pestilence that walketh in darkness, / nor for the sickness
    that destroyeth in the noonday.
A thousand shall fall beside thee, and ten thousand at thy right
    hand; / but it shall not come nigh thee.
Yea, with thine eyes shalt thou behold, / and see the reward of the
    ungodly.
Because thou hast said, 'The LORD is my refuge', / and hast made
    the Most High thy habitation,
There shall no evil happen unto thee, / neither shall any plague
    come nigh thy dwelling.
For he shall give his angels charge over thee, / to keep thee in all
    thy ways.

– Psalm 91:5–11

PROLOGUE

I awoke alone and in pain. Both feelings had been alien to me until recently. "Recently" had been alien to me until … My thoughts moved in weary circles like an animal pacing a cage. I was indeed in a cage of sorts, and I was in pieces, or almost in pieces, tenuously filmed together in places by naked will, the whole mess bounded and constricted by a vessel of stone. I felt at once fragmented and compressed.

The other alien thing that I felt was shame. The shame made it difficult to think; it dampened and suffocated my intelligence, which was to say my gift, my self.

I remembered a summons, and a smoky room. *Speak, and I will come to you* … I remembered being surprised and outnumbered. I couldn't recall by what. I knew it had been shameful.

It is good that you are alone, I said to myself in my shame, or my shame said to me—I was so broken that it was difficult to tell. *It would be awful to be seen like this. It would be awful to be apprehended as the weak, flickering thing that you are now. How could you have allowed this to happen?*

I had thought that voluntary unconsciousness—sleep—might help me to repair myself, but it seemed only to have increased my anxiety. That too was shameful.

With an effort, slowly and carefully moving the intelligence that is my self under the blanket of shame and pain that lay on it, I thought about the world outside of the stone vessel. It is full of people who are capable of compassion as well as cruelty. Cruelty had been visited on me over and over again in the preceding … in the time that had preceded—I thought that "months" was the right term for it, but I was not sure. Compassion, I decided, from someone outside myself (though probably from myself as well), was what I needed now. Slowly and carefully I began to think about how I could get it.

Chapter One

AN INTERESTING LIFE

The police sergeant consulted his notebook. "Squadron Leader Boult, I believe?"

"That's right," said Charlie. "What can I do for you?"

"We're here about a suspicious death. The body of a man in his fifties was found in the water off Horrey Head just south of your base. Judging by the condition of the body, he met his death some weeks ago, not by drowning but from a bullet wound."

The sergeant paused, a little too dramatically. Charlie wanted to say that there had been a lot of that going around—bullet wounds—what with the war. He managed to keep this witticism to himself. It was not in very good taste.

The inspector, who had been looking around the officers' barracks rather idly, drew breath to speak, but the sergeant ploughed on before he could, reading from his notes again.

"The victim was in civilian clothes, and the bullet which was retrieved belonged to a .32-calibre weapon, which, as you will know, sir, is not standard issue for any of our servicemen. We are treating this as a murder investigation."

"Right," said Charlie.

"But you can well imagine," said the inspector, with a ruefully confiding air, "after weeks in the water, the poor fellow won't be easy to put a name to. There was nowt in his pocketbook, nowt at all on his person to help us."

Charlie winced sympathetically. "You're wondering if I've mislaid any of my men at around the right time."

"Aye. Around the thirtieth of January, according to what the medical man tells us."

"We haven't lost anyone," said Charlie, "that we can't account for. But January 30 was the day of that crash at Newingthorpe, and they shut down the runways there. We had a lot of extra planes coming our way, including some civilians. I can look at my records, but there won't be any names."

The policemen waited while he found the logs of the days on either side of January 30, and the sergeant copied down the entries. They thanked him, and Charlie watched them walk away toward their car. He wondered if they felt there was something poetically absurd in what they were doing: trying to track down the identity of one particular untenanted body when there were so many in Europe, unclaimed and even unburied.

There was a shaded spot outside the officers' barracks where somebody had set out a couple of chairs, and you could sit there and look away from the grey hangars and the whitewashed barracks and the runways, out over the North York moors, green and brown in the afternoon sunlight. After the policemen left, Charlie stood in the doorway, looking at the chairs and considering the possibility of sitting in one. He had an errand to run, and work to do after he got back, and on the whole he didn't really have time.

Someone had left a newspaper on the seat of the nearer chair, and the latest headline about the end of the war shouted encouragingly up at him as the pages lifted and rattled in the breeze. He thought about the celebrations that would greet the end when it came, but the best he could summon was a kind of wistfulness. He was tired in a way that he couldn't imagine being remedied by any amount of sleep.

Latham came around the corner of the barracks at a stroll, hands in his pockets, curly brown hair blown into an extravagant mess, pale features set in their habitual look of tragic boredom. He was obviously headed for the chairs and the view, but he stopped when he saw Charlie.

"Might as well enjoy the view while you can," said Charlie, leaning against the doorframe. "If you believe the papers, we're not going to be here much longer."

Latham looked out over the moors, hands still in his pockets. "Oh, are we speaking to each other today?"

They were quite alone in the corner of the barracks. Charlie sighed. "Speaking to each other wasn't what we stopped doing, Latham."

"No? Well, I thought it went with the territory. Are you coming or going, or what?"

"Going. I'm on my way down to the Hall to visit Anderson. The men packed up some things for him, and I said I'd take them down."

Latham shuddered exquisitely. "Better you than me. I've never been able to stand hospitals. That reminds me—did I tell you I've had a letter from Ros?"

"No. Have you?"

He nodded, still intent on the view. "She's coming to see me. Apparently she knows the people who own that place. Or knows people who know them. Anyway she's got herself an invitation to come up for a few days. Thought you'd be interested to know."

Charlie rubbed a hand over his face. "Interested. Yeah, I guess so. I'd be interested to know what you're going to say to her."

"But I don't see that that's any of your affair."

"No," said Charlie, looking out over the moor now too. "No, you don't, do you? That's the whole problem."

He left Latham alone with the view, and set off for the hospital with the bag of stuff for Anderson. Lafferty was going that way in one of the jeeps, so Charlie hitched a ride, got off at the gate, and cut across the grounds. The hospital was a converted manor down the hill from the airfield, which was on land that belonged to the estate. It was a hodgepodge of a house, half Tudor and half Georgian. The facade was harmonious enough, in a stodgy way, if you approached from the front, but when you came at it from the side, as Charlie did now, it looked like two different buildings, one of which was trying to eat the other. At the back he spotted a little outbuilding that looked so pristinely medieval it had to be Victorian.

The main entrance in the stodgy facade opened onto a standard-issue Palladian entrance hall, coolly columned and tiled, now set up to serve as the lobby of the hospital. A makeshift reception desk stood under a niche that held a statue of a bored Apollo. The man behind the desk look as bored as Apollo, though that was the extent of the resemblance.

A tall, blonde girl moved through the hall like a knife cleaving the atmosphere. Charlie turned to give her an appreciative stare. This was mostly for the receptionist's benefit; she was the sort of girl it would look odd not to stare at. Having got that over with, he turned back to the man behind the desk.

"Morning. Squadron Leader Boult to see Flying Officer Anderson," he reported.

The receptionist gave him an unfriendly look. "Did you leave your jeep blocking the front steps, or did you pull it around in front of the stables as you're supposed to?"

"Neither. My ride's already left."

The receptionist looked as if he didn't believe him. Charlie wondered what had happened to the dark girl who had been behind the desk the last time he visited the hospital. She had been businesslike, but not actually unfriendly.

A nurse was summoned to take him to Anderson, and Charlie was led into a Georgian drawing-room converted into an administrative office, and through a corniced doorway into the older part of the house. The Tudor great hall, with its flagged floor and dark-beamed ceiling, was being used as the main ward. Two dozen hospital beds lined the panelled walls under tapestries and tall mullioned windows, and the nursing station was tucked under the hood of the great stone fireplace. Not a bad room to be in if you had to spend time on your back staring at the ceiling, Charlie thought, craning his neck to admire it. Anderson was not in his bed, so the nurse led Charlie on, down a narrow service corridor, past a modern elevator which had been installed in a back stairwell, to a library full of beautiful Jacobean woodwork and worn wingback chairs.

"He's still very weak," the nurse told Charlie, pointing him toward a pale figure in a wheelchair near one of the windows. "You mustn't stay long."

Anderson looked not only as if he had lost weight but as if he had shrunk all over. One leg was gone below the knee, and the other was in plaster. Charlie took a peek in the bag he was carrying, and found it contained Anderson's boots along with his service dress uniform. Even the uniform probably wouldn't fit any more, and the boots might make the poor man cry. Charlie extracted the cigarettes and chocolate and the paperback novel that were at the top of the bag, and dumped the bag itself out of sight behind a side table before approaching the window. How stupid of someone to have packed those boots. And it looked like Anderson wouldn't be needing the clothes for a while, either.

But it was a good visit. Anderson seemed happy to see a familiar face, even a little honoured that his commanding officer should take the time to come. Charlie related some anecdotes from the squadron, mostly cheerful stuff, and they talked about the likelihood of the war being over soon.

"Where's home?" Charlie asked, and Anderson told him all about it: a village in the south, the girl he was going to marry, and the hotel that they were going to take over from her parents.

"But you're much further from home, sir. You're Canadian, aren't you?"

"That's right. Our own air force wasn't up to speed when I joined up, so I've been with you boys the whole way. It was my first time in England, coming here in 1940."

"We're glad you came, sir," said Anderson seriously.

The nurse reappeared to frown at Charlie and offer to wheel Anderson back to the ward. Charlie said goodbye and retrieved the bag from behind the table. He waited until the nurse had gone, and then took another door out of the library, not the one that led back to the passage they had come down to get here. He had a half hour to kill before Lafferty would be back to pick him up. If challenged, he planned to pretend that he had gotten lost, but the truth was that he just wanted to look around the house.

He wandered through a number of uninteresting ground-floor service rooms before he found a pokey flight of stairs, and got into trouble. Coming down the stairs as he was about to start up them was the dark-haired girl who had been on reception before. She was young, probably under twenty, but very severely dressed in grey, her curly hair pulled into a tight knot. He assumed she was some kind of nurse, though she wasn't wearing the standard uniform. He tried smiling at her, and she glared down at him. She was very small, and he was six foot three, but she was above him on the stairs, so she glared *down*. He pretended he had been headed for the door to the outside at the bottom of the stairs, and turned away, trying not to look amused.

Outside, he found himself in a large, roughly square courtyard belonging to the old part of the hall. He wandered around admiring the Tudor windows, and walked out through a back gate that looked as though it had originally been the front entrance of the house, before the Georgian additions had reoriented it all to the south. He passed the stables where he had been instructed to park, and found the faux-medieval outbuilding he had noticed before, on the other side of an ill-kept lawn, nestled among the trees at the edge of a fringe of woodland. A gravel path led there from the front-back gate. He walked down it.

For such a small building, the summerhouse—or whatever it was—had entirely too much architecture. There was a crenellated turret, a Perpendicular window, an oriel, gables, gingerbread, and Romanesque chimneys rising up out of an Italianate tiled roof. It was like a fever-dream of Victorian medievalism. Charlie didn't know whether he hated it or loved it.

A new-looking padlock hung from a rusted loop on the door. Charlie tugged it, not expecting any result, and was startled when it fell open in his hand. Serendipity, he thought. He nudged the door open and went in.

It was disappointing, of course; it was being used as a storehouse for garden furniture and croquet sets and things under sheets. But it was dark and tranquil, and he was tired and had time to kill. There was a bench near the door, where he sat and stretched out his legs. He realized it had been a long time since he had been alone on the ground. Being alone in the sky was quite different: louder and more tense, not so easy to think. He wasn't one of those pilots who was crazy about flying. It had certainly been a fine way to spend the war, and he might miss it when he was back home, but he didn't think he was going to write poetry about it or anything. He planned to go home and go on much as he had before.

He thought about that. Most of the men in his squadron prob-ably wanted to do that, thought they were going to do that, and for many of them it was just wishful thinking. There were the ones who had been wounded, like Anderson, who would never be whole. Then there were the ones who had lost people: families killed in the Blitz, girlfriends who had got engaged and married to other men. Even the men who thought they were just going to go back to their old jobs—whose employers had had to find ways to make do in their absence—might be disappointed. But there was no reason why he should be. He was uninjured, worked for himself, had no family, no girlfriend. He would go back to his life in Toronto: the good, well-ordered life that he had been living. He wouldn't pine for airplanes, and he wouldn't pine for anything else, either.

In a month he would be 35. By that age you should have a few things sorted out, and Charlie thought that he did. Recent evidence to the contrary notwithstanding.

He heard the door open and close. He opened his eyes. It was the little black-haired nurse, or whatever she was. She had stopped just inside the door, looking at him with surprise.

"I am sorry to disturb you," she said quickly. She spoke with some kind of foreign accent, light and pretty. "You came in here to pray."

"Um, well. To think," he admitted. He suppressed the instinct to get to his feet. She was no longer on the stairs, and he didn't want to tower over her. "But that's—that would be a good idea."

She nodded curtly. "The best idea, always."

He grinned, and this time she smiled restrainedly back.

"But I shouldn't be in here, should I?"

"No," she admitted. "It should be locked—it usually is. I came in to see …" She let her voice trail off, as if embarrassed by her mistrust.

"I'm not making off with the croquet mallets, don't worry. I'll get out if you want."

"No, that is all right." She smiled again. "I will leave you to pray."

She went briskly out, leaving him alone in the dim interior, and he thought, well, after that how could he not at least try to pray?

So he tried, closing his eyes again and opening his mind, half-heartedly at first, because he wasn't sure how honest he was prepared to be with God about his current situation, about how similar it was to a lot of past situations … And without warning he was aware that he was not alone in the little building.

It was totally different from the arrival of the black-haired nurse, whom he'd simply heard opening the door. This wasn't a noise, and he knew that when he opened his eyes, he wouldn't see it. This thing—whatever it was—had been there all along. And it was crying, very softly and faintly, for help.

He opened his eyes and sat for a moment longer on the bench, his muscles rigid. He knew where the thing was, and finally he made himself look at it.

It was on the other side of the room, beyond a stack of wicker chairs and an old suitcase. It was a wooden crate, nearly but not quite the size of a man, set on the floor under the window, with smears and footmarks in the dust around it, showing that it had been placed there, or at least interfered with, recently.

Every new mission he had flown, every time his plane's wheels had left the runway, he had been in the habit of thinking, *Suppose this is it. Well, I'm still young, but no one could say I haven't lived an interesting life.* He would take that private satisfaction with him into the sky.

But there was one thing in that interesting life that stood out from the rest of the narrative—and at the same time was folded more deeply into it, because it wasn't a thing you could talk or even think straightforwardly about. It was a formative experience of his youth, but he hadn't thought anything like it would ever happen to him again. He got to his feet and stepped around the piled furniture to look down at the crate, knowing he had been wrong.

※

The wooden box was an outer shell around another box made of something that he guessed was alabaster. The word *sarcophagus* suggested itself distastefully. The lid, which had been broken and repaired, was carved with a busy mythological bas-relief. It had a grubby, shopworn look to it.

The stone box fit tightly inside the crate, and it took Charlie a few tries to get enough of a purchase on the lid to ease it up. The voice from inside the vessel—if "voice" was even the right word for something so faint and vague—had ceased, and it would have been easy at this point to convince himself that he had imagined it. He hadn't the least interest in doing that.

"Just give me a sec," he said under his breath. "I am *gonna* get this open."

As he said this, the lid became easier to lift, and he realized this was because it was being pushed from the inside. He slid it carefully off to one side, balancing it on the edge of the crate, then lifted it off and laid it gently on the ground.

He looked down on the open box. The interior was roughly carved and plain. There was something inside, but he could not properly look at it. It was too bright, and too smoky, and—somehow—too many things at once, like a shattered mirror reflecting a confusion of images.

He felt a slight, gentle touch in his mind, a question slowly and carefully posed:

What

do

I

look

like

to

you

?

He was not aware that he had answered the question, but the smoky, fragmented light began to resolve itself, after a little, into something else: a human form. For a moment it glowed from within, an apparition; then abruptly it was solid and really there, filling up the alabaster box, squashed and crammed down into it. The light extinguished, it was darker now in the room, too dark for him to see clearly at first.

It was—it looked like—a young man, and it was in very bad shape. The long, supple white hands were torn and freshly bloodied, and a trickle of blood ran down from one corner of the parched lips. Heavy curls of bright red hair fell back from the white face. The features had a childlike softness, yet it was an adult face, serene and beautiful. The eyes were closed. The body lay twisted, knees drawn sharply up on the left, because the box was not long enough for him to lie flat. He was vested as a deacon, with a red stole, thickly embroidered in gold, lying across his chest, and a red cope around his shoulders, but he was barefoot, which would never have gone over at any church Charlie had attended. The front of his alb was stiff with blood.

Crushed and packed into the box around him were a lot of blood-red feathers—huge, long feathers, patterned with iridescent eyes like a peacock's tail, but bent and broken and stained with actual blood, dried dark and muddy.

The chain that fastened the red cope had ridden up so that it was tight across the young man's throat. Automatically, Charlie reached in and slid two fingers gently under the chain to loosen it. The young man's eyes opened. They were a smoky grey, unexpectedly human, and they squinted up at Charlie with the guarded look of someone who expects pain.

"It's okay," Charlie said, carefully slipping the hook at the end of the chain out of its mooring—though it was doubtful he could have noticed the cope choking him, with his other injuries. "I'm not going to hurt you."

The guarded look gave way to a kind of exhausted relief. It was plain that he didn't have the strength to sit up, much less get out of the box. Charlie leaned over the box and reached in to lift him. He slipped one hand under the young man's neck, trying hard not to touch the feathers and not to think about what they were. But they shuddered and moved as he touched the body, confirming—sickeningly—what the crushed shape on either side had been. Charlie froze, teeth set. The smoke-grey eyes looked up into his for a moment. The young man moved his shoulders effortfully back, as if shrugging off something heavy, and the broken wings fell away into nothing. His eyes rolled upward and shut, and his head dropped back and clunked against the bottom of the box.

"Shit," said Charlie.

He got his forearm under the young man's shoulders now, and

his other arm under his knees, gathering up the red cope with him, and lifted him out of the box without too much difficulty. He was not small, but he was slight, just a bundle of loose limbs in his bulky vestments. Charlie carried him across to the bench under the window where he had been sitting, and laid him down, still cradling his head and shoulders, the red hair spilling over the sleeve of his jacket. He looked down at the unconscious face for a moment. He thought, *This is probably very stupid*, but he did it anyway: he touched the white throat, slipping his fingers under the folds of the amice and pressing them there until he could feel, faint and slow, a heartbeat. *Well, of course. What was he going to be—dead?*

There were several long rents in the bloodstained front of his alb. Charlie gingerly lifted the torn cloth open with a finger to see whether he could assess how badly the young man was injured. What he saw was horrific. He quickly withdrew his hand.

He was going to slip his arm out from under the young man's neck, but before he could do it, the grey eyes opened again, and then Charlie didn't like to move for fear of hurting him.

"It's okay," Charlie whispered. "It's gonna be okay. I've got you. Nobody'll hurt you or put you in a box again on my watch." His diction had become rough, something that always happened when he made an effort to be gentle. "We clear on that?"

There was a tiny spasm in the white face that he took to mean, "Yes." In fact, it looked as though it might have been an attempt to smile. Charlie's grip on the slight body tightened, and he smiled in return.

"That's right. You know you can trust me, eh?"

This time the young man made a definite attempt at a smile, and even managed to raise one red eyebrow slightly. Charlie felt the compassion and awe that already filled him make way for something like plain affection. This was so surprising under the circumstances that he almost wanted to laugh aloud.

His greatcoat was draped over the back of the bench, and he

took it now and bundled it up to tuck under the young man's head, gently withdrawing his arm.

"That okay?"

"Mm." It was the first sound the young man had made, and it was just somewhere between a sigh and a grunt, but it was thrillingly musical.

"Can you talk, at all?" Charlie asked.

Apologetically, the young man opened his mouth, just long enough for Charlie to see that his tongue was gone. His mouth was full of dried blood.

"Oh, God. How did that … Yeah, I'll maybe just ask you yes-or-no questions, huh? It looks to me like you've been … " What? Carved up? Gutted? "Pretty badly hurt. Do you need, um, medical attention? We are at a hospital."

Slightly but firmly he shook his head.

"You'll heal on your own, eh? Because you're not … you're not human, so … that kind of makes sense. And you don't want anybody else knowing about you, maybe. Yeah? So is the most helpful thing I could do—would it be getting you the hell out of here?"

"Mm-*hm*." It was faint but emphatic.

"You got it," said Charlie.

Chapter Two

THE AWFUL DECLINE

Evvie closed the file drawer and looked out the window. The view was depressing. In late summer, when the heather bloomed, it covered the landscape in a delicate purple fuzz that was quite pretty. Now, though, in March, the plants were a carpet of brown lumps, giving the moors a mangy, desolate appearance. And it was cold. So cold. Cold indoors, in the draughty old house with its rattling windows and big rooms and tiled floors, cold outside, where the wind scoured across the upland. Evvie wore thick socks inside her sturdy shoes, and a woolly cardigan over her plain grey dress, and kept a cup of hot tea on her desk when she worked in the office, partly to drink, partly to cradle in her hands to warm them. In the evenings she remembered with homesickness the sun dropping golden into the Aegean, its last warm light gleaming on whitewashed walls as the bells rang for Vespers.

The police had been there that morning. A man's body had been found in the water off Horrey Head. He was nobody from the hospital—that had been easily established—but it was an unsettling beginning to a day that would have had a cloud over it anyway.

There had been another suicide attempt overnight. This one had been very feeble: not so much an attempt, Evvie thought, as an attempt at an attempt. Sergeant MacGregor had been found by the duty nurse sitting in the anteroom by the supply closet with a handful of pills and a glass of water. Just sitting there—trying to work himself up to the deed, perhaps, or already thinking better of it, it wasn't clear which. But the fact that he'd been able to get into the closet, which was kept locked ever since Rutger's second, successful attempt, was bad enough—and a bit of a mystery. MacGregor wasn't able to give a very good account of himself, but as far as anyone could tell, he must have got a key from somewhere, since the lock hadn't been broken. Everyone was on edge that morning, and when Evvie saw Josephine Good bearing down on her clutching a tract with the title SUICIDE: IS IT A SIN? she found herself pointing to the door and saying quite fiercely, "Out!"

Miss Good gave a surprised little jump and stared at Evvie for a moment, and for a moment Evvie considered backing down apologetically. It was unlike her to bark orders at people, even people whom she disliked as much as Josephine Good. But something prompted her to stand her ground and fold her arms sternly, and in another moment Miss Good had turned on her heel and scurried out the way she had come.

Lady Rathburn came into the office, interrupting Evvie's reverie. Evvie pushed herself away from the file cabinet and plopped down at the little desk in the corner that she had claimed for her use.

"You look like you could use a break," said Lady Rathburn, pulling out the chair behind her own desk.

"Do I, ma'am? I'm sorry—I didn't mean to."

Lady Rathburn smiled. "It wasn't a criticism. Why don't you go see what Rosalind and Daphne are up to? They were in the billiard room looking bored a little while ago. They can't be too comfortable with all this talk of murder and suicide going on. Well! It isn't easy for any of us."

It was an ambiguous suggestion. Evvie wasn't sure whether Lady Rathburn was mostly concerned that she should take a break and amuse herself, or that she should entertain the two female guests. Either way, she wasn't enthusiastic about it.

Rosalind and Daphne had arrived at the house the day before, along with Ernest, a friend of Lady Rathburn's nephew Leo. Ernest had been a frequent visitor in the year Evvie had worked at Adderley Hall, and Leo lived there, but the two women were new.

"It will be nice for you to have some female company your own age," Lady Rathburn had said to Evvie at the time.

And it might have been—the six nurses who staffed the small hospital, all hand-picked by the head physician, Dr. Sheppard, were women of Evvie's mother's generation. Evvie had liked the look of Rosalind when she saw her at dinner the night before; she was a thin, freckled girl with limp dark hair and a hopeful expression. But she was accompanied by her cousin Daphne: older, fashionably dressed, stunningly beautiful, frostily disdainful of the world. Evvie didn't know how to talk to someone like Daphne, wasn't sure that she really counted as "company of her own age," and was sure Daphne would not wish to be so described.

It was love that had brought both women to Adderley Hall, apparently. Rosalind had a fiancé in the RAF, whose squadron had been moved to the Adderley base a few months ago, and Daphne was engaged or betrothed or somehow connected to Ernest.

They weren't in the billiard room when Evvie looked for them there, and they weren't in the long gallery upstairs. She found them, finally, in the courtyard, sitting on the edge of the dry fountain. Rosalind's feet dangled, and she looked chilly and awkward. Daphne was tall enough to perch on the edge of the fountain with the toes of her elegant shoes still on the flagstones, and she had a shawl, not a flimsy, gauzy thing but a lush, substantial rectangle of bright red, tossed casually around her shoulders. Rosalind was smoking; Daphne was not.

Daphne was talking as Evvie approached, in a cool, authoritative tone.

"What happens to ordinary couples is a kind of emotional erosion. It starts with some little thing that seems harmless at the time, and then before they know it their love has been eaten away and there's no solid ground left beneath their feet. It won't happen that way with me and Ernest because I am on guard every moment against it. Lately I have had to be even more vigilant. I ask myself, *Is this the thing that will begin the awful decline?* But then Ernest proves the solidity of our love, and it's all right again. But that's what you have to do. That's what it's like."

She really was beautiful. Her blonde curls, tighter than Evvie's, were pinned into an artless-looking cascade, so that they bounced when she moved. Her skin was porcelain-white, her figure like an hourglass. She was dressed very simply in white, and made up very simply, and wore hardly any jewellery. Clearly she knew that she didn't need to. It was this, rather than anything about her face, that made Evvie think she was in her thirties rather than her twenties. She was too coolly confident in her own beauty to be very young.

"It's rather rotten," said her cousin. She sucked at her cigarette and darted a glance at Evvie, as if wondering whether it would be a good moment to include her in the conversation. But Daphne had apparently decided not to.

She went on: "He was married when we first met, to this conventional little woman. Of course *in a sense* he's still married to her. But what I meant was that in those days he was really married— emotionally married, you know, married in his heart. Now it's just a legal thing."

"I see," said Rosalind. Evvie, deeply shocked herself, willed Rosalind to look horrified, and was disappointed when she did not.

"But you see," Daphne concluded. "*she* wasn't on her guard. That was why she lost him."

"Right," said Rosalind. "Hello, Evie! It is Evie, right? Or …"

"It's Evvie," said Evvie. It felt petty to insist, but she had never liked the idea of people thinking that her given name was "Eve."

"Oh, yes. Sorry! You've met my cousin Daphne, right?"

"Last night," said Daphne. "You were there."

"She was giving me advice about life," said Rosalind. "Apparently I need it. Cold out, isn't it?"

"Yes," said Evvie. She wondered what Rosalind had done or said to make Daphne think she needed that kind of advice.

Rosalind said, "Leo told me his aunt doesn't like smoking in the house. Cigarette?"

"No, thank you."

"Oh, you probably don't smoke! That's good." Rosalind put her cigarettes away and looked ambivalently at the one in her hand.

"You could, though," said Daphne, giving Evvie an appraising look. "I can't—it's terrible for my skin. But you're quite dark."

"She has a lovely olive complexion," Rosalind blurted hastily. "And—and an accent. You must be from somewhere. Somewhere interesting, I mean."

"I'm from Greece originally, but I've lived in England since I was ten." Except for those nine beautiful months in 1940.

"But you still have an accent," Daphne observed.

"So I am told."

She smiled at Daphne. She hated being reminded of her accent, and couldn't understand why people thought it was an acceptable thing to comment on. But it was funny: she could tell that Daphne was being deliberately rude, whereas Rosalind was just awkward. But Daphne's cattiness bothered her much less than Rosalind's gaffe. Maybe it was because she could never have pictured being friends with Daphne, but Rosalind had seemed like a good prospect.

They sat in awkward silence until Rosalind had finished her cigarette and hopped down from the edge of the fountain.

"I'm frozen," she said. "Let's go in. What is there to do around here, Ev?"

"She works," Daphne pointed out, as if she thought the idea was in rather poor taste.

"Right, but when you're not working?"

"Generally at this time of year when I'm not working, I find a seat as close as I can to a good fire and work on my embroidery, or I curl up in my bed with a book," said Evvie, shaking out her skirt.

Daphne was looking at her as if she hadn't expected to hear such a long sentence from her lips.

Evvie said, "They have a very good library here."

"We saw it already," said Daphne. "It was full of sick men."

"Well," said Evvie, deadpan, "this is a hospital."

Rosalind giggled, and Daphne gave her a poisonous look. They went in by the side door that led to the kitchen area.

"Nymphs!" cried a man's voice.

Evvie looked up and saw Ernest and Leo coming around the corner from the kitchen, with plates of food they must have got from the pantry. The two men had gone on a drive together that morning, leaving after the police finished questioning everyone, and missed lunch. It was Ernest who had greeted them.

"Nymphs?" Leo repeated sceptically.

"What else would you call them?" Ernest asked, around a mouthful of cold pie.

Both men were in their late thirties. Leo was fair-haired and probably would be considered handsome by people who admired that kind of sharp-featured, thin-skinned look. Ernest, by contrast, was one of those men on whom ugliness conferred distinction. He had a jutting jaw and pock-marked cheeks, a stringy, restless, muscular body, and a kind of magnetism that was hard to explain. In civilian life he had been some kind of artist. He wore his army officer's uniform, as usual, though he had not been on active duty for more than a year. He tried to give Daphne a kiss, but she dodged away from the pie, while somehow managing to convey a teasing sexuality rather than fastidiousness. She was very good at it.

"I don't know that I quite like being called a nymph," said Rosalind with a smirk. "It doesn't sound quite decent."

Evvie wanted to point out that they were very obviously only honorary nymphs, but felt that if she said so in front of Ernest she would trigger an outburst of gallantry that she would find embarrassing.

With Leo, the danger was just the opposite. It was no good trying to fish for a compliment from Leo. He'd been in a bad mood after the police arrived, and the drive didn't seem to have cheered him up at all.

"Come on, Ernie," he said irritably. "Let's go eat."

"I'm going to my room to take a nap," Daphne announced sultrily.

Evvie watched the way Ernest looked at her, and thought about his wife. *Now it's just a legal thing.* Did it seem like "a legal thing" to *her*?

"Did you want to go to the library?" Evvie asked Rosalind, when both Daphne and the men had departed, in opposite directions.

"Sure," said Rosalind with a shrug. "Though I'm not much of a reader."

The library was in the old part of the house, in the north range at the back, and Evvie liked it, although it was as cold as the rest of the manor. She found them a window-seat at one end.

Rosalind leaned her head against the many-paned window. "Why are there so many amputees here?" she asked. "It seemed like almost everyone at dinner last night was *missing* something."

"It's a specialized hospital. For the treatment of amputees."

"How grisly!"

"Not really. They don't *do* the amputations here. They do rehabilitation and prosthetics. It's actually a calm kind of hospital—especially for wartime. Hardly anybody dies here. More or less everybody's on the mend. But keeping up morale is a challenge."

"And what do you do?"

For a moment she wanted to say that she was in charge of digging little graves for all the severed limbs, but she wasn't sure that Rosalind would appreciate being made fun of in that way.

"File things and fold laundry, mostly. Officially I'm Lady Rathburn's assistant. I'd wanted to join the WAAF, but my parents didn't care for that idea—probably sensible of them, as they know I'm not really very mechanically minded—and they found this situation for me. My stepfather was at school with Lord Rathburn. He heard that Adderley was being turned into a hospital and Lady Rathburn was looking for a girl to help with the administration."

The only thing Rosalind could come up with to say to this was: "Would they have let you in the WAAF? You're not English."

Evvie looked at her for a moment to see if she would think better of that. "I'm a naturalized subject, actually. And you know that Greece has been on the Allied side since the beginning of the war."

Rosalind looked as though maybe she hadn't.

"Well, anyway," said Evvie, "helping to administer a hospital isn't glamorous, as war work goes, but it is useful."

"Oh yes," said Rosalind. "I expect so."

And Evvie, who had been hoping to goad Rosalind into saying something about how she wished she herself could be useful, felt simultaneously disappointed in her for not being goaded, and guilty for doing the goading.

Across the library, she saw a tall RAF officer who had been visiting one of his men leaving by the wrong door.

"I think that man is going to get himself lost," she said. "Will you excuse me?"

"Oh sure," said Rosalind. "You've got work to do."

And as Evvie left, she wondered if she hadn't succeeded in making her feel bad after all.

This, on top of the unpleasant encounter with Daphne, and the cold, and everything else, put her in a cross mood, so that when she finally did find the tall airman—he must have got himself spectacularly lost—she glared at him quite fiercely, although he was doing nothing more untoward than coming up the back stairs. Of course, he had no business being there, and something about the look on his face told her that he knew that, and suggested that maybe he hadn't been lost after all. He was a big man, good-looking in a tough, unassuming way, with black hair combed back and eyes and skin as dark as her own, though a different, warmer hue. She found him intimidating, though she was pretty sure he was trying not to be. He turned away toward the back door, as if that had been his original intention, but she didn't believe it.

She went on down the stairs and back into the library, but by this time Rosalind was gone. Instead she found herself waylaid by Ben Sherwood, one of the civilian patients, who wanted someone to complain to about being forced to give up his private room to accommodate Leo Rathburn's guests. Ben Sherwood had been a cricketer and a conscientious objector, and had lost his left hand in an accident only loosely related to the war, and he would tell any-one who stayed within earshot for long enough how unfair all of this was, how the hospital where he was initially treated shouldn't have amputated his hand in the first place—he had the word of a Harley Street specialist who was his personal friend—and so on. It was his way of coping with a terrible situation, Evvie could see. She couldn't blame him for being miserable; it was just hard to agree with his implied assessment that of all the people under that roof, he was *the most miserable*.

She escaped Ben Sherwood by pretending that she had to go help take in the laundry that was drying on the north lawn, but of course it was still wet, and so she was left standing by the overgrown back drive with nothing to do. Her mind returned to the odious things that Daphne had been saying about love. *Is this the thing that will begin the awful decline?* How terrible to feel one had to watch one's beloved every day like a hawk, waiting for some sign that his affection was waning. Was that really what it was like? What if I behaved like that? Evvie thought. *This thing that's happened, does it mean that you don't love me? Does it? Does it?* It would be the worst kind of sin.

That was when she noticed that the door to the lodge was stand-ing ajar. The lodge was a funny little building at the back of the house, beyond the stables, where the gardener used to store his tools in the days when there had been a gardener at Adderley, before he had joined up. Now it was largely unused, although Leo and Ernest sometimes went in there.

Evvie had a moment of déjà-vu as she walked down the drive toward the lodge. Hadn't she done something like this before? Yes, she remembered going out here one night last summer while the full blackout had still been on, because there had been a light. What had happened after that? She couldn't recall.

She pushed the door open and looked in. The dark-haired airman from the stairs was sitting just inside the door, and she saw him as soon as she stepped inside. Unfortunately, he opened his eyes and saw her too. She was surprised into saying the first thing that came into her head.

"I am sorry to disturb you. You came in here to pray."

At least, she thought as she went out, closing the door carefully behind her, he did not seem to think she had been following him. Or if he did, he wasn't interested, bless his heart.

After that she decided that she had loitered uselessly about the house and grounds long enough, and Lady Rathburn could not object if she went back to work. She found Archie at the reception desk, and asked if he wanted a break—a good bet, as he almost always did. She took over his chair and found the embroidery that she had left in a drawer of the reception desk the last time she had taken over for Archie, and settled down to work while Archie lounged off to have a cigarette.

She was working on a monogram for Wing Commander Stewart, a complicated design involving an airplane and the lion from his family crest. It kept her happily occupied until Archie returned. He came back followed by Leo, who seemed to be trying to pick a fight with him.

"I *did* park it in front of the stable," Leo was saying angrily. "I *never* leave it out front! What the hell did you mean by moving it?"

"I didn't touch your car. I don't know what you're talking about.

And you can damn well apologize. All I said was that *if* you parked it in front of the house—"

"Oh, shut up! If you didn't move it, who did? And where is it?"

Evvie scooted out from behind the desk so that Archie could install himself there and ignore Leo. She beat a retreat to the office, with her embroidery, before Leo could accuse *her* of moving his car. She didn't know how to drive, and wouldn't have cared for Leo's car even if she had—it was a big old boat of a thing—but as with everything about Leo, he had no sense of humour about it.

It was later in the afternoon, when she went out to help Nurse Graham take down the laundry, that she thought to check the door to the lodge again. It was securely padlocked now, so she picked up her basket and headed back toward the house. She knew there would be nobody in the lodge now that the door was locked, but for some reason, as she came around the corner, she paused to glance over her shoulder at the window in the side of the little building. There was nothing to see; it was dark inside, and the window reflected the darkening sky. But as she turned from it, she saw that she had been observed: Ernest was coming over from the direction of the stables. He paused for a moment, looking at her, his expression unreadable. Evvie hefted her basket in a businesslike way and walked on down the drive. He smiled faintly and nodded as he passed her.

She put away the clean laundry, went to the family quarters in the west wing to ask Lady Rathburn if there were any special instructions for the cook for dinner, and then went back down to the kitchen and ran into Ernest again. He was in the back passage, and Leo was there too; it was his voice she heard first. He sounded agitated, almost hysterical.

"It's gone, Ernest. The lid is off. The box is empty."

There was a pause. She was around a corner and could not see them, nor they her.

"What the hell does that mean?" Ernest asked finally, his voice casual.

"It got out."

"It can't have. Can it?"

"I don't know! I didn't think so, but it has."

"Maybe it stole your car."

"Why would it need a car?" Leo's voice rose into a squeak.

"I have no idea. I was joking."

"Ye gods. How can you joke?"

"Not sure."

Leo made a strangulated noise, and Evvie heard the dining room door bang as he went back into the house. She couldn't tell whether Ernest had left or not. She debated sneaking back the way she had come, but decided to press on to the kitchen. He could have no reason to think she had been listening to their conversation. Even if he did—what could he do about it?

He was leaning against the wall, hands in his pockets, as she turned the corner. He looked up.

"Evvie. Did you touch that box or take anything out of it?"

"What box?"

He looked at her appraisingly. "Well, good. There might have been a dangerous article, in a box, that shouldn't have been taken out. That's all. I didn't think you were the type to take it out, but it's always better to be safe, isn't it?"

"Of course," she said. Clearly he thought she was just the type to take the thing out of the box, whatever it was. Since he had given her an opportunity to end the conversation and go on her way, she thought about taking it, but she paused. "Was the box in the lodge? Is that why you asked me?"

He still looked thoughtful. "Yes, that's right. But you didn't see it?"

"I didn't see anything," she said honestly, "because I didn't go in there. I was checking that the door was locked."

"And was it?"

"Yes. I'd seen it open earlier in the day."

He looked at her sharply now. "When?"

"About three."

She waited for him to ask what she'd done then, whether she'd gone in, or why she hadn't locked it. She wouldn't lie to him about seeing the tall airman in there, but she decided she also wouldn't volunteer the information. The man hadn't been doing any harm. But Ernest seemed distracted by his own thoughts and did not ask. This time she did take the opportunity to end the conversation, and went on into the kitchen, thinking she would certainly have to go back out to the lodge as soon as she saw the chance.

Chapter Three

FEAR NOT

Charlie pulled the car to the side of the road and turned off the engine. He looked over his shoulder at the slack, still figure curled up on the back seat. The blue sky, the moors, the road, the car itself all seemed unreal. The only real thing was what was lying there: the still, pale form of it, mutilated but beautiful …

Use the word, he told himself sternly. *It's not as if you don't believe in it.*

He had found a plaid blanket in the car's trunk when he opened it to stow Anderson's bag, and he had laid it over the cope for extra warmth. Against the blazing red and gold it looked absurdly ugly. He had not taken the time to put up the car's top, but it hadn't rained, and they had met no one on the road.

He looked at his hands on the steering wheel, trying to remember why he had stopped. His stiff shoulders and back reminded him. He got out of the car and stood in the grass by the side of the road and stretched. He had driven north, more or less, for a couple of hours. He had no destination in mind, his only idea being to get as far away from the hospital as possible. He was avoiding determinedly a certain train of thought, the one that dealt with what happened next, that spelled out the possible consequences of his actions.

He turned to lean on the side of the car and look down at the angel. The late afternoon sun flamed in the red hair, which was brighter than it had appeared in the dim interior of the Victorian monstrosity. Charlie suddenly realized that he had seen him before, and where. He even had a name for him.

"Hal!" he said softly.

The angel's eyes snapped open, and he looked up at Charlie in confusion.

"Sorry, sorry. I'm sure that's not really your name. It's, uh … somebody you remind me of, is all." The full explanation seemed too complex, and probably too silly. "No doubt you've got a name, but to be honest, even if you could talk, I'm not sure I should hear it."

The beautiful face had relaxed into a smile.

"Anyway, if you don't find it completely undignified, that's what I'll call you for now." He slid back into the driver's seat and shut the door. "My name, for what it's worth, is Charles."

Odd that he didn't say "Charlie." Nobody really called him "Charles."

He started the car and drove on, heading north on the same road for another hour, until they began to lose the light. Since the angel closed his eyes and seemed to fall asleep again, he did not attempt to talk. He found a track leading off into the moor, and carefully manoeuvred the car down it, until he could pull off behind a lumpy hill studded with rocks, which hid the car from the view of the road. When he turned off the engine, for a moment it was completely silent and still. Then a bird gave a mournful cry somewhere in the distance, and that was worse.

He got out of the car and stood looking down at the angel again. The cope and the plaid blanket had fallen to one side. He looked again at the bloodstains and remembered the damage he'd glimpsed beneath. It had looked methodical, almost surgical. What had done that to him? There was a patch of blood lower down, suggesting a kind of injury that one wouldn't necessarily have thought an angel could suffer.

Revolted, Charlie turned away from the car and walked a little way out onto the moor. The bird cried in the distance again, but after a moment he noticed another, more welcome sound, and discovered a stream of clear water running through the bracken. He knelt and filled his hands to drink, then went back to the car to look for something in which he could bring water to Hal. He found an empty bottle in the trunk, rinsed it in the stream, and filled it with the cold water.

Hal was awake when he came back, and had made a partially successful attempt to sit up and look around, clearly worried that he had been abandoned in the car.

"Hey! Fear not. I haven't left."

The angel looked up at him and laughed with pure delight like a child. This was almost too much for him; he collapsed on the car seat, one hand pressed to his stomach, and looked for a moment as if he might faint. But he recovered and smiled.

"To tell you the truth," said Charlie, "I'd been looking for an opportunity to say that."

He opened the door on the passenger side so that he could kneel by the angel's head and lift him gently to help him drink. Hal had difficulty swallowing, either because of the missing tongue or from inexperience with the procedure. He choked and coughed up much of the water before he managed to get any of it down, and he began to look pitifully frustrated and—surprisingly—embarrassed.

"It's okay," said Charlie. "Take your time."

He felt strangely calm. The light was fading in earnest now, and in the shadow of the hill it was quite dark. When Hal had drunk most of the water, Charlie tipped the remainder out onto his handkerchief and wiped the blood from the angel's face and hands.

"Best I can do at the moment," he said. "Do you think you'll sleep again?"

"Mm."

"Is that a 'yes' or a 'no'?"

"Mm."

"I'm glad to know you have a sense of humour."

Actually, it seemed kind of miraculous.

He put the top of the car up, tipped the driver's seat back, and stretched out as best he could. He was too tall to get really comfortable, and his stomach was beginning to complain about his missed dinner. He pulled off his tie and unbuttoned his collar. He was tired enough that he thought he might be able to sleep a little, eventually. When the sun went down altogether, there would be nothing else to do out here, anyway.

He opened his eyes to the dawn.

The air inside the closed car was chilly, but he was warm enough, with the plaid blanket spread over him. He looked into the back seat. The angel was sitting in a corner of it, with his feet drawn up on the seat and the red cope over his knees. He swept back his hair with one hand and held up the other, two fingers together in a casual rendition of the gesture that angels make in paintings when they have something to say.

He said, "Good morning, Charles." His voice was deep and musical, like church bells or the sound of a well-tuned engine.

"Oh. Uh. Good morning." Charlie sat up stiffly and rubbed his eyes. "You're … feeling better."

"Yes. Much better."

"You've got your … You can talk. Good Lord. I'm a master of stating the obvious this morning."

The angel smiled. "I must thank you for what you did. I am almost tempted to say that you saved my life, though that would be meaningless and untrue." He lifted his red eyebrows quizzically. "Still, it is not something that I have been tempted to say before. You must not think me ungrateful."

"Of course not. I mean it was my pleasure. I mean …"

"You found it easier to talk to me when I couldn't reply. Where are we?"

"Middle of nowhere. Roughly. I don't know where we are, honestly, but I'm not too worried about that. I took the same road all the way up, and I know we were travelling north, so in effect we can't be too lost. The real problem is this car."

"It won't go?" the angel guessed helpfully.

"No, it'll go. There's a full can of gas in the trunk, too—probably bought on the black market. It'll go quite some distance yet. The problem is it's not my car. I stole it."

The angel looked at him with wide eyes, as though nothing in his angelic experience had given him resources to cope with this kind of information. Not really surprising.

"I don't know how else I could've got you out of there," Charlie explained. "But when I saw this parked in front of the stables … This make is so easy to start without a key, it's like they were designed for stealing. And for an older car, they're pretty fast. This one's a 1935 model. I didn't know whether they were still making them with the ignition terminals under the dash in '35—that's what makes it child's play to get at them. Anyway, it turns out they were. Sorry, that's got to have been pretty unintelligible, huh?"

"I think," said the angel slowly, "that this is not the first time you have stolen a car."

"No. I used to boost cars for a gang, when I was a kid. I was eventually caught and did time, sort of—I mean, it was a juvenile correctional facility, not exactly a chain gang. I pulled myself together after that and went straight, and that was twenty years ago. I don't ordinarily think of myself as a car thief any more."

"I suppose this isn't ordinary."

"You can say that again. So. Where are we headed?" It was a more monumental question than the mere words made it sound.

Hal frowned slightly. "When I asked, 'Where are we …'"

"You meant in general," Charlie guessed. "You didn't know where we were when we started. Yorkshire. A place called Adderley—a hospital in a converted manor house. Does that help?"

"Yes. So we are in England."

"Yeah. Sorry—I didn't know you needed the real basics. We're in the north of England, it's 1945, March. I'm not English, I'm Canadian—if maybe my accent was confusing you."

The angel gave a surprising, unangelic snort of laughter. "I can't even tell what language we are speaking unless I concentrate—and I am still not very well able to do that."

Charlie took a moment to consider this, but found he couldn't really. "That's okay," he said finally. "So you know where we are—where do we need to be?"

"Jerusalem," said Hal after a moment, apologetically.

"No kidding?"

"I think so."

"Right. Well, you do know—*do* you know there's a war on?"

"Still? Oh. Yes. You are a soldier."

"I'm an airman—a fighter pilot. But I don't think I can fly you to Jerusalem. At least not any time soon. Does it have to be soon?"

Hal shook his head. "I don't know. Perhaps it is not where I need to go. A better idea might be to go back to where we started. You could return the car and explain that you borrowed it in an emergency."

"But I thought you needed to get away from there."

"I did—to recover … a little. But I think perhaps I should go back." He pinched the bridge of his nose, a very human gesture. "I wish I could think more clearly."

"Well … maybe I can make a suggestion. I can't see how it's safe for you to go back to the hospital, especially if you don't feel a hundred per cent. We don't know that the people who had you—who put you in that box—might not still be there."

"Yes, I see. You think they would present a danger, but I don't think so. They would not be able to recognize me."

"No?"

"No. This," he gestured at himself, "is not how they saw me. This is a form that you gave me."

"I gave you? How … What?"

Hal sighed, not irritably but with simple lassitude. "It is difficult to explain, and I am still quite tired. When you looked at me, this is how you thought I should appear, and so … you gave me this form to use. I am very grateful. Had you been frightened, or disbelieving, or lacked … context, and not seen me in this way, I could not have inhabited a human form at all. I was too badly injured. As it is, you gave me wings, which cost me some effort to be rid of." He smiled. "Though they were handsome wings. I should like to have them again."

"But couldn't I have given you a form that wasn't … so beaten up?"

"No. That had happened already. Do not blame yourself for that." He turned in his seat to look out over the moor. "There is a source of water somewhere. You brought me water to drink last night."

"There's a stream close by. You want some more water?"

"No, I thought I might bathe. This form seems to need it."

"Yeah, sure—though the water's apt to be freezing. Actually, I've got clean clothes you can wear after. I'd think Anderson's uniform would fit you."

The angel pushed aside the red cope and swung his legs down from the seat. He moved gingerly, like someone carefully testing new physical limits.

"Do you need a hand?" Charlie asked, opening the car door on the side closest to the stream.

Hal slid across the seat and grasped Charlie's hand and the side of the car, and got out onto the grass. On his feet he was surprisingly tall—shorter than Charlie, but not by more than an inch.

"Thank you," he said with dignity. "I will be all right."

He walked barefoot down the bank and disappeared into the trough where Charlie had found the stream.

He came back after a few minutes, dripping and naked.

"It *is* cold! May I have the blanket?"

His body was pristinely young, and decidedly male. His skin, with its almost pearlescent whiteness, was unmarked now, his abdomen smooth and discreetly muscled. The damp curls around his genitals were the same flame-red as the hair of his head.

Charlie reached into the back seat and tossed him the blanket.

Hal caught it clumsily and wrapped himself up in it. He was shivering, and his lips were starting to turn blue. He was slender to the point of thinness, awkward and graceful at the same time, like a young animal. Why, Charlie thought miserably, when I could have imagined a sappy, swooning, pink-and-white Victorian girl angel, or a fat baby—why in the hell did I do this to myself?

"You spoke of clothes," Hal said. "If you give them to me, I will dress."

"Sure." Charlie opened the trunk to extract the bag with Anderson's things. "I'm not sure exactly what's in there," he said as he handed it to Hal. "You can figure it out—I mean, can you?" He thought about suspenders, ties, bootlaces, and the possibility of having to help the angel dress.

"I can," said Hal coolly. "I am unused to these things, but I am intelligent. Intelli*gence*, in fact, under normal circumstances." He swung the bag over his bare shoulder, hitched up the blanket, and picked his way back down to the stream.

He was gone much longer this time, so long that Charlie was on the point of going to see what had happened to him, when he finally came back. At first Charlie thought he had done a half-hearted job of dressing: his jacket was unbelted, the collar of his shirt open, his tie stuffed into a pocket. Then Charlie realized that his own tie was stuffed in his own pocket, and that Hal had exactly imitated his state of dress. Anderson's uniform was a good fit, though Hal was slimmer than the pilot had been. He had taken Anderson's greatcoat out of the bag and packed up his bloodstained vestments in its place.

"Looks good," said Charlie. "Though the long hair's not remotely regulation."

Hal tossed the bag into the back seat and gave what looked like a deliberately sketchy salute.

"What am I dressed as now, exactly?"

"A flying officer in the Royal Air Force."

"And you?"

He tugged at his cuffs with their stripes. "Squadron leader. I outrank you."

"You *do not*. Your clothes outrank mine—that is not the same thing." Hal fished something out of one of his jacket pockets. "I found this with the clothing. I thought you might want it."

It was a chocolate bar. There must have been two in the bag, and Charlie had found only the one to give to Anderson.

"I'll share it with you," he said, taking it. "You must be hungry too."

"Not literally."

But he looked with interest at the chocolate as Charlie unwrapped it, and accepted a square. He made three bites of it, and seemed to enjoy it, but politely refused to take another. They sat side by side on the hood of the car.

"So," said Charlie, when the chocolate was finished, "do we go back now? Is that our plan?"

Hal looked down at his boots for a moment, then nodded. "I think that is our plan."

"All right. You can sit in the front now, if you want." Charlie slid down from the hood and opened the car door.

"Thank you," said the angel, "but I don't think I will. I think that it would be good for me to sleep some more, so I will stay in the back."

Charlie couldn't deny that he felt a bit relieved.

Hal curled up in the back seat again—he was too tall to stretch out—and Charlie pulled the car out of its hiding-place and began to retrace their route back towards Adderley. Maybe because the angel was less uncanny with a tongue and dressed in Anderson's uniform, maybe just because things always looked different in the morning, Charlie found he was beginning to be dogged by some fairly mundane worries. He had been absent without leave for a shockingly long time now, he had stolen a car, and he truly did not know where they were. They had no food and not much money, either. And Hal had admitted that he was not thinking clearly.

Though what "not thinking clearly" meant for an angel, Charlie wasn't at all sure.

He hadn't tried to explain this to Hal, because he vaguely assumed the angel would have worked it out already, but when he had found the car parked in front of the stables outside Adderley Hall, he had taken it as a sign from God. For another man, God might have needed to arrange for the car to be left at the front steps with the key in the ignition and the engine running in order for the message to get through; but Charlie had been a car thief. He realized now that he hadn't just assumed that taking the car was the right thing to do; he'd also assumed it was the *only* thing he needed to do, like giving the correct password, the secret thing that would make everything afterward smooth sailing. Which was just stupid.

*

They had been on the road for about an hour when they passed a crossroads which Charlie remembered from the day before. The road signs were gone, of course, but he could see a grey, sleepy village in a valley on the left-hand branch of the road. A village might offer the possibility of food. He turned onto the left-hand road. Sure enough, there on the side of the road just before the huddle of buildings was a pub. He was ferociously hungry; the chocolate had done little more than taunt him with the fact that he had now missed two meals. He pulled off the road onto the gravel by the side of the pub and turned off the car. He sat for a moment wondering whether to wake Hal. The angel had said he wasn't literally hungry, but then Charlie remembered the way he had savoured his one square of chocolate, and wondered what "not literally hungry" meant, anyway. And Hal wasn't, as it turned out, asleep, when Charlie looked into the back seat.

"Breakfast," Charlie said. "I thought we could get something to eat."

Hal sat up, raking back his long hair, and smiled. "That sounds very good."

Charlie hesitated, taking the time to tie his tie and button his jacket. He didn't quite know how to ask whether Hal knew enough about human life to deal with breakfast in a pub. Whether, in a word, he knew how to *pass*. He decided there was no way to put the question, so he just got out of the car. Hal put on Anderson's coat, which he had been using as a blanket, and followed him. He still moved tentatively, almost clumsily, like someone who had just woken up, or—as was presumably the case—wasn't quite used to his body. He had not put on his own tie, though he had buttoned the collar of his shirt.

The pub was low-ceilinged and dark, empty except for a couple of old men sitting at the bar, and the bartender polishing glasses as if he planned to make the task last all day. All three of them stared at the strangers as they entered. They would have stared at anyone who came through the door, but they went on staring at Hal.

Charlie tried to remain nonchalant. "What would you like to eat?" he asked, turning to Hal.

The angel thought a moment. "Bread? I like bread."

"Yeah, I think we can do better than that."

"I like cake as well. And fruit."

"Okay … how about eggs and bacon? Though they won't have eggs. Sausages?"

"No, thank you. I do really like bread."

Charlie went up to the bar, Hal following with his hands in the pockets of Anderson's coat, and ordered sausage and potatoes for himself, and toast for the angel. And a pot of tea. He paid for the food, took the tea and cups, and led the way to a table in a corner by the window.

"How do you take your tea?" Charlie asked.

"With sugar. Lots of it. What?"

"I didn't expect you to have an answer to that."

The angel arched a red eyebrow at him. He had picked *that* up pretty quickly. "Why then did you ask?"

"I don't really know. As a joke, I suppose."

Charlie poured the tea, and added sugar to Hal's. The angel settled back into the dark, high-backed bench by the window, shrugging off his coat.

"Thank you," he said, accepting the cup with a smile, and curving his long fingers around its warmth. "I like things that taste sweet. I'm not sure why. It is very kind of you to feed me."

"No problem. Least I can do."

They sat in silence until their food came.

"Toasted bread!" said Hal, as if it were a delicacy, and began spreading butter on it. "Do you think they would have jam?"

"Maybe so. Would you like me to ask?"

"No, don't get up. I will."

He was out of his seat before Charlie could stop him. And Charlie would have stopped him, though he wasn't sure exactly what he was afraid of. Hal was leaning on the bar now, smiling at the innkeeper, putting his request in a totally natural manner, saying, "Splendid!" when he was told that there was jam and that it was homemade from wild blueberries by the innkeeper's wife. Actually making small talk about the superiority of blueberries to raspberries while the innkeeper's young daughter went to get the jam. And Charlie felt his heart strangely constricted. *He can handle himself just fine. He'd be okay without me.* It was a devastating thought.

On his way back with the jar of jam, Hal stopped for a moment in front of a picture frame that hung near the door. Charlie realized that it was a mirror, and the angel was looking at his own reflection. He slid back into the booth opposite Charlie.

"I wondered why the men at the bar were looking at me with such wide eyes," he said. "I think I see."

"They're just jealous. You look great."

Hal gave him a startled look, and Charlie felt that had been an incredibly stupid thing to say. He was still staggered by the way that he had felt when he watched Hal across the bar.

"You do look maybe a little young to be wearing that uniform," Charlie admitted. "Sorry about that. To me, you look like an angel."

Hal cocked his head to one side. "That is the first time you have used that word." He unscrewed the lid of the jam jar, and began spreading jam on his toast.

"Well, this doesn't happen every day. So what do you normally look like? I mean, when you appear to people."

Hal was silent. He set down the knife. For a moment he sat with his slender hands pressed between his knees, but when he tried reaching for the knife again, they were still shaking. His face was completely calm.

"You okay?" said Charlie. "Want to go outside?"

What kind of psychological damage could you carry if you were a being of pure intelligence? Probably a staggering amount.

"Outside?" Hal looked surprised, and it seemed to distract him from his anxiety. "No, why?"

"Um, I just thought …" *I found you in a BOX.* "This room is a bit close. I wondered if it was making you nervous to be in here." It would be another thing that his experience had prepared him to deal with.

"No. Your question distressed me." He didn't sound remotely distressed.

"Which question?" He had lost the thread of the conversation. "'What do you normally look like'?"

Hal nodded. "What distressed me is that I can't remember."

"I see," said Charlie gently. "Amnesia? That makes sense."

"Sense?"

Hal looked up at him, and for a fraction of a second there was something in his smoke-grey eyes that was like what Charlie had seen at first in the alabaster box: something smashed up, broken beyond repair, but *not at all* human.

When it was gone, and Charlie had collected himself, he said: "You've been through an ordeal, right—that's the sort of thing that can happen. I mean, it's a human explanation, but you're in human form, so …"

Again Hal seemed distracted from his anxiety, this time by curiosity. That was maybe the way to deal with it, Charlie thought.

"You have some experience meeting angels in human form, I think," Hal said.

"Not proper angels, no. I met a devil when I was a teenager. Not met, exactly—uh, encountered. And it wasn't in human form at first. But you're right, that is what prepared me for you. The same way my years with the gang prepared me for taking that car. I think … I think I was meant to do this."

Hal, to Charlie's surprise, frowned. "I certainly meant for you to do it," he said diplomatically.

"I meant more …" He made a vague gesture suggestive of the cosmic. "On a larger scale."

"I know what you meant," said Hal.

There was silence again. Hal went back to spreading jam on his toast.

"Do you want to talk about it?" Charlie asked.

"About what?"

"Well, about what you *do* remember."

"Not really."

Hal took a bite of his toast and sighed with satisfaction. He cut the next slice of jammy toast in half and put one half on the edge of Charlie's plate without comment. Charlie tried to offer him a sausage in return, but he refused it firmly.

"You want to know what happened, how I ended up in that box," Hal said finally.

"The question has crossed my mind."

"I remember very little about how it happened. I've … It is like looking off a cliff, and there is nothing down there." He shook himself slightly. "I was imprisoned in the box, some … I think months ago, but I am not sure—I think it would be difficult for a mortal to tell time accurately in the absence of cues, and unfortunately I have less facility with time than you do. So I cannot tell you how long it was. It *could* have been years."

"We could figure it out, if … "

"If I remembered anything about the circumstances of my imprisonment, which I don't. I remember that I like tea with sugar, that I prefer blueberries to raspberries, but not what happened to me."

"Right. So. You were in there for months or years … But some of your injuries were fresh—were they torturing you?"

"I suppose they must have been. They … " He shook his head. "I don't wish to talk to you about this, Charles. I am afraid it will horrify you, and you will not wish … consciously, you will wish to have compassion on me, but in your secret heart you will associate me with horror and wish to distance yourself."

"Damn. It must be awful to worry about things as deep down as that." Charlie speared another piece of sausage. "I can't promise anything except how I'll react consciously."

"I didn't intend that you should." The angel sounded slightly stung. "You are laughing at me."

"A little bit," Charlie admitted. "But in an entirely friendly way. Look, you don't need to tell me what they did to you—I mean, you *can't* really tell me any way but metaphorically, and I already know that version. They cut out your tongue, castrated you—I think—eviscerated you, and held you captive for a period of … months or years. The only reason you didn't die is because you're immortal. You made yourself a human form out of something you found in my mind—but I think that was the first and last time you've had access to my mind, because I felt that, kind of, and I haven't felt it since. I'm guessing that's because you just don't have the strength to do that again. And I'm also guessing that all you did, when you healed your human form, was make the metaphor less exact—I'm guessing you're still carrying that damage, you're just not letting me see it."

Hal looked mildly impressed. "Not exactly. It is as if … when you found me, I was bleeding in the dirt, and now I am washed and bandaged. You are right, I am not healed, and will not be for …" he gestured hopelessly, "a period of time which I have truly no idea how to quantify. But I *am* in a much better state than I was. I could have made the metaphor more exact for you, but I did not see the point."

"No, it would just have been awkward. And unrealistic anyway—people's tongues and, uh, things don't actually grow back, so there was just no way of making that look natural."

Hal nodded. Charlie didn't expect more, but he appeared to make an effort. "It is not true that I remember nothing. I remember certain things. There were two of them. My captors. Two men. They wanted—well, one of them, the one who knew what he wanted, had an idea that I could grant wishes, and he had a list of requests. People whose lives he wanted to prolong, and others whom he wished dead … Many things. If any of them ever were in my power to grant—which I doubt—they are not now, in the state I am in. The other man … just liked hurting me. He did it almost playfully. I don't know what I appeared to them, what they thought they were doing, physically. I had been very badly hurt before I was imprisoned—not, I think, by them."

"Right," said Charlie, after a space of silence indicated that this was all Hal had to say. "So. Next question. Jerusalem?"

Hal gave him a blank look. "Jerusalem," he repeated.

"You wanted to go there, earlier this morning. I'm just wondering why."

"I remember." He thought about it for long enough to make it seem like that might not have been true. "I think it is where my former captors mean to go," he said finally.

"I see. And you think … there's some reason you need to follow them? That's what we're doing now, isn't it—going back to the hospital in case they haven't left yet?"

Hal nodded.

Charlie thought about all the people he had seen at the hospital: the crabby receptionist; the little nurse who had thought he was praying; the blonde girl who had breezed through the lobby; Anderson, shrunken and feeble in his wheelchair. He couldn't begin to connect any of them with Hal's appalling metaphor for what had been done to him.

"And the reason you need to follow them … "

Hal spread his hands wide, his expression still impassive. "I feel a sense of incompleteness. As if I have a mission which I have not accomplished."

"I see."

Hal had been distracted by something outside the window. He frowned.

"What is it?" Charlie asked.

The answer was one he was not prepared for.

"A policeman," said Hal softly. "I think he is looking at our car."

*

They left the pub with a show of nonchalance that was surprisingly effective. Charlie's main fear was that Hal somehow would not be able to manage this—but his concern was totally unfounded. Either the angel just wasn't that worried, or he was able to use the loose connection between his mind and his body to his advantage. In any case, he sauntered very convincingly out of the pub, and made it all the way down the main street of the village without even seeming tempted to quicken his pace. Charlie, who felt like running most of the way himself, was impressed.

At the edge of the village, they turned off the road and took refuge in the shadow of a barn. They sat down on the far side of the building, leaning back against its rough wall. Ahead of them was a bleak expanse of country, rocky and treeless, where two men on foot would be visible for miles. The policemen didn't seem to have noticed them, and certainly had not followed them. But the locals could not have failed to connect them with the car, and if any kind of determined search was made, they couldn't hide for long.

"At least we didn't leave anything incriminating in the car," said Charlie, speaking for the first time since they had left the pub. "Did we?"

Hal looked at him. "I think we did."

"Oh, shit. Anderson's bag. And your vestments! They'll think I murdered a priest! Stole a car and then murdered a priest. No, murdered a priest on Palm Sunday and then stole the car later. Well, I doubt they'll work that bit out."

After a moment he realized that the expression on Hal's face was the result of his attempt not to laugh. The mind-body thing apparently only worked up to a point.

"Yes, I agree," Charlie said drily. "It's hilarious. Perhaps I won't be court-martialled for desertion after all. Perhaps I'll hang for murder instead."

"Desertion?" Hal looked serious now. "You are absent without leave? You did not tell me that."

"I wasn't sure you'd understand."

"Of course I understand," said Hal. "I am myself essentially a soldier."

Charlie hadn't thought about it that way. "Right. But you couldn't exactly desert, could you?"

Hal opened his eyes very wide. "Is that what you think? Your theology is very defective. Of course I could."

"Oh. Free will. Yeah, I did know that. It's not such a serious business for me. My Wing Commander is a friend—we came through the Battle of Britain together. He might well believe me if I told him ... well, some sort of story."

It was serious enough. By this time, losing his command and his rank, dishonourable discharge, "Lack of Moral Fibre"—all that was probably inevitable. He just couldn't begin to explain to Hal how little that mattered to him right then.

"I wonder if this barn's locked," he said, to change the subject. "We might buy ourselves some time if we could get inside. At least we could hide more effectively." He stood up and tried the door. It swung easily open. For a moment Charlie stared into the dim interior, not believing what he was seeing.

Hal got to his feet too, and peered around the other door. "It's an airplane," he observed.

"It is an airplane." But it was, very clearly, more than an airplane. It was like the car. It was another sign from God. "It's a Tiger Moth. I learned to fly on these."

"Your criminal past also involved airplanes?"

"My ... no! I trained with the RAF in Canada. Utterly aboveboard. It just happens that I learned on one of these. Well, most everybody does. Not that it would matter—I'm a good pilot. I could figure out an unfamiliar plane. Of course," he said, coming back down to earth somewhat, "it's probably not operational, and certainly not fuelled—I mean, what would be the chances?"

"Slim," said Hal.

"You know you don't have to answer the rhetorical ones."

He walked around the little biplane. It was painted in camouflage colours, quite freshly, without any military markings, and everything looked in working order. When he climbed up into the rear cockpit, he found the fuel gauge registering three-quarters full. He let out a whistle and slid back down to the floor of the shed.

"So much for rhetorical questions. It looks ready to fly."

He tried not to wonder what the plane was doing there—what it was doing there other than waiting for him—but he was comforted by the thought that the owner of a civilian plane in good working order, fuelled and ready to fly, hidden in a shed during war time, couldn't have been up to any good. It might be no bad thing for the plane to disappear.

"Let's do it."

Hal gave him a wide-eyed look. "Do what? Steal the plane?"

"Yeah. It's just sitting here asking to be stolen. And it'll get us out of this place in style. Come on."

He propped the barn doors open wide and looked critically at the grassy field that would have to pass for a runway.

"Now, flying in an open cockpit without goggles or flight jackets won't be fun. It'll be noisy and windy and *cold*. We might be a good hour from Adderley—these little Moths don't go very fast—but we can't land there with no radio, and we might freeze if we try to stay in the air for that long anyway. We'll just get safely away, and then come down in some likely spot and rethink our plans. All right?"

Hal nodded mutely.

Charlie flicked back the lapel of Hal's coat and pulled Anderson's tie out of the pocket where Hal had stuffed it. "I'd recommend you tie back your hair, or it'll be in your face the whole time."

Hal fumbled with the tie, the complexity of gathering up his hair and tying a knot without looking at what he was doing almost too much for him.

"You get in the front, here," Charlie directed, flipping down the side panel at the front. Hal gave him a worried look. "You're not afraid of flying, are you?"

Hal laughed, distracted again. He swung up into the front seat, and figured out the safety harness before Charlie had a chance to explain it to him. (Intelli*gence*, under normal circumstances, Charlie reminded himself.)

"Don't be alarmed by the instruments and stuff," Charlie said. "There are two sets of controls because it's a training plane. You don't have to do anything."

"Ah," said Hal. "Good."

Charlie flicked the ignition and spun the propeller to start the plane's engine. The sound brought back pleasant memories, the exhilaration of his first flights. He vaulted happily into the rear seat, and they taxied out onto the moor. The Tiger Moth bumped along over the uneven ground, Charlie turned them into the wind, and they took gently to the sky.

Climbing in the little biplane, the wind in his hair and roaring in his ears, Charlie felt oddly in his element, like a swimmer naked in the ocean. He remembered how he had congratulated himself for not taking a romantic view of flying; well, why the hell not, though? It *was* a romantic thing, a miraculous, glorious thing. It was his ticket to saving Hal, being able to operate this machine, to fly.

He levelled out at a conservative altitude, reining in his exuberance. The wind had torn the tie out of Hal's hair and hurled it away. Hal gathered up his hair and pulled it forward over his shoulder, looking back to smile at Charlie, a beautiful, confiding smile. A trusting smile. Charlie's heart soared, well above a conservative altitude.

But Hal was no longer smiling now; he was pointing back behind them. Charlie looked and saw a speck beyond the plane's tail, in the sun. Another plane.

His first thought was that if it were a German, he was a sitting duck; the Tiger Moth was unarmed. His second thought was that it wouldn't be a German, but that he'd made a terrible mistake. There was an American squadron stationed near here that he'd entirely forgotten about. He had taken off perilously close to them. The plane in the sun behind them grew rapidly, and he could see that it was indeed an American, a Mustang. He could picture the pilot on the radio, trying to hail the strange biplane, knowing from the silhouette that it couldn't be an enemy aircraft, but still deeply suspicious of it. Getting no answer. Radioing his base to ask for instructions.

"We may be forced to land!" Charlie shouted, hoping Hal could hear him over the wind and the engine noise. He could barely hear himself.

And if they landed, then where would they be? How could he possibly account for what he had been doing and where he had got this plane? His plan had not been well thought out. He felt sick, ashamed of his stupidly exultant mood of a minute ago.

The American was getting quite close now, flying behind them with a determination that gave Charlie a sinking feeling. He waggled the biplane's wings in what he hoped looked like a friendly gesture. The American's warning shot whined overhead.

Their pursuer was more than suspicious. He'd heard back from his base. He knew—thought he knew—who was flying the Tiger Moth. He'd had orders to shoot him down.

Or he was an overzealous Yank taking matters into his own hands; it amounted to much the same thing, as far as they were concerned.

Hal was twisted around in his seat again, loosened hair flying around his face, looking back at Charlie with concern. His white face looked childlike.

"It's okay!" Charlie shouted. "We're—"

The whine of another shot. Stupid, impatient American!

"All right, all right, I'm landing!"

Charlie banked, scanning the landscape below for a safe place to come down. He didn't see anything remotely helpful. It was all hills and woods.

The American fired a third time, and Charlie, unthinking, evaded, executing a piece of fancy flying that must have looked deeply suspicious to the Mustang's pilot. He stopped taking chances at that, fired on the Tiger Moth in earnest, and the little plane shuddered at one solid hit, then another.

It was only the second time Charlie had taken such a direct hit in the air. He felt it almost as if the shots had struck his body: the grim corollary to that delirious sense of oneness with the plane that he'd felt on their way up. They were dropping, out of control, leaking fuel, smoke streaming like blood.

For a few terrible moments Charlie felt so overwhelmed with failure that he couldn't make even the simplest move to control the plane. To be shot down by an Allied pilot, to have made it almost to the end of the war and to die now—but most of all, to have failed to save Hal, to have failed the commission from God that had been granted him after all this time …

He got control of himself, and, after a fashion, of the plane. But—assessing the situation coolly now—they were too high, and descending far too fast, to land safely.

"We're going to crash," he said, his voice surprisingly calm.

Wrong again. You're not going to be shot or hanged. But this, after all, had always been the most likely outcome.

Hal was looking back at him through the smoke. Charlie thought he must have undone his harness. At this point, it couldn't matter.

"This will likely kill me, but you'll be okay—won't you?" He shouted over the shuddering noise of the engine.

"What will kill you? The impact with the ground?" Hal seemed barely to have to raise his voice to be heard. He was kneeling backwards on his seat now, holding onto the rear windscreen with one hand, the other trying to keep his hair out of his face.

"Yes, obviously! What a stupid fucking question! And you didn't answer mine—will you be okay?"

"That is actually a much stupider question. Let's avoid hitting the ground."

"Do you think I hadn't thought of that? We can't! The plane is going down."

"Yes—let's not stay in the plane, though." Truthfully, Hal was almost out of it himself already. He was standing on his seat now, reaching up to grip the edge of the upper wing to steady himself.

"We don't have parachutes! Hal—stop that! We don't have even one parachute between the two of us—getting out of the plane won't ... "

Hal was looking down at him with a very sweet smile. He had climbed up onto the fuselage between the front and back seats. He stood upright, balanced above Charlie, and into the roaring blue sky he snapped open his huge red wings.

"Undo your harness and put your arms around my waist."

Charlie did as he was told.

He held onto the angel, and the plane dropped away from beneath them. He could feel the bones of Hal's slim hips through the fabric of Anderson's trousers, hear his heartbeat under his ribs. He had never held onto anyone so tightly. There was nothing natural about this, no exuberance or triumph. He was being carried, as helpless as a child, as a lamb in the talons of an eagle. He was terrified, and at the same time he felt completely, blankly calm. Hal grasped his arms, hauling him up higher so that he could hold onto him, wrapping his own slender arms around Charlie.

"Sorry I'm so heavy," Charlie heard his own voice choke out.

"You're not," said Hal.

He could see, and feel, the power of the great red wings as they beat the air, stretched against the wind to glide, beat again, hard, to slow their descent. He had imagined himself rescuing Hal by piloting a machine, but this was so different, this was Hal's body— metaphor though it might be—straining to bring him safely down out of the sky.

Was the American seeing this? he wondered. Would this be the moment for him when everything changed, as it had twenty years ago for Charlie?

The Tiger Moth fell away, just dropping now, pilotless, to the distant ground. It hit with a small sound and a small explosion like a firecracker, and now Charlie and Hal were descending gently, spiralling down with the wind. The sky was vast and quiet around them. The American plane was nowhere in sight.

They came down out of sight of the wreck of the Tiger Moth. Charlie let go a few feet from the ground, dropped, and rolled out of the way. Hal landed gracefully, dropping to one knee and steadying himself with his fingertips on the ground. He rolled back to lie outstretched, wings spread.

Charlie tried to gather his legs under him to stand, but found them too shaky. He half-crawled, half-scooted across the bracken closer to Hal.

"You okay?"

The angel tipped his head to one side to look over at him, without otherwise moving. He managed a slight smile. He looked exhausted.

"I thought you'd got rid of the wings," said Charlie.

"I had. But was it not handy that I knew how to restore them?"

"Yeah. Very."

Hal gathered the wings in a little; iridescent red feathers brushed against Charlie's shoulder. Charlie felt a strong temptation to lie down among them.

Apparently it was obvious that he was thinking this, because Hal said, "Go ahead."

"I, uh—I don't want to hurt you."

"That part is just feathers. There's no sensation."

He lay down very carefully in the crook of Hal's wing, his cheek on the smooth flight feathers, trying to keep still for fear of disarranging them. His head was filled suddenly with the scent of incense, unmistakable and instantly familiar: the incense from St. John's. It made a kind of sense. They lay quietly for a while.

"What does it mean?" Charlie whispered. "Why would the plane get shot down? Does it mean I wasn't supposed to take it after all?"

The feathers around him rustled. Hal's voice sounded distant, very tired: "Charles, I am afraid you may be thinking about this the wrong way. Of course you were not supposed to take the plane. It belonged to someone else. You weren't supposed to take the car, either. You weren't really supposed to open that box in the first place. It was someone else's property and clearly none of your business."

"But I heard you calling for help!"

"Exactly. So you opened the box. And I told you I needed to get away from that place, so you took the car. You didn't take the car just because you thought God was telling you to do it—you took it because there wasn't any other good way to get away. I don't think that was a mistake. I do think taking the plane may have been a mistake. We could have stayed hidden in that shed and got away later on foot. I think you took the plane not because it was the best idea but because it looked so much like the coincidence with the car that you thought it meant something."

"Why didn't you tell me then I was making a mistake?"

"I didn't know. Like you, I have limited foreknowledge."

Charlie laughed. "Unlike me, you mean. You forget. I'm human—I have no foreknowledge at all."

"You can discern causes and anticipate effects. When you see that the plane has been shot, you know it will crash. That is the kind of thing I mean. Strictly limited." After a moment he added, "I should have told you I had misgivings about taking the plane. That was my mistake. I'm sorry."

"No, I wasn't listening—wouldn't have heard you. All's well that ends well."

He sat up, out of the nest of feathers and the smell of home. He looked down at Hal and realized suddenly that all *wasn't* well. He wasn't sure how he could tell, but the angel wasn't just tired.

"You're hurt."

Hal returned a wan, apologetic smile. "Metaphorically ... I think my back may be broken."

"Oh, God. Are you—literally—in pain?"

"I don't ... I can't tell the difference any more. Yes, I suppose so. I can't move very much. And I'm afraid I can't get rid of the wings. I'm sorry—I overextended myself."

"Saving my life," said Charlie miserably. "Which was not supposed to be the point of our acquaintance."

Hal made an extraordinary noise that could only be described as a growl. "You don't know that. *I* don't know that—you *certainly* don't."

"No, you're right," said Charlie, chastened. "I'm sorry." Remembering how distracting Hal always seemed to help, he added, in as frivolous a tone as he could manage: "I kind of like it when you pull rank like that."

"Ah! You—bastard—it—hurts to laugh."

"I'm sorry—I keep forgetting you have such a hair-trigger sense of humour." He knelt over the angel, and gingerly brushed the back of his fingers along the top edge of one wing, smoothing the feathers. "What can I do? Is this another one where you just need time, and rest—or is there something I can do? If you need time to think about it, that's okay too."

Hal had closed his eyes. Charlie sat stroking his red feathers and looking down at him, his pale face slack and exhausted, his bright hair spread on the bracken. He looked very slight and vulnerable. His hands with their long fingers lay loosely, one on the feathers of his other wing, one on the front of Anderson's coat. There were neat slits in the fabric of the coat to accommodate the wings; Charlie could just see the openings where the coat was bunched about his shoulders. I guess, Charlie thought, if you can grow wings on command, details like that don't present much of a problem.

He knelt there for a while in silence. They were on a bare, exposed slope, in the middle of nowhere. The sky above them was streaked with clouds. There was a lot of sky, and it seemed unnaturally quiet. The American plane, mercifully, seemed to have moved on. A breeze brushed across the landscape, ruffling Charlie's short hair. He had long ago lost his cap.

He began to think that it was unfair and unwise to expect Hal to tell him what to do. But he had little trust in his own ability to make proper decisions. Hal had been right; he had been led down an irrational path looking for signs from God. It had almost got him killed, and it had hurt Hal badly.

He stood up and took a few steps away from the supine angel, up the slope behind them. He thought he could see the smoke from the wrecked plane, a faint thread against the sky. There would be no sense going that way, then. It was the most likely way to be reunited with the American, and besides, he had no desire to see what had become of the Tiger Moth. He looked down the hill. There was a rough track at the bottom of it, he could see now. From this vantage it appeared to lead from nowhere to nowhere, but that couldn't really be true. On the other side of the track, dark trees climbed up the opposite side of the valley.

Charlie returned to kneel beside Hal, and touched the hand that lay on his chest. It was chilly, and didn't move under his touch, but Hal did open his eyes.

"You wanted me to tell you what to do," Hal said, recollecting himself.

"No, no. Don't worry about that."

"But I've thought about it," the angel pursued, speaking slowly and apparently with effort. "You will have to leave me."

"I'm not gonna do that."

"But you have to. I can't move. You can't stay here. You have to go back to your base."

"I won't leave you and walk back to Adderley by myself. I just won't. I'll phone my second-in-command with some kind of story—accident, unavoidable delay—it needn't even be a lie, exactly."

"But … if you have to telephone … you can't stay here. You will have to leave me."

He had a point.

"Let me carry you down under those trees, out of the open," said Charlie, "and we'll talk about it."

Carrying Hal with his wings was a difficult proposition; the wings were very light, and didn't add much to his weight, but they were huge and fragile and awkward. Charlie gathered him up as carefully as he could, and picked his way down the slope, across the track and in among the trees, where he managed with some manoeuvring to find a place to lay him down. Hal found that he was more comfortable lying on his side, which allowed him to fold his wings completely. Charlie arranged him as gently as he could. He tried to give Hal his folded-up greatcoat to use as a pillow again, but the angel refused it.

"You'll be cold," he said.

So Charlie settled for taking off his jacket and giving Hal that.

"I've decided not to argue with you," he said finally, putting his coat back on. "I'll go. I'll phone Benson at the base, first place I find, and I'll see about some food and drink. Cake, for sure, and the best beer money can buy—well, the best beer *my* money can buy, in the middle of nowhere, which is actually not a very exciting prospect. Then I'll be back. I have an *exceptional* sense of direction, and a great memory for places. I will be able to find you—don't worry about that."

Hal looked up at him, and for a second time Charlie could see that wreckage in his eyes, the terrible state he was in. He didn't want Charlie to leave him; he was going to worry about every possible thing, the entire time Charlie was gone. He wouldn't be able to help it.

"I'll stay until you fall asleep," said Charlie firmly, sitting down on the forest floor beside Hal, and realizing to his alarm that he had just had to resist a strong impulse to call the angel "darling." He'd never in his entire life called anyone "darling."

Chapter Four

OPUS ANGLICANUM

Breakfast at Adderley was served in the dining room, with its butter-coloured walls and huge paintings and tall windows draped like a theatre stage. The family and the residential staff breakfasted when it suited them, while most of the patients took the first meal of the day on the ward or in their rooms. Saturday morning, Evvie was able to breakfast without encountering Leo or any of his guests. Lady Rathburn was there, fretting about the fact that the patient being sent up from Newingthorpe that afternoon was a woman, which would mean rearranging the bedrooms again.

There had been a bad accident a month earlier at the Newingthorpe airfield, south of the Adderley estate. The Adderley base had been built to replace Newingthorpe, which was poorly situated and plagued by dangerous fog. Two planes had collided in the air trying to land at Newingthorpe, killing both crews and several passengers. One survivor, who had been pulled from the flaming wreckage and clung to life in the Newingthorpe infirmary, was to be sent to Adderley Hall to recuperate. Newingthorpe hadn't been receiving planes since the accident, and was finally scheduled to be shut down completely. Evvie wondered whether the survivor of the crash would be as bitter as Ben Sherwood about being injured in a wartime accident rather than a bomb blast or actual combat.

"Maybe I should just let Ernest and Daphne bunk up together after all," said Lady Rathburn. "Am I being too, too Victorian, do you think, Evvie?"

"No! Not at all," said Evvie quickly. She wondered whether to tell Lady Rathburn that Ernest was an adulterer, but that seemed like something Josephine Good would do.

"Perhaps you're right. One must keep up some standards, mustn't one? I was forgetting that you're such an old-fashioned girl yourself."

Evvie didn't think "old-fashioned" was quite the right word for it, but maybe Lady Rathburn knew better.

"It won't be any trouble to free up another private room," Evvie assured her. "Captain Carter is doing much better, and I think he's bored being by himself all day and might like a change."

And if he didn't, she would talk him into it.

It didn't come to that, as he was quite willing to go. Nurse Fitzgerald went to fetch a wheelchair to bring him down to the ward, but while she was gone, Carter told Evvie he wanted to try getting down there on his crutches. She thought about how she would justify this when the nurse caught them at it and berated them. Dr. Sheppard had given a stirring speech the other day to the staff, in the wake of MacGregor's suicide attempt, about the importance of keeping up morale. Surely this fell into that category. If the man wanted to try to get down to the ward on his own two—well, under his own power—why not let him? There were plenty of chairs on the way where he could take a break, and she could always fetch the wheelchair if he overtaxed himself completely.

Captain Carter was very young, not much older than Evvie herself, and he had been very sick—that was why he had been in a private room—but she could tell that before his injury he had been what her younger sister Aphrodite would call a cutie, with blue eyes and straw-coloured hair and a snub nose.

They set off down the passage from his bedroom. The private rooms for the patients were in the east wing, at right angles to the long gallery at the back of the house, where the elevator had been installed. They made slow but steady progress down the passage towards the gallery. They would have gone faster if Captain Carter hadn't insisted on talking to Evvie the whole time. She didn't like to discourage this, because she thought he was doing it to cover his awkwardness with the crutches, but she had a sinking feeling that she knew where it was tending.

When they had reached the gallery, and she suggested he sit down on one of the upholstered benches and take a break, she wasn't surprised when he patted the seat beside him and said, "Unless you've got a jealous sweetheart who'd object."

"No," she said, and flinched at how sad her voice came out sounding. He'd be sure to misinterpret that.

Fortunately, no sooner had she sat down next to him than the elevator gate clanked open and Nurse Fitzgerald emerged with the wheelchair.

"Oh, you made it all this way by yourself, Captain," she said, obviously struggling to look pleased about it. "Good. That's very good."

"And I'll make it all the rest of the way, too!" Carter declared. "I'm determined. Evvie has been a great encouragement to me." He flashed her a smile that hinted at just what a cutie he had once been—and would be again. Evvie wished there were some way she could tell him that without sounding flirtatious, could assure him that there were plenty of girls in the world who could fall for such a nice-looking, good-humoured young man, even when he had only one leg. She just wasn't one of them.

"I'm sure she has," said Nurse Fitzgerald. "But now I think it would be better if Evvie went back to your room and finished packing up your things. I can accompany you the rest of the way to the ward."

"I know you'll do great," said Evvie, feeling perversely a little sad to be forced to abandon him now. "I'll see you later."

Captain Carter gave her a tragic look, as if he thought Nurse Fitzgerald was playing the role of the Hellespont separating Hero and Leander, and said, "I'll look forward to it."

Evvie went back to his empty room and packed up the rest of his personal effects, looking hopefully for a picture of a sweetheart but finding only one of his mother. As she came back out into the hall with the box in which she'd stowed everything, Josephine Good was coming out of the room next door.

She was dressed as usual in one of her stylish suits. She had an elegant wardrobe, but since her conversion she had started making odd pairings of smart outfits with unflattering hats and ugly shoes. Evvie wondered if she was trying to show her contempt for the world without the expense of an entirely new, ugly wardrobe. Today she carried a shapeless, threadbare handbag clutched under one arm, and had put her hair up very sloppily.

"Captain Carter is not leaving us, surely?" she said, looking with surprise from Evvie's box to the door she was closing behind her.

"No, we're moving him down to the ward," Evvie said, since she couldn't very well ignore the question. She wanted to, though; even giving Miss Good the slightest piece of information was somehow annoying.

"What a tragedy for such a good-looking young man to be so maimed, don't you think?" Miss Good said with a wistful expression. She wore a strange-looking ring on the middle finger of her left hand, with a flat red stone incised with a design. It must have been loose, because she twisted it with the fingers of her other hand as she spoke. "But I am forgetting," she went on with a trill of laughter, "that you give no thought to such things—I'm sure you don't even notice whether men are handsome or not, do you? *So* commendable! Here, have you seen my brother's latest? He wrote it only recently." She stopped twisting her ring to reach into her handbag, and produced a pamphlet which she offered to Evvie. It was called HARNESSING THE POWER OF THE ANGELS.

"Makes them sound like horses or electricity or something," said Evvie, allowing Miss Good to go on holding the pamphlet out, not shifting her hold on the box in order to take it.

"Don't you think that they *are* a kind of electricity, though, properly understood?" Miss Good placed the pamphlet neatly on top of the picture of Captain Carter's mother in the box.

"I really must get back to work," said Evvie.

Maybe she was being unfair to Miss Good, Evvie thought as she marched down the hall. Everyone said she had turned over a new leaf and wasn't it wonderful. But she had betrayed Evvie's confidence, rather badly, before the leaf-turning, and she had never apologized for it. Evvie didn't think it quite fair for her to suddenly act as though they were friends. And really—*a kind of electricity?*

*

She removed the pamphlet about harnessing angels and deposited it on the waste-paper pile in the office before going in to deliver Captain Carter's things. She found him happily chatting with the airman in the bed next to his, and heard that the police had just turned up with Leo's missing car. It had been found parked in a village some 90 miles north of Adderley, but how it had got there remained a mystery. That wasn't the only mystery about it, either. Evvie was still tidying up in the ward when two police officers came in to talk to Flying Officer Anderson. They were the same pair who had come about the body off Horrey Head the day before.

"Yes, that's my kit," she heard Anderson say, "but I haven't had it since I got shot down. It was at the base. Anybody could've … Yes, I mean, really, anybody could have taken it."

"And what about these? We found these rolled up inside the bag."

"What the …"

Evvie looked across the room to see what it was, and nearly dropped the vase she was holding. Spread across the foot of Anderson's bed between the two police officers was a stunning red silk garment, stiff with gold embroidery. She thought at first it was a phelonion, the outer garment worn by priests in the East, but she saw quickly that it was a Western-style vestment, like a cloak, whose name she couldn't remember. In England, her family had always gone to the kind of church where they didn't use vestments. One of the policemen produced a narrow, Western-style orarion of matching silk, with a gold fringe, and laid it on the bed as well.

"I've never seen that in my life," said Anderson with conviction. "I don't even know what it is."

"It's some kind of fancy dress," said one of the policemen.

Evvie had put down the vase by this point, and now she saw her opportunity. She was dying to get a closer look at the needlework.

"It's a priest's vestments," she said, approaching the men by the bed. "Or a deacon's—I think in the Western style they look the same. Pardon me for interrupting. I couldn't help noticing. It's very impressive work."

"I told you that's what it was," said the other policeman. "Do you know owt about it, Miss?" he asked Evvie.

"I've never seen these before, but I do know something about … about embroidery. May I look at it?"

"I don't quite see what that … " the first policeman began, while the other one said, "Go ahead, Miss."

She picked up a corner of the garment delicately, and studied the stitches. It was incredibly fine work, in a style that she remembered having seen on display in an English museum: *opus anglicanum*, the technique made famous by English embroiderers in the Middle Ages. But the cope—that was what it was called, a cope—wasn't old. The fabric was stained and creased in places, but the colour was still vibrant, the silk had a brand-new sheen to it, and none of the stitching was coming loose. If it hadn't been dirty, she would have said it had been made yesterday.

"It's new," she told the policemen, realizing that this might be a useful piece of information. "And it's *very* well made. A lot of work went into it. But it's not been cared for as you would expect."

"Expensive, would you reckon?"

"Oh, yes." But she was slightly distracted.

She had just noticed something bizarre about the cope. She wasn't familiar with Western vestments, but surely a cope didn't normally have two slits in the back like that. They were reinforced and bordered with embroidery, like giant buttonholes, and there were two exquisite little gold clasps above each one, to fasten them closed up to the neck. She couldn't think what they would be for.

"Well," said Mr. Anderson into the silence that had fallen, "I wish I did know something about it, but I'm afraid it beats me. You say this was in my bag?"

"Along with this," said the first policeman, the one who hadn't known about vestments, reaching into the canvas bag that they had brought with them. He pulled out a bundle of white cloth and shook it out. When both Evvie and Anderson gasped, he couldn't help looking slightly satisfied.

It was, as Evvie had expected, the Western kind of sticharion, a simple white robe, but it was gashed and dramatically bloodstained, as if someone had not long ago been killed in it. She and Flying Officer Anderson stared at it in dismay.

"Do you have any idea how this came to be in your bag, sir?"

"Absolutely none!"

"We didn't expect you to," said the other officer, the one without the dramatic flair. "It's pretty obvious you had nowt to do with this. We're just a bit flumoxxed, as you can imagine."

"If I were you," said Evvie, "I would ask at some of the local churches. Maybe they have had vestments stolen recently." Or had one of their deacons gruesomely murdered.

"Aye, I thought of that," said the policeman, glancing at his companion as if to say *I told you so* again. "But I can't think of any that would have something like this. They're all lower than a snake's belly in that part of the country. I mean," he explained for Evvie's benefit, "they're very Protestant, if not outright Non-Conformists. They wouldn't go in for vestments and the like."

"No," said Evvie, who had understood the reference to the snake's belly perfectly well, "of course not."

The other officer folded up the bloodstained sticharion. As he was about to put it back into the bag, Evvie noticed that it too had slits in the back, neatly hemmed, with buttons to fasten them at the neck. And she suddenly thought of a situation which would warrant permanent matching slits in both inner and outer vestments, with buttons above to fasten them. She was afraid she might begin to giggle crazily.

She decided not to tell the policemen her theory that their murder victim might have had wings.

"You're religious, Evvie?" Mr. Anderson asked, out of the blue, when the officers had left.

"Am I … oh. Yes."

"You just seemed to know a lot about that stuff."

"Well, my father was a priest." This was true, but beside the point. Her father had died when she was a little girl; the real reason she knew about vestments was more complex and tended to leave people not knowing what to say to her.

"Oh, a clergyman's daughter!" Anderson smiled. Evvie liked him, and was pretty sure he was safely engaged, so she smiled back.

"I don't know if any of the things you expect would necessarily be true. Orthodox priests are very outlandish, you know, with bushy beards and black hats."

Anderson laughed. "But I'll bet they bring their daughters up to have a very moral outlook, don't they?"

"I'm sure mine tried, while he lived."

"I wonder what you think I should have done, Evvie."

"Done?"

"Well, whether I should have told those policemen everything, or not."

She took a moment to let that sink in. "Of course without knowing anything about it, I *do* think you should have told them everything—but then I imagine you must have felt you had a good reason not to?"

"I guess so. It's just that when they asked about the bag, I realized that I *had* seen it recently. My squadron leader came up yesterday to visit—it was really thoughtful of him, and he brought some stuff from the base. And I think he had the bag with him. Anyway, he had a bag—I suppose it could have been his, but I figured at the time it was mine, and that he'd brought my clothes and boots, and took them away again because he realized I ..." Anderson sighed. "I wasn't going to need them. He's a good chap. I thought that might have been what it was. I thought that was considerate of him."

"It was," said Evvie. "And if he took the bag back with him, then it *was* at the base, and as you said, anyone there could have taken it."

"So you don't think I should have told them?" Anderson looked hopeful.

"No ... I do think you should have told them—I don't think you need worry about incriminating your commanding officer, because if he did take the bag back to the base with him, then the police will be able to work out, as we both did, that anyone could have taken it. And if he *didn't* take it back there, then he can tell them what he did do with it."

"Yes, I see what you mean. It's just that ... they said that it had been found in the boot of a car that belongs to a chap from Adderley, and that it went missing yesterday some time after three o'clock. And ... "

"That's when your commanding officer was visiting you," Evvie guessed.

Anderson nodded.

"What does he look like?"

Anderson looked worried. "Squadron Leader Boult? Um ... tall. Black hair. Thirtyish. Why?"

"Oh, I just wondered if he was who I thought. I saw him yesterday, I suppose that was after he'd been visiting you."

He had been on the stairs, heading up to a part of the house that he had no reason to go to, and then later he had been in the lodge, near the stables where Leo parked his car. And there had been something dangerous in a box in the lodge, and now it was gone. *Maybe it took your car*, Ernest had said. And Leo, hysterical: *Why would it need a car?*

Exactly. Why would it need a car? It had wings.

Of course none of that added up to a coherent picture of anything, and it was all quite absurd. But Evvie was left, somehow, with a conviction that Anderson's squadron leader and Leo Rathburn and his friend were on two opposing sides of some strange conflict, and she wanted to know more about what it was before she could say which side ought to win. She was not sure this represented a moral outlook that Anderson would have expected of a priest's daughter, or indeed that her own father would have approved. But—well, she was not sure.

"I don't think you should tell the police after all," she said, straightening Anderson's sheets, which had been disarranged by the police officers laying things on the bed. "I think you were right about that."

"Right," said Anderson, leaning back against his pillow. "Yes, I'm glad you agree. Being a clergyman's daughter and everything."

Something small had fluttered to the floor from the folds of the bedsheet as Evvie moved it, and she bent to pick it up. It was a tiny feather, soft and curled and bright, iridescent red.

*

"I think there's a croquet set around somewhere," said Evvie to Rosalind at lunch. She was pleased with herself for having successfully manoeuvred the conversation to this point. She knew very well where the croquet set was.

"It's a bit cold for croquet, don't you think?" said Rosalind doubtfully.

"Yes, I suppose so," said Evvie. She addressed Lady Rathburn across the table: "But there is a croquet set around somewhere, isn't there, Lady Rathburn? In the lodge?"

"Yes, I think that's where Gifford stored it. Did you want it? I would have thought it was a bit cold for croquet."

"I just thought of getting it out to make sure all the mallets and things are there," Evvie embroidered, once more pleased with herself. "So that when it warms up we can play."

"Oh, yes, if you like. I can give you the key after lunch. I don't have it on my ring with the others—I never go out there. Leo and Ernest were using the place for something … but I don't suppose they did anything with the croquet set."

They left it at that, as Lady Rathburn's attention was drawn by her nephew, who came in fuming about being victimized by the police.

"It's bad enough having my car stolen, without having to put up with insinuations that I might have bought contraband petrol and murdered someone in the back seat! It was *stolen*—how should *I* know how some bloody clothes ended up in it?"

Which gave Evvie the distinct idea that Leo knew plenty about it.

After lunch, she reminded Lady Rathburn of her promise of the key to the lodge. Rosalind tagged along as she went out to open it.

"What a cozy little place," said Rosalind, following her into the cold, stone-walled room.

"Cozy?" said Evvie in disbelief.

"Well, it could be, if it were fixed up. If I lived at Adderley, I'd make this my private retreat. I'd put floral curtains on the windows and an overstuffed chair in front of the fireplace and a rag rug on the floor."

"That sounds nice," said Evvie, and it did, but she couldn't connect Rosalind's comfortable picture with the cold interior of the lodge.

They found the croquet things and began pulling them out to assess the completeness of the set. Evvie cast her eye to the far corner of the room, where there was a bare patch of floor, as if something had recently been moved from there. Was that where Ernest's box had been? She couldn't see any other boxes; the rest of the space was taken up with furniture and gardening equipment. She made a pretty thorough search in the end, in the guise of looking for the green croquet ball, which did seem to be conveniently missing, but found neither the ball nor the box that she was really looking for. It was disappointing.

As she walked back with Rosalind towards the house, clutching her cardigan closed against the chilly wind, Evvie admitted to herself that she had been excited about the possibility of the dangerous thing in the box. Why was that? she asked herself sternly. Well, she was bored, and lonely, and homesick for a place that had never properly been her home. A nice juicy mystery, with Ernest the adulterer and the disagreeable Leo in the villains' roles—it could have been satisfying. It might even have given her something useful to do, something more interesting and of more obvious importance than hospital administration.

She'd been turning over several different possibilities since the discovery of the bloodstained vestments that morning. Perhaps the dangerous thing in the box was the murder weapon. Leo's car had obviously been stolen after he'd disposed of the body but before he had been able to destroy the evidence of the vestments. Or perhaps the body had been hidden in the box, and it was "dangerous" only in the sense that it would be a danger to Leo and Ernest, the murderers, if it were found. But why murder somebody in vestments in the first place? That certainly hadn't taken place at Adderley Hall; she would have heard about a priest in a red cope wandering around. And what about the actual body that had been found off Horrey Head, shot, apparently, not slashed with a knife?

More importantly, what about the red feather and the wing-slits—if that's what they were—in the vestments?

"I'm in the mood for croquet now," said Rosalind as they reached the back gate of the house. "Too bad it's so beastly cold! I know what—why don't we try to talk the boys into teaching us to play billiards?"

Evvie could think of nothing she'd like less, but fortunately—she'd been feeling guilty over using Rosalind in her pathetic little ploy to snoop in the lodge—she was spared actually having to say that.

"I'm afraid I've got to get back to work," she said instead, since it was true. "There's a prosthetist coming up from York, and we have to get ready for him."

On the way in, she passed Leo using the telephone at reception, while Ernest perched on the edge of the desk and thumbed through a train timetable. The lobby was otherwise empty.

"Etruscan, alabaster, very good condition." Leo scribbled irritably on the pad by the phone with a pencil. "Yes, well, tell him I wasn't in a position to sell it before, but I am now, that's all. If he's interested, good. If he's not, I'll find another buyer."

Leo slammed down the receiver and glared at Ernest. Archie was nowhere in sight, so Evvie stationed herself discreetly behind the two men at the desk, ready to claim she was just here to take over reception, but actually interested to hear their conversation.

"How can you be so unconcerned?" Leo demanded in a low voice. "That civilian plane they're talking about that crashed this morning? That was my plane. It's going after me, Ernest. In some roundabout way, it's going after me. Why do you think they never found the pilot?"

Ernest shrugged. "He bailed and parachuted safely to the ground. Or he didn't and he's dead somewhere. He was probably a German spy. Do I even want to know what you were doing with a private plane?"

"Business, Ernie." Leo was trying to light a cigarette with shaking fingers. "Just business. It's all business."

"Antiques, or … your other business?"

"Does it matter? Farren's saying he doesn't want to buy the sar-cophagus now—he wanted it last summer, but not now, and I had a big job lined up that I can't do without that plane. Everything's going to Hell in a hand-basket."

Ernest gave a snort. "I don't know what kind of basket it is, Leo, but Hell? Yeah, that's probably about right."

*

The patient from Newingthorpe arrived at quarter to two that afternoon. Evvie was surprised to find, seeing her in the lobby soon after her arrival, that the only survivor of the terrible crash was a girl younger than herself.

She was a tiny, fragile thing, fine-boned and wasted with illness. Her right leg had been amputated above the knee, and her right arm was in a sling. Her straight, honey-blonde hair had been chopped off seemingly at random in an unbecoming mess, and the right side of her face was disfigured with traces of old bruising. In spite of all this, she was still impishly pretty. She had beautiful blue eyes, and she smiled at everybody, in what Evvie though was a deliberate attempt to reassure them all that she was really much better than she looked. This was probably true. She was able to manoeuvre her wheelchair surprisingly well with one hand and the toe of her remaining shoe, and she was very talkative. She had a cultured American accent, and Evvie, who was in the lobby waiting for the prosthetics expert from York to arrive, heard the girl telling Archie that she was from Boston, Massachusetts.

"I'm Fee St. Clair," she said. "Fee is short for Fidelity, which is dreadful, isn't it? Hence 'Fee.' I work for a woman's magazine you wouldn't have heard of—they had me doing a story on the Air Force, to help stir up patriotism on the home front. When we crashed, they just replaced my story with a feature on Victory Gardens."

"You're a lady reporter?" Archie said sceptically. "How old are you?"

She sighed. "Twenty. I know—believe me, I'm used to being told I look younger. I guess in a couple of decades it will start to seem flattering."

Since Evvie had made the same mistake about the girl's age, she was grateful for Archie's tactlessness. She saw Fee looking curiously towards her where she stood in the corner of the lobby, and in another moment she would have stepped forward to introduce herself.

"Here she is!" said Lady Rathburn, coming in from the family wing of the house with Rosalind in tow. "Fidelity, this is Rosalind Lake, whom I mentioned. Rosalind, you'll show Fidelity around and make her feel at home, won't you? I know the two of you will find you have heaps in common."

"How d'you do?" said Rosalind awkwardly, sticking out a hand and then going blank-faced with embarrassment as she realized that Fidelity's right arm was immobilized.

The girl in the wheelchair just beamed up at her with that reassuring smile.

"It's so nice to meet you, Rosalind. Do please call me Fee—everybody does."

"Oh, you're American!" Rosalind cried. "How thrilling! I've always wanted to be from Abroad. I'm a very standard-issue English gentleman's daughter—I expect you'll find me terrifically boring."

"Not at all!" Fee said warmly. "I'm liable to find you much the more fascinating of the two of us. I know nothing about English gentlemen's daughters. Do you live on a country estate and everything? I'm technically the heiress of a soap empire, since my brother Calvin got himself written out of Daddy's will—but of course the business is only a shadow of its former self."

"A soap empire?" Rosalind repeated doubtfully. "Is that ... I'm so ignorant—is that American slang for something?"

Fee laughed. "No, it's quite literal. My father owns a soap company. St. Clair Soap. You won't have heard of it. They were going to expand overseas in the twenties—before I was born—but then the stock market crash happened, and everything went to pieces, and Daddy barely managed to hang onto the company. Of course, I've only ever known life in the aftermath. We're like Europe after the fall of the Roman Empire, all stories of past greatness, and eking out an existence among the ruins."

"Gosh," said Rosalind.

Evvie thought it was a magnificent image, and that "Gosh" didn't quite do it justice. She wished Lady Rathburn would introduce her to Fidelity so that she could be part of the conversation. But the mistress of the house, obviously feeling she had done the best she could at the moment for poor Fidelity, was taking her leave and telling Rosalind to take her new friend out onto the terrace. Rosalind turned the wheelchair awkwardly towards the front door.

"What happened to your hair?" Evvie heard her ask as she wheeled Fee out to the terrace.

"It caught fire," the girl said coolly.

Rosalind, to Evvie's relief, didn't say "Gosh" to that.

Chapter Five

THE WALLS OF ZION

"*And neither have I … wings to fly*," Charlie sang to himself, jumping down on the far side of yet another stile into yet another field occupied only by sheep. He paused to survey the far corners of the field, but saw no sign of any human habitation. He set off diagonally across the field, singing again: "*Give me a boat that can carry two, And both shall row, my love and I.*"

He was not a particularly good singer, and his repertoire of gloomy folksongs was not doing much to lift his spirits. But that wasn't really what he was going for.

He had been walking all day. Apparently he and Hal had come down at the furthest point removed from a telephone anywhere in the British Isles. He had encountered two farm houses in the course of the afternoon. At the first he had been given a meal and vague, roundabout directions to another farm where his hosts thought they might have a telephone. And they might have, but they had also had dogs and a shotgun and a fixed idea that he was a German spy.

"*A ship there is, and she sails the sea.*
She's loaded deep, as deep can be;
But not as deep as the love I'm in,
That I know not if I sink or swim."

The sheep in the field looked at him stupidly as he passed by. He'd lost a lot of time backtracking after the farm where they tried to shoot him, and by then there had been no one home at the first farm to direct him towards some other civilization. Wary of losing his means of finding his way back to Hal, he had kept on the track he had been following, although he was beginning to think it really was a trail from nowhere to nowhere. But half an hour ago he had seen a road from the brow of the hill he had been climbing, and decided to strike out across the sheep fields toward it. He couldn't remember the rest of that song, so he started a new one.

"A blacksmith courted me, nine months and better.
He fairly won my heart, wrote me a letter.
With his hammer in his hand, he looked so clever,
And if I was with my love, I would live forever."

He reached the edge of the field, climbed over another stile, and landed on the narrow grass verge of the road, just as a cream-coloured Vauxhall surged around the curve and nearly ran him down.

The car pulled to the opposite side of the road and stopped a few yards past him. The man behind the wheel was thin and grey—grey-haired, grey-faced, dressed in grey flannel—and the woman beside him looked enough like him to be his sister. She was much younger, her hair under her severe and unattractive hat a lustrous chestnut colour. They glanced at Charlie, then conferred gravely with one another for a moment, obviously discussing whether or not to offer him a ride. When they looked back in his direction, unsmiling, it was not clear to him what they had decided.

"Are you in trouble, young man?" the woman asked. She had a surprisingly deep, attractive voice.

"You could say that, yes," said Charlie, approaching the car. "I crashed my plane in the hills back there. I need to get to a phone to report to my base, and send someone to pick up my friend, who hurt himself."

Hopefully they wouldn't ask what on earth he had been doing flying in his dress uniform (without his cap and jacket, now).

"We will help your friend," said the woman. "Tell us where he is."

Something about the way she said it struck Charlie as odd, quite apart from the impracticality of the offer. It almost sounded as if she had been waiting for him to mention his friend. Of course that didn't make any sense. Charlie decided he had spent too long alone with

Hal, and wandering in the hills being shot at by paranoid farmers, and had somehow lost the ability to deal with normal people.

"That's very generous of you," he said, "but do you think you could give me a lift into the nearest town instead? The thing is, we'll both be in a lot of trouble if we don't report back to base."

"But if your friend is hurt …" said the man, glancing at the woman.

"Yes," she said. "We should go to him."

"I don't think you'll be able to get to him with the car," said Charlie, hoping that he still sounded reasonable. "He's not badly hurt—he'll be okay. But he had to stay with the plane. It's protocol." He shrugged apologetically.

"In that case," said the man, again glancing at the woman as if for approval, "I do think it would be best for us to drive you to Zion, where you can use a telephone."

"To where?" Charlie blurted, startled.

The man smiled greyly. "To our home. Please get in."

Charlie opened the back door of the car, mumbling suitable words of thanks, and got in. He found himself sharing the back seat with a large cardboard box with the name of a printer on a label pasted to the lid. As the man started the car and pulled back onto the road, Charlie tried to read the rest of the printing on the label to see what the box contained. It was five hundred copies of something called BALM FOR THE TROUBLED SPIRIT.

By this point he wasn't really surprised when the man glanced over his shoulder at him and said, "Young man, you will pardon my asking, but are you saved?"

Although he had half-expected the question, he had no idea how to answer it, and various disastrous options flashed through his mind. Finally he said, "I do go to Mass every Sunday, and Confession in Lent, if that's what you mean."

"It isn't," said the woman, with a musical laugh. "I feel sure you knew that. But don't worry—my brother won't throw you out of his car over a theological difference. Not when you are a soul in need."

Looking at her brother, she added, "You catch more flies with honey, Jeremiah, remember."

The brother laughed in his turn, much less musically. "Of course, Josephine. Of course. Forgive me, young man—we have not introduced ourselves. I am Dr. Jeremiah Good, pastor and director of the Zion Retreat Centre, and this is my sister Josephine."

"Charlie Boult. RAF squadron leader. Pleased to meet you. Looks like you've been picking up some tracts from the printers?"

"Yes," said the man, "we are very pleased with how they turned out. Do have a look."

Charlie opened the box and pulled out one of the low-budget, black-and-white pamphlets packed inside. It was badly laid out and embellished with very amateur line-drawings. He scanned the text, becoming more and more dismayed about the people who had picked him up. The Zion Retreat Centre was peddling some kind of heresy; his theologian friend Henley could have dissected it handily, he was sure. Oh Lord, Charlie found himself thinking irritably, why is everything always about fucking *church*?

"Very interesting," he said, stuffing the tract back into the box.

It was one of those soft-focus, sugar-coated heresies, all about beings of light and universal love, and very woolly on the subject of sin. If there'd ever been a time in history when that kind of thing could be said to fly, Charlie thought savagely, now was really not it.

The woman smiled back at him. In spite of the unflattering hat, she was striking, elegant-looking.

"It must be a relief for you, in a way," she said thoughtfully, in her beautiful voice. "Being out of the sky."

*

The Zion Retreat Centre was in the middle of nowhere, and it was in ruins. It was a large stone farm house that looked as though it had taken a direct hit from a bomb, knocking the whole back of the building into sticks and rubble, and leaving a section of the roof hanging precariously in the air without support. A white tent looming behind the house had obviously taken over some of the duties of the building.

"It happened last July," Dr. Good explained, as Charlie followed him from the garage, carrying the box of tracts. Miss Good had gone on ahead of them to the house. "A stray bomb, they said—most unlucky. In all likelihood a bomber headed for York had a malfunction and had to jettison its payload. My sister Josephine was nearly killed in the blast—a very near escape indeed, a genuine miracle. And do you know, it transformed her character. I am afraid Josephine was an apostate before the bomb fell. Her heart was hardened. But now she has become a tower of strength. So instrumental to me in my ministry. We have been holding services in the tent since it happened, while we raise money for repairs. A slow process. Fortunately we are still able to use most of the rooms, except when it rains."

Charlie heard all this, but he was distracted by the state of the building's roof.

"Did you say that it's been like that since last summer?" he asked Dr. Good.

"Yes. The twenty-sixth of July was when the catastrophe occurred." His host noticed that Charlie had stopped on the path, and turned to look at him with a worried expression.

"That's actually very dangerous," said Charlie. "Do you see the way that section of roof isn't supported by anything? It could fall down any time, and it would probably take that whole side of the roof with it."

"Oh dear. Do you think so?"

"Yeah, I think you're lucky it's lasted this long. I'd recommend you get some of the men from your congregation together—actually, get the girls out too, they can probably be a lot more help than you'd think—and get some temporary supports up right away. Don't worry about how it looks, and don't wait until you've raised money to do it nicely. You need to do it *now*."

"How kind of you to take an interest. How Christian of you."

"No, it's my profession—I'm an architect. Back home I had a business renovating churches." He laughed. "I feel as if I should give you my card, but oddly enough, I don't have one with me. But I can help you, if not with the actual work, at least with a plan. I can show you what needs to be done."

Dr. Good shook his head wonderingly. "It is Providential, young man. Providential. The Lord be praised!"

"I'm just happy to be able to help," said Charlie.

The building was chaos inside. Charlie got the sense that, quite apart from the havoc wreaked by the bomb, the Zion Retreat Centre was in the throes of an identity crisis. There was a faded sign propped in a corner that read simply "Zion," and a new, flashier sign waiting to be put up. There were stacks of newly-printed books with Dr. Good's name on the cover piled on an old secretary desk pushed in behind a brand-new reception counter. In the library visible through an open door off the front hall, the gleaming modern furniture blocked access to the overflowing bookshelves. It seemed as though the Goods had completely lost perspective. They had been redecorating and printing books and tracts while there was a gaping hole in the roof.

Miss Good appeared in the front hall, her face a study in gracious apology.

"I'm afraid our telephone is out of order, Mr. Boult."

"Not again?" Dr. Good exclaimed. "But how vexing! I thought last time that the problem had been repaired once and for all."

His sister shook her head. "You mustn't blame the repairman, Jeremiah—I am sure he only did his best. Of course it is a nuisance for us, but I am most concerned for you, Mr. Boult. You will not be able to contact your base. How terrible that we have taken you out of your way with a false promise of aid which we cannot fulfil!"

"Josephine …" Dr. Good frowned.

"Yes, Jeremiah?"

"Never mind."

"Don't worry about it," said Charlie hastily. "It's bad luck, but if you can just point me in the direction of the nearest village …"

"I wouldn't dream of it," said Dr. Good. "I will drive you to Newingthorpe myself. It is not far at all, a matter of half a dozen miles."

Six miles from Newingthorpe? Charlie tried to work out what that meant about where he and Hal had crashed, and whether it made sense. On the whole, he thought it didn't, and that worried him. He hadn't been exaggerating—he didn't think he had been exaggerating—when he told Hal he had an excellent sense of direction. The simplest explanation was that he had got turned around when he was fleeing from the American plane. He wished he could feel more convinced that was all it was.

"Oh, but Jeremiah," Miss Good was saying now, in an agony of apology again, "you are forgetting the meeting at four o'clock. It is quarter to four now."

"I have not forgotten," said Dr. Good, unconvincingly. "Mr.—Squadron—"

"Charlie," Charlie suggested.

Dr. Good coughed awkwardly and plainly didn't know how to address Charlie at all now. Charlie felt suddenly quite kindly towards him.

"Josephine is correct," Dr. Good went on finally. "I do have a meeting to lead at four o'clock. But it will likely … that is, there is a good chance it will be over very quickly—almost before it starts, in effect—as I am not at all sure that anyone intends to come."

"Oh, Jeremiah …" Miss Good sighed.

"And in any case, I will drive you to Newingthorpe immediately afterward. I assure you it will still be much faster than for you to walk there on your own. In the meantime, Josephine will make you some coffee—she has managed to procure real coffee from somewhere, such a mystery to me how she does it! And if you are hungry—are you hungry? you must be hungry—she will make you a sandwich. Won't you, Josephine?"

"Of course, Jeremiah, of course!"

You've forgotten my story about the injured friend, Charlie thought, *and how eager you were to go to his rescue when you first heard about him.* But they were clearly very odd people, and perhaps it was too much to expect any kind of consistency from them. He felt a profound desire not to hang about their falling-down farm house eating sandwiches and drinking coffee while Dr. Good conducted his pathetic prayer-meeting—always supposing he would be allowed to sit it out, which he guessed wasn't very likely. He thought about Hal lying under the trees where he had left him, anxious and hurt and unable to move, and the dark descending on him. And he thought about the way he had wanted to call the angel "darling," and he thought: six miles to Newingthorpe, that would take me two hours to walk at this time of day, with how tired I am—more if any of it's uphill—and chances are old Jeremiah doesn't really know how far it is, and it might be more like eight or nine miles, and even if I made it in two hours, by that time it would be six o'clock, the garages will be closed, and I can't risk stealing another car, so the fact is I'll end up having to spend the night in Newingthorpe any way you look at it, and *God,* could I use a coffee.

"Sure," he said, "that sounds fine."

The kitchen, mercifully, was in one of the intact parts of the house, and it was warm and welcoming. Miss Good motioned him to a high-backed bench by the fireplace, with a worn, striped cushion on the seat, and he sank down gratefully on it. She had taken to calling him Charlie.

"How do you take your coffee, Charlie?" she asked, putting water on the stove.

"I can't even remember, it's been so long since I had real coffee."

She laughed melodiously.

"Black, I think," he said. "Yeah, black sounds good."

"Black it is. And what would you say to a ham sandwich?"

"I don't want to put you to any trouble. I can get dinner in New-ingthorpe." He preferred to cling to the notion that he was going to be in Newingthorpe by dinner-time.

"It's no trouble—indeed, I feel I owe it to you, for taking you out of your way like this."

"No, please. Don't worry about that. A ham sandwich would be terrific."

She laughed again. "You are American, aren't you?"

"Canadian."

"Oh, I do beg your pardon!"

"Not to worry. I've got nothing against Americans." *Except that I got shot out of the sky by one this morning.* He wanted to tell her that she didn't need to make conversation; he would be happy just to sit there. He leaned his head against the back of the bench and shut his eyes.

When he opened them, Miss Good was cutting thick slices from a ham on the scrubbed wooden table in the middle of the kitchen. "And you are Catholic, are you?" she said conversationally.

Here we go, Charlie thought. Something odd got into him, and he said, "Do you think? Maybe I was just saying that about Mass and Confession to get a rise out of your brother."

"Oh, how I would like to believe that!" she said, her eyes flashing with mirth.

"Go right ahead," he said, and then they were both laughing.

And somehow he had the impression that what she took him to mean was that he didn't believe in any of it. He didn't do anything to correct her.

"I think I must remind you of your mother," she said. "That's so, isn't it?"

"What? Good grief, no!" He judged she was at most five or six years older than he, for one thing. But what he said was, "You wouldn't want to remind anyone of my mom."

"Oh, dear. Why not?"

"Well, she was just real young when she had me, and didn't know the first thing about raising a kid. Or want to learn, really." He realized after he said this that it sounded bitter, as if he regretted that his mother hadn't involved him in her horrible life, when really, what she'd done for him had been the best possible thing.

"But she did a good job in the end," said Miss Good. "You've turned out well."

"Thanks, but she had nothing to do with it. My gran was the one who raised me."

"Ah, I see. And did you not know your father at all, then?"

"Oh, I knew him all right. He and my mom were married—or she always claimed they were married, anyway." Again, he didn't know why he had said that. Nobody had doubted that they were married, not even his grandmother, who had plenty of reason to wish they weren't. And it wasn't the sort of thing his mother would have lied about.

Miss Good set down a steaming mug of coffee next to the plate with the freshly made ham sandwich, and Charlie got up from the bench and sat at the table. She took the chair opposite him, and curled her hands around her own cup of coffee. She wore a curiously masculine ring on one hand, with a red stone. She tipped her head to one side as she looked at him warmly.

"And I hope there is another woman in your life," she said. "A younger woman?"

"No," he said, smiling and sipping his coffee. It was strong and delicious.

"No?" She looked sad and a little sceptical.

"Well, not at the moment."

Where was he going with this? he wondered.

"So there was someone!"

"Yeah, but—it didn't work out."

He hoped she would let him leave it at that. He took a bite of his sandwich.

"This is great," he said. "The coffee too. Even better than I remembered it."

"Tell me about her," she said.

"What? Why?"

"Because it helps to talk about these things."

"I don't know what there is to talk about," he said, after finishing another large bite of the sandwich. All of a sudden, though, he realized she was right; he did need to talk about it, desperately. "She was dishonest with me. There was somebody else."

"She cheated on you?"

"No, I was the person she was cheating with. But she hadn't told me. She didn't see why I would care."

"How thoughtless! Of course you would care. Your sensitivity is obvious even to me, and I have only known you such a little while. She must have seen it herself. How could she think you wouldn't care?"

"It doesn't—I'm not sensitive. It's something anyone should care about. It's next door to adultery." Of course there was also another name for it.

"She was married?"

"Engaged."

"Was this at home in Canada?"

"No."

She nodded. "I thought not. So it was here, in England. The war has upset so many things, don't you think? People behave in ways they never would in peacetime, but you know, they are just trying to grasp a little happiness for themselves, in the face of such danger. Thinking they might lose everything tomorrow. I'm sure you can understand that."

"Yes, I do. That makes sense."

"Perhaps you should forgive her."

"Sure. I did. It's not as if I'm still angry. We talk. It's okay between us."

"Then perhaps there is a future for the two of you after all." She said it in a gentle whisper. "A future together. Engaged isn't married, after all, is it?"

"There's no future for us," said Charlie coldly.

"No, perhaps you are right. If she could cheat on one man, what's to say she wouldn't cheat on another? It was certainly very generous of you to forgive her. Very loving. I hope you aren't missing her terribly."

"No … I don't think so." In fact, he was so mired in this fiction that he didn't know what to think any more. He tried to work out whether, given that he hadn't been talking about an actual woman, any of what she said had any possible bearing. He wasn't sure.

"What made you decide to join the Air Force?" she asked after a moment. "Did you know how to fly planes before the war?"

"No, I learned after I joined up. I don't know why I picked the Air Force. I guess I was trying to impress someone." Really?

"Another woman?" She smiled.

"No, a man."

"And did you? Was he impressed?"

Charlie shook his head. "Of course not. He doesn't give a damn about me, when the chips are down." He stopped dead, the coffee cup halfway to his lips. "Sorry! Pardon my language." But that wasn't really what had frozen him.

She leaned forward across the table, looking into his eyes. "You care more about that than about the girl, don't you?"

For a dizzying instant he had the strangest feeling, as though she were about to read the whole story out of his head, as though she were opening the book, flipping past the title page, scanning the table of contents, looking for the chapter headed "Father Underhill."

He pushed his chair back from the table with a squeal of wood on flagstones, and banged the book shut.

"Of course I do," he said, trying not to shout. "Of course I care more about him than about some lousy affair that lasted a month, that was wrong and stupid from beginning to end—of course I do. And it isn't remotely true that he doesn't care about me. He does. It's his goddamn *job*."

"Goodness," she said.

He got to his feet. The coffee was not finished, but that was just too bad.

"I have to go," he said. "Thanks for the food. Tell your brother I'm sorry, but I realized I really can't wait."

She got up from her chair and started to say something, but he was out of the room before he could properly hear it. He crossed the front hall in a few strides and let himself out the door.

Of course it wasn't so much that he couldn't wait as that he couldn't wait there, with Miss Good. In the time it had taken him to eat a sandwich in her kitchen, he had maligned his mother, insulted a man he respected and loved more than anyone in the world, and come near to denying his faith. What had happened, he decided, was that somehow, sometime in the recent past, the bottom had fallen out of his spiritual life, and he hadn't seen it until now.

Once outside the door, he put a decent distance between himself and the half-destroyed farm house as quickly as he could without actually running. He had a queasy moment when he reached the road and realized that he didn't know which direction to head for Newingthorpe, and he wondered briefly whether he was overreacting and should slink back to the house and make some kind of excuse and wait for Dr. Good after all. But reason—at least, it was partly reason—prevailed, and he worked out that he should still be north of Newingthorpe, and figured out from the sun which direction was south, and set off along the road. And as luck would have it, he was shortly overtaken by a man on a bicycle, who was able to confirm that he was headed the right way.

That was as far as his luck held. The rest of the walk was a kind of low-grade waking nightmare. It began to rain, not hard but steadily. It got dark. The road to Newingthorpe was almost entirely uphill, and Dr. Good's six miles was definitely more like ten. By the end of it Charlie was ready to curl up in a hedge by the side of the road and sleep out the rest of the night. If it hadn't been raining, he would have done it. He thought about Hal under the trees where he had left him, and wondered if his wings were waterproof. He wondered what his newly discovered spiritual breakdown had to do with his failure to save Hal.

This was a new thought, at least. Up to that point he had just been turning over and over the things that he had said in the kitchen, until his mind felt as blistered as his feet. When he finally limped into the main street of grey, rain-soaked Newingthorpe and saw the lighted windows of a pub blessedly beckoning, he realized that he had wasted hours which he could have spent perfecting the story he was going to tell Flight Lieutenant Benson. But he was past caring. He dripped his way to the bar and ordered a pint of ale, which he took with him to the pay phone in the corner. He took several long draughts while he waited for the operator to connect his call and for someone at the Adderley base to fetch Benson.

"Boult! What can I do for you?"

This was not how he had expected the conversation to begin.

"Well, I expect you've been wondering where I am."

"No, no. Well, we were a bit puzzled yesterday, but Addison-Carmichael put us wise."

"Addison-Carmichael," Charlie repeated stupidly. It took him a moment to remember that this was Latham's surname. But then a wholly unexpected possibility began—blessedly—to take shape in his mind before he could say anything more damning. He managed to keep his tone perfectly light as he said, "Addison-Carmichael, right. What did he tell you?"

"Just that you'd got another secretive MOD summons and gone tearing off to Newingthorpe." Benson laughed. "He said he didn't know if you'd remember telling him, you looked so distracted."

"No, I remember telling him. I remember telling someone, anyway. I'm down at Newingthorpe now, and I don't know exactly when I'll be back."

They spoke for a little longer, while Charlie adjusted to the idea that he wasn't AWL after all; he was seconded to some obscure MOD department on a classified mission. It was plausible, actually. He had flown a few such missions in the past. It wouldn't hold up as a story if Wing Commander Ogilvy found out about it, but maybe there was no need for him to find out. Charlie felt slightly giddy thinking about it, and realized he wasn't hearing what Benson was saying. Before he hung up, he said, "Please make sure to thank Latham for passing on the message for me."

He replaced the receiver and sat nursing his glass and looking out across the bar, thinking yet again about what he had said in Miss Good's kitchen—but this time about the one bit of it he hadn't felt guilty for. He had vented his bitterness about Latham to a stranger, caricatured him as a cheating woman. And Latham in the meantime had done him a tremendous favour, had lied for him, unasked, and at some risk to himself, since he actually could have had no idea where Charlie was or what he was doing. Charlie had cut him loose in some kind of belated fit of scruples, and Latham had behaved—in a morally questionable and court-martial-worthy way, admittedly—like a friend.

Though it was an entirely mundane piece of good fortune, it felt surprisingly like a miracle. By this time he had enough sense not to imagine he'd done anything to deserve it.

Charlie took another swallow of his drink, and lifted the phone receiver again. He asked to be put through to the Newingthorpe air

base, and thought about how best to frame a request to borrow a
jeep. What odds? he thought. He was seconded to the Department
of Angel-Rescuing, after all. And there was no way he was going
to sleep that night.

Chapter Six

FIDELITY

Evvie didn't get an opportunity to talk to Fee until dinner that night. The "family"—Lady Rathburn, Leo, and Dr. Sheppard, Lady Rathburn's brother—took most of their meals in the dining room with the patients and staff of the hospital, except the nurse on duty and any of the amputees who were too sick or self-conscious to eat in company. The family-style meals were thought to be good for morale. But eating at a long, linen-covered table under giant paintings and winking chandeliers wasn't really "family-style" to anyone normal, and the result was an odd atmosphere, with patients and staff outnumbering family, and Dr. Sheppard being in both camps anyway, and everybody trying to be on their best behaviour. Evvie, as an employee with a personal connection to the Rathburns, was midway between staff and family, and sometimes sat with the patients, to contribute to morale, and sometimes with the family, to avoid the wistful flirtation of young men like Captain Carter. That evening she found herself sitting across the table from the new girl in her wheelchair. Rosalind, sitting on Fee's left, was chatting to her about film actors as they ate their soup. Then Daphne appeared, late and lacking Ernest. She looked Fee over critically, sat down on the other side of Rosalind, and said, "Introduce me to your friend."

"Oh, sure. Fee, this is Daphne Montague, my cousin. Daph, Fee St. Clair. Fee's an American soap heiress."

Fee beamed as usual, and said, "Lovely to meet you," but Evvie cringed on her behalf. And there had been just an infinitesimal pause before her smile clicked on; she was tired, Evvie thought, and she didn't like being summed up as a "soap heiress." Well, who would? Especially when she had a career of her own, and had been horribly injured doing her patriotic duty at her job.

Daphne looked at Fee as if she had been presented as the punch-line of a not-very-funny joke. "What kind of soap?"

"All kinds," said Rosalind. "Right, Fee? Her father owns a soap factory."

"Three," Fee corrected her politely. "Three factories, actually. One for the luxury products, one for laundry soap, and one for miscellaneous." She gave a diffident little shrug, as if to apologize for knowing all this. "Daddy did get a military contract when the U.S. entered the war, and that was what made it possible to open the third factory. Besides, it's been good for business. We did an advertising campaign with pictures of handsome GIs washing with our St. Clair Pearly White Toilet Soap—it's been selling like stink ever since."

"And who is 'Daddy'?" Daphne asked. "Would I have heard of him?"

"Gregory St. Clair. And no—we haven't expanded overseas."

"I'm sure I know some St. Clairs from New York, though," said Daphne.

"You might," said Fee quickly, "but they wouldn't be relatives of ours. At least, I wouldn't know them. The truth is, Daddy's family is complicated—and we're the black sheep because we're on the wrong side of the Catholic-Protestant divide."

"I think the New York St. Clairs I know are Catholics."

"Exactly. And we're Baptists, you see. In spite of the name. And nobody talks to anybody—it's really quite sad."

"I see." Daphne looked bored. "And, my dear, *what happened* to you?" She managed somehow to make the question sound critical, as if Fee's condition were her own fault, something she had done on purpose to offend Daphne.

"She was in that plane crash at Newingthorpe," Rosalind supplied. "She's really very lucky to be alive."

"Oh, I'm sure," said Daphne blandly.

And she proceeded to talk to Rosalind about some couple they both knew, casually excluding Fee from the conversation. Fee did not look as if she minded.

The servants removed the soup bowls and brought out the main course, and Evvie saw Fee take her fork in her left hand and stick it glumly into the chop on her plate. She looked around hopefully for assistance, but Daphne was still monopolizing Rosalind, and all the nurses were busy helping the men.

"I've got it," said Evvie.

Fee's blue eyes flicked up to meet hers across the table, surprised.

"I'll cut up mine and we'll swap," Evvie suggested. "Is that all right?"

"Brilliant. Thanks." Watching Evvie cutting the meat into little pieces, she said, "It's funny what you can learn to be grateful for. Anywhere else, I'd be complaining about not being able to use my right hand—but you know, at least it's still attached to me."

Evvie smiled at her. Finished cutting up her food, she stood to reach across the table and switch the plates.

"Ta dah!" she said under her breath as she sat down with Fidelity's plate.

Fee giggled. "You're a life-saver. Thanks! What's your name?"

"Evgenia." She thought that someone named "Fidelity" could probably appreciate what it was like to go around with a name like that.

Fee's eyes widened. "So beautiful!"

"Thanks. Everyone calls me Evvie."

"I'll bet they do. Ev-yeh-*nee*-a—is that right? It isn't hard to say. What does it mean? Oh, um, don't tell me. It's like a nicer version of Eugenia. 'Well-born,' right?"

"That's right. I'm not, particularly."

Fee laughed. "No? But are you, for instance, a dish-cloth heiress or anything?" She lowered her voice a little as she said it, and just glanced in Rosalind's direction.

"No, nothing so glamorous."

"I saw you in the lobby when I arrived. You work here, don't you?"

"Yes. I'm Lady Rathburn's general factotum, and I do miscellaneous mending and sewing as required. I've even … well, this afternoon I got to learn from a prosthetist from York how to mould a leather socket for a new kind of limb that they're testing out."

"How tremendously useful of you!" said Fee brightly, but Evvie could see she was brought up a bit short by the idea of prosthetic limbs. They weren't just an abstract idea any more, but something she was going to have to become acquainted with if she ever wanted to walk again. That was why Evvie had hesitated before mentioning that part of her work. But Fee struck her as the type of girl who wouldn't want the conversation censored for her sake. "Were you a seamstress or a shoemaker or something on civvy street?"

"No, nothing practical like that. But I did needlework—silk embroidery, mostly."

"Oh, swoon! I so admire people who can do things like that. My godmother has tried three times to teach me to knit, and it's never taken. Though maybe I'll have to give it another try now, just because—you know, *two hands*! Hooray! She does embroidery too, my godmother does. Do you have any of yours here, or did you have to leave it all at home?"

"I had to leave it, yes. I was working on a big piece when the war started—rows and rows of lilies … I wonder what has happened to that now." She pictured it sitting forlornly in the whitewashed room where she had left it—although of course Sister Irene or someone would have had the good sense to pack it away. "I do monograms for some of the patients, when I have spare time."

"I'll bet they like that."

"I could do one for you."

"Thank you!" She looked genuinely pleased by the idea. She was really beautiful when she smiled, Evvie thought, in spite of everything. "Could you put a lily in it? *F.—lily—St. C.?* Like that?"

"I could try."

"It could be another flower, if you don't think the lily would be quite right. I don't want to be presumptuous."

Evvie was about to say that lilies seemed just right, when Rosalind turned to involve Fee in an argument she was having with Daphne about the name of some American product. For the rest of the meal, Evvie was on the outside of the conversation, but she listened in unabashedly. She listened to Fee talk about her cousin Graham, who worked for the Foreign Office and whose house she had been staying at before her disastrous flight to Yorkshire. And there was her other cousin George, at home in America, who had tried not to show it but envied her for being able to go overseas to do something to help the war effort, being himself too young to enlist. She was a good story-teller; you could picture Graham and George as she talked about them. Evvie thought she must be good at her job, and wanted to ask her what she had written about. But Rosalind was too busy telling Fee about the murder investigation, and how the police had been searching for a gun and questioning everyone at the hospital. Fee acted gratifyingly impressed. After dinner, Nurse Porter and Nurse Griggs swooped down on her and began to fuss over her chopped-off hair.

"I think if it was feathered at the sides it could look quite decent," said Nurse Griggs.

"I don't know," said Porter, petting Fee's head critically as if she were on display in a shop. "I think the best thing to do would be to curl these longer bits and pull back all these short pieces at the sides with a nice broad ribbon and some barrettes. A permanent wave might help."

"Maybe. My hairdresser back home would know what to do with

it. She can work wonders! I wish I knew how she did it. But we'll figure something out, dearie." She patted Fee's arm.

Fidelity smiled very sweetly and said nothing.

*

That evening, as most evenings, the family and their guests sat in one of the private drawing rooms for a while after dinner. Evvie had brought Wing Commander Stewart's monogram to work on, and she sat in her favourite spot at the end of a couch near the fire. Sitting with her embroidery in her lap, she let her gaze drift around the room, wondering, if she were Lord Peter Wimsey or Inspector Grant of Scotland Yard, with which of these people she would strike up a conversation that would deliver the appropriate clues to solve "The Adderley Affair" or "The Mystery of the Red Cope," or whatever it would be called.

There was Rosalind, flipping desultorily through a fashion magazine at the opposite end of the couch. She had already talked to Rosalind, and Rosalind did not seem a good source of clues. There were Lady Rathburn and her brother, at the card table, playing gin rummy. Lady Rathburn was in her forties, red-haired, and wore tweed suits like a uniform. Evvie liked her. She liked Dr. Sheppard, too, who was older than his sister, equally red-haired, and taciturn about everything except his professional speciality. She knew both of them too well to feel that there were any important secrets she could learn from either of them.

Her eyes lighted on Daphne, who was standing by the window, arms folded, looking out on the dark grounds and displaying a beautiful three-quarter profile to the rest of the room. Yes, Daphne was the one Lord Peter Wimsey would have struck up a conversation with, Evvie decided, and he would have learned all kinds of telling things—things Daphne probably wouldn't want him to know. But it was all very well if you were Lord Peter Wimsey; Evvie wasn't, and she didn't want to talk to Daphne. She picked up her embroidery.

She'd made only a few stitches in the lion's mane when the drawing-room door opened and Leo and Ernest slouched in, both with demoralized, hangdog expressions. Lady Rathburn laid down her cards and turned in her chair to give them a dissatisfied look.

"You missed dinner, Leo—you might have told us you would be out."

"We're frightfully sorry, Lady Rathburn," said Ernest. "It won't happen again, though. We were haring about the countryside in search of some artifact Leo had his heart set on, but we didn't find it, and we're done searching for it, so you can count on seeing us at dinner from now on."

Leo flung himself down on the couch across from Evvie, then started up again in order to poke savagely at the fire. Ernest went to the window to join Daphne.

"It beats me why the two of you still hang out together so much," said Rosalind, glancing between Ernest and Leo. "It's not as if you're really friends."

Leo subsided angrily onto the couch again, frowning at Rosalind, who had gone back to her magazine. "Of course we're friends," he said. "Of course we are. Certain things happen, but it doesn't mean anything's different. It doesn't change anything—why would it?"

Rosalind seemed to have lost interest, and when Leo looked up to see that Evvie's eyes were on him, he merely scowled at her. But a moment later she saw him twist in his seat to look over his shoulder at Ernest, who stood with his arm tucked tightly around Daphne's waist, their heads bent together, the two of them deep in their private world. *Certain things happen* … Daphne was the obvious explanation. Daphne had happened to Ernest, and he would never be the same, no matter how much Leo tried to pretend otherwise. Evvie wondered if that was it.

Chapter Seven

TO KEEP THEE IN ALL THY WAYS

With a map and a vehicle, but without the ability to cut across sheep fields, it took Charlie a couple of hours to retrace his day's walk, and after the added time spent at Newingthorpe airfield acquiring dry clothes and provisions, and stopping briefly at the pub on the way out of the village, it was midnight by the time he reached the grove where he had left Hal. At least he thought it was the grove where he had left Hal.

The night was a deep, thorough black. The jeep bumped slowly along the track between the hills, following the juddering beam of its headlights. It had stopped raining.

"*For he shall give his angels charge over thee,*" Charlie chanted under his breath, knowing that he hadn't got the tone right. "*To keep thee in all thy ways. They shall bear thee in their hands : that thou hurt not thy foot against a stone …* "

He was very tired, but the panic and despair of the evening were gone—maybe just because he was so tired.

Tree trunks marshalled palely at the edge of the headlights' beam, and he slowed the jeep to a crawl. Was it here? He didn't remember there being this many trees, but the dark was disorienting. He was on the point of stopping the vehicle to get out and search on foot, when the ghostly beam ahead of him fell on a figure in among the trees, huddled against the base of a trunk: a white face, a dark coat, the collar turned up, blazing red hair.

He stepped on the brake and threw the jeep into park. "Hal! It's me!" He jumped down from the driver's side.

"Charles." It wasn't an exclamation; it was barely more than a whisper, but it was full of joyous relief.

The wings were gone, and Hal's curly hair was short, in a neat, modern cut. In the headlights' harsh light, he looked frail and ill, and he plainly couldn't stand up.

Charlie flung himself down on his knees and gathered Hal into his arms to hug him tightly. The fabric of Hal's coat was soggy; evidently his wings hadn't kept him dry, or maybe he'd got rid of them before the rain started. He was trembling in a way that might just have been cold, but might also have been crying.

"It's okay," Charlie said. "I'm here. I'll never abandon you. Never. I promise that. I swear it."

He could feel Hal's forehead resting against his collarbone, Hal's hand gripping the front of his shirt. He wondered if the angel's hair smelled like incense. It would have been very easy just then to find out. He loosened his hold slightly.

"Sorry … I've had kind of a long day. Guess I'm a bit overwrought." He tried to laugh.

After a moment Hal stirred, let go of Charlie's jacket, and sat up. He touched the side of Charlie's face. His fingers were ice-cold; it took an effort not to flinch away from the touch. His eyes, Charlie saw, were dry.

"Nor will I abandon you. I make you the same promise."

Charlie let out the breath that he had unintentionally been holding. "You've no idea—maybe you have some idea—how much I needed to hear that."

Hal nodded.

"I'm sorry it took me so long to come back," said Charlie.

"I didn't expect you before morning."

"I know—me neither. Still, you've been on your own a long time, and I'm sorry. I phoned my base and everything's okay. Bizarrely, miraculously okay. I've got a jeep—do you want to lie down in the back, or …"

"If you don't mind, I'd rather sit in the front with you."

"You got it."

"I don't think I …"

"Can get up? No, I figured. Here, why don't we get you out of this wet coat first."

Hal let himself be stripped of the soggy coat, lifted into the passenger seat of the jeep, and wrapped in a dry blanket. Charlie rummaged in the back for the food and drink he had brought from Newingthorpe.

"I couldn't get cake at this hour," he said, "but I did get beer." He produced two bottles. "And cheese sandwiches, crisps, chocolate, and a couple of apples. What would you like?"

Hal laughed happily. He was tugging at the wet laces of his boots. "I'd like a beer, please. And a sandwich. I don't think that I know what crisps are."

"Potato chips. You'll like them."

Charlie climbed back into the driver's seat and opened the beer bottles with his penknife. Hal had got his boots and socks off, and was rubbing his bare feet with the edge of the blanket and looking more like himself. Charlie handed him a bottle and a paper-wrapped sandwich. He opened the crisp packet and balanced it on the gear-box between the seats. He turned off the jeep's headlights, and they sat in the dim glow of the lights on the dashboard. The night was quiet and immense around them. Hal sat with his feet tucked up on the seat and the blanket wrapped snugly around him. He took a long swig from the beer bottle and sighed happily.

"You must have had a worse day than I did," Charlie remarked. "I see you got rid of the wings, but it looks like that just about did you in."

Hal took a bite of his sandwich, and looked happy about that too. "Somebody came—a farmer with a dog. I just managed to hide. To turn invisible, I mean. I did not want to frighten him to no purpose. After that, I did find the strength to … to reconstruct my form without the wings."

"And you cut your hair. So to speak."

"I noticed that the long hair made me conspicuous. Why have I never had these before? They are *very* good." He had tried one of the crisps. "And I discovered that short hair was an acceptable variation to the form as I originally learned it from you. Whereas altering my height or the colour of my eyes would not have been."

"I see. That's what you were distracting yourself with, is it?"

Hal laughed again, and Charlie thought he was happy to find himself so well understood.

Charlie's eyes had adjusted to the darkness enough that he could see Hal fairly well. He sat for a moment in silence, watching the angel hedonistically eating potato chips and licking salt off his beautiful fingers. The short hair suited him. Charlie wanted to run a hand through it, feel the clipped curls slip through his fingers. He wondered what Hal would do if he did that. What if he leaned over and undid the top button of Hal's shirt, and kissed his white throat, just in that hollow where his collar came together? What if he … Charlie felt sick to his stomach. *He's the most amazing thing ever to happen to you. Can you just this once not be like that?*

"It's an okay body, right?" he said, successfully recalling what they had been talking about. "I mean, you're not wishing I'd come up with something better, are you?" *For instance, if you knew I was sitting here getting hard wondering whether you would stop me kissing you, would you wish you were a woman?*

Hal just smiled at him. "Where did it come from?"

"A stained-glass window." Charlie took another swig of beer and shifted carefully in his seat. Thinking about St. John's cooled him off somewhat. He wondered just how much Hal *did* know about what he had been thinking. "Back home, in my church, there's this one window with a lone angel in it. There used to be a whole set of them, in the narthex, but the others were destroyed in a fire, long before my time, and there's just this one left. He has red hair, red wings, and a red cope. And the rector's daughter, when she was little, nicknamed him Hal, and for some reason it stuck."

"And that's me," said Hal thoughtfully.

"That's why I call you Hal, yeah."

"It feels like my name."

It occurred to Charlie that Hal didn't remember his real name. He wondered why he hadn't thought about that before.

"A weird thing happened to me today," he said.

Hal raised an eyebrow. "*A* weird thing? Really, Charles."

They laughed about that for a minute. Charlie looked at Hal curiously.

"Say that again?"

"What?"

"'Really, Charles'—but say it the way you said it."

"Why?"

"Because I never noticed before that you have an English accent."

"Really, Charles?"

"Yeah, you do—you have all along, it just didn't register somehow."

"I'm sure it's a metaphor for something."

They laughed about that too.

"Well, okay. *Several* weird things happened to me today—yesterday, I mean—I think it's tomorrow by now."

"Have mercy."

"Sorry. I ran across this place … Well. When you said your captors were going to Jerusalem … are you sure that's the word they used? Only I remember you said you have trouble telling what language people are speaking, and I wondered if it was possible they used another word. Say, Zion?"

"Yes. That is possible."

"Because I ran across a pseudo-church place today called the Zion Retreat Centre. I wondered if that might have been where they were going. Do you think it's possible?"

Hal nodded.

"What were they going there for, do you know?"

"They were going to take me there. They thought it would be safer. They have a friend there, and they said something about an old man who would never know."

The idea of Dr. Good pottering around with his tracts about light while Hal was being eviscerated in his basement made Charlie queasy. It was somehow all too plausible.

"Huh. Well, it was an odd place. I did get a kind of sinister feeling about it—about one of the people there, anyway."

"Tell me."

He tried to explain about Miss Good and his feeling that she had been about to read him like a book. "It was subtle," he admitted, "and maybe I'm just going crazy. But she seemed to know about you, somehow, and she kept asking these funny, pointed questions, and I … well, it brought out the worst in me. I kept saying awful things."

"Like what?"

"Like I was flippant about my religion. And you've got to understand, I'm *never* flippant about my religion, it's incredibly important to me—it's … the anchor of my life. I don't mean that I'm some kind of saint—far from it—it's just I've always gone to church, the same church, I've been an acolyte there ever since I was a kid. It's home. And I acted, just for a minute, like that might not have been true. And then it all went to shit from there. I started saying these mean-spirited things about my mother that I don't even think are true. They're the kind of things you might imagine I'd think, you know, if I were a character in a story or something. A pretty trite kind of story, though. And then she started asking whether I had a woman in my life …"

"And you went on acting like a character in a story?" Hal suggested. He had finished his beer, and reached down to put the bottle on the floor of the jeep. He peered into the crisp bag and offered the remaining fragments to Charlie.

"No, you have them. I'm getting a kick out of just watching you eat them."

"That sounds like the sort of thing I should say," said Hal wryly. He tipped the last of the chips out of the bag into his palm. "But continue. Did you make up an imaginary wife to impress this strange woman?"

"Just an imaginary girlfriend, but yeah." He found it a little unsettling that Hal had been able to guess this. "It's not as if that's something I've never done before. Back home, I had a deal with my friend Vera that if I need a fake fiancée, she's always available to play the role, and her standard line with men is that she's just had her heart broken by the love of her life, and if anyone asks for details, she describes me. Although the last time I heard from her, she'd met a guy she didn't tell that story to, so that may be a good sign. Her problem is just that she doesn't like men all that much, but my problem …" Why was he even talking about this?

"Is that you do." There was something extraordinary about the way he said this, something so calm and compassionate that Charlie didn't quite know how to deal with it.

"Am I just telling you a bunch of stuff you already know?" he said, sounding more surly than he intended.

"Of course not. Anyone might have predicted how that sentence would end." Again he spoke very gently—not as if he didn't care about it, but as if he cared only because he knew that Charlie did.

"Well, stop me if you get bored." He gulped down the last of his beer. "I'm sorry, I shouldn't have said that. I …" He waited for Hal to finish that sentence too, so that he could snap at him again.

Hal said nothing. He was fastidiously trying to wipe the grease from the chips off his hands without involving his clothes or the blanket, and it wasn't working. After a few moments of watching him do this, Charlie dug a handkerchief out of his pocket and offered it to him.

"Thank you. You take such good care of me." He wiped his

hands with studied attention. "I knew there was something about you, Charles, some pain that you keep hidden. I am not surprised to find this is what it is."

Charlie felt himself relax into the possibility that they were going to talk about this, that it was somehow going to be okay. "Yeah? People usually are surprised. I guess I don't seem like your typical homosexual."

"No?"

"I'm not effeminate or anything. I've always felt as if … it wasn't part of me, you know? Well, you probably don't. And I'm not sure that's what I mean. Not *supposed* to be part of me, I guess. As if I had one idea of what my life was supposed to be about, and this just didn't fit."

"Tell me," said Hal after a moment.

"Well … Did you want the chocolate? You seemed to like it before, that's why I got it for you."

"Thank you. Yes."

Charlie got down from the jeep again to get the chocolate. "Listen," he said as he got back in, "I'm not trying to change the subject, but …"

"I don't need the whole thing. Break it in half and have some yourself."

"If you insist. But what I was going to say is, we should drive. If we sit here much longer, I'm gonna get sleepy and not be able to make it back."

"Then let us drive. Charles, that isn't *half*."

"It's okay—you have it. The question is, where do we drive?"

"Oh. It does seem to me that we should go to this place called Zion."

"Yeah, I figured that too. I did promise the guy there I would help him repair the roof—I have to go back at least for that. And if the place is where your captors were headed … it's something that needs looking into, pretty clearly. Okay, that's what I thought you'd probably say. We'll drive back to Newingthorpe, then, and try to find a room. Two—*two* rooms, obviously. Or they might be able to put us up at the base—it's nearly empty, as they're shutting it down."

He started the jeep, and pulled in among the trees to make a U-turn and head back in the direction he had come. Hal broke his chocolate into its component squares and ate them one at a time.

*

"Okay," Charlie said as the jeep bounced along the track between the silent hills, through the huge black night, "here's the story about me. I'll start at the very beginning. In case there was any possible way you couldn't tell this, I come from pretty humble origins. My grandmother was Mohawk, and lived on an Indian reserve when I was born. I don't actually know what my grandfather was, so I could be half Indian or a quarter, I'm not sure. My dad for sure was white. He was bad news—a small-time gangster, in and out of prison all the time, and drunk and violent when he was out. My mom was pretty level-headed about everything except him, but she was just a teenager when she married him and had me. She'd run away with him to Toronto, and when he got put away just shortly after I was born, she wrote to my gran asking for help. Gran came to Toronto and pretty well took over raising me. When I was eight, my dad died in the flu epidemic, and my mom moved in with a new man, even worse than him in some ways, who didn't want anything to do with me. I didn't see her much after that—eventually she moved down to the States, and would've taken me with her, but Gran wouldn't hear of it. Gran did really well by me. She worked hard—cleaning houses—and took me to church with her, and tried to raise me to be decent. It wasn't her fault that I got mixed up with a bad crowd when I got older.

"I told you about that, how I stole cars, and got caught and sent to an industrial school instead of prison, because I was only fourteen. And Gran I think was afraid I was taking after my father, and nothing she'd done to raise me properly was going to pay off after all. She more or less told me so one time. She was upset. She didn't think it would get through to me, of course, because she thought I was already too far gone. I don't blame her for that, either. But it *did* get through, and it about killed me. I thought she was right, it was just in my blood to be bad, you know, and there wasn't anything I could've done about it. If something else hadn't happened, if God hadn't sent something else my way, I don't think I would've reformed at all after that. But he did, and it happened in kind of a funny way. I didn't really see it, how it all worked, until much later.

"So I was living in this institution with a bunch of other delinquent boys, and I was fifteen by this time, and thought I might be pretty much a lost cause. So I had indeed got up to some stuff … sex, I mean. But it was just what was available under the circumstances—it was part of being a delinquent. I thought the fact that I liked it as much as I did, well, that was just another bit of proof that I was probably irredeemable.

"Then a couple months before I was set to come up for parole, we had this exhibition—it was a new school, and the administration wanted to show off how it was working out. We were learning woodworking, and we had to show what we'd been making to the public, and be on our best behaviour. I wasn't planning to do anything, you know, delinquent, but a couple of my friends had been talking about how they might try to steal some watches. I was never good at that kind of thing, but I figured if they did do it, I'd probably end up helping them hide the stuff. That was how I felt about everything then—just fatalistic. As it turned out, though, that never happened. My friends got interested in this girl instead, and forgot all about the watches. They came up to me at one point, all excited, saying, 'Charlie, you've got to see this girl.' Well, she wasn't a girl, she was a woman, a classy, grown-up woman in her twenties—I don't know what they were thinking. She was pretty, sure, but as far as I was concerned she might not even have had a face. She was with this beautiful man. It honestly amazed me that anyone could look at her when she was next to him. He was a priest—not a Methodist minister in a suit, but a proper priest, in a Roman cassock with buttons down the front—but he looked like a film star. He would have been about thirty then—twice my age. And I guess I fell in love with him right away, although for a while I didn't know that's what it was.

"I forget how it got started, but he was asking for a demonstration of one of the machines—just being nice, you know—and then somebody started suggesting other things we could demonstrate, and one of my friends said, 'Charlie could teach you a thing or two—he knocked down a teacher once.' Which was true. That teacher was a bastard and had it coming—but that's another story. So he looked at me, with kind of a glint in his eye, and more or less said, 'Think you could take me?' That's not how he talks, but that was what he said, if you follow me. I wasn't expecting that. But I was about his size, when I was fifteen—he's not all that big—and so I said that yeah, I thought I could. Well, I couldn't, in a million years—not just because he was a priest, and I was in awe of him, but because he was fast, and knew what he was doing. He's really much more of a fighter than I've ever been. I'm just sort of a big guy—I don't have to try very hard. He did end up going down, but only because he stepped on his cassock, which is easy to do—I wanted to tell him not to be embarrassed, because the number of times I'd nearly fallen on my face when I was serving at church, you wouldn't believe. But we were on the floor in the workshop with a bunch of people standing around, and it just wasn't the right moment.

"Then somebody suggested the gym, and he jumped at the idea—I didn't expect that, either—and he showed me how to do a couple of real wrestling moves, and let me throw him just to prove to me that I could. By this time, some of my friends wanted to fight him, and this one kid, Jimmy—not one of my friends, not anybody's friend, a real crazy little shit—got so mad at being thrown the first time, he just laid into Father Underhill the second time like a rabid dog. I think he actually bit him. He definitely kneed him in the balls. And I felt responsible, somehow, like I'd led him on, made him think we were all sportsmanlike and civilized, when actually we were these savage beasts, and it had been naïve of him to trust any of us. One of the teachers had to help me haul Jimmy off—I mean, Father Underhill could've defended himself, for sure, but maybe not without breaking Jimmy's neck, and he was trying not to do that. Oh, and by this time some old ladies and Methodist ministers had shown up and were disapproving of him for brawling with the delinquents, and being Catholic, and everything.

"Well, you can figure out what he did. He was *gracious* about it. He shook my hand and said, 'Thanks for a good match,' and I stammered something and felt like a failure. And then he left, and I didn't guess I'd ever see him again—I didn't know his name, or what church he was at, or even whether he was Roman Catholic or Anglican. But what I knew was that … he was the real deal. It was like he made everything else in my life seem kind of fake and stupid. And that was what I needed just then—that was how God made that happen for me. Two months later I impressed the parole board, and I went home to try to impress my gran, too. One of the wardens at her church gave me a job in his shop, and I was allowed back in the Acolytes' Guild. And that's what I mean about the story I thought I was living: that's what I thought it was. I was the Prodigal Grandson—I had my criminal inheritance from my dad to fight against, but that was just what I had to do, and what had gone on at the school, everything that had gone on there, that was part of my criminal past.

"Only it wasn't. So while I'd been away, the rector of our church, Father Britton, had begun to talk about retiring. It was a settled thing by the time I came back—his daughters were already starting to pack up the rectory—and the only question was where to find a suitable vicar. That was the big debate for a while. I told you my boss was one of the wardens, and he used to get his stock boys to do odd jobs around the church—we were on the clock, so it was generous of him, but I was the only one who was actually a parishioner. So the day before Epiphany, I was in the church, helping the sexton take down the Christmas greenery, and a couple of the Altar Guild ladies came in giggling about something, and said, 'We just met the new vicar! Wait till you see him—he's a dream!' And I knew right then it was him.

"So the Altar Guild ladies went on their way, and the sexton laughed and said to me, 'Stupid old biddies—why would they think *we* care what he looks like?' And I thought, if he had any idea what I felt just then, when I thought about that beautiful, gracious, splendid man being in charge of my church … well, he wouldn't have thought it was funny. So I guess that was how I realized I really was a homosexual."

They had reached a place where the track diverged, and Charlie had to concentrate for a moment on which fork to take, and then on steering the jeep down a sharp, gravelly incline toward the road below.

Of course it hadn't been quite as simple as he had just made it sound. It was only looking back now that he could see that he'd begun to grasp the truth about himself in the empty church that afternoon. That didn't mean he hadn't gone on trying to deny it, just that the denials from then on had been noticeably more feeble and unconvincing. And he wondered how different it would seem, looking back on it, if that first object of his affection had been someone who just passed out of his life, or someone he had discovered he could not like or respect.

"But here's the other thing," he said, when they had safely gained the road. "By this time I'd had lots of benefactors, people who'd helped me when I didn't deserve it, and I was grateful to them. Father Underhill wasn't one of them, not really. He came on the scene—permanently, I mean—after I'd already turned my life around and been offered my second chances. He never even knew, for years, what it was that I'd done to get arrested. He was good to me, he treated me like a friend and an adult—but I didn't owe him anything. I loved him just because I loved him. It's hard to explain, but it felt like a luxury. To be able to offer love that wasn't in return for anything—it felt like Grace. And the funny thing is, he knew. I don't know how, exactly, but he knew—not just that I loved him, but what it meant to me to be able to love him like that—and he didn't try to do anything about it. He didn't take me aside and say, 'Listen, son, don't you think it's about time you took an interest in someone your own age, and *not* your own sex?' or … anything. He didn't even try to turn my love into something useful, to transform himself from my idol into my mentor. It made me wonder if he thought … no, it made me really believe that he did think there could be Grace in something like that—in that kind of a perverse love. And that was kind of an amazing thing to think. I don't know that he was *right*, but it was an amazing thing to think.

"He got married eventually, to this woman who … " Charlie smiled. "You wouldn't peg her for a vicar's wife in a million years. But even I had to admit she's worthy of him. I really like her—I wanted not to, but I couldn't help it. And as for me, well, I slipped up a few times when I was still a teenager, but all through my twenties, for ten solid years, I didn't, um … I was chaste. For a decade. I thought I was getting so good at it. Which is pride—and that's a worse sin, isn't it?"

"That is what I have heard," said Hal.

Charlie glanced at him. "Are you getting bored?"

"Of course not."

They drove on in silence for a minute. Charlie tried to think where to go from there. There were so many different ways you could explain the path that his life had taken. In some ways, of course, the big event was that Saturday before Easter, 1926, when the supernatural had burst casually onto the scene. But he had been basically a bystander to those events, and couldn't so easily trace a "before" and "after" for that day in his own life. Others, much quieter and altogether mundane, had made a far greater difference to his trajectory. He remembered one evening that summer, coming to the rectory with some message from Mr. Oates, and intercepting Father Underhill and his fiancée on their way out, coming out the door hand in hand, deep in some happy private conversation. They were such a pleasing couple to look at. Everyone remarked on it, though no one stopped to analyze why it was—no one, apparently, except Charlie. It was because his beauty was so straightforward, and hers so unconventional. Together they presented both harmony and interest to the viewer. Charlie had worked this out.

Their ways of being in love with each other seemed complementary too. He was frank and enthusiastic, always eager to talk about her and show her off to people, and she treated him gently, almost reverently, as if she had understood something about him, maybe about the limits of his strength, that was opaque to everyone else.

That day Charlie had waited in the porch, crushingly embarrassed, while Father Underhill went inside to find the answer to Mr. Oates's query, and Miss Nordqvist, as she was then, stood there in her pretty summer dress, probably missing the beginning of the picture or whatever it was, but being very nice about it. And out of the blue she had said, "Charlie, do you ever think about going back to school?" He could trace a "before" and "after" from *that.*

"It was his wife—before she was his wife—who talked me into trying to get into university. I think it was probably his idea, and he put her up to it, because he wanted us to be better friends, but I don't know that for sure. She helped me to study for the entrance exam, too. She was working on her doctorate, and we used to kind of encourage each other.

"At some point I got the idea that I wanted to study architecture. I remember telling him that I was thinking this, and how enthusiastic he got about it. He lent me some books on church architecture that he had, and promised to introduce me to someone he knew who was an architect. He did, too, eventually—it just took him a while, because he was distracted around that time by his own wedding.

"Then it was about a week after they got back from their honeymoon that my friend Henley, who had been an acolyte with me for years but still had to be reminded what order to light the candles in, and *always* turned the wrong way after censing the congregation, he dropped his bombshell about what *he* wanted to do with his life."

"He wanted to be a priest," said Hal.

"Yeah. 'Felt called,' or whatever. And so now he's having *long* conversations with Father Underhill, and they're thick as thieves about it, and of course I couldn't help thinking, *Well, shit. Why couldn't that happen to me?* Mind you, it turned out Father Underhill thought Henley might do better as a seminary professor than a parish priest, which was right on the money, but also kind of meant Henley didn't follow quite in his footsteps, and I found that a bit comforting—more than I should have, for sure. So anyway, I didn't go completely off the rails and pretend that I also thought I was called to the priesthood, because that would've been grotesque. But I did … that was the one time I … I got up to some stuff that I really regret, because I was feeling sorry for myself. Anyway. After that I swore it off, and that was the beginning of my decade of chastity.

"I did get into university, and did my BA in architecture. And it's an amazing thing, having an education. My gran never learned to read, and neither of my parents graduated high school, but here I am with a university degree. A *university* degree. I went on a scholarship, of course—I couldn't have afforded it otherwise. The scholarship dried up after a year because of the stock-market crash, and it was hard going getting through the rest of my degree. I'd had a good job, stocking shelves at the grocery store, but I could only work part-time during term, and I had to take a pay cut—everybody did in those days. Then my gran got sick, and I had to drop everything to look after her. But she made me promise I'd finish my degree after she died. And I did. It's the thing I'm proudest of having done.

"After I graduated, instead of joining a firm, I rented a little studio and set up shop by myself. I figured I could get enough work, of the kind people could afford to pay for in the depression, just from people I knew at church who were proud of my achievement and wanted me to get on, and them recommending me to their friends and their friends' friends. It was a good strategy. I got plenty of work—mostly helping people fix up their houses, you know, so that Great-Aunt Mabel or unemployed Cousin Joe could live in the basement, that kind of thing. Nothing you needed a Bachelor of Arts to do—but I'm a good worker, and people liked that I had the qualifications but didn't think any job beneath me. I got a bit of a reputation. I put a sketch of a Gothic spire on my card, and decorated my studio with pictures of imaginary churches I had designed, and I started to get a bit of restoration work on actual churches. That was what I wanted to be my specialty. I was able to pay back the people who had loaned me money, and I lived frugally, and before the war I had saved enough to buy a small lot in my old neighbourhood, near St. John's, and I was going to start building my own house. I didn't start on it, though, because when the rumours of war were getting pretty definite, I made up my mind that I would enlist, and I thought a vacant lot would be a better thing to leave behind, in case I was killed, than a half-dug foundation or something sad. But I turned out to be a pretty decent pilot—well, I'd had an inkling that I would be—and so here I am, still alive after all, squadron leader even, and now the rumours are about the end of the war. It's starting to look like I'll get to build my house after all."

"You have designed it?" Hal asked, apparently interested.

"Yeah."

"Does it have a Gothic spire?"

"The house?" Charlie laughed. "No, it's a very ordinary design for a house—a little bungalow, a cottage-type thing, with a peaked roof over the porch, and a fieldstone chimney, and exposed rafters in the eaves, and cedar shingles, and a dormer, and little bits of stained glass in a couple of the windows. All the things I like, but nothing original about it. I don't approve of architects putting up weird avant-garde follies for themselves on streets of working-class cottages. It's bad taste. I feel that having a university degree entitles me to talk about taste—otherwise I wouldn't."

"Will you live there by yourself?"

"Of course."

"Of course?" Hal repeated curiously. "You don't think you will ever share it with anyone?"

Charlie frowned. "No, I wouldn't do that." He wasn't really sure what Hal meant.

"Why? Are you still in love with your priest?"

"No, I stopped that when I was twenty."

"Just like that?" Hal sounded surprised.

"No, but … Well, kind of." It was another of those "before" and "after" moments; there were more of them in his life than he'd realized. But this one he'd seen for what it was at the time. "What happened was, that fall, my gran and his dad both died within a week of each other, and we had their funerals at St. John's, and they were buried in the churchyard. And one day a couple of weeks after his dad's funeral, we ran into each other there, and I think we were both grieving in the same way by that point—you know, like we were both just exhausted by it. And he invited me into the rectory for a drink, which he'd never quite done before. I thought he meant sherry or something—that's kind of what he's like—but it turned out he meant beer. We sat on his back steps and drank beer out of bottles."

"As you and I did just now."

"Yeah. And he talked about his dad a bit, and I talked about my gran—nothing spectacular, just reminiscing. And at some point I thought, you know, this business of being in love with him is bull-shit—we're friends."

Hal was silent for a while. "So you still love him," he said finally, thoughtfully.

"A lot. But I'm not *in* love *with* him. Is that a distinction that you get?"

"Oh, certainly."

"You're not very emotional, I've noticed—that's why I wondered. Is that typical?"

"Yes, entirely typical. We are without passions. In our natural state—which, you understand, I am no longer in."

"Right. So … you feel things that you wouldn't normally?" He wanted to hear more about this. He was starting to feel sleepy, and he was tired of talking, just physically tired of it.

"Yes. What happened to your friend, the one who wanted to be a priest?"

"Tom Henley?" Charlie took one hand off the steering wheel to rub his eyes. "He did get ordained, and didn't take Father Under-hill's advice, and did a curacy at some Low Church place where they almost turned him out on his ear. Then he went back and got his doctorate, and he teaches theology now. He wrote a book … *Hypothermia in Cyril of Alexandria*, or something."

"Hypothermia?" Hal repeated sceptically.

"No, but something like that. I haven't read the book, although he gave me a copy. It's a big joke between us—'Well, you'd understand that if you'd read my book, Charlie.' Any time I ask him something. It's interesting you ask about Henley, because there *is* more to the story, and I guess it has something to do with him." He felt more awake again. "I guess I'd never quite got over the feeling that I was cheated, somehow, because Henley got that call and I didn't. And then … the war started, and there was no question I was going to enlist, and do you know why? Can you figure out why?"

"I suppose your priest fought in the previous war," said Hal, without having to think about it.

"Exactly. Fought, and was wounded and decorated and everything. He was nineteen when he joined up, so he was just an enlisted soldier, although he rose through the ranks—but I had my university degree, so I started out an officer. And I thought finally I was going to have done something that would make him genuinely proud of me—and don't try to tell me he was certainly already proud of me for getting my BA and starting my own firm, *I know that*, but that's not what I was thinking. I was thinking that here, finally, was my chance. I picked the Air Force because he'd made some offhand comment once about thinking he would have liked to have been a pilot. And what do you suppose happened then?"

"You found your friend Henley the theologian had already joined up as an Air Force chaplain, and they were cosily chatting about it when you came in with your news."

"No! You see, I knew you would guess that. No. Henley's asthmatic and short-sighted and no recruiting officer would look twice at him. The one who'd already joined up as a chaplain was Father Underhill. He'd rejoined his old regiment, of course—an infantry regiment. They were sent to Sicily in '43. He's probably seen more actual fighting than I have. I was imagining myself taking up the torch or something, making him proud of me finally—I suppose in my heart of hearts I imagined myself being killed and him missing me. I don't know what I was thinking. He was forty-five, a veteran, married, with four young kids—anyone would have said he could decently sit this one out. *Of course* he'd joined up before me."

For a moment he lost himself in that memory, which was not a happy one. He'd felt so stupid, as if everyone—Elsa, and Henley, and Sara, and everyone—could see what he'd been thinking, how entirely he'd been wrapped up in a selfish fantasy in which Father Underhill was only a kind of symbol for something. Telling himself that probably nobody was thinking this, simply because nobody cared that much about him and his dumb preoccupations, had only made him feel worse.

"And?" Hal prompted. "I can't guess what the next part of the story is."

"And … he wasn't actually proud of me for enlisting. He tried not to say so, but he was kind of upset about it. He *clearly* thought that the Air Force was a stupid idea."

"But what happened to him? You said that he went to Italy. Did he … Is he … "

"Alive? As far as I know. Except I don't really know. We parted badly. We've corresponded, but not … not much. It's mostly my fault—it's entirely my fault. He doesn't write a lot, but it's always good stuff—postcards with just a few lines on them, you know, but all to the point—and always prompt. I'm the one who doesn't write back for months, and then I send these stupid, rambling letters … Basically, I haven't written to him in a year, and the last postcard I had was six months ago. Somewhere along the line I realized, you know, I'm just a fucking pastoral problem for him, and he's got enough to do right now looking after his own men. Also … by the time I wrote last … "

"Your decade of chastity was over."

"Yeah. Well and truly."

He caught again that sense of quiet, sympathetic sorrow, the sense that Hal was sad about it in the same way that you would be sad for someone who was in pain. He didn't know where he was getting all this from; he was very tired, and maybe his imagination was just misfiring.

"So there's someone else you're in love with now?" Hal said, after a long stretch of straight, dark road.

"In love with? No, it's not like that. It's just sex. No, that's not true. I try very hard—I'm very strict with myself. I can have one or the other: sex or love. I can't have them both at the same time in the same place. I want to, but it's not an option."

"Why not?"

"Because it's wrong! It's perverse. It would be like … pretending that it wasn't."

Hal took a while to consider that.

"So … you find celibacy untenable, but you have somehow convinced yourself that a life of fornication and unrequited love is preferable to a mutually loving liaison? That doesn't make any sense."

"When you put it like that, no, it doesn't. Obviously that's not how I think of it."

Hal was giving him a look that suggested that he didn't see how there was any other way to think of it.

"I did get fond of someone," Charlie said, both to be honest and to divert the conversation from what seemed too difficult a channel for this time of night. "A pilot officer in my squadron, Latham Addison-Carmichael. He's young, only twenty-three." *Though not a teenager like you*, he almost added. "He didn't think he was gay—I was his first experience. It was all very … I don't know, I guess I felt *tenderly* toward him—not in love with him exactly, but like I wanted to look out for him. He's an incredibly shitty pilot—he got an officer's commission because his grandfather is an earl, but he should never have been allowed to fly anything ever, and I was able to get him a safe job on the ground, which he was grateful for. Then when we'd been … you know, when it had been going on between us … for a month, he finally mentioned his fiancée."

"Oh."

"Yeah. He 'didn't think it mattered.' He honestly didn't understand why I would care. And I guess sometimes I see his point of view—if it's just sex, as I claim, why should it matter? No emotions involved, right? I don't think there's much emotion involved in that engagement either, honestly—it sounds like it's next-door to an arranged marriage. But I don't know. It did make a big difference. I didn't want to touch him after that. I guess that's it, basically. It made him less attractive to me, finding that was what he was really like, so it was easy to end it. No virtue necessary.

"But now I think I might have been unfair to him." And he explained about the phone conversation with Benson and how Latham had lied on his behalf.

"That was kind," was Hal's comment.

"It was, wasn't it?"

The road took a series of serpentine curves that Charlie remembered from the drive out, which meant they were more than halfway to Newingthorpe. As the road straightened again, Charlie began to whistle "The Water is Wide" softly.

"Do you know that one?" he asked.

"No."

"Ah. No reason you should, I guess. It's a folk song—my old boss used to sing things like that around the shop, when he thought nobody was listening. He had a great voice—sang in the church choir, of course, but on weekdays it was always folk songs about miserable, doomed lovers." Charlie chuckled, remembering that unexpectedly romantic side to Mr. Oates. "That one has a line about wings—that's what put it into my head." He hummed another verse. "Your turn. Sing something for me—and not a lullaby, I need to stay awake."

There was a strange silence.

Finally Hal said, "I can't sing anything for you, Charles."

"No? How come? I'd have thought you would be pretty good."

"It isn't that. I don't remember any music."

"Oh. Well, that's all right."

"It is not remotely right," said Hal quietly. "It is another metaphor. It is the truth that I have been trying not to look in the face ever since you released me. I don't remember Heaven."

Charlie had to fight to keep from replying in a wholly inappropriate way, with some kind of profanity. "I'm sorry," he forced out finally. "When you said you'd lost your memory, I didn't realize it meant that."

"No. I did not intend that you should."

Charlie glanced across at him. He sat with the blanket loose around his shoulders now, one knee drawn up, looking out at the night, expressionless. The breeze stirred his short curls. To Charlie at that moment he looked quite human, his lack of emotion nothing more exotic than the buttoned-up stoicism of someone who "didn't want to worry you."

Charlie wanted to touch him, but in a completely different way than he had wanted it earlier in the night; he wanted to hold him and comfort him. But there was no possible way to do that now. He longed for something to call him that would sound as caressingly intimate as "Charles" for some reason sounded to him every time the angel said it. But there was nothing; he didn't know Hal's real name.

"It must be awful," Charlie said finally.

Out of the corner of his eye he caught Hal's glance in his direction, his fleeting smile, before he looked away into the darkness. "It has become less so. Thank you."

Now Charlie felt a need to talk both to break the soporific silence and to dispel the desperate sadness that he felt building in his chest on Hal's behalf. He said the first thing that came to mind.

"I told you I haven't written to Father Underhill in a year," he said, "but I got a postcard from him six months ago. So that's six months after he last wrote to me, and I haven't written back—and I don't have the excuse of being dead or even wounded or anything. Pretty unforgivable, right?" This wasn't helping. In fact, he felt that if he went on he might start to tear up. He went on anyway. "The postcard … it's a picture of a church with a Gothic spire like the one on my business card. And on the back he wrote, *Dear Charlie, Whenever I see one of these, I think of you. I hope you are hanging on okay.*"

He could picture it clearly: the neat, schoolboy handwriting, the way it was signed, so casually.

Love, Kit+

It had taken him pages and pages of dense nonsense to try to convey as much as Father Underhill had managed to fit into two words and a little cross at the bottom of a postcard.

"It doesn't sound to me like he thinks of you as a pastoral problem," said Hal mildly. "Didn't that make you want to write back?"

"No, the truth is it didn't. The truth is … the truth is I couldn't stand being forgiven like that. It was the last straw."

A minute went by in silence, the headlights ghosting along the hedge ahead of them.

"I expect that doesn't make any sense to you," Charlie said finally.

"It shouldn't," said Hal. "But it does."

Chapter Eight

IN THE SPIRIT ON THE LORD'S DAY

Fidelity arrived for breakfast in the dining room the following morning with a stylish and perfect man's haircut.

"I asked Dr. Sheppard who cuts the men's hair," she explained, without preamble, when Evvie sat down next to her. "And it turns out—you may already have known this—that Corporal Marsden is a barber in civilian life, and he's been cutting all the men's hair since he got here." She raked back her newly dapper blonde fringe with her good hand. "This cut is the standard 'short back and sides.' He didn't even try to talk me out of it. I like Corporal Marsden."

"It's wonderful," said Evvie raptly.

She didn't mean just the haircut, although it was far more dignified, and probably prettier, than anything that the two nurses or their hairdressers back home could have contrived with ribbons and curling irons. She was awed by Fee's whole approach to the problem. The girl had the use of only half her limbs and seemed eager to be agreeable to everyone; but she was in command of her own destiny. She wasn't having anyone doing anything stupid with her hair.

Evvie said, "It's like Alexander the Great cutting the Gordian Knot."

Fee smiled a slow, private, and very pleased smile, and Evvie realized that they were friends.

*

It was a Sunday, so after breakfast they went down together to the prayer service in the tiny Adderley chapel, and afterward Fee whispered, "Do you mind if we sit here until everyone else leaves? I like this place." And Evvie, who liked the chapel too, didn't mind at all. They sat quietly together until Rosalind showed up and looked eager to resume her duty of amusing Fidelity. Evvie, who had promised to accompany some of the patients into the village that morning, excused herself reluctantly.

That evening, after dinner, she looked for Fee in the library where most of the patients were gathered to listen to the wireless, but she was not there. She debated for a while about going to Fee's room, and finally decided to risk it. She tapped on the door, trying to formulate an excuse for being there. *I thought you might be lonely and might like … I'm lonely, and I was hoping that …*

"Yes?" came Fee's voice from inside.

"It's Evvie. I …"

"Oh, Evgenia! Come in!"

She slipped through the door, shutting it quietly behind her. Fee was sitting up in bed with a book in her lap, her bandaged arm out of its sling. She looked even smaller and frailer in her nightgown, against her piled-up pillows, like a doll pulled out of the rubble of a burnt-down house.

"I know it's only eight o'clock," she said, "and I'm not really sleepy, but I felt a migraine coming on earlier, and I asked the nurse to help me get ready for bed so I'd be left alone for the rest of the evening."

"Oh, if you want to be left alone," said Evvie uncertainly.

"No, not by you—I *like* you." She patted the coverlet with her good hand. "And the migraine never materialized, after all. Come and talk to me about yourself—or about anything, really, so long as you don't want to hear about me and my fabulous American soap family. I'm sick of talking about them."

"Don't worry. They sound nice, but I'm not dying for more details."

"Thanks."

"What are you reading?"

"A Dorothy Sayers." She turned it over to show Evvie the cover. It was *Strong Poison*. "I found it in the library, in the cupboard where they keep the déclassé paperbacks and things that don't have swank leather bindings."

"Yes, I'm glad you found that cupboard. I was meaning to tell you about it."

"I've read this one before—my father's a fan of hers and has them all—and I remember who did it, but I don't remember exactly how, and it's fun the second time anyway. Do you read mysteries?"

"I love mysteries, and love Lord Peter, but I haven't read that one yet."

"You can have it after I'm done. I meant to ask—do you like to be called Evvie or Evgenia?"

"Oh, either. At home it was always Evgenia, but I think English people find Evvie easier."

Fee nodded. "Then I know what I'll call you. Where's home, if you don't mind my asking?"

"Well, I was born in Athens. But I haven't lived there for a long time—it's not really 'home.'"

"I've been there, you know. Athens. When I was ten, with my family. I even know a little bit of Greek. I can order coffee, and tell you about the wrath of Achilles—both with an equally bad accent."

"How very useful!"

"Oh, tremendously, yes. But you said Athens wasn't really home."

"No. Well, my father, who was an Orthodox priest—"

To Evvie's surprise, Fee perked up instantly at this. "Oh! That's … how interesting that must be! I'm going to stop interrupting you."

Evvie laughed. "Are you sure? I don't mind. He died when I was six, so I don't remember him as well as I'd like."

"I'm sorry."

"Then my mother remarried when I was ten, and we moved to London. My stepfather's English, and my two half-sisters have never lived in Greece. They could *maybe* ask you how Achilles takes his coffee, but that would be about it."

Fee laughed. "What about your mother?"

"My mother?"

"Yes, what does she do?"

Nobody ever asked "What does your mother do?" Mothers were just mothers; it was self-explanatory.

"It's funny you should ask that," said Evvie. "She writes novels."

"But that's delightful!" Fee reined in her enthusiasm tactfully. "No, you don't think it's delightful, do you? What kind of novels? Mysteries?" She sounded hopeful.

"No … romances. Her pen name is Charlotte Delisle. No, you haven't heard of her. I'm afraid she's not very good."

Fee made a sympathetic face.

"She married an English archaeologist, you see," Evvie went on, "and then she wrote a book about a Greek woman who married an English archaeologist."

"Oh, cripes!"

"Exactly. My stepfather loved it, and got it published for her, and the critics who said it was bad were just envious of their love, or something. She's done seven more books since then."

"Have you read them?"

"Every one. I love my mother."

"Sorry, I shouldn't laugh. It's just something about the way you said it."

"I know. I'm *such* a dutiful daughter. But I remember when it was just me and my mother, after my father died. I feel as if I owe her a little for that time, because she was very strong then, even though she was very unhappy. And now she's happy, and the books are part of it, so. Of course Aphrodite and Hero are good daughters too, though they don't read her books."

"Aphrodite and …"

"Hero. My sisters. I know. They're ridiculous names. My step-father chose them."

"It sounds as if you have the type of family that's more fun from the outside looking in. Or maybe I'm being presumptuous."

"No, I think you're being sympathetic, and that's a nice way of putting it. But it is my fault—I should be more charitable."

"My father says that's the hardest thing to do, be charitable to your own family. Because they're so close to you—you expect more of them than of other people. Even … you know, think about the Wedding at Cana—it might be just the way it's translated, but it really sounds like Jesus absolutely snapped at Our Lady for trying to get him to do a miracle before he was ready, or whatever it was. Like, you know, he expected her to know better. That's a scandalous thing to say, isn't it?" she finished cheekily.

"Yes, completely, and I am scandalized. But I think I see what you mean."

"So … maybe you can explain something to me that I haven't been sufficiently tactless to ask Rosalind."

"I'll try."

"Who is she, and what's she doing here?"

Evvie laughed.

"No, I mean it," said Fee. "She's not a patient or staff—neither is the ghastly Daphne or her ghastlier gentleman friend—"

"They're friends of Leo's. It's a country-house party, like P.G. Wodehouse, you know, only it's all happening in the midst of a hospital because of the war."

"All right. But—what's Leo?"

"He's Lord Rathburn's nephew."

"Lord Rathburn being …"

"The owner of the house. He's away in London, doing secretive war work. Lady Rathburn stayed on to administer the hospital. I don't know whether Leo lived here before the war or not. He has

a lot of stuff here, so perhaps he did. He deals in antiques. And …
I think contraband too."

"Cripes! What kind?"

"I'm not absolutely sure—I've just heard him saying things. He
owned a private plane that he said was 'for business,' and when his
car was stolen—supposedly stolen, anyway—the police gave him
a hard time, when they found it, about the amount of petrol that
he had."

"Hm. And Ernest is just a friend of his?"

Evvie nodded. "He's an artist, but he worked as a cartographer
for the government during the first years of the war. Then he had
some kind of breakdown—I think he was nearly killed during the
Blitz—and he hasn't gone back to work after that."

"And that weird proselytizing woman?"

Evvie shuddered. "Josephine Good. She's … at least she used to
be friends with Leo."

"You're joking!"

"I know, it's very odd. She used to be different—more like Leo.
But she had a brush with death, too—"

"How original of her."

"I know, everybody's doing it. Anyway, in her case it changed
her character, supposedly. She started helping her brother with his
mission work."

"Mission work—you mean those tracts she hands out? She tried
to give me one, and I made believe I had some 'literature' I was very
keen to give her in exchange. That shut her up."

"I expect it would have!"

"You said 'supposedly' it changed her character."

"Well … if you ask me, she was a busybody before, and now she's
a busybody with tracts. I don't really consider it an improvement."

Fee looked at her with satisfaction. "You're quite hard-headed,
you know?"

"I try. What kind of 'literature' were you going to give her? You're a Protestant, I think I heard you say?"

"What? Oh, yes. Baptist."

"I don't know much about their beliefs."

"Oh, well." She looked up at the ceiling. "No icons, no incense, no vestments … lots of singing, but not the kind you're used to. Very long sermons, terrifically long sermons. And you're saved by faith, and works are a waste of time, and … oh, there's something about the Holy Spirit that we believe that you don't—but I'm afraid I can't remember what that is. The something-or-other clause."

"It's the line in the Creed about proceeding from the Father and the Son. But that's just a fundamental difference between the East and the West." And the other things she had described sounded much like Evvie's stepfather's Low Church Anglican parish. "You're not … exactly a *convinced* Baptist, are you?"

"Oh! Well, it's got a lot to recommend it—all the really strong traditions do, I think. And I'm a convinced *Christian*."

"I figured that out this morning in the chapel." Evvie smiled. "I expect we could still be friends if you weren't, but it certainly does give us much more common ground."

"Yes!" Fee changed the subject unapologetically. "So you've lived in London since you were ten?"

"No, we were only in London for a year before we moved to Oxford."

"Oxford? But that's—oh, shut *up*, Fee!"

Evvie laughed again. "Well, I'm glad you think it's exciting. My stepfather teaches at the university."

"So your family must have got out of Greece in the nick of time then, right before the war."

"No, not really. It was in 1937, when I was ten. I'm eighteen now."

"Oh, of course. And the Italian fascists invaded in the fall of '40, didn't they?"

She knew a surprising amount about it. She said that this was because her elder brother Calvin was a naval officer stationed in the Mediterranean. Evvie thought that this didn't fully explain it, because he couldn't have been there before 1941, when America joined the war. But she said nothing.

"This has become a very masculine conversation, hasn't it?" said Fee presently. "Perhaps I had better say something to stem the tide. Um. Hm. I know! Do you have a sweetheart?" She said it as if reciting something by rote, deliberately silly.

"No," said Evvie seriously. "I have a husband. At least I—I consider—in my heart I do. And that is the important thing."

Fee cocked a sceptical eyebrow at her. She had a very pretty way of doing it. "Well, I'd have said it was at least a little important whether he also ... Oh. You mean Our Lord, don't you?"

"Yes."

Fee looked at her with awe. "You're a nun. Or ... you *were* a nun?"

"Only a ... you would call it a novice. I had not taken permanent vows—that is why I was able to leave at the beginning of the war. I'd gone back to Greece, you see. And that is why I don't wear the isorassa ... the clothes of a nun—the habit. But it is what I am meant to be."

"I think that's splendid. Really splendid. I did wonder, when you talked about embroidering a big thing with lilies—I thought that sounded like a nunnish sort of thing to do, and I thought maybe you'd been at school in a convent or something. But I didn't say anything then, because, well, I thought you'd tell me if you wanted to. You don't tell many people, do you?"

Evvie shook her head. "I suppose I should. I did, at first. But some people don't understand—they think that I left because I didn't want to take vows, or that I'm glad to be out, as if it were prison. And then ... I've found there are some men who take it as a challenge—who like a challenge."

"Oh, how *vile!* I'd thump them on your behalf, if I could. Run over their feet with my wheelchair, at least. But I'm not really one of the meek who shall inherit the earth. I don't know if you'd noticed."

Evvie smiled. "You have other excellent qualities. There are a few people around here who know. I told Miss Good, early on—in confidence, I thought—but she went and told Leo, and he was … well, he made fun of me. He didn't tell anybody else, as far as I know, because he's the sort who likes knowing a secret, likes feeling he's 'got something on you.' Another thing that makes me think he's a smuggler or a black marketeer, or whatever you would call it. Anyway. Do *you* have a sweetheart?"

"No, no, never yet, nor a husband. And I am absolutely dead keen on yours, I really am, but I don't think I'm meant to marry him."

"Of course not. You're a Protestant."

"Right. Well, it looks as if talking about boys might be a dead end after all. Something of a relief. I'm picturing you in one of those severe black habits now, looking *ravishing*."

"That's not really the idea."

"For a bride of Christ? Well, why not?"

Evvie laughed. "Anyway, the novice's cassock is white."

"Still. I bet you looked dead smart. Tell me about your convent. Whereabouts in Greece is it?"

"Patmos."

"*Really*? As in Revelation—'in the spirit on the Lord's day'—that Patmos? How terrific!"

"Do you just get excited about everything?"

"No, not at all—only genuinely exciting things."

"Well, I'm glad. I entered the monastery when I turned thirteen. The reason I went to Patmos was because …" She paused. She was about to tell this girl something that she had only told a handful of people. But they were friends; she went on quickly, ashamed of the pause: "I experienced a vision, during the time that I was beginning to … beginning to discern my call to the monastic life."

"A vision?" said Fee raptly. She was excited, certainly, but not notably more moved by this than by any of the other things about Evvie that seemed to please her. She certainly didn't seem sceptical. "Oh, terrific! What was it—how was it—I mean, were you awake or asleep, or … you know, because there are different kinds, aren't there?"

"Yes, some people get messages in dreams, and that would be a kind of vision, too. I was awake. It wasn't a dream. An angel visited me."

"Oh, my! Really?"

Evvie nodded.

"What kind of—I mean, what did he—no, no, forget I said anything. I expect it's difficult to talk about, and I shouldn't ask silly questions."

"It's not silly to ask about it, but it is difficult to explain. I'll tell you about it some day, though."

"I'd like that. I believe you right now, though, by the way. I've never seen an angel myself, but I've … sort of heard a devil."

"You have? How?"

"My cousin Graham, you know, the Foreign Office one? He used to be stationed in the Middle East, and he collected things. Artifacts. He has this ring that supposedly belonged to King Solomon. I don't know about that, but sometimes when you put it on you can hear voices—mean, whispery voices saying 'What is thy will?' and things like that." She wrinkled her nose at the memory, and seemed to be about to say more, but then stopped. "Actually, let's not talk about that—it's quite unpleasant. So you were visited by an angel, and you went to your convent on Patmos—did you like it there? Of course you did, that's another silly question."

Evvie wanted to hear more about the ring that supposedly belonged to King Solomon, but she let Fee direct the conversation back to her own past in Greece. "I loved it, from the first day. I did miss my family, of course I did, but at the same time I was so happy. That is what no one ever understands."

"Well, I guess most people think the monastic life would be hard.

I suppose I'm no exception. I think I'd find it hard. But I mean people think it's *supposed* to be hard."

"Yes, and if it isn't, you are doing it wrong. But what I think is, why shouldn't God give you the capacity to enjoy the things he's called you to do? Oughtn't that to be one of the signs that you're called to do them?"

"It makes sense."

"So why shouldn't I be called to be a nun and made to like it at the same time? Why is it deluding myself to say I think I wouldn't find the celibate life difficult? Couldn't that just be the way God has made me?"

"Well, of course," said Fee. "Does anyone seriously claim otherwise?"

"Maybe not seriously, but people like Miss Good and Leo Rathburn always say things like, 'You just haven't met the right man yet,' and 'You'll regret it when you're older.' My mother and stepfather always seem to imply something similar, if they don't say it outright. At first they thought I was just too young, then they thought I was traumatized by my father's death, or my mother's remarriage, or her silly books, or something."

"Oh, pish tosh!" exclaimed Fee.

Evvie laughed. "My stepfather's one of those well-meaning people who believes in everything and nothing, and he was particularly horrified by the idea that I wanted to go all the way back to Greece to a monastery. At first he convinced himself that it was really just homesickness, and started suggesting family trips and places I could go to school. When that didn't placate me, he got it into his head that the reason I wanted to go back to Greece was just because there aren't any convents in England—"

"Which isn't true."

"Which isn't true—there are. I'd visited one, and it was lovely. It just didn't seem to be the place where I was called to go. But it suited my stepfather to believe there weren't any monasteries in England.

That way he could suggest alternatives. 'Well, if you want to do good works, Evvie, there's always the Something-or-Other Mission Society.' Or 'I know you like praying, so why not join the Guild of St. Whoever.' But I don't just want to do good works, I don't just like praying—I want to be a bride of Christ. I'm convinced that is what I was made for."

Fee sighed happily. "How *exciting*."

"Well, at first. But I also don't want to be disobedient to my parents, so when they wrote begging me to come back to England at the beginning of the war, I left Patmos and came. Patmos—it's Greek, of course, I mean the people are Greek, but it's in the Dodecanese, which belonged to Italy. So in 1940, everyone who could was trying to get out. People thought I was lucky to have family in England—and I was. But I can't wait to go back."

"Won't you be able to go back soon? Greece and Italy are out of the war now, and you're eighteen, so you don't need your parents' permission, do you?"

"No, but the Dodecanese are still occupied by the Germans. Your brother Calvin didn't fill you in on that, I guess? Besides, I need money to make the trip, and I haven't enough."

"Oh, rats!"

Evvie shrugged. "It's all right. I am useful here, and so long as I'm useful, I should stay anyway. And to tell the truth, some of the things I miss are worldly things—the weather, and the food, which was good, even in the monastery. I miss my sisters, and my habit, and the colour of the sea. None of that's particularly admirable of me, but there it is."

"Yes, I see what you mean. You liked living in your monastery, so you're not a sort of saint for wanting to go back there. But equally, you're not a sort of nutcase."

"I was there for such a short time, though. Only about nine months. Sometimes I'm afraid I'm romanticizing it in my memories.

I've been *here* longer now. So I don't know. I have had no second vision to guide me."

Fee was silent for a bit. "The war has made everything weird. Everyone's been landed in such odd places, you know? And doing odd things that they never would have thought they'd be doing. There are Italian prisoners of war in the Orkneys who built a beautiful chapel dedicated to the Blessed Virgin out of a Nissen hut. Somebody told me about that. I think you're kind of like them."

Evvie smiled at the image. "What about you?"

"Me? I fell out of the sky and *caught fire*, Evgenia—and lived to talk about it. I think I may be the luckiest person I know."

Chapter Nine

THE WATER IS WIDE

Charlie parked the jeep between the abandoned hangars of the Newingthorpe base and walked into the village. It was late, the sky already dark, clouds drifting over the moon. He had been longer than usual today, attending to paperwork about the transfer of some planes to another base. He'd meant to be back in Newingthorpe for supper, but then work had taken so long that he'd stayed to eat with the men before leaving. He climbed the steep main street into Newingthorpe, heading for the lit windows of the Feathers.

For more than a week, he'd been driving back and forth between Newingthorpe and Adderley every day, spending all his off-duty time in Newingthorpe. At the base, he'd stayed on top of things, handily making up for the time he'd been away. He'd flown two missions, relieved to discover that he hadn't developed any awkward fears of flying after his run-in with the American and Hal's spectacular rescue. He'd said nothing about his secret mission, which is what he would have done if it had been real, and he was letting everyone think, without exactly lying about it, that he was visiting a girl in Newingthorpe on his off-duty hours. He had thanked Latham for covering for him.

"That was more than I deserved," he had said.

Latham shrugged. "I don't think so," he admitted.

"No?" That was surprisingly touching. "Well, thanks."

He wondered what he should do about Latham, how he could repay his loyalty. He thought about raising the subject of the fiancée, seeing if there was something Latham wanted to talk about there.

He remembered now how Latham had brought her up on the day when he went to the hospital to see Anderson, and thought there might have been something he had wanted to say then, or something he wanted Charlie to say. But Charlie was wary of giving the younger man false hope. *I think you should break it off with your fiancée, because* … well, because he thought that would be the honest thing to do, and better for both of them, but it was easy to see how Latham would hear that as, *I want you back*. And he didn't.

He had been back to Zion, seen Dr. Good, but managed to avoid being alone with his sister, and drawn up a plan for the repairs to the farm-house roof. He had promised to come again to help with the restoration, as he was able, once Dr. Good had assembled a team of workers.

Dr. Good had given him some tracts. One was called SINS OF THE FLESH, and contained a cozy narrative about how sexual perversions could be miraculously cured through prayer. Dr. Good said Josephine had been particularly anxious for Charlie to have that one. There was another about angels, which painted a wholly insipid picture of them as some kind of supernatural telephone-exchange operators. Charlie thought again about Hal's captors planning to bring him to Zion to carry on their program of torture in peace, while Dr. Good was busy writing more twaddle like this. He wondered whether the sympathetic friend Hal had heard them mention could be Dr. Good's sister. But that was probably unfair. He hadn't liked her, but he had no reason to suppose she was really *that* sinister. He had thrown the tracts away at the first opportunity.

He reached the Feathers, passed through the cozy bar and up the stairs to his room. He shucked off his uniform tunic and discarded his tie, and went back out into the passage to tap lightly on the door of the adjacent room.

"Come in," said the voice that had become his favourite sound in the world.

"It's just me," he said, slipping inside and shutting the door quietly behind him.

"I know," said Hal. "I can tell when it's you from the way you knock."

He was in bed, of course—he'd barely left his bed since their arrival at the inn—but it didn't look as if Charlie had woken him. The lamp on the nightstand was turned on, casting a warm pool of light on the head of the bed. Hal was lying propped up against his pillows. There was an empty teacup and a plate on a tray beside him, and a book open face-down on the coverlet.

Charlie pulled up the chair which he always replaced against the wall when he left, and sat, stretching out his legs.

"How—" he started, as Hal started to say the same thing. They laughed.

"You first," said Charlie.

"I was only going to ask how you spent the day—if what you were about to say was less banal, you should go first."

"Not really. I was going to ask how you were feeling."

"Better."

"That's what I thought. You look better. Like you're feeling better, I mean. What have you been reading?" He reached for the book, turning it so he could see the title. It was called *Watch Over Me*, and the cover featured a pair of golden-haired children ignoring a very pink-faced, doe-eyed female angel. "Do I even want to know?"

"Perhaps not. Mary found me reading the Bible that I discovered in the nightstand yesterday, and offered to bring me something from her own library."

"And this was what she brought? Seems insightful of her."

"No, I chose this one. She brought me a selection—the others are on the dresser." He gestured toward a pile of paperbacks. "Though she did say this one was her favourite."

Mary was the landlady of the Feathers, and Charlie had mixed feelings about her. She had been very kind to Hal, and obviously liked him. But she had insisted on sending for a doctor when the two of them first arrived at the inn, with Hal barely able to stand, and Charlie had made a fool of himself trying to stop her. Now he felt that she regarded him with suspicion, and to tell the truth he was jealous of the way she had taken over caring for Hal—and the way Hal had let her. Charlie's concern about calling the doctor had been unfounded; the doctor had come, said Hal was suffering from "nervous exhaustion," and prescribed rest and wholesome food. Charlie had babbled out something about amnesia and a plane crash, at which the doctor had nodded, unsurprised, uninterested in the details of who Hal really was and where he belonged. Mary too had been blessedly unconcerned by his lack of ration book or official identity. Maybe it was because Charlie seemed above suspicion himself, though he doubted it; he thought it was more likely something about Hal that made people just want to help him.

Hal had spent the next six days sleeping, waking only to eat toast and porridge and politely refuse the landlady's offers of beef tea. It was only on Saturday that he had begun to sit up and take notice of the world again. On Monday, Charlie had come back from Adderley to find Hal and the landlady's four-year-old grandson playing with toy cars on Hal's bed. Hal had invented a narrative about the drivers of the cars and their city that had kept the little boy entranced for an hour—a feat, Mary had assured Charlie. When Charlie arrived, Hal had wrapped it up neatly by driving all the cars back into their garages, and said, "Georgie, why don't you go downstairs now. I want to talk to my friend." And Charlie, who had found himself feeling embarrassingly jealous of the four-year-old, hadn't been able to keep the grin off his face.

"I've passed a bookstore in the high street," Charlie said, returning the sappy angel book with a shudder. "I'll stop in and pick something up for you tomorrow. Maybe I can find you *Hippopotamuses of Alexandria.*"

"Your friend Henley's book?"

"That's the one."

"Please. I long to find out what it's actually called."

They talked for a while. Charlie told Hal about his day, the latest developments at Adderley, and the news from Europe. Hal read him a funny passage from the landlady's sentimental novel. When they ran out of things to say, there was silence, but it was so charged with affection that for the moment it seemed to Charlie that nothing was lacking.

"Want to come downstairs for breakfast tomorrow?" he suggested.

"Yes, that's a good idea."

Hal yawned and stretched. He didn't have pyjamas, so he had been sleeping in shorts and undershirt. His arms and smoothly sculpted white shoulders were bare. He rubbed his face, his fingers chafing the exquisite sheen of red stubble on his chin. Charlie hadn't yet had the courage to ask about the beard, which grew faster than his own—probably at a normal rate for a red-haired white man of Hal's supposed age. The doctor had asked how old Hal was, and Charlie had experienced another moment of unnecessary panic before Hal had said quite collectedly, "Twenty." It was just plausible.

Charlie tried hard to recapture that feeling that nothing was lacking, and failed.

He left soon after that to go back to his own room. He drew back the curtains and stood looking out at the night. The clouds had uncovered the moon, and the countryside behind the inn was whitened by its cool light. It occurred to Charlie, not for the first time, that his best course would be to tell Hal what was going on. It wasn't as if it would come as a surprise to him. It wasn't right to conceal it, and it was quite possible that Hal would have some suggestion of what Charlie might do to get over it.

He had to admit, though, that the reason he hadn't brought it up yet was that he wanted to make a proper declaration. He realized that this was ridiculous and shameful, but there it was. He undressed and changed into his pyjamas—he *did* have pyjamas—and lay for a little while with his hands clasped behind his head, staring at the ceiling and indulging in a fantasy of different ways he might tell Hal he was in love with him. Eventually he fell asleep.

*

It was one of those dreams where he knew he was dreaming. He was back in Toronto, at St. John's, in the sacristy cleaning up after Mass. For some reason he was by himself—everyone else had gone off to a party to which he had not been invited—and he was feeling hard done by. He opened a drawer and discovered that it was full of forks and knives. That was just typical.

Then he realized he wasn't alone. He looked to the doorway. Hal was standing there, leaning against the open door, arms folded, watching him. He wore deacon's vestments again, not the ones Charlie had found him in, but the new white dalmatic made for St. John's the year before the start of the war. His hair was long. He was barefoot, and his wings filled up the doorway behind him.

For a moment Charlie wondered why the angel was not at the party with everyone else. After all, he'd been a hit at the Mass— though someone was going to have to talk to him about wearing shoes.

Then he remembered that Hal was waiting for him. In that way that things do in dreams, it all fell into place. He felt unbelievably happy.

The angel folded his wings a little to come through the doorway into the sacristy. His feathers were swan-white to match the dalmatic. In the dream, Charlie had always known that they changed with the seasons.

"I won't be long," he said. "Just have to finish up here." The counter was covered in chalices, dozens and dozens of them, and he realized he had no idea where they belonged. He was supposed to have asked someone about it, but he had forgotten. "It's nice of you to wait for me, but …" He was never going to be finished. He couldn't keep his friend away from the party indefinitely.

Hal frowned at the forest of chalices, and there were only two of them on the counter after all.

"This is St. John's, is it?" he said.

"Yeah, do you like it? They let you deacon at the Mass—you remember that, right?"

"Of course not."

"No—you don't remember stuff, that's okay. I remember it. You were great."

"Yes. Thank you. I'm not nearly as much in control of this narrative as I would like."

"Let's go upstairs," said Charlie, pointing to the spiral staircase that suddenly took up most of the middle of the sacristy. It led up, as he remembered now, to the church roof. "It's okay that we're a bit late. I'll introduce you to Elsa—Dr. Underhill, you know, the rector's wife. She wants to meet you."

"Some other time," said Hal.

He took hold of the front of Charlie's surplice and pulled him toward himself and kissed him on the mouth.

*

When Charlie woke, his first thought was that actually, he *didn't* remember Hal being deacon at the Mass. For a moment he was so dismayed about this that he forgot the thing he should really be fixated on. Then he remembered. He sat up in bed, horrified. This was what came of indulging in fantasies before bed; his subconscious had finally crossed the fatal line. The last moment of the dream had been so vivid that he could still conjure up the feeling of Hal's lips.

It had been a real masterpiece of a kiss: just passionate enough to send an unmistakable message, not so much as to risk awkwardness, which was always a possibility when you tried to do too much too soon. It was exactly the way he thought a first kiss should go. Which, since it was the product of his own imagination, wasn't really surprising.

Of course he'd had embarrassing dreams about men before. He remembered several he'd had as a teenager about Father Underhill that had made him want to skip church afterward. They still made him feel slightly sick to recall. But they had all been voyeuristic dreams, nothing like the travesty of imagining Hal kissing him in the St. John's sacristy, *in vestments*. And avoiding Hal that morning was even more out of the question than skipping church had been when he was a teenager.

In fact, avoiding Hal would have had to involve jumping out the window or hiding under the bed, because it was Hal who knocked at Charlie's door before Charlie was fully dressed.

"It's me," he said from the other side of the door.

"Just—just give me a minute!" Charlie called, then realized he had sounded absurdly guilty, but couldn't figure out what to do about it.

There was a pause. "Sure. Take as long as you need."

He scrambled into his clothes in a pointless hurry, and in his haste tugged so hard on one of his bootlaces that he broke it. He had a spare pair, but had to hunt for them, and then to relace the boot, and the whole thing took a ridiculously long time. He finally emerged on the landing, looking sheepish. Hal was lounging on a bench by the stairs.

"Sorry for—" he started to say, getting up from his seat, just as Charlie started to say the same thing.

They laughed, perhaps a little more than they needed to.

"You're looking well," Charlie said.

"I feel well."

He was dressed in Anderson's trousers and a grey-blue plaid shirt that must have belonged to the landlady's husband or son, the sleeves rolled up, the collar open. He was clean-shaven, and his hair was damp as if he had washed it, the wet curls pushed back from his forehead. He looked painfully lovely.

"I thought I might walk with you to the air base," he said, as they descended the stairs.

"I don't know that that's a good idea—it would be a long walk back uphill by yourself. You've only just got out of bed. You'd maybe better take it easy."

"Oh, well, then I won't. If Mary insists on serving me bacon, will you eat it for me?"

"Of course."

"Will you be flying today?" Hal asked, as they sat in the sun by the front window of the bar.

Charlie nodded. He had told Hal about the previous week's missions only after the fact, then regretted that, although Hal hadn't offered any particular reaction.

"It's just—" he started, then realized that the sentence shouldn't contain *just*. "It's a combat mission, but not the most dangerous thing I've ever done. The war is almost over—the likelihood is we won't be engaged."

Hal nodded. "Well, be safe."

"I'll try."

The landlady came with their food, and said how happy she was to see Hal up and about. He beamed up at her and waited until she had gone before he discreetly transferred the bacon from his plate to Charlie's. Charlie smiled across the table at him. A sudden, satisfying image formed in his mind: an image of himself, Charles Boult, thirty-four years old, in the prime of his life, with his rough background and his university degree, his semi-artistic career and his discreetly impressive war record, and a beautiful and brilliant young friend who shared his interests and his convictions, even his sense of humour, who wanted to share his life and his bed …

He nearly choked on his bacon. It was a fantasy as bad as—worse than—the dream about the kiss in the sacristy, but somehow as they sat there in the sun with their breakfast, it felt dangerously, seductively real.

Hal was spreading honey on his toast. He took a bite and looked up at Charlie. His red eyebrows arched in a wordless question.

"What? Oh, nothing. Just thinking."

"Mm." Hal swallowed his mouthful of toast. "I would pray for you," he said, "if I knew how."

It took Charlie a moment to realize he was still talking about the mission.

Chapter Ten

CROQUET AND CHAMPAGNE

By the time Fee had been at Adderley a week, her right arm had healed sufficiently that she was able to propel her wheelchair everywhere by herself, and she had begun exercising with crutches. Dr. Sheppard said that she would be ready to be fitted for a prosthetic soon. That Monday, in honour of Evvie's day off, they secured the loan of Lady Rathburn's car, and got Rosalind to drive them the thirty miles to Newingthorpe, where they ate at a tea room, tried on hats in one shop, bought books in another, and visited a squat little grey English church.

The rest of the week passed on uneventfully. The bond between Fee and Evvie had become such a settled thing so quickly that it scarcely needed speaking of—though Fee, who had a more sentimental streak than Evvie, did occasionally speak of it. Whenever Evvie was not actually working (and sometimes when she was) they would spend their time together, in Fee's room or in the library or, as the weather grew warmer and Fee became daily more mobile, in the courtyard or out on the lawn. Evvie had read *Strong Poison*, and they had thoroughly discussed it. Fee had made a stab at learning to embroider, and Evvie had finished the handkerchief with *F.- lilies-St. C.* on it. They had not talked again about angels or rings that summoned devils.

On Thursday morning, the long-delayed game of croquet that Evvie had proposed was finally to take place.

"You'll join us, won't you?" said Rosalind at breakfast. "After all, it was your idea."

"It sounds like fun," said Evvie, taking a couple of slices of cold toast at the sideboard. She peeked under the silver lids of the other dishes, and glumly scooped a few withered-looking mushrooms and charred tomatoes onto her plate. "But I have to help inventory a big shipment of supplies that came in yesterday, and then I have a pile of sewing to finish."

"Oh, sorry!" said Rosalind, grimacing. "I keep forgetting you work."

Evvie looked at her for a moment to see if she would realize that was a bit insulting, but she didn't. She dumped her plate on the table and sat down. Evvie poured herself a cup of tea.

"Do you think Fee might like to join us?" said Rosalind. "I mean, obviously she can't play, but it's a nice day to be outside, and if you're so busy, she might be bored."

Evvie could see that this was aimed—probably unconsciously— at putting her on the defensive and drawing her into a discussion about whether or not she unfairly monopolized Fee's time. She didn't take the bait.

"That's a good idea," she said, sitting down with her plate of unappetizing English food. "You should ask her."

She remembered the reason why she had brought up the subject of croquet, nearly two weeks ago. It seemed like a different era al- together. She had lost all interest in investigating Ernest and Leo and their dangerous boxes and stolen planes. Even the mystery of the bloodstained vestments had become merely a strange story to tell Fee—who had listened with wide eyes and looked appropri- ately chilled at the sight of the red feather—and the rest of it she hadn't even mentioned. Fee had filled the void in Evvie's life much more effectively than sneaking about eavesdropping and concocting mysteries ever could have.

The croquet players assembled on the front lawn, where Evvie could see them out the office window while she worked on her inventory. She saw Ernest standing with his arms wrapped pro- tectively around Daphne, as if to shield her from more than the weather—which was, in fact, very pleasant. Whatever it was for her, Evvie thought, for him it looked very like it was love.

"He thinks he's Prince Hamlet or something," Fee had said in private the other day, about Ernest. "It's *deeply* boring."

"Prince Hamlet?" Evvie wasn't sure; she thought the comparison unflattering to a favourite literary character.

"Like he's the only person he knows who's ever thought seriously about the fact that life might be really awful, and evil might—gasp!— actually exist, and that kind of thing. And he thinks I should be so impressed with him for coming up with these insights. Like it's his mission to go around sowing black little bits of despair in people's hearts and then looking at you soulfully and feeling *so tragic* about it. Blech! I haven't time for it. Actually though, I quite swoon over the real Prince Hamlet—I mean the *fictional* Prince Hamlet."

"You had me worried for a moment," said Evvie.

She thought Fee might be right about Ernest. There was something about him—a look as if he wanted you to know how deeply he had suffered. But that didn't mean he didn't love Daphne.

Daphne herself called it "sympathy" or "synchrony" or something. She had been holding forth about it in the library the night before, as the young women sat together.

"In the case of that other woman, you see, there was no physical sympathy, and that's the thing that makes it really true." Evvie realized that she was talking about Ernest's wife again, and that she either didn't know, or refused to pronounce, the woman's name. "Without the physical, it's all just a lot of words, completely hollow. Ernest and I have that connection, so even when we fight about intellectual things, our bodies are still in absolute synchrony. Sometimes my mind tells me I can't stand him, but my body always knows otherwise. You see, it's that connection that makes us essential to one another."

"But," said Evvie, taking Daphne by surprise by speaking, "what does it really mean, for bodies to be in synchrony?"

"I was wondering just the same thing!" said Fee with a little laugh. "Only I didn't want to admit that I didn't know."

Rosalind held very still, as if she had been frozen, and Evvie could tell she didn't want to commit herself to a side until Daphne had given her answer.

"Actually," said Evvie, not letting her, "it wasn't a real question. What I meant was, I don't think one should deify sex attraction. I'm sure it's very nice, a very nice part of the created world—but one ought to keep things in perspective."

Daphne rearranged herself in her chair, making minute adjustments to her dress and her hair.

"Have you ever been with a man?" The question was undirected, general.

"No," said Evvie, and decided to draw Daphne's fire. There was no need to let her start in on beautiful, crippled Fee, or even poor, waffling Rosalind. "And I don't ever mean to be. After the war is over, God willing, I'll go back to my monastery in Greece and become a nun."

Daphne looked up at her with something like horror. There was a strained silence, which Rosalind broke by laughing nervously.

"She means it," said Fee witheringly.

Later that night, in Fee's room, Fee had said, "I was so proud of you *declaring* yourself like that."

"Declaring myself?"

"How you told Daphne about going back to your monastery. It must have taken courage. Proclaiming your allegiance, you know, to someone you knew would be hostile. I just remembered how you said people don't understand, and so you don't like to talk about it."

"Yes, and that's wrong of me, isn't it? I just did it now because I didn't want her to start in on you, and whether you have a boyfriend."

"Which you know I don't."

Evvie waved a hand. "You will when it suits you. You'll have your pick of boyfriends, and get engaged to the one you like best, and walk down the aisle with your father on your wedding day. And your future husband will be lucky to get you, Fee, and if he's worthy of you, he'll know it."

She watched Ernest and Daphne embracing on the lawn, and Fee sitting in her wheelchair while Rosalind flitted back and forth, chatting to her and organizing the croquet game, and thought how strange it was that so many different things in the world could go by that same name of "love."

*

Evvie was in the upstairs workroom, busy with her pile of mending, when Fee came in, walking quite well with her crutches.

"Oh, look at you!" Evvie exclaimed, hopping up from her seat to clear her work out of the chair next to her and make room for Fee. "You came all the way up here by yourself?"

"In the elevator," said Fee. "It's not so much of an accomplishment."

"What's the matter?" Evvie asked, suddenly noticing how white and ill Fee looked.

Fee made one of her little faces: an *oh-it's-nothing* face. "Bad migraine came on all of a sudden."

"Want me to close the curtains?"

"What? Oh, the light? No, it doesn't bother me, actually." She rubbed her forehead. "I don't get typical migraines—they go away quickly. But … I just had a disturbing conversation with someone. I shouldn't have let it get to me." She sat down in the chair, propping her crutches next to her. She was wearing a long pleated skirt that fully hid the stump of her missing leg.

Evvie remained standing, her bundle of mending in her arms, looking down at her friend. Fee looked up at her, and didn't try the *oh-it's-nothing* face again.

"Who was it?" Evvie asked.

157

"It's not really important," Fee tried again. "It was that woman—Josephine something?"

"Josephine Good." Evvie put down her bundle and perched on the edge of the table in front of Fee. "What did she say to you?"

"Well, I'm sure she didn't mean it to sound so horrible, but she more or less said that she didn't think I had any reason to go on living."

"She *what*?"

"I'm sure she didn't mean it that way."

"No?"

"Well … nobody could, could they?"

"Nobody who wasn't a fiend in human form."

"Don't joke about that."

"I wasn't joking. But Fidelity—"

"Oh, please don't call me that."

"I'm sorry."

Fee shook herself a little. "*I*'m sorry. You just wanted more syllables to be sympathetic in."

Evvie got up and went to the corner of the room, where there was a gas ring, to put the kettle on. "I'm making tea," she said. "To prove what a naturalized English subject I really am."

That got a little snort of laughter out of Fee. Evvie came back and sat beside her to wait for the water to boil.

"Do you—would it help to tell me what she said?"

"Yes, I suppose so. I can't remember it exactly. But I had a funny feeling *I* was going to tell her things, you know. Things I didn't really want to tell her. I mean, I don't know her, and she was being rather horrible, so why should I want to tell her anything? She said … something about how sad for my parents, how I must have been their perfect daughter, and now … now it was like I'd ruined their happily-ever-after. She did actually use those words."

"That's monstrous!"

"Isn't it? It *is*, isn't it?" Fee sighed, as if relieved to have it out in the open. "But the truth is, my parents did have a beautiful love story, and everyone does think they're a romantic couple. And I had this feeling that in a moment I was going to tell her all about them. Or … that she was going to *know*, even if I didn't tell her—she was going to know all my secrets."

Evvie didn't ask what it was about Fee's parents that was a secret. Maybe she hadn't meant that.

"And that's when she started to sort of hint about how if she were in my position, she'd … kill herself." She looked up at Evvie steadily. "I am not thinking of taking her advice, Evgenia. Please don't worry. But it was horrible, how she seemed to know exactly what would get to me. I mean, if she'd talked about how hard it'll be for me to find a husband or something, it would barely have bothered me. But talking about my parents like that … " She shivered.

"You know you're not just sort of an epilogue to your parents' love story, no matter how romantic it was. You can't be. Nobody is that kind of thing."

"I guess so." She sounded unconvinced. "I guess I didn't *mind* thinking of myself that way, when I felt … when I felt like I wasn't spoiling the story."

Evvie wanted to say that of course Fee's parents didn't think of her that way either, but the truth was she couldn't be sure of that. Reasonable people wouldn't, but she couldn't be sure Mr. and Mrs. St. Clair were reasonable. She pictured them floating about in a cloud of self-satisfaction, thinking of their beautiful daughter as an accessory to their romantic story of love in genteel poverty, or whatever it was. Of course she didn't know that's what they were like, but she still felt a strong desire to bonk their heads together.

The kettle boiled, and Fee changed the subject to talk about happier things while the tea steeped. Evvie picked up her mending again, and they were still sitting together like this later in the afternoon when Rosalind returned from an outing with her fiancé and sought them out. She looked glum too.

"Here, there's another chair if you want to sit," said Evvie, pulling it out from under the table. "We had some tea, but I think it will be cold by now. Shall I make some fresh?"

"Thanks," said Rosalind, dropping into the offered chair. "I could use some tea."

"Where did you go on your date?" Fee asked, as Evvie went to the cupboard to get another mug for Rosalind, and back to the sink to refill the kettle.

"Oh, we just walked around a bit. Latham didn't have much time—he didn't have proper leave, just a bit of free time."

"It sounds nice, though," said Evvie.

"Oh, it was. It's just that the moment I got in, there was a letter from my father waiting for me."

"Not bad news?" said Fee.

"No! Nothing like that—just the usual nagging. He thinks Latham and I should have married before the war, and he thinks it's my fault we didn't. He's never forgiven me for it."

"But you'd have been awfully young, wouldn't you?" said Fee.

Rosalind shrugged. "I was eighteen when we got engaged. I'm older than you two, you know. Anyway, being too young isn't a problem as far as Papa's concerned. He just wants to see me sorted, and is afraid I can't manage it on my own. The problem with fathers, I find, is that they're only really interested in sons."

"Not my father," said Fee loyally. "I mean, that doesn't invalidate your point—I expect he's the exception that proves the rule."

Rosalind looked sceptical. Evvie was on the point of jumping in with some change of topic, to get the conversation away from fathers, but Rosalind pre-empted her by asking, "Do you have brothers?"

Fee was silent for so long that Evvie replied for her: "Just the one, just the one older brother, right, Fee?"

"Oh. Yes. Calvin. But … Daddy doesn't prefer him over me, or wish that I were another son, or … If anything, I think sometimes I'm the one who gets preferential treatment, because I'm the only—

the daughter, you know, and … fathers and daughters can share some nice things, actually. With sons they have to be all *man-to-man* and *one-day-all-this-will-be-yours*, and keep up appearances, but with daughters they can be sentimental and show their affection if they want, and boast about how pretty you are, and …" Her voice trailed off, and she looked out the window. "Sorry! Uncharacteristically mopey! I was just reliving a happy memory. Dancing with my father at Florence and Rick's wedding last summer. Her brother and his friends played the music—they aren't very good, but they were having fun, and so were all the guests, and Teddy Chapman asked me to dance, and every second step he took was on my toes, and Father took pity and rescued us. Rescued me, I mean, but Teddy was pretty relieved, too. I guess waltzing with your father is kind of little-girly, but we enjoyed it. It's just a bit sad to think it won't ever happen again."

Evvie sat looking at Fee with a sympathetic expression, waiting for when she would look up and meet her friend's gaze. It was all you could do; there was nothing to be said except, "I'm sorry," which you could just as easily say without words.

Rosalind cleared her throat awkwardly. "I wouldn't have thought Baptists danced at weddings," she said.

Evvie wanted to jump up and strangle her.

Fidelity gave her a magnificent look. "It wasn't a Baptist wedding. There was *also* champagne." She seized her crutches and got up from the chair quite neatly. "If you'll excuse me," she said, and left the room. Evvie caught the look she gave over her shoulder, which said, *Deal with Rosalind; don't worry about me.*

Rosalind sat looking wretchedly into her half-finished mug of tea. "Gosh, what a stupid thing to say. I feel like such a fool. I'm no good with sympathy."

"Why's that, I wonder," said Evvie, looking out the window.

"Hm?"

"Never mind. It can be difficult."

"I mean, no doubt her dad's fabulous and all that, but still. Sounds like a bit of an Elektra complex to me." When Evvie said nothing to this, she started to elaborate: "That's when—"

"Thank you. I am Greek. So you had a nice visit with your fiancé?"

Rosalind shrugged. "It was all right. It's not a love match, you know."

"What's not?"

"My engagement. I mean, it's a tremendously good thing, for everyone—his father is the younger son of an earl, and mine is tremendously rich, and our families are on the best of terms. And Latham is tremendously handsome and well-bred and we've been friends since we were kids and we're crazy about each other." It sounded like something she had memorized. "It's absolutely the perfect thing for us to get married, nobody questions that. It's just not a love match."

"Perhaps I don't understand. If you are crazy about each other … " She thought, *Please don't use the word "tremendously" again.*

"But that's just something we say. I don't even know what it means."

"Right," said Evvie. It made a depressing kind of sense.

"I guess it means we love the *idea* of getting married to each other. I know I love it, anyway. My father loves it, too—it's the first thing I've done right, as far as he's concerned. My mother is happy enough, though she'd prefer I ran off with a chauffeur or something—more romantic. I wonder if she drank that champagne."

"What?"

"Fee. I wonder if she drank the champagne at that wedding. I sometimes think she's a bit odd. I mean, you have to wonder what her precious Daddy would think of that haircut!"

"I don't think he'd be shocked if he knows his daughter at all. And I suppose he must—it sounds as if they are good friends." Which was a little surprising, given everything else Fee had said about

Gregory St. Clair, but there was always something else surprising to be learned about Fee.

Rosalind squeezed her hands together in her lap. "I don't know what's the matter with me, Evvie. I think I must just be jealous." She thought about that for a moment, and looked stricken. "How awful! I'm jealous of a girl with *one leg*."

But that was the thing about Fidelity, Evvie thought. She made it so hard to feel sorry for her, you could actually come right out the other side and end up envying her. In fact, how could you not envy someone so resilient, so fortified by nature to endure her fate? Especially if you were Rosalind, with nothing going on in your life but an engagement to a man you didn't exactly love.

To Rosalind she just said, kindly, "When you think about it like that, it doesn't make sense, does it?"

Rosalind finished her tea and left, and Evvie waited a decent interval before going in search of Fee. She found her in a corner of the library, by herself. It was clear that she had been crying, but she was dry-eyed now. She looked up at Evvie's approach.

"Isn't human life complicated, Evgenia?" she said.

Evvie sat down on the window-seat beside her. "Yes. But some things are very simple."

Fee grinned and clearly knew what she meant. "I'm glad you stuck by Rosalind when I went off in a huff. You did, didn't you? Don't worry—I'm not going to ask what she said about me behind my back. It doesn't matter. We have to stay friends with her because her only other recourse is the horrible Daphne, and we can't abandon her to that fate." After a moment she added, "It's not easy. I expect you'll have noticed I'm very possessive."

It took Evvie a moment to work out what she meant by that. "Oh, Fee!" she said when she did. "You don't have to be possessive about *me*. I feel exactly the same way!"

Chapter Eleven

ORDINARY TIME

The studio was at the very top of an old house, literally a garret, but a nice one, with a high, sloping ceiling, painted white, and a tall dormer window that caught the afternoon light. Charlie's sketches of churches were pinned on the walls, keeping company with his framed university diploma. His drafting table stood under the window. A second-hand couch opposite gained an air of slightly bohemian elegance from several brightly coloured cushions made by his fashion-designer friend Vera. It was all much as he had left it.

He was sitting on the stool at the drafting table, with his back to the window, not working but waiting for someone. He must have nodded off, though, because he couldn't remember who. Not a client, but a friend, someone he had been looking forward eagerly to seeing. Vera? Henley? He thought not. Father Underhill? No, that didn't make sense; he never had reason to come out here. But it was someone like that.

He heard steps on the landing, and a knock at the door. He crossed the little room in a couple of strides and flung the door open. He had remembered who it was.

It must have been Ordinary Time, because Hal's wings were green, a beautiful iridescent gold-shot green that made a striking contrast with his short red curls. He had to fold them down until the longest feathers brushed the floor to get through the low doorway. He was dressed in a style that Charlie himself often affected: rolled-up sleeves and a waistcoat without a jacket, like an office clerk or a newspaperman. His trousers and waistcoat were dove grey. Charlie had always thought redheads looked good in grey.

"You were expecting me?" he said, smiling and stretching his wings. The high ceiling and sparse furniture let him arc them up over his head, shaking out the feathers.

"Sort of," said Charlie, watching enraptured as the sunlight flashed gold and green on the tremendous architecture of the wings.

Hal laughed. "I didn't know whether you wanted me to come back, after last time." He started to fold his wings.

"Last time?"

"Yes, the way you reacted—it's not your fault, I took you by surprise—but I wasn't sure … " He settled his wings fussily, giving Charlie a sidelong look, as though he hoped he might finish the sentence for him.

"It's okay," said Charlie warmly, not knowing what he was talking about. "Do you want some coffee?"

"Coffee?"

"Yes, actual coffee, not pretend wartime swill. I was about to make some for myself …"

"Ah." There was a pause. "Thank you. That would be nice."

There was another pause. The hotplate and percolator were on top of the bookcase on the other side of the room. Hal and his wings took up all the space between the couch and the drafting table, but he didn't seem to realize that he would have to move to let Charlie get by.

Very naturally, as if it were something he'd done many times before, Charlie reached out a hand to edge him out of the way so he could get past. His hand came to rest on Hal's waist. They smiled at each other. Hal's hand came up, and Charlie caught it and lightly kissed his white fingers. He released him casually and moved past him towards the coffee things.

"Sit down," he said. "Make yourself comfortable."

When he turned back from putting the water on to heat, he

saw that Hal was perched on the stool at his drafting table, facing into the room. Of course; he couldn't really sit on the couch with his wings.

Charlie stood for a moment with his back to the bookcase, just looking at Hal, overwhelmed with the magnitude of his happiness.

"What are you doing?" Hal asked.

"Looking at you. Thinking how much I love you."

Something very young seemed to blossom in Hal's expression. "You are? You do?"

"Hal! Of course I love you."

"And you know that I love you—do you?"

"Yes. Of course."

Perhaps he shouldn't say *of course*, as if it were something that should go without saying. Hal got like this sometimes—he had anxiety about things, and of course his memory was unreliable—but in truth Charlie didn't mind, and he didn't want to make it seem like he minded. He crossed to the drafting table and gave Hal a long, reassuring kiss, tipping his head back and tangling his fingers in his hair. Hal's hands pressed against his back, and when Charlie bent to kiss his throat, he gasped.

"I could get to like this," Hal said thoughtfully, when Charlie had gone back to see to the coffee.

"What?"

"Whatever is going on here. Are we in the future, do you think, or the past?"

"We're in the *present*. I know you're not so hot on the passage of time, but come on."

"Yes, I see."

Charlie poured coffee into two mugs, and remembered that Hal took his with lots of sugar and milk. He brought it to him, and went to the couch with his own cup of black coffee. He picked up the sketchbook which was lying on the cushions.

"Do me a favour?" he said. "Toss me a pencil—2B if you can find one—and then turn to your right, so I can see your wings in profile. There's something happening with the sun on your feathers that I want to try to sketch."

He flipped through the sketchbook, past all his earlier drawings of Hal: precise renderings of the structure of his wings; studies of his hands; a few attempts at full-length portraits, one of Hal at church, in a cope, another of Hal wingless and naked, sprawled asleep on their bed. He opened to a blank page, smoothed out the paper, and woke up.

*

The thing to do, he decided, as he sat by himself at what he had already started to think of as "their usual table" by the window in the bar, was to tell Hal about the dreams. He had already made up his mind that he had to admit how he felt, and this would be a particularly clear and vivid way of doing it. But the thought made him want to cry.

The first dream had left him alarmed and disgusted that he had foisted his perverse desires subconsciously on Hal. The second dream had mostly just made him sad. The whole thing had been so tender and idyllic: the coffee, the drawings, Hal perched on the stool in his studio, anxiously asking whether Charlie knew that he loved him. It hadn't been completely coherent, of course, but the details had been right, down to the patterns on Vera's cushions. The sketches of Hal had looked like things that Charlie might have drawn. And Hal had seemed very much like himself. That was possibly the worst part.

"Is he not bahn to come down today?"

Charlie looked up with surprise to find the landlady standing beside their table.

"What? Oh, I don't know."

"I hope he didn't tire hissel out yesterday," she said. "He was a grand help with Georgie, and they do get on like a house afire, but I'm afeared that bairn is a handful."

"I'm sure he's fine," said Charlie. "He didn't seem tired last night. He said he had fun—sounds like Georgie's a real pro at hide-and-seek."

"Bless his heart! If he does want breakfast in bed, though, he's welcome."

Charlie pushed his chair back from the table. "I'll go see whether he's up."

He climbed the stairs reluctantly; he didn't want to encounter Hal in bed that morning, looking sleepy and beautiful and semi-naked.

There was no answer when he knocked on Hal's door. He turned the knob after a moment and looked inside. The bed was empty, the covers thrown back, and the pillows disarranged.

So that's it, Charlie thought. *He's gone*. He didn't know what to feel.

Across the hall, the bathroom door opened. Charlie looked up with a start. Hal emerged, hair damp, a towel around his waist. He saw Charlie, and a smile lit up his face.

"Charles! Good morning!"

"Oh. There you are. I was just …" He moved out of the doorway. "Better get some clothes on."

That sounded stupid. They were the only guests in this wing of the house, so there wasn't much danger of anyone else seeing him. And Hal probably wouldn't have minded if anyone had.

"It was my intention," Hal said dryly. He pushed the door of his room open all the way. Charlie's eyes followed the twist of his torso, dropped down the gentle curve of his spine to the smooth twin hollows in the small of his back. "Come in," Hal said.

"What?" Charlie looked him in the eye, startled and dismayed. "No, I'll … I'll just wait out here."

Hal gave him a look of complete bafflement. "Fine," he said after a moment. "Why don't you go downstairs and order breakfast, in that case."

Charlie went downstairs, feeling utterly wretched. He managed to pull himself together sufficiently to tell Mary that Hal was coming down for breakfast, then he slumped in his chair at their table and wondered what was to become of him.

There was no way he could tell Hal about the dreams now, he decided. Not after Hal had looked so puzzled—even offended—by his refusal to be in the same room with him while he dressed. He had thought the angel was a little more savvy than that. Actually, he'd thought he was a lot more savvy. Hadn't something been said about intelligence? Was it possible that he didn't realize he was attractive? He knew that Charlie was homosexual. Had he somehow not been able to put the pieces together?

By the time Hal came downstairs, wearing another borrowed plaid shirt, Charlie had worked himself into a state of being actually annoyed with him.

As it happened, Hal also seemed annoyed with Charlie, and they ate their breakfast in an unusually cool silence.

"What are you going to do today?" Charlie asked finally, reaching across to spear the pieces of bacon that Hal had left on his plate.

Hal pushed the plate towards him. "I think I will go outside and sit in the sun." He smiled, and Charlie felt weak with relief; he hadn't realized how desperate he had been for Hal to regain his equanimity.

"That sounds dreamy." He grinned. "If you see any planes overhead, one will be me, on my way down to London to pick up a general."

"I will watch for you."

A previous occupant of the bar had left yesterday's paper on the table, folded open at the crossword, with the pencil that had been used to fill in two of the clues. Hal pulled the paper to himself across the table, glanced down the list of clues, and filled in the rest of the grid, as rapidly and methodically as a shopkeeper writing a receipt.

"I don't know why they call them 'puzzles,'" he remarked, laying down the pencil.

Charlie took the paper away from him and turned it face-down on the table. "You've got to stop doing that."

"Why?" Hal asked, deadpan.

"It makes you look very unusual."

Charlie peeked at the completed crossword, then slapped the paper back down again. He'd have to take it upstairs with him to dispose of; this morning Hal had filled it out in a sort of pristine medieval calligraphy. The day before, though he'd done it just as quickly, he had formed all the letters in an exact imitation of the newspaper's typeface. Charlie wondered what Hal's actual handwriting would look like. He must *have* handwriting, the same way that he had a specific accent to go with his current form. Other details, such as his preference for sugar in his tea and his refusal to eat meat (which he had admitted to Charlie was nine-tenths squeamishness), were clearly genuine parts of his personality that had survived the wreck of his memory.

"Am I very unusual?" Hal asked, looking off out the window, apparently thoughtful.

"Well, no. That's the point. Most of the time you're not. You're very good at passing for human."

"Thank you, but that was not what I meant. I was wondering how unusual my current situation is."

"Yeah, I would think that's pretty unusual."

"So would I, but I don't actually know." He frowned. There were times when something about his expression, the depths of pain and dislocation behind it, chilled Charlie with horror. But they never lasted long.

*

He came back early that evening, found Hal's room empty again (though the bed was made this time), and prowled around the inn looking for him. He found him eventually in the kitchen, peeling potatoes while the landlady told some story about her daughter-in-law.

"There now, love," she said, when she saw Charlie. "Thi friend is back. Take thissel off, now, and leave me to finish up." She took the peeler and half-finished potato away from Hal. "He's a dear lad," she said to Charlie, in an undertone, "but I don't reckon he'd ever peeled a potato afore in his life."

"Could be," said Charlie.

He and Hal went out the back door into the paved yard behind the inn. It was still light out, though the shadows were lengthening. Charlie hadn't had much leisure that day to dwell on the problem of Hal—the mission to fetch the general had been unexpectedly involved—and he had no plan for what to say now. In fact, his only plan was a way to avoid having to talk to Hal at all.

"I was thinking of driving out to Zion," he said. "Since it's still light. I haven't heard from Dr. Good—their telephone might be down again—and I don't know if he's made any progress on the repairs."

"I'll come with you," said Hal. "Unless … May I come with you?"

"Sure," Charlie said readily, although he had thought it was the last thing he wanted.

They set off in the jeep that Charlie had brought up to the inn for the purpose, and fell easily into conversation about the events of the day. Hal was amazingly good company; his understanding was so quick, his interest in everything so lively and genuine, his sense of humour at once bone-dry and childlike. He was content to listen to Charlie talk without interruption, but he told his own stories readily when Charlie wanted to hear them. In his fantasies about confessing his love, Charlie had sometimes imagined explaining the reasons for it.

"I met your Miss Good in the village today," said Hal. "She gave me the creeps."

"The what?"

"The *creeps*. It is a slang expression. It means—"

"Oh, you're hilarious. How did you know it was her?"

"I heard someone speak to her in the post office. Then she stared at me, and I thought she wanted to speak to me, so I left."

"What were you doing in the post office?"

"Posting letters," said Hal airily. "Is that not what one normally does?"

"Yeah, it is. Who're you writing to?"

Hal laughed. "They were our landlady's letters."

"Right! That makes more sense."

"I found something else you might like," said Hal after a moment. "The little church at the other end of the village, the one whose bell-tower I can see from my window, has a noticeboard in front that refers to their Sunday Eucharist as 'Mass.'"

"Do they indeed?"

"Yes. I asked Mary if that was because it is a Roman Catholic church, and she said no, 'They call themselves Church of England.' She herself attends the Methodist chapel, as I learned. But I thought: Church of England, Mass, beautiful medieval stonework ... " He ticked the items off on his fingers. "That sounds like my Charles."

"Thanks," said Charlie, touched. "We'll go on Sunday, for sure."

They arrived at the Zion Retreat Centre as the sky in the west was beginning to redden. The ruined farm house stood just as it had when Charlie first saw it; clearly no repair work had begun yet. They parked the jeep by the gate.

"Now how to do this without running into Miss Good ... " said Charlie, getting down from the driver's seat. He was mostly joking; he was embarrassed when he thought back on his panicked reaction to their previous encounter.

He was relieved, though, when it was Dr. Good who opened the door.

"Squadron Leader Boult! How good to see you again. And this

must be your friend whom I am afraid we left stranded—it was very remiss of us. But you are recovered fully, I hope?"

He shook hands anxiously with Hal, who seemed to have gone quiet and merely nodded in response. Charlie wondered briefly how Dr. Good had known who he was, but supposed it must have been the RAF greatcoat that he was wearing and a lucky guess.

"Josephine will be so sorry to have missed you," said Dr. Good, beckoning them into the cluttered entryway of the house. "She is over at Adderley Hall visiting the poor souls there—I believe they appreciate her visits very much, and so of course even though it is inconvenient for me to be without the car all day ... " His voice trailed off and he frowned slightly.

"Do you need a ride anywhere?" Charlie offered.

"What? Oh, how very good of you. I—but no, it is late, and I should not be out when Josephine returns, it would not be right. But now! Can I offer you young men a drink? I have some very tolerable sherry. And then you must tell me how I can help you."

"Well, it's more a question of me helping you," said Charlie. He glanced at Hal and mouthed, "Sherry?"

Hal looked uncomfortable, Charlie thought, but not obviously so, and he shrugged slightly. They followed Dr. Good into the library, where he dug out a sherry bottle from a sideboard while Charlie and Hal sat in two of the brand-new wingback chairs in the middle of the room.

"Help me?" Dr. Good said vaguely. "Oh, yes. Your kind offer to assist with the repairs to the house. Yes, yes. I'm afraid ..." He peered into the sideboard. "There don't seem to be any glasses. Pardon me one moment."

He took off in the direction of the kitchen, the sherry bottle clutched in one hand. Charlie looked across at Hal.

"You all right?"

Hal nodded, but he still didn't look happy. "I don't like this house."

"Neither do I!"

"Good," said Hal. He shifted in his chair, and for a crazy moment Charlie thought he was about to reach over and take his hand. But he just leaned on the arm of the chair to look around at the shelf behind them.

Charlie followed his gaze. "Oh, those are their tracts. I've had a look at a couple of them, and they were rubbish." He reached around and pulled one off the shelf at random. "'Suicide: Is It a Sin?' Well, surely they can't go too far off the rails with that one." He opened it and scanned through the contents, thinking he knew what he'd find.

It was quite different from what he'd expected. He found himself going back to the beginning and reading more carefully, with a horrified fascination.

"What does it say?" Hal asked.

Charlie looked up. Hal had a strained, tired look on his face, and Charlie saw him again as in his dream of the night before: anxious, damaged, vulnerable. He understood better than he ever had before why people kept things from those they loved sometimes. He wanted very much to keep the contents of that tract from Hal.

Dr. Good came back into the room before he could reply—he would, in the end, have replied—and saw what Charlie was looking at.

"Ah, I see you are perusing some of our literature!" He set the sherry glasses down on the sideboard and began filling them carefully. "That one is a favourite of Josephine's to bring to the poor souls at the hospital. Many of them are prone to despair, you see."

"I can imagine," said Charlie. "But is this really the right thing for them? Isn't it a bit … pro-suicide?"

"Pro-suicide?" Dr. Good turned to face him, two brimming sherry glasses in his hands. "Dear me, I hope not! Of course I abhor the idea of suicide, Mr. Boult. Of course I do. To throw away the life that God has given you …" He shuddered. "And yet, one must show compassion to those in despair—and one must not breed despair in the hearts of loved ones, by condemning the poor unfortunate who has taken his own life. These are the complexities I tried to address in that pamphlet."

"I see," said Charlie. He did, in a way, see how Dr. Good's intentions could have matched his name. But the tract as it stood went a fair bit further than "showing compassion" to suicides. It really seemed almost to encourage them.

He set it aside to accept the glass of sherry that Dr. Good offered, then tried to steer the conversation back to the question of repairs on the farm house.

"So kind of you, really," Dr. Good mumbled. "But I am afraid it will be some time before anything can be done. I turned the whole matter over to Josephine, you see—she is much more adept in these practical matters than I—and she tells me there has been some unexpected difficulty about ordering the necessary supplies. Timber and shingles and so on. The exigencies of wartime, I fear."

Charlie tried to emphasize again the importance of getting the work done soon, and suggested that Dr. Good might call upon members of his congregation to donate supplies, and at all of this their host nodded and repeated how kind it was of Charlie to be concerned, and that he would speak to Josephine about it. There seemed no more that could be done.

Hal had finished about half of his sherry when he put the glass down suddenly and got up from his chair.

"Excuse me," he said. "I don't feel … well."

"Fresh air?" Charlie suggested, getting to his feet. He remembered suddenly that they were in the house where Hal's captors had intended to bring him. How could he have forgotten that? Well, he hadn't forgotten it, exactly, but he certainly hadn't been thinking about it.

Hal nodded and hurried out of the room.

"Oh dear," said Dr. Good. "Is there anything I can do?"

"No," said Charlie. "Sorry. We'd better be on our way. He's been a bit shaken up ever since the crash."

Dr. Good nodded sympathetically. "Poor fellow."

He accompanied Charlie to the door, said again how sorry Josephine would be to have missed them both, and shook hands in parting. Charlie found Hal leaning against the jeep by the gate.

"Feel any better?"

Hal looked up. He certainly looked as if he was feeling better.

"Yes. I am sorry for making a scene."

"Oh, pff! Don't worry about it. I should've … " He was starting to say he should have been more sensitive, or something, but remembered that wasn't the right tack to take with Hal. "What got to you? Was it the sherry?"

Hal cracked a smile at that. "No, the sherry was fine. It was the house. And that man."

"Care to be more specific?"

"No." He shook himself irritably. "It was similar to the aversion I felt to Miss Good in the post office. Is that more specific? I don't know what it was, exactly. That is part of the problem. I *can't bear* this physical existence, Charles—all this uncertainty, *feelings*, vagueness. It's … " He sighed. "No, I misspoke. I can bear it very well. I just don't always understand it. That frustrates me."

"I get it," said Charlie.

"I know."

They stood leaning against the jeep for a minute longer in silence. The sky was quite dark now in the east, but the sunset still flamed in the west. Charlie tried to think what else to say. Then something told him that Hal was enjoying the silence, and he realized that, when he let himself, he was too. In the failing light, something flickered at the edge of his vision, and he felt the slightest breath, like the passage of feathers. He looked, and there was nothing there, but Hal caught his eye and gave him a smile of an incredible, private sweetness, before looking coolly away into the sunset. Charlie asked himself how he could possibly want any more than this.

Chapter Twelve

THE MOST MAGNIFICENT OF FRIENDS

Fee had tired herself out traipsing around the house on her crutches, and later in the afternoon she returned willingly to her wheelchair, and even intimated that she wouldn't mind if Evvie pushed it for her. They had been in Evvie's room, which was in the west wing with the family's quarters, and they were about to head down for dinner. Evvie pushed Fee's chair out of the west corridor into the long gallery. The lift opened at the east end of the gallery, at the junction with the corridor that housed the patients' bedrooms. It was easier going in this direction with a wheelchair, because the floor sloped noticeably down, towards the lift.

As they rounded the corner from the west wing, Evvie heard shouts from the far end of the gallery. Looking out, she saw one of the patients, a naval officer named Reardon, standing at the end of the gallery, facing the door to the east wing. He had a pistol in his hand, which he was waving back and forth between the doorway and his own head, threatening alternately himself and whoever was standing in front of him.

"I'll do it!" he was shouting. "I'm going to do it!" Confused cries of protest came from the patients' corridor.

Evvie grabbed for the handles of the wheelchair, thinking only of getting Fee and herself out of the range of Reardon's waving gun. But Fee had already rolled herself out into the gallery. Moving quickly, she swivelled the wheelchair so she was facing a big sideboard that stood at the end of the gallery. In an instant Evvie grasped what she had in mind. It was completely mad—heroic and brilliant and completely mad, and she was just going to do it, without a second thought. She pulled herself towards the sideboard, bracing herself against it. It probably wouldn't work, Evvie realized, unless—

"Wait!" Evvie hissed.

She wriggled in between Fee and the sideboard, adding her own weight to shove the wheelchair as hard as she could down the long gallery. Fee and her chair shot down the sloping floor towards Reardon. She braced herself as the chair slammed into him. It caught him by surprise, and he went down heavily—he had a prosthetic leg and wasn't used to it yet. By the time Evvie and the astonished nurses from the west wing had reached her, Fee had wriggled out of the toppled wheelchair and taken charge of the pistol which Reardon had dropped.

"Sorry about that, my man," she was saying to the fallen Reardon, struggling into a sitting position, the gun cradled in her lap. "But I had to do something."

Reardon lay on his side, looking at Fee as if he couldn't decide whether he wanted to throttle her or propose to her. Fee herself was white-faced and must have been in pain, but was trying not to show it.

"How did it happen?" Nurse Griggs wailed.

"The brakes must have gone on the wheelchair," said Nurse Fitzgerald. "Poor thing—are you hurt?"

"I'm fine," said Fee.

"The *brakes?*" said Anderson, who had been in the patients' corridor in his own chair. "It's a wheelchair, not a car—she must have been pushed." He looked at Evvie.

"Of course I wasn't pushed," said Fee, with enormous dignity. "I shoved off from that credenza thing. Evgenia didn't have time to stop me."

"She was very fast," Evvie agreed.

Reardon by this time had buried his head in his arms on the floor, and looked as though he might be weeping. As the nurses were fussing over Fee, Evvie knelt beside him and touched his shoulder gently.

"Let me help you up," she said.

He looked up at her with a face full of pain.

"I don't know what I just did," he murmured. "What did I just do?"

"You were upset," said Evvie.

"I was … out of my mind. That woman … where did that woman go?"

"Which woman?"

"The woman with the tracts." Evvie felt a stab of cold down her spine. Reardon had pushed himself up onto his elbows, and looked more collected than Evvie had anticipated. "She came to talk to me, and started asking me these questions. I think she sent me out of my mind."

He looked up at her with embarrassment then, as if he'd said more than he intended. She didn't pursue the question. The nurses helped him up and bustled him back to the ward, and Dr. Sheppard was summoned, and there was a discussion about whether to move Reardon to a private room, and he said—crying now in earnest, and too miserable to try to hide it—that he didn't want to cause anybody any more trouble. The pistol had been taken away, and there was a long and fruitless discussion about where Reardon had got it from—he said he couldn't remember, and no one seemed to believe that, but they were trying to be gentle with him and did not insist. He didn't mention Miss Good again. Fee and Evvie hung around through all of this, so that the nurses could satisfy themselves that Fee had not seriously hurt herself. Anderson hung around too. Finally he found an opportunity to speak to Fee.

"I just don't see how," he said quietly, "even if you shoved off from the credenza, you managed to gain enough momentum—you absolutely rocketed into Reardon."

"Of course Evgenia did push me," Fee whispered back. "You're right—it probably wouldn't have worked if she hadn't."

"I knew it!" He looked at Evvie with respect.

"Just keep quiet about it, will you?" said Fee. "*We* know that she did the right thing, but I don't want her to get fired for bowling patients down hallways into other patients. I can see where an unenlightened person could take a dim view of it."

Anderson laughed.

"I *was* going to shove off by myself," Fee added. "Only the most magnificent of friends would have pushed me."

Things quieted down finally. Dr. Sheppard shooed the nurses away from Reardon's bed, and Fee rolled herself over there. Evvie helped Anderson back into his own bed.

"I guess that's our excitement for the day," he said with a grin.

"It seems like enough," she agreed. "I wonder … did you see who was talking to Reardon before he …"

"Before he went off his head? Yes, it was that woman, Miss Good. I've seen her around once or twice before. Handing out tracts and talking to some of the men."

"And did she ever talk to you?"

"No, I always pretended to be asleep when I saw her headed my way. It's just not my cup of tea … I'm sure she means well and all … " He looked embarrassed.

"I'm not sure of that, actually. Reardon says it was her talking to him that made him try to kill himself."

Anderson stared at her and shuddered slightly. "That's creepy, Miss."

Fee had come across the ward to join them, and tipped her head at Evvie to indicate she wanted to talk alone. Out in the back passage, Evvie looked at her with raised eyebrows. Fee glanced around the corner to make sure they were alone, positioning her chair where she could see down both angles of the passage.

"Evvie, I don't know anything about guns, but when the police were here asking about the murdered man, did anyone tell them about that one, do you suppose?"

"The one Reardon had? I don't think so. They did ask about guns. Ernest showed them his service revolver, and Lady Rathburn told them about her husband's hunting guns, but they said—well, the talkative policeman said—they were looking for a much smaller weapon, because the bullet had been small."

"Yes, and that was a small gun, wasn't it? Small and old-fashioned-looking. I think I could have fired it myself, and I've small hands. And, you know, it had been fired. There was a round missing."

Evvie felt cold inside. She really had almost forgotten about the police investigation. "You think that was the murder weapon."

"I think the police ought to know about it."

"Do you mean we should … take it to them?"

"Maybe, but that wouldn't help them figure out whose it is. I think we should make sure its owner takes it back, and then tell the police who has it."

"How can we do that?"

"That's the question. But can we work out whose it is likely to be?"

"We could make a list," Evvie suggested, thinking of detective fiction again, and then felt silly.

"Well, let's just think," said Fee. "It wouldn't belong to any of the servicemen—it wasn't a very military sort of gun—and that lets Ernest out too. Are there other civilian patients besides me?"

"There's Ben Sherwood, and Mr. Brant, the math teacher. They're the only ones right now."

"They're possibilities. I can't see why anyone would bring a gun to the hospital with them, but there is a war on. Rosalind?"

"Oh, I doubt it."

"Me too. It *could* belong to one of the nurses, or to Dr. Sheppard, but why didn't they say so when everyone was fussing about it this afternoon?"

"Too embarrassed."

"Could be. It might be Lady Rathburn's, but then why didn't she mention it to the police along with her husband's guns?"

"She might have forgotten about it."

"Yes, or she might have neglected to mentioned it on purpose, because she knows it's the murder weapon. So might Dr. Sheppard or any of the nurses, or Daphne, or Leo. But in fact, Daphne and Leo weren't there this afternoon to be questioned about it, and my money's on one of them as the owner of the gun. I could just see Daphne owning a little gun like that. Or Leo. It looked like an antique gun."

Evvie nodded. "So how do we get one of them to take it back, if it is theirs?"

"Leave it lying around where they'll happen upon it," said Fee promptly. "Only we can't very well do that without stealing it ourselves."

"I know—why don't I tell Lady Rathburn that we thought we heard Daphne or Leo talking about losing a gun, and *she* can give it back? Along with a lecture about keeping it safe from suicidal thieves in future."

"Brilliant!"

"Do we say Daphne, though, or Leo? It'll only work once, so we'd better give it our best shot."

Fee needed only a moment to consider. "Leo," she said, decidedly. "My money's on Leo."

"Right. So you think Reardon stole the gun, then?"

"I suppose he must have."

"Yes," said Evvie, but she was thinking of Miss Good and wondering if it hadn't been given to him.

"It may not have been in Leo's room, mind you," Fee went on. "If he—or someone—did do a murder with it, it may have been hidden somewhere else in the house, and Reardon just found it. Speaking of whom, I think I should go back and sit with him for a bit. He looked like he could use some sympathetic company."

Fee sat by Reardon's bed for the rest of the afternoon. For a long time she even held his hand. She talked to him, but softly, intermittently, not in the animated stream of chatter that Evvie had become used to. Even with her injuries and her boy's haircut, she was a very pretty girl, and she was a fellow-sufferer, maimed in the same way as Reardon, and she used both of those things, deftly and deliberately, to comfort him. And she had been ready, at an instant, to barrel down the gallery and crash into him while he was waving around a gun. While Evvie busied herself with little tasks around the ward, she watched her friend, so filled with love that she felt as if she might burst.

Chapter Thirteen

MICHAELMAS

Charlie was in his tidy bachelor apartment in Toronto. It was late afternoon, and he was getting ready to go out. He was knotting his tie in front of the bathroom mirror when the knock came at the door. He went to answer it.

"Hal! I wasn't expecting you."

"No? Well, I've given up trying to predict how these things are going to go. I brought you something." He held up a bottle of wine, an expensive-looking red. He was dressed in an impossibly sharp charcoal-grey three-piece suit. "Perhaps we could have a glass before we go out? I assume from your clothes that we're going somewhere?"

"Church. You're welcome to come, of course, but I'm afraid I don't have time for a drink."

Hal narrowed his eyes at him for a moment. "Church? It's not Sunday."

"Of course it's not Sunday. It's Michaelmas."

"Oh. Checkmate. Well. What time is the service?"

"Six—but I have to get there early to set up, and there's rush-hour traffic to contend with. I'm afraid I do really have to go. But look—we'll come back after and drink your wine, all right? I can even make us something for dinner."

"All right," said Hal, uncertainly. "It does sound lovely. But you are speaking of *hours*. I'm not sure that I can stay that long."

"Oh?"

"I will try. You know I would do anything for you."

"I know. What happened to your wings?"

Hal looked at the floor, blushing slightly. Charlie realized he had never seen him blush, and hadn't known that he did.

"I thought they might get in the way."

"Oh. Hal … I'm sorry! I do—do want that too, but I *really* have to go. How could you forget about Michaelmas?"

"Indeed."

Charlie knew that he should leave without touching Hal because, as had been proven before, if they once went down that road, it was very hard to turn back. He knew that.

They moved together of one accord. They kissed hungrily, Hal backing Charlie up against the wall and undoing his tie in one sharp motion. Charlie had forgotten how strong he was.

"Okay, okay," he gasped. "Slow down." Hal drew back immediately, and Charlie pulled him close again to show him that he wasn't displeased. "You know I'll like it any way you want it, but it would be our first time together—maybe your first time period, I don't know."

"Yes. That time in Sodom, nothing actually happened."

"That time in … Hal! It's not going to be like that! Does it seem to you it'd be like that?"

Hal leaned with straightened arms on either side of Charlie's shoulders. "That was a joke."

"Oh. Yeah, okay, that was pretty good. But the point is … " He had undone several buttons of Hal's waistcoat, and slid his hand inside. Hal closed his eyes.

"The point is?"

"Can you make it so it's not Michaelmas, and we can take our time?"

"Certainly."

Outside the window, the sky darkened and a streetlight came on. Snowflakes drifted down.

"Thank you," said Hal. "You made that very easy."

"Well, I want this too."

He scooped Hal up and carried him to the bed.

*

He woke up with a sweet taste in his mouth, like honey. It took him a moment to remember what had tasted like that, in the dream, and then he struggled out of bed and staggered to the wash stand to rinse out his mouth. He stood there shaking and wiping his lips convulsively with the back of his hand.

Mercifully, he couldn't remember all the details of the sex, just that it had been tender and—in the end—relatively brief, because Hal came very quickly, like a teenager.

He bathed and dressed and stood for a minute outside Hal's door, trying to decide whether to knock or not. When finally he did, there was no answer. He cracked the door and looked in. Hal was still asleep, lying on his back, one arm flung up onto the pillow above his head.

He remembered the process of taking off Hal's clothes, teasingly slow, the way that Hal had moaned when Charlie's hands finally slid over his bare skin.

He shut the door silently and went downstairs.

The landlady stopped by the table as he sat there alone. "And how is Henry this morning?"

Charlie stared up at her and was about to say, "Who?" before he realized that she must mean Hal. He wondered whether to tell her that his name wasn't really Henry, but decided that would just be confusing. Besides, for all he knew, Hal had already told her that it *was* his name.

"Still asleep," he said. "I decided not to wake him."

She nodded. "Poor angel."

Please go away, Charlie thought. But she was a nice woman; he was being very uncharitable. There was no one else in the bar, and she lingered, clearly wanting to talk.

"Happen he'll have to go back to his squadron soon? Now that he's feeling bravely."

Charlie made some noncommittal noise.

"If 'twere me," she went on, confidingly, "I'd drag out t' ailment a little longer. I mean, t' war's almost over, isn't it?"

"Seems like it."

"Well, I wouldn't 'a made a very good soldier. I'm sure Henry knows his duty better." She smiled, and Charlie tried to smile back. "I suppose he's got a lass waiting for him somewhere, does he? He is a bonny one. Is he courting, then, or …"

Charlie remembered Hal's body under his on the bed, the soft warmth of his skin, his hands moving eagerly.

"No. Not as far as I know."

"I expect he'd have told tha. Tha's a good friend to him."

"Well, I try to be."

Hal came down the stairs into the bar, dressed but looking sleepy. He hadn't washed his hair this morning or, apparently, combed it, and it was a mess, the curls flattened on one side. His shirt was untucked, the buttons misaligned. He smiled sweetly at Mary and dropped into the chair opposite Charlie.

"How's tha faring this morning, love?" the landlady asked.

"Me?" said Hal. "Fantastic."

She looked surprised. "Well, that is good to hear. I'll be reet back with thi tea."

"I think I alarmed her," Hal said, putting his elbows on the table.

"Your shirt's done up wrong," said Charlie.

"Oh, so it is." He started to unbutton it. "That is what comes of dressing in a hurry. I thought it might be later than usual—though perhaps it isn't—and I did not want you to leave without me."

"I'm just going to the base as usual."

"I know. I want to walk with you."

"Oh. Okay."

He tried again to recreate the feeling from the previous evening at Zion, and from the other mornings at breakfast, the feeling that he had everything he could want, that he could simply relish every moment in Hal's company, and it would be enough. He watched Hal's fingers redoing the buttons of his shirt. He remembered pressing them to his lips and whispering, "Of course. The best ever. Do you doubt it?" He remembered settling Hal's head against his bare shoulder, stroking Hal's back, cupping his hand around the perfect curve of Hal's ass, Hal's dick soft and spent against his thigh. He remembered the whole damn thing, in fact. He'd been wrong to think it had been brief; that had been just the first time, but there had been more after that. They had uncorked the bottle of wine and drunk out of mismatched glasses, sitting on the floor by the bed, and later made love again, twice more—unprecedented in Charlie's waking life—and then finally Hal had fallen asleep in Charlie's arms, and Charlie had woken up.

The landlady returned with their tea, and stayed to chat, and this time Charlie was actually grateful for it.

After breakfast, Hal ran upstairs to get his coat, and came back down pulling it on, and they walked out into a misty, cold morning.

"I don't think this is going to be very pleasant," said Charlie.

"Nonsense," said Hal.

They walked along the road leading out of the village, hands in their coat pockets, not talking. The morning was very still. It was lovely, in spite of the cold.

"It is nice, isn't it?" Charlie admitted.

"Mm."

"I usually leave the road here and cut across the fields," he said, indicating a gate and a footpath snaking away into the mist.

"Then let's do that."

"Well, it'll be wet."

"I don't mind."

Charlie opened the gate, and they went through onto the footpath. It was wet, but it was beautiful. The path led along the side of a forest, and they could hear birds singing into the stillness.

"I have to tell you something," said Charlie.

"Yes?"

"I'm afraid I've been acting like a bit of a bastard the last couple of days, and I wanted to explain why."

"You don't have to—you haven't been acting like a bastard, and you don't have to explain. You're in a strange situation, and you are trying to negotiate it. I understand. It is strange for me too."

"No … but listen." He stopped walking. He looked into the forest rather than at Hal. "The last three nights I've dreamt about you. I told you that I'm a … a sexual deviant, but I don't know if you realize that your human form is very appealing—to me, really very appealing. But it isn't just that—it's everything about you. I've wanted to tell you, I knew I *should* tell you, but I couldn't decide how. And then, apparently, my subconscious took matters into its own hands, because I've had these dreams. Only in the dreams, you—you feel the same way. I mean exactly the same way. And I'm … I'm deeply ashamed, and I've found it difficult to talk to you for the last few days because of it. That's all I wanted to say."

Finally he looked at Hal, and found Hal staring at him with an expression of blank horror. It was worse than the worst thing he could have imagined.

"I'm sorry, I … I thought you ought to know. I can see I should have kept it to myself. I … "

"Oh, Charles. What have I just put you through? I am so sorry. I thought that you knew."

"Knew what?"

"I *was* beginning to wonder if perhaps you did not know, but then you asked if I could stop its being Michaelmas, and I thought … "

"I did … *what?*"

"You don't remember that?"

"Of course *I* remember it—*I* dreamt it. How do *you* know about it?"

"Know about it?" Hal's normally deep voice rose to a hysterical pitch. "Charles, I was there. Did you honestly think you came up with all that on your own? Is that what your dreams are normally like?"

"No," Charlie admitted. "They were very unusual dreams."

"Of course they were! I thought it would be safer that way, easier for you. Besides, I … I wanted to show off that I was well enough to do that. I didn't mean to put you through this torment—I thought you would figure it out, that you had figured it out. It's—it's in the Bible! It's what we do. Oh, Charles. I'm sorry. I'm so sorry."

"Stop apologizing!" Charlie cried. "I'm so far from being mad at you, I don't even know if I can say 'I forgive you' with a straight face. Hal! We're lovers? And I *didn't know?*"

"Apparently."

"To say that this is the best thing that ever happened to me would be such an understatement."

Hal looked for a moment as if he wanted to say he was sorry again. Then his face relaxed into a smile: an amused, self-mocking smile that made him look much more than twenty. And again, as in the sacristy at St. John's, he was the one who made the first move. He stepped up to Charlie and took his face between his cold hands and kissed him, and it was real.

Gingerly, Charlie slipped his hands inside Hal's unbuttoned coat and around Hal's slender waist. He remembered clinging to Hal as they soared from the crashing plane, his arms cinched tightly around him. He felt Hal's long fingers on the back of his neck, strong but gentle. Images from the previous night came back to him, and he had to make an effort not to hustle them guiltily out of his mind.

Hal brushed the side of his face against Charlie's. His skin was whisperingly soft except for a slight tickle of stubble. "It distresses me to learn that I hurt you without meaning to," he said.

Charlie tightened his hold. "Don't give it another thought. It was nothing—honestly. It was perfect. I wouldn't have had it any other way."

"You are so good to me."

"It's easy. You're just everything I've ever wanted—could ever have wanted, if I'd had the brass to want everything I could imagine. I love you."

They stepped apart, after a moment, and Hal's hand slipped into Charlie's, as naturally as if it belonged there. They turned to walk on.

Hal said, "You did not make it easy for me, you know. The dreams. You may say your subconscious wanted me, but from where I was standing, it looked as if it was dead set against me. It kept throwing up the most absurd obstacles—vestments and church services and … " He groaned. "You have no idea how hard I had to work to drag you to a weekday last night, and to get you to let me lose the wings and wear that grey suit."

"That was a very sharp suit." He remembered unbuttoning the waistcoat and tossing it onto the chair by his bed.

"Yes, obviously!" said Hal archly. "I didn't just buy it and hope you'd like it—I found it in your memory, associated with a handsome red-haired man you saw once and admired. I noticed, too … there wasn't a lot of that sort of thing."

"Admiring men? I do that all the time. I try not to, but I do."

"No, I meant men who look like me. If I had expected to find your imagination full of androgynous young redheads, I would have been disappointed. You seem to prefer older, more masculine men—from the little that I saw. I found it flattering."

"You mean because you're not my regular type, but I still fell for you?"

"That's what I mean."

"Is that … looking in my mind, is that how you found out how I felt about you?" The idea was obscurely disappointing.

"No, oh no. I really did not do much of that, Charles—only what

I had to in the context of the dreams. You see, your dreams are made up largely of memories, so if I go in there, I walk through certain corridors of memory as a matter of course—I have to, in order to search for raw material, and so … "

Charlie pressed his shoulder against Hal's and grinned, charmed by the way his explanation had become suddenly technical. Hal shoved back against him, as strong as he had been in the dream.

Hal said, "I found out how you felt about me by *guessing*. I watched you, and I wondered if you felt the same way that I did."

"And how was that?"

"In love," he said serenely.

"Wow. So you figured that out on your own."

"Pure intelligence, Charles."

"That's your favourite line."

"It is so often apt. Shall I tell you something funny? I sought inspiration in some of Mary's novels."

"Inspiration for what?"

"For what to say to you, how to behave with you. They were unhelpful—absolutely so. There were many accounts of lovers and their declarations to one another, but none of them suited. I shall tell you about them some time, and you will be incapacitated with laughter."

"I could've told you books like that wouldn't be much help."

"I know. But I wanted to offer you something quite specific. It is for the same reason that I tried to direct you to familiar places in your dreams. I wanted it all to be ordinary."

"Is that what turns you on?"

Hal gave a shout of laughter. "For you, Charles—ordinary for you. None of this is ordinary for me."

"Why did you want it to be ordinary for me?"

"Do you want a serious answer?"

Charlie stopped walking and looked at Hal. His grey eyes were dark and unreadable. "Um … sure."

"I think you imperil your soul with this nonsense of segregating sex and love. I wanted you to see, in the most ordinary terms, what it might be like if you did not do that, so that you would not be tempted to do it again."

"Oh. That *was* a serious answer."

"And not ordinary at all, but I have given up on that." He sighed. "I hope I haven't made a thorough mess of this."

"No, not at all. I'm still just a bit stunned." He turned to walk on, then turned back. "The wings changing colour—was that your idea or mine?"

"It was a bit of both."

They walked hand-in-hand to the other end of the footpath, and kissed again while they were still hidden from the road by a hedge.

"You have to go fly your planes now," said Hal airily, stepping back. "I'll be there when you return, waiting for you. Thinking about you. As I have been all week."

Chapter Fourteen

THE CAVE OF THE APOCALYPSE

"Lady Rathburn—"

"Do call me Heather, my dear Fidelity."

"Heather, I wondered whether you'd told Leo that we found his gun?"

"Yes, oh yes, I did, and he was quite put out when I said I would keep it locked in the office safe from now on. He tried to tell me a story about its being an antique that he means to sell, but I said when he has a buyer for it, then I'll get it out of the safe for him. It was very careless of him to leave it lying around where poor Reardon could get at it."

"It was *very* careless," Fee agreed. "Well, I'm glad you've locked it away, though, Heather, and that we know whose it is now. Oh, I was thinking, by the way, that I'd like to go down to the village this afternoon, and I wondered, could I bring Evvie with me? Can you spare her?"

In the village they made straight for the police station. It served the whole region, so it was a bigger one than you would expect in such a small, sleepy place as Adderley.

Fee explained their mission briskly to the officer on duty. "We think we may have information about the unsolved murder—the man who was found in the water last week. We think we may know where the murder weapon is."

She told the story of the discovery of the gun at Adderley in a cool, journalistic style, while Evvie just listened, nodding when the policeman looked at her for confirmation. In the end, he didn't say any of the things Evvie had been expecting: *Are you sure you weren't imagining things?* or *Don't worry your pretty heads about that,* or anything of the sort.

"Of course it may be a completely different gun," said Fee in conclusion, "and even if it is the murder weapon, you won't know for certain who fired it—but we did think it was something you might want to investigate, all the same."

"Quite reet, lass," said the policeman. "And very sensible tha's been about it, if I may say."

"Thank you," said Fee demurely.

Evvie turned to open the door, but Fee still had more to say, now in a lower tone—Evvie almost wondered whether she were intended to hear this part.

"Also, Constable, I had an idea about the victim. It's just an idea. He didn't happen to have a pocket watch with a bird on it, did he? An etching of a bird, on the inside of the lid."

The constable looked startled, though no more than Evvie.

"'E did," he admitted. "That was about t' only notable thing left on 'im. Nobody round 'ere knew it ti look at it."

"They wouldn't have," said Fee grimly, "because he wasn't from around here. At least, if I'm right. Do you have a pen and paper I could use? If I write down a name and an address for you, will you look into it?"

The officer reached across the counter to hand a notebook and pen down to her. "We'll do our best, lass."

Evvie decided that if Fee wanted to tell her what she had written down, she would, so she said nothing, then or later. And neither did Fee.

*

"Can I tell you about my vision?" said Evvie.

They were sitting on Fee's bed, early on Friday evening. Fee had retired to her room before dinner, in her effort to convince the nurses that she was taking it easy after the drama of the previous day.

"Of course!" said Fee. "I was hoping you'd … I mean, if you want to. I'm sure it's very private, but I'd love to hear about it."

"It happened when I was twelve. I had been very sick, but I was on the mend. I wasn't feverish any more—even the doctor admits it. I was wide awake, and lying in bed, in our house in Oxford. I had been woken by the clock striking on the landing. There was a man standing beside my bed, someone I'd never seen before, dressed in Eastern vestments—deacon's vestments, all embroidered in gold and green. I didn't see him appear, I just looked, and there he was. He said, 'Don't be afraid,' in Greek. I think I knew he was an angel even before he said that. I couldn't really tell you what he looked like, because … I had a sense that it didn't matter. It would have been like admiring someone's handwriting without reading what they wrote.

"He smiled at me the way you smile at a friend, and went to the door, and beckoned me to follow him. I understood that he couldn't help me up from the bed because he was a vision. But he waited there patiently for me." She remembered folding back the coverlet, sitting up gingerly, poking her feet over the edge of the bed, and finally sliding down to the floor, pulling down her nightgown, which had ridden up awkwardly, and noting that it was an old, faded one, and that her hair was matted on one side from lying on it.

"I realized I looked a bit of a fright, and that I should feel embarrassed about that, but when I looked at the angel's face, I knew it didn't matter. It didn't matter in the same way that how he looked didn't matter. So I tottered my way down to the foot of the bed, and then he slipped out the open door, and I followed him, holding onto things, and then we were somewhere quite different.

"We were in a cave. The ceiling was all lumps and bumps of rock, and it was dim, but there was a little sort of chapel in a corner, with icons and hanging lamps burning. There was a bench, and he sat down on it. I sat on the stone floor at his feet. And he leaned down when I did that, like … like this." She put her forearms on her knees, the way the angel had done. She remembered that gesture very clearly; it had been such a funny, human thing for him to do, and him so obviously otherworldly. "And he said, 'Evgenia, do you know this place?' I shook my head. He said, 'It is the Cave of the Apocalypse, on the Island of Patmos.' And I felt as if I had to say something, so I said, 'It's lovely.' And he laughed—I can still hear the sound of it, so beautiful—and disappeared, and I was sitting on the floor on the landing in my parents' house.

"My stepfather found me there a few minutes later, and I babbled out, 'I've just seen an angel, and I have to go the Island of Patmos and become a nun!' I was so excited about it. I expect I sounded like a girl who'd just been told she was getting a pet pony or something."

"I bet that went over well," said Fee.

"Oh, terrifically, yes. They thought I was still sick, and raving. And I admit there were times when I wondered myself whether it had really happened, or if I was right about what it meant. But the place really was the Cave of the Apocalypse—where St. John had his visions that he wrote in *Revelation*. I found a picture of it, and I recognized it, down to the last detail. And the angel was real—he was a vision, but a vision of a real angel. It's hard to explain why I'm so sure of that. The best I can say is that it seemed to me like he had a personality. I only doubted it all in that way that you sometimes doubt things you know perfectly well."

Fee nodded. "Like when you write an exam at school, and you're suddenly not sure of things you knew cold when you were studying. Did your parents eventually come around? They did let you go off to Patmos in the end, so …"

"I don't know what they really believe. At first they tried to reason me out of it. Then they tried just not talking about it, to see if I'd come to my senses and want to forget the whole thing. Then I think they talked it over together and decided that the best strategy would be to tell me that they both believed I'd really had a vision, and thought it was wonderful, but that it didn't mean I had to go be a nun on Patmos. Maybe it meant I just had to make a pilgrimage—maybe it meant that I had to join a mission society at a church of St. John. There I was on shakier ground, because I'd described the vision exactly—over and over—and it was true that the angel hadn't said anything about my becoming a nun. He'd just beckoned for me to follow him, and taken me to the cave and told me what it was. It was easy to see how that meant I should go to Patmos, but harder to be sure what I was meant to do when I got there. That wasn't exactly part of the vision. It was more … an idea that I got from seeing it. My idea was that somehow, if I became a nun, I'd be … don't take this the wrong way, but I'd be like my angel. That angel, I mean—he's not mine. I'd be like him because I'd be doing my job. Does that make any sense?"

"Yes!" said Fee. "Perfect sense. Oh, but I see how difficult it would be to explain." After a moment, as if the idea had just jumped up and bit her, she said, "Did he have slits in his vestments for his wings?"

"He didn't have wings."

"Oh, drat. Of course."

Evvie settled herself back against the head of Fee's bed, drawing her knees up and smoothing out her skirt. She looked at Fee in the lamplight. A little gold cross that she wore peeked out at the collar of her blouse.

"Did you ever see him again?" Fee asked.

"Who? The angel? No."

"No, of course not. That was a funny question to ask, wasn't it? I don't know why … I somehow thought you might have." She shook her head with one of her humorous expressions. "Thank you for telling me about your vision. It feels a real privilege to have heard about it."

Evvie smiled up at her; she was sitting up straighter than Evvie, so that she looked down at her.

"Fee, I'll miss you when you go back to America."

"I'll miss you too! But it might be a while yet."

"I don't know. I believe it when they say the war is winding down, you know."

"Oh, yes. That's true."

"What will you do when you go home, do you think?" She put the question with a deliberate lightness. It was not something they had talked about before, and she wasn't sure Fee wanted to talk about it.

"Oh, I don't know. Maybe I'll marry my cousin George."

"What!"

Fee laughed. "I'm joking. Though I *could* marry him, if I wanted. As far as the law's concerned, and as far as he's concerned, too. Technically he's my second cousin, and only by marriage. He's *much* too fond of pointing that out."

"Oh, I see!"

"It's not that he's in love with me. It's much sillier than that. I think he thinks he's in one of those stories where the heroine marries the solid, dependable fellow whom she's known all her life, after having her heart broken by the handsome rake."

"That was the plot of my mother's second and third books."

"Maybe George has read them. He is certainly a solid, dependable fellow, and I have certainly known him all my life—he's a year older than I am, and our families are very close. The only thing is, I haven't yet had my heart broken by a handsome rake." She looked thoughtful. "Of course, I only have one leg. I doubt a handsome rake is really in the cards any more. Even my cousin George might think twice. I wonder ... " She looked at Evvie with a kind of twinkle in her eye. "Do you suppose maybe I *am* the handsome rake? This is the kind of thing that would happen to him. It would alter his character, of course, and I don't know that mine has been altered at all."

"I don't think you're a rake, Fee. And I can't see you letting such a person break your heart, either."

"You think Cousin George may be out of luck?" She waved her thin hand with a frown. "No. This fake bravado is just self-pity in disguise. I had much better be honest about my feelings. I don't want to be reduced to hoping that George might still want me as the heroine in his story."

"Fee …" Evvie began thoughtfully, "if you think that you are the handsome rake who had to get terribly burned in order to learn a lesson about something, then … well, then George is the heroine of his own story."

Fee shook with laughter. "He wouldn't like that *at all*!"

"You know," said Evvie after a moment, "I do think lilies were the perfect choice for you. Delicate, you know, but a bit … spiky."

Fee's eyebrows went up. "Absolutely. That's me in a nutshell."

"About your cousin George, though …"

"Yes?"

"Well, I couldn't help noticing. You said just now he's a year older than you."

"Mm-hm."

"Only I remember a story you told about him when you first got here, and you said he wasn't old enough to enlist."

"Oh. So I did."

"And that would make him younger than you, wouldn't it?"

"Oh. Right. Yes."

"I just thought perhaps you might not have noticed, that's all."

"No, you're right. I hadn't."

She seemed to be waiting after that for Evvie to ask, "So which is it? Is he older or younger?" And Evvie thought about asking that question. She could think of several other questions. Certain details had been accumulating in her mind. Fee had said early on that she was heiress to the soap empire because her brother had been disowned, but later she had told a story about his emotional leave-taking that made it sound like father and son were reconciled. And there was the godmother who had tried three times to teach her to knit; Evvie was fairly sure Baptists didn't have godmothers.

She didn't think they referred to Mary as Our Lady or the Blessed Virgin, either. She wasn't sure what all of this added up to.

"I don't think it is really fake bravado," Evvie said.

"No? What do you think it is?"

"Courage. Really and truly. I think you're being incredibly brave."

"Thanks. I don't have much of a choice though, do I?"

"Maybe not." *I know I shouldn't ask*, Evvie thought. But no—no, she didn't know that. "Why is that? What's happened to your family?"

"I don't know," said Fee in a very small voice. She looked like the doll pulled out of the burnt house again, and she sounded suddenly much younger than twenty. "That's the truth. I think my father might be dead, and I don't know what's happened to the rest of them, why I haven't heard from them. I don't know. Evgenia? Thank you for asking—really, thank you. But please don't make me talk any more about it. I'm sorry." Her voice had sunk to a tiny whisper. "I just can't."

"Of course, Fee, of course. I'm so sorry."

"Thank you." Fee looked up and managed another of her reassuring smiles. "You really are a magnificent friend. If … if you should at any point hear me telling Rosalind something about why I haven't heard from my family, please don't think … It won't be true—it'll just be something I made up to stop her asking me about it. I don't know what it will be … "

"Oh, well—tell her you *have* heard from them," said Evvie easily. "The staff at Newingthorpe sent them a telegram after the crash, of course, and they cabled back, and wanted to bring you home right away, but of course you're not well enough to travel, and besides, it's still too dangerous. Your father wants to come get you himself, but your mother won't let him leave America, she's too scared something will happen to him too. Your brother in the Mediterranean—he is still in the Mediterranean, isn't he? He wants to come get you too, but he can't leave his ship. You've had a letter from him, but your parents are more the telegram-sending type, I think, so they cable rather than writing."

"Evgenia? I love you."

"I love you too, Fidelity. I can arrange for you to get a telegram if you think that would help. Much easier than trying to fake a letter from America."

"I'll keep it in mind as an option. It sounds like I should have asked for your help in the first place. You're quite good at this."

"Better than a nun ought to be, maybe. If there's ever anything else I can do to help … "

"I know. Thank you."

For a moment she felt an impulse to say, "Fidelity? I just made up a totally fictitious story about your family, and you didn't bat an eyelash. Why is that? Who are you really?" But she knew who Fidelity was really. It didn't matter that she strongly suspected some of the details were made up.

Chapter Fifteen

PURE INTELLIGENCE

"Gone above to wash, poor love," Mary told Charlie that afternoon, when he asked where Hal was. "He's been helping me with my spring cleaning, and got hissel filthy."

A long story about the progress of the spring cleaning followed, and Charlie listened good-humouredly, noticing that he was no longer even slightly jealous of Mary. She liked Hal, and he loved her for that.

Upstairs, he found Hal lying on his back on the bed, wearing only his trousers, with one of Mary's novels open facedown on his bare stomach. He had plainly fallen asleep reading, and been woken by the door opening. He blinked and rubbed his eyes.

"Tired?" said Charlie, closing the door behind him.

Hal picked up the book, looked at it, and set it aside without marking his place. He linked his hands behind his head. "Yes," he said.

"Ah." Charlie hesitated between his usual chair and the edge of the bed. "In the human world—I wouldn't expect you to get this from those tame romance novels, but 'I'm tired' is usually code for, 'Sorry honey, I don't feel like sex.'"

"Ah," said Hal. He shifted on the bed, arching his back a little, and took one hand out from under his head to unbutton the waistband of his trousers. "What's the code for, 'I just meant it literally, darling'?"

"I don't know," said Charlie, slightly shocked. "But, um—message received."

He moved back to the door, locked it, then went to the window and drew the curtains. He unknotted his tie.

Hal lay and watched him undress, and Charlie felt awkward and silly and didn't mind.

The feeling remained when he joined Hal on the bed. It didn't help that he remembered the dream-Charlie of the previous night being suave and confident. How had he not noticed before the complete ridiculousness of that? The bed sagged and creaked under him as he knelt on the foot of it, and he wanted to put some clothes back on. Hal, still in his half-unbuttoned pants, shifted again to make room for Charlie between his legs. Charlie knelt there, planting his hands on either side of the pillow and looking down at Hal, who was looking up at him with a new, intent expression.

"It's different," said Charlie, his voice sounding thick and husky, "when it's physical like this."

"Yes." Hal's voice sounded the way Hal's voice always sounded.

"It matters more."

"It matters a lot."

Hal smoothed his hands up Charlie's thighs to his hips, and pressed them there a moment, fingers splayed. He pushed one thumb slowly down into the crease between thigh and groin, watching what he was doing with the same intent look, then drew it up, following the trail of black hair up to Charlie's belly. He brushed his fingertips lightly down again, and stroked the heel of his hand up Charlie's erection. Now he was looking into Charlie's eyes. Charlie's breath shuddered out of him in something like a sob.

Hal's seriousness disappeared after that, as if he had made his point, and he turned playful, pushing Charlie back and rocking up into a sitting position, knees clenched around Charlie's waist, to kiss him almost ferociously. But Hal playful and Hal serious and intent were both equally wonderful, and everything after that, on the sagging, creaking bed, was perfect. They were so warmed and lit and lifted beyond themselves by their shared love that they couldn't get it wrong. Even clumsiness and uncertainty were made beautiful.

It was what Charlie imagined a wedding night would be like. He felt, in the end, as if his own body had become as much a metaphor as Hal's, and all that it meant was love.

He held Hal close after they had spent themselves thoroughly. His mind was buzzing with pleasure.

"I'm not going to wake up now, am I?" he said, his words muffled in Hal's hair.

"On the contrary, you sound as though you might fall asleep."

He laughed low in his throat and gathered Hal's hard angles and soft skin more comfortably against him. "I won't, though. I'm not sleepy." In fact, he felt talkative. "Do you remember I told you I have some leave due? I'm going to take it next week. Three whole days. We could go somewhere, if you wanted—drive to one of these picturesque seaside towns and rent a cottage, maybe."

"Like a honeymoon, you mean," said Hal, apparently seriously.

"A little bit like that, I guess." Charlie found the idea far less embarrassing than he would have expected. "If we're going to talk like that … well, I've been thinking all day about the end of the war, and what that will mean for us. I don't want to be the kind of man who stops thinking just because he's started *feeling*, you know—you deserve better than that."

"I cannot imagine why. But tell me what you have been thinking."

"Mostly what I've been thinking is how I might redo the plans for my house. I thought you might like a cathedral ceiling upstairs so you can stretch your wings."

Hal twisted out of Charlie's arms and sat up, the sheet that had covered them both falling down around his waist. He looked speculatively around the room, judging distances. Charlie grabbed his arm.

"Don't do them here! Have some sense. What if you couldn't change back again, what would we do with you?"

"I'd be *fine*," Hal scoffed. "But I don't think I have room in here."

He remained sitting up, looking down at Charlie fondly. Charlie pushed the pillow back against the head of the bed and propped himself up on it, hands clasped behind his head.

"I know what I just implied is ridiculous," he said. "I know we probably have only a short time together, and that you can't make me any promises. You've got to go back to—to Heaven, when you get your memories back. If you think about it, that's no different from any normal couple. Nobody knows how long they've got. But while you're here, I'll look after you. Well, I swore to you that I would. And when I go back to Canada, if you want to come with me …"

"Of course I want to come with you. Cathedral ceiling or no cathedral ceiling. I am frankly much less enamoured of those wings than you are." He stretched out again, laying his head on Charlie's chest. "Of course I want to come with you," he repeated.

*

After a while, Hal remembered that he had promised to run an errand for the landlady, so they got up and dressed and went down together. Georgie came charging out of the back room, eager to tell Hal some story about a cat. Hal sat down at the bottom of the stairs to give the child his serious attention, while Charlie went through into the kitchen. He collected the package that Mary wanted delivered to her sister-in-law, and came back out to find Hal attempting to fix one of Georgie's toy cars that had lost a wheel. Charlie leaned on the bannister and watched Hal's beautiful fingers twiddling the wheel until finally it popped delicately back into its place.

"There you go," said Hal, passing the car to a delighted Georgie. "We have to go out now. See you later!"

As they walked down the steep grey main street of Newingthorpe, Charlie said, "I was just thinking about the last time we went for a walk together, and how much has changed."

"That was this morning."

"Indeed."

Hal laughed. "I'm surprised you didn't notice how little I wanted to be out of your sight these last few days."

"I did notice, actually. I just didn't think it could mean … you know."

"No? But I think it only reasonable that it should. You rescued me and cherished me, and I am damaged and confined to a physical form—the logic of it seems almost ineluctable to me."

"The *logic*? It's got nothing to do with logic!"

"For me it does. For you …" He shrugged. "I will admit that your love may not be logical. That does not offend me."

"Every so often, just when you start to seem perfectly human, you say these things …" Charlie grinned, slung an arm around Hal's shoulders, and let it slide casually off again. He felt almost obscenely happy.

They passed in front of the little grey church and down a narrow lane that sloped so steeply toward the bay that it broke into shallow steps halfway down. Because of the angle, they were able to see Miss Good climbing up from below, shopping basket on her arm, well before she saw them.

"Her again," said Hal under his breath. "Hm."

Before Miss Good looked up, Hal had caught Charlie by the front of his jacket and backed him up against the blank wall of a house behind him and kissed him, hard and assuredly. Miss Good passed them by without comment or acknowledgement. Hal released Charlie and stepped back.

"What did you do that for?" Charlie asked in alarm.

Hal was looking after Miss Good with a curiously intent expression. It was a moment before he looked back at Charlie and said, "She has designs on you. I don't know what they are, but I wanted her to know that they will fail because you are mine."

"She's—she's much older than me, and I don't go for women at all, Hal, even young, pretty ones. I thought I'd made that clear to you."

"I didn't say I was jealous. I said she had designs."

"Yeah, maybe—but you don't have to worry about them. It's a little ridiculous."

Hal shrugged. "Maybe."

"No, listen, Hal—you can't go kissing me in public."

"I haven't been."

"Or in front of people, at all. She could talk about that—she could tell somebody, and it could get back to my squadron, and I could be in a lot of trouble." Actually he thought it was more likely that she would take matters into her own hands by trying to have another frank little chat with him, or sic her brother on him or something. But that didn't make what Hal had just done any better.

"I understand that, Charles. She will not tell anyone."

"I'm sorry, Hal, but you don't know that. Please just promise me you won't do that again."

"I promise. I am sorry."

*

Their errand accomplished, they set off along the road towards the edge of the village, and struck out onto the moor. The late afternoon sun glowed on the green and brown of the landscape and warmed the air.

"Let's head for those rocks," Hall suggested, pointing to a formation in the distance.

They bent their steps in that direction, and after a few minutes Hal left Charlie's side and took off toward the rocks at an easy run. Charlie watched him for a moment, noting with pleasure how strong and well he looked. Then he gave chase, and Hal sped up, laughing, until they were racing each other across the rough ground. Charlie outran Hal in the end and reached the rocks first. He stood catching his breath as Hal staggered up and collapsed with his back to the rock.

"You all right?" Charlie asked. "You didn't tire yourself out too much?"

Hal was too winded to speak, but he grinned. Charlie laughed.

He climbed up onto the rocks while Hal walked around their base. Hal sat down on the far side, where the sun hit the rock. Jumping down beside him, Charlie sprawled full length on the ground. Hal lay down too, perpendicular to Charlie, his head on Charlie's stomach.

"I like this," said Charlie.

Hal just smiled, eyes closed.

"So what do you think we should do with my three days' leave? It could be whatever you like."

Hal opened his eyes, turned to lie on his side, looking up at Charlie past the landscape of blue shirt and buttons. "Why whatever *I* like?" he asked lightly.

Charlie put his hand inside Hal's coat, resting it just above his belt. Hal smiled and drew in his knees a little, curling up around Charlie's touch.

"I don't suppose it matters," Hal answered his own question. "We seem to like the same things."

The sun came out from behind a cloud, very low in the sky now, its light tracing a fine line of searing gold around Hal's red curls as he lay looking up at Charlie.

"You know," said Charlie, "I'm finding it awfully easy to forget about this, but we've still got to sort out this mystery about Zion and the men who were holding you captive."

Hal shifted slightly. "Do we? No. Let's forget about that."

"Really? Do you think that's … Well. If I ask whether you think that's smart, you'll just hit me with your standard wisecrack."

"Absolutely." Hal had closed his eyes again.

"So I won't. But if you change your mind …"

"Let's enjoy your three days, and then see."

"All right," said Charlie. "I like that idea."

Chapter Sixteen

CLERGYMEN'S DAUGHTERS

Evvie was taking a shift at the reception desk when Miss Good came through the front door in her brown coat and squashed-looking hat, carrying her handbag and a bundle of tracts. She set off across the lobby without giving Evvie a glance, clearly intending to march straight through to the ward.

"Excuse me!" Evvie called.

Miss Good glanced back briefly as if she didn't think the words could be addressed to her.

"Miss Good," said Evvie, coming out from behind the desk. "Excuse me. I need to speak to you for a moment."

"Yes, dear?" Miss Good shifted her hold on her tracts as she turned to face Evvie, so Evvie could see that today's title was SINS OF THE FLESH: IS ABSTINENCE THE ONLY SOLUTION?

"Lady Rathburn has asked me to tell you that she has decided not to allow tracts to be distributed in this hospital any longer."

Miss Good's grey eyes bored into her. "Is that true?"

"Yes, ma'am."

"She would deprive the poor maimed souls in this place of the solace of the heavenly teachings contained in our publications?"

"It's not their souls that have been maimed," said Evvie. Miss Good looked nonplussed. "And Lady Rathburn is not sure that your teachings are heavenly—or very good for the patients."

"You put her up to this, didn't you?"

"Yes, ma'am." Evvie folded her arms and met Miss Good's gaze steadily.

It was true that Lady Rathburn had forbidden the tracts, and told Evvie to pass on the message. And it was true that she had done it at Evvie's urging. They'd had a long conversation about it the night before in Lady Rathburn's dressing-room after dinner. But how Miss Good could have guessed this, Evvie didn't know. In fact, though, she was glad Miss Good had made the thing personal.

"I told her what you said to my friend Fidelity the other day. She was as horrified as I was. I don't know how anyone who claims to be a servant of the Gospel could be so cruel. I wanted her to ban you from the hospital, but she said that perhaps you had spoken thoughtlessly. I think that's charitable of her, but I don't buy it."

"I am sure if I have injured your friend's feelings, it was unintentional. It is very natural that you should take her side, but—"

"Lady Rathburn was clear. No more tracts. And you're not to talk to any of the patients alone."

"I beg your pardon?"

"You're not to talk to any of the patients alone."

"What does your friend claim that I said to her?"

"If you'll give me the tracts, we can go in to the ward together. Otherwise, you must leave."

"Has it ever occurred to you that you don't know everything about your friend Fidelity? Do you think there are no secrets she keeps from you?"

"Would you like to give me the tracts, Miss Good, or would you like to leave?"

"I have never been so insulted in all my life! How dare you presume, you insolent girl—"

"Get out. Now."

It was only after Miss Good had scuttled across the hall and back out the front door that Evvie realized she had spoken that last command in Greek.

Miss Good must have met Leo on her way off the property, because he came storming in through the front door shortly after she left and marched straight to the reception desk where Evvie was again sitting. He put his fists on the desk and glared at her.

"Look here, I don't know what you think you're playing at, but calling Josie names and ordering her out of the house? It's not on, you understand?"

Evvie pushed her chair calmly back from the desk. "I didn't call her names. I was obeying your aunt's instructions when I told her to leave the hospital."

"You bloody well put Aunt Heather up to that, and you know it."

"Please don't use that language, Mr. Rathburn."

"I'll use the bloody language that I bloody like. Did you or did you not put Aunt Heather up to it?"

"I don't think it makes any difference whether I did or not."

"Don't you, by Jove? Josie says you cursed and swore at her."

"She is lying."

"You dirty little hussy. You like to act the part of the pious novice, but you're the one who summoned a great big, flaming devil when all Ernest and I could manage was puffs of smoke. Don't you forget that!"

"What?" said Evvie, with a feeling as if the ground beneath her had turned to water.

Leo gave her an unpleasant sidelong look. "Oh, but you *have* forgotten it, haven't you? I never liked that idea much. Maybe it's time you were reminded."

"I don't know what you're talking about," said Evvie. Her face felt numb, and she wondered whether she could continue standing up.

Leo scratched his chin and went on glaring at her for a few moments. He straightened up and folded his arms, looking smug now. Evvie thought at first that he was going to leave without explaining, but he began to speak: "It was last summer. Ernest and I had picked up a few choice items in London. It was Ernie's idea, and the thing he was keenest on was this ring. Belonged to King Solomon, apparently. Gift of the Archangel Michael. Mystical powers. Blah blah. You slip it on, and you summon demons to do your will."

"Don't be ridiculous," said Evvie weakly.

Leo sneered at her. "Right. 'That's not in the Bible'—that's what you said at the time."

"Of course not, but ..." But it was the story that Fidelity had told her, about the ring that belonged to her cousin. Leo had heard it somehow, and was just embroidering on it.

"No, you just listen to me. We had this ring, and Ernest wanted to try it out. He had a list of names, demon names, out of some book. But he told you all this at the time. You see, you burst in on us, out in the lodge, as we were working our way down his list. Something about breaking blackout—you were being officious as usual. We hadn't been having too much luck, but I thought to myself, here's little Evie, little Sister Evie, virtuous little nun—wouldn't it be funny if she gave it a try? You didn't exactly jump at the idea, but I was right, you have what it takes to summon devils, no doubt about it. You summoned up a real peach. *Voi-thi*-something, you called it. Scared the living daylights out of Ernest." He laughed roughly at the memory. "I can still see him cowering with his arms around his head like an ass! Well, the thing did make me quake a little in my own boots, I'll admit."

"You're lying," Evvie breathed. "I don't remember any of that. I would never have done that."

"Well, you did," said Leo, petulantly. "I'm not lying." He shrugged. "In any case, it wasn't much use, that devil—it looked good, but it wouldn't do much."

"What ... what did it look like?"

"Oh, I don't know. Flames or something. Fancy your not remembering at all, eh? *That* part worked all right. I rather thought you were pretending, but I suppose not."

*

Of course she wasn't pretending. She *still* didn't remember anything about it, although when Leo had said "flames," for a moment she had thought … some kind of an image had formed in her mind, but she didn't know where it came from or what it might have to do with anything.

After Leo left, she sat at the desk again, trying to collect her thoughts. She still thought he might have been making the whole thing up—it was too much of a coincidence that his story should have involved the same ring that Fee said belonged to her cousin. But then, she thought she remembered the night in question, now that she came to consider it. She did remember seeing lights in the lodge one night last summer, and going out to do something about them, and then … she didn't know what had happened after that, and that was either because it had been wholly unmemorable and happened half a year ago, or because she had somehow been made to forget.

Of course, Leo had said they "picked up" the ring in London. Could that mean he had stolen it from Fidelity's cousin?

Archie came slouching in to take his turn at the reception desk, and Evvie got up gratefully and went upstairs to the workroom. She gathered up some mending and took it back to her own bedroom and shut the door. She wanted time to think, and she needed to do it alone.

There was no question she must tell Fee what Leo had said, but she dreaded it. Why should Fee believe any of it? The story of her vision was one thing, straightforward and almost cozy. It made her seem special, blessed. But this? It was horrible, if it was true, and it didn't sound true, anyway. Especially if Fee herself were making up stories, it would surely sound as if her friend were doing the same thing, only much less skilfully.

Then again, she admitted to herself, there was the simple fact that she didn't *want* it to be true. She remembered how before Fee arrived she had hoped there was some mystery to be solved about the lodge and Leo and Ernest's strange behaviour. But all that had been forgotten in the pleasure of having a real friend with whom to talk endlessly about real things. She'd even convinced herself that there was no mystery there at all, just her own imagination. She wished she had been right.

*

She had already avoided Fee for longer than they would have spent apart on any ordinary day, but she couldn't spend all day in her room sewing. At half past eleven she returned her finished mending and went down to the office. As she passed through the lobby, Archie was being unhelpful to a grey-haired man in a once-smart black overcoat that looked like he had recently been sleeping in it.

"I understand that," the man was saying doggedly, "but I have very little information to go on. Could you look in your records to see whether her name appears … whether she was here at some point?"

Archie gave an aggrieved shrug. "I'm very busy, and I didn't recognize her from the photograph. It wouldn't do any good to look in the records."

He started to turn away, but the man reached across the desk and seized the front of his waistcoat, not violently, just the way one might have done with a misbehaving child, to get its attention for the delivery of some important lesson.

"I am sorry," the man said. "You are busy. But *I don't know whether my daughter is alive or dead.* If you think that I wouldn't gladly reduce this building to rubble, patiently, one brick at a time, if that might offer me the slightest hope of finding her—well, I would suspect that you don't have children." He let go of Archie's waistcoat. "Look in your records."

Evvie felt sorry for the man, but she wanted to cheer for the way he had taken Archie to task. It was just what someone ought to have done to him ages ago. She had to go hastily out of the lobby for fear she would start to laugh.

She spent some time tidying her desk in the office, and went to the French windows that opened onto the terrace at the front of the house, where she drew back the curtains and opened one door to assess the weather. The grey-haired man from the lobby was there, by a bench that stood next to the window, folding up some papers and putting them back in his overcoat pocket with the air of a sleepwalker. He turned without seeing Evvie, put his hand on the back of the bench, and got stiffly to his knees on the ground. His clasped hands dropped to the seat of the bench, and he buried his face between his arms. She stood motionless, embarrassed to witness this obvious breakdown in a stranger. He was not in a strictly private place, but he must have thought he was unobserved. She tried to pull the window shut silently, but of course it creaked. The man sat back on his heels and looked up, dry-eyed and surprisingly composed. He had been praying, not crying.

She noticed several other things at once. He was much younger than she had supposed, certainly not out of his forties, in spite of the grey hair—it was a sandy, attractive grey, and his two or three days' worth of beard was a similar mix. He had beautiful blue eyes. He looked up at her with an attempt at a reassuring smile, which was surprisingly successful.

"You're Fidelity's father!" she burst out, flinging the window wide and stepping out onto the terrace in her excitement. "You're Gregory St. Clair. You must be."

His smile faded to a look of bafflement. "Must I? I'm afraid I'm not."

"No," Evvie admitted. "And you're not a soap millionaire either, are you?"

His coat was open, and his scarf had fallen away from his clerical collar.

"I'm ... not," he said, "but that *is* the sort of thing Sara might have made up."

"Sara," Evvie repeated. "Her—her name isn't Fidelity?"

"Absolutely not. At least—my daughter's name is Sara. I have a picture of her." He fumbled in his pockets, still kneeling by the bench, and after a moment held out a photograph for Evvie's inspection.

It was a snapshot of Fee standing on a bridge, her blonde hair long and braided, the wind pressing her skirt against her legs. It was recent—you could see barrage balloons tethered in the background—but she looked so much younger, like a child. It was no wonder Archie, glancing inattentively at the picture as he must have done, hadn't recognized her. But Evvie would have known her anywhere.

"She is alive, Father, she is here, she is alive," Evvie said all in a rush. "She is well, she is doing well. She was badly injured—she lost her leg—but she is so strong, she has borne it better than most of the soldiers."

Then he did cry, and didn't seem to have the energy to try to hide it.

"I'm sorry, I …" He made a face that again reminded Evvie powerfully of Fee. "I don't know why I'm apologizing, Sister—you're obviously something quite Mediterranean, you'd probably think it was embarrassing if I *didn't* cry."

A surprised laugh escaped her. "I am Greek. But you are English."

He wiped his eyes with his handkerchief. "Yes … Ah, you were expecting me to be something else."

"American."

"An American … soap millionaire."

"Yes, St. Clair Soap, from Boston."

"No, we live in Toronto, in Canada. Sara is Canadian."

By this time she was sitting on the bench, and he on the ground facing her. She was wondering again about his age. If he was Fidelity's father …

"You don't look old enough to have a twenty-year-old daughter," she said frankly.

He stared. "I absolutely am, but I *don't*. She's sixteen."

Sixteen. Of course that made sense of her cousin George, who was older than she but too young to enlist. Though Cousin George was probably, like everything else about Fidelity—her name, her nationality, her age, her parents—a fabrication. There was a small, tense silence. Hovering between them was the question of why Sara, who was sixteen and Canadian and a priest's daughter (like Evvie), was passing herself off as a twenty-year-old Baptist soap heiress from Boston. Evvie had a feeling that her father knew *why* she was doing it—he just hadn't known *that* she was.

"I am so sorry, Father!" she said, popping up from the bench. "I must not keep you talking like this. You want to see Fee—Sara—this instant."

"No," he said quickly, gathering himself up but then not rising from the ground. "No, it's quite clear that I can't see her."

"Oh? But …"

He shook his head. "The man at the front desk looked at her picture and told me flatly she wasn't here. And she isn't. There's a girl named Fidelity who looks something like her, but tells an elaborate story about a life that's quite different from Sara's." After a moment he added, lightly, as if it might mean anything, "I know my daughter, Sister, and in spite of what you may be thinking, she wouldn't make up a story like that for a lark."

Like tripping on a lump in the pavement, her mind in racing along over these words stumbled at something quite irrelevant. He had been calling her "Sister."

"How did you know that I was a nun?" she blurted out.

He looked up at her then; he had been looking away. "A nun? No, I didn't know that. I called you 'Sister' because I assumed you were a nurse."

"No, I am not. I just do—I do work for the hospital, but on Patmos I was a nun." She realized the implication of his mistake. "Oh, no—I am not a nurse. You think I have been caring for your daughter, but I haven't—I just help with the administration, and the laundry. I don't have anything to do with caring for her. I only—I only—"

It had all come crashing down on her suddenly. She had thought Fee was fudging some particulars of her life, it is true, and she had decided it didn't matter. But Fee had lied about everything, *everything*; her whole life had been a fiction. The friend Evvie thought she had did not exist.

"You befriended her," Sara's father finished the sentence for her. "Or you thought you did—and now you find out she has been telling you a lot of lies."

"No no," said Evvie, with a poor attempt at nonchalance. If he thought it was important to pretend that Fee wasn't Sara, the least she could do was go along with it. "I quite see that she hasn't—I do see that she is a different person, as you say. It's unfortunate for you, because … but it's just a coincidence, isn't it?"

The conversation seemed to have turned into a nightmare.

He looked like he was thinking the same thing. He rubbed his eyes and looked very tired. "Why don't you sit down," he suggested.

She did so, surprised.

"What is your name?" he asked. The reassuring smile was back. How was it that they were both so *good* at that?

"Evgenia."

He repeated it carefully. "Lovely. Mine's Christopher. And our real surname is Underhill. It's not connected with any brand of soap that I'm aware of."

She managed a weak laugh.

He said, "Sara was doing some work for her cousin—intelligence work. That's why it's taken me so long to find her. I don't have any kind of security clearance, so I couldn't tell you any more than that if I wanted. I think I can trust you with that much. I realize Sara didn't, but you must make allowance for the fact that she is only sixteen, and is following orders."

The first thing she felt, when she had taken this in, was ashamed. He shouldn't have had to tell her any of that. If she had been the magnificent friend that Fee thought her, she wouldn't have needed to be told. She should already have worked out that people who told elaborate fictions about themselves in wartime were probably spies.

"Thank you for trusting me," she said, because she quickly realized that what she should actually feel was gratitude. "Thank you, thank you." She found herself leaning forward, clutching the lapel of his coat, before she knew what she was doing. "That you could think of me and what I feel, when you have suffered so much and must be so tired! You will not regret it."

He gently extracted his lapel from her grip without touching her, and she sat back on the bench, embarrassed. He was, like Fidelity, a very attractive person, and like her he knew very well how that affected other people. Evvie thought it was not the first time he had needed to detach an hysterical young woman from his clothing. She noticed the plain gold band on the ring finger of his left hand. It was coming into fashion now, in the West, for men to wear wedding rings, but for someone of his age, it would have been a bit of a statement.

"Father," she said, trying hard to regain her dignity, "I cannot let you go without seeing her at all. In five minutes I will bring her down to the lobby. You go back inside and wait. We'll just pass by, but you will see her. That will be some comfort, at least."

"Thank you, Sister," he said composedly. "That is very good of you."

She ran inside rehearsing what she was going to say to Fee, but then she found her in the library between Rosalind and Daphne, pretending—Evvie thought she would have known it was pretending even before she found out that everything about Fee was pretend—to be interested in the cynical conversation they were having about marriage.

"It just lulls them into a false sense of security," Daphne was saying, "and makes them think a man is *theirs* for good, even if they let themselves go and get fat and slovenly."

"I know," said Rosalind. "I know, and so I'm not going to do that. I mean, I know nobody takes the marriage-vows seriously any more."

Fee had spotted Evvie, and looked a desperate plea from between Rosalind and Daphne, clasping her hands in a petitionary gesture.

"I've been looking everywhere for you, Fee," said Evvie, presenting herself, and feeling that her line lacked conviction, that Fee's fake name sounded fake on her lips. "Don't you remember you said you'd meet me on the terrace?"

"Oh, is it that time already? Rosalind, why don't you come out with us? You said you were dying for a smoke."

And so Rosalind trailed after them to the door, and Evvie knew that Fee was bringing her along solely to extract her from Daphne's clutches—and had cleverly mentioned smoking, which Daphne abhorred, in order to discourage her following them—but all the same, she felt as if it was still Fidelity, and not herself, who was in control of events.

Father Underhill was there, when they came into the lobby, making a pretence of looking up train times. He glanced up at their entry, and Evvie realized she had been naïve to think he would feel simply comforted, seeing his daughter. Fee looked much better now than she had when she had first arrived at Adderley, with her arm in a sling and her face bruised, but she was still very different from the healthy girl on the bridge in the photograph. The expression that crossed her father's face when he saw her was horror. He got that under control quickly, though, and managed a smile that was entirely plausible for a kindly stranger seeing a passing girl in a wheelchair. They made it through the lobby and out the front door to the terrace.

"Actually, you know, I fancy a walk," said Evvie, as Rosalind got out her cigarettes and perched on the rail. "Can I push you around, Fee?"

"Sure," said Fee. "If you like." Her expression was totally unreadable.

"Well, I'm just going to sit here," said Rosalind mercifully.

Evvie pushed Fee's chair down the wooden ramp from the terrace to the lawn. Most of the things that she had felt at first—anger and grief and betrayal—had melted away by this time. Her friend did exist, and she had probably been as honest with Evvie as it was safe for her to be; in fact, if Evvie was honest with herself, she could see that Fee had taken some risks with her. She remembered how excited Fee had got when Evvie said her father was a priest, and guessed how close she must have come at that point to saying, "Mine too!" and admitting that the soap millionaire was a fiction. She remembered how Fee had let her make up the story about her family, although she must have known how that looked. No, Evvie wasn't really angry with her on her own behalf any more. There was just one thing, she thought, that still bothered her. And so when she had wheeled Fee's chair down onto the lawn and they were safely alone, the first thing she said was not, "Don't worry, Sara—I know all."

It was, "How could you do it to him?"

Fee looked up at her. "How could I do what to who? To whom," she corrected herself prettily.

That didn't help; now Evvie found herself getting angry again.

"No, you do not get out of this by being cute. I am talking about your father, *whom* you saw as well as I did. He has been looking for you for a month, and couldn't find you because you have been pretending to be someone else."

Fee let her pretty eyebrows rise incredulously. "Do you mean that rather fetching middle-aged clergyman who was in the lobby just now? You think I'm his daughter?"

She saw her mistake instantly, but Evvie saw it too. She had strayed into a line of imposture which she could not sustain.

"He *was* rather fetching, wasn't he?" said Evvie, tipping her head to one side. She couldn't keep this up either, of course, but she was pretty sure she wouldn't have to.

"I suppose," Fee backtracked. "Not really my type."

"Whyever not?"

"Oh, you know. Too old. Nearly fifty." Another mistake. "I'd have said," she amended carelessly.

"*Would* you? That's funny, I'd have said he was younger. But I expect you prefer *much* younger men. Boys, even. Since you are only sixteen."

Fee gave a hard, bright little laugh. "Who's only sixteen? *What* are you talking about?"

This time she was really shaken. Evvie could have—indeed had—guessed that she was the priest's daughter just by looking at him, but her age couldn't have been a guess. And for a moment Evvie could see that she really was sixteen, that the picture of her on the bridge, with two legs and her hair in girlish braids, had been taken only a few months ago.

She knelt in front of the wheelchair. "Fee—Sara. I am sorry for being so brutal. I was upset. Your father told me the truth about what you have been doing. A bit of the truth—he said it was the only part that he knows. He told me because I had already realized that you were not who you said you were—that was not his fault, he hadn't any idea of your false identity, he was just trying to find out whether you were alive or what had happened to you. But when I told him about Fidelity, he could see that must mean you were still undercover, and he said he wouldn't see you. He must have realized that part of what you were doing was trying to protect him. But he decided to tell me, so that I would understand too why you lied to me. And—I didn't understand this part until just now, because I was thinking only of myself—and he told me so that you might have an ally. So that you would not have to go on lying, at least not to one person. Oh, Sara, please believe me."

She was silent for a long time. "Of course I believe you. The— the—when we passed in the lobby like that, was that ... was that Father's idea or yours?"

"It was my idea. He was going to leave without seeing you at all.

But I don't think—I don't think he quite knew how worried you were about him."

She shook her head. "Of course not. It's not as if I had any real reason to think he—was—dead. His regiment wasn't involved in active fighting any more. But, I mean, anybody *could* be dead during a war, couldn't they? And I hadn't *any idea* that they hadn't told him where I was. They *knew* my cover story, I assumed they'd tell him, and he'd come here looking for Fidelity St. Clair—I was so looking forward to the hard time he'd give me for making him pretend to be a ruined Protestant soap magnate! That was probably quite irresponsible of me—I should just have said that my father was the Reverend Mr. Gregory St. Clair, because he couldn't really be convincing as anything other than a clergyman. But they obviously didn't tell him anything at all. If he didn't even know where to find me … "

"Oh," said Evvie suddenly. "Did he … Does your father have a pocket-watch with a bird in it?"

"You mean what I asked the police constable about, in the village? No, my father wears a wristwatch. That's not who I thought the man in the water might have been." She was silent for a moment. "Evgenia, I can tell you what I have been doing here, at Adderley. Precisely nothing. My cousin Graham, the—"

"Foreign Office Graham? He's real?"

"He's quite real, and I've been working for him. Unofficially. He was going to meet me here, and I've been waiting for him ever since … ever since the crash. All the while my poor father has been looking for me without knowing what name I've been using or even if I'm alive or dead. I think … I think something has gone awfully wrong. And my cousin Graham does—well, *did*—have a pocket-watch with a bird in it."

"Oh," said Evvie. "I'm sorry."

That was when it hit Evvie, finally. Her friend was a spy—next door to a spy, anyway. At sixteen, which was really even more impressive than being a magazine journalist at twenty. There *was* a mystery, but it would be all right, because they would figure it out together. She didn't need to fear telling Leo's terrible story after all. And she had been mourning the loss of Fidelity St. Clair, but she should instead have been rejoicing about properly meeting Sara Underhill, who seemed like she might be an even more exciting person.

"We'll figure it out," Evvie said. "The two of us. We'll figure it out together."

Sara smiled gratefully.

That was all they had time for, because Rosalind came lounging across the lawn to join them, her cigarette finished. It was time to go in for lunch.

Chapter Seventeen

KING SOLOMON'S RING

It wasn't until late in the afternoon that Evvie finally had a chance to talk to Sara alone again. Daphne had not turned up at lunch, and Ernest, strangely frantic, had insisted on mobilizing the whole staff to look for her. They had gone over the house and the grounds, and Evvie had been treated to an embarrassing commentary on the episode by Nurse Porter.

"I heard them fighting before lunch—that's what he's so worried about. He thinks she's gone off and left him. Or thrown herself down a well in despair, maybe." Nurse Porter chuckled at the idea. "Yes, my dear, depend on it, that's what he thinks she's done—made away with herself because he won't leave his wife. That's what they were arguing about. Can you credit it? He won't ask for a divorce. Trotted out some rot about how *he* doesn't need their love sanctioned by church or state—so noble of him, I'm sure! But think about it from her point of view. She probably wants to have a kid. And she's not getting any younger. These artistic men, though—they make themselves out to be such rebels, but when push comes to shove, what they're really looking for is a nice dependable woman, same as any man. If he's got a wife who'll stick by him while he gallivants about the country pretending to be shell-shocked and carrying on with sultry blondes—why'd he want to give that up? It only stands to reason."

Evvie was forced to admit that it did.

In the end, though, it seemed Daphne had neither abandoned Ernest nor thrown herself down a well. She had gone for a long walk on the moors, and turned up again of her own accord, and couldn't understand what all the fuss was about. Ernest acted as though going for a long walk was about as alarming as throwing herself down a well, and Evvie saw Nurse Porter and Nurse Griggs giving each other highly significant looks.

Finally finished her work for the day and free to seek out Sara, Evvie found her sitting on a bench in the courtyard, with her crutches beside her, enjoying the last of the daylight in the company of an unfamiliar young man in civilian clothes. He had the look of one of those wispy English angels in a church window: thin and pale with light brown, curly hair. He was sitting coiled up on the bench, hands loosely clasped by his ankles, looking up at Sara and laughing. He uncoiled himself and got up when Evvie approached.

"This is Latham," said Sara. "You know, Rosalind's Latham. More properly Mr. Addison-Carmichael. Latham, my friend Evgenia."

"Ev-yee …" He floundered, embarrassed.

"Evvie," she supplied.

"Evvie, how d'you do? Seen Ros around?"

"Rosalind? Yes, she came back from Newingthorpe just now. She's gone upstairs to change. I should think she will be down shortly."

"Ah, well then. I've just been entertaining Fee while she waits for you, so I'll shove off." He pushed his hands into his pockets and clearly didn't want to leave.

"That's all right," said Evvie, sitting down on the other end of the bench. "I didn't mean to interrupt your conversation."

Latham subsided bonelessly onto the bench again. "We were talking about detective stories," he said with a grin. He really was remarkably handsome. "Comparing notes on our favourites."

"I see," said Evvie. "And do you agree or disagree, in the main?"

"In the main we agree," said Latham. "Though Fee claims she guessed the ending of Agatha Christie's latest."

"And he doesn't believe me," said Sara. "But I think it was obvious."

"Have you read it? You haven't—we'd better stop talking about it."

Sara rolled her eyes. "As if there's any surprise to ruin."

"So Mr., um … " Evvie realized to her shame that she couldn't remember his double-barrelled surname. "May I call you Latham?"

"Oh, of course!"

"So are you not flying a mission today?"

Latham gave her a surprised look. "Oh, Lord. Ros hasn't been telling you I'm a pilot?" He looked embarrassed. "Never mind. I don't actually fly, I'm just a glorified mechanic. I did try flying, after my uncle got me the Air Force commission—he was an ace in the last war and all that. But I'm terrified of heights, and I panic under any sort of pressure. I was just hopeless. So my squadron leader found something for me to do on the ground, and I try to make myself useful."

"That's the most any of us can do," said Sara.

"Did Ros tell you I'm a pilot? I'm not trying to get you to tell tales, only I feel bad. Poor Ros—I expect she's embarrassed by me."

They assured him that they didn't remember whether Rosalind had actually said he was a pilot or not, but that they had assumed it.

"You must be grateful to your squadron leader," said Evvie, to change the subject.

Latham's face lit up. "He's brilliant! I'll never forget how he behaved after I crashed my plane on the runway the second time. I was trying to keep a stiff upper lip, but I was shaking like a leaf, and when he ordered me into his office, I thought he planned to rake me over the coals. But he didn't—he said, 'We're going to figure out something for you to do on the ground.' I started to cry in front of him, I was so relieved." Latham looked wistful for a moment, then shook himself and grinned sheepishly. "Fancy admitting that to a couple of girls! Ros is right to be ashamed of me."

"I'm sure she isn't," said Sara in her comforting way. "I think it's good to be honest about things." She shot Evvie a look of ironic apology.

"I suppose so," said Latham.

They reverted to talking about detective fiction, and presently Rosalind came out the door and said, "Latham! There you are!"

"Hullo," he said, uncoiling himself from the bench again, with what Evvie thought looked like a forced attempt at enthusiasm. "I've been chatting with your friends."

"Yes, I see that," said Rosalind tartly. "I *thought* you'd come to see me."

"I did," Latham replied uncomfortably. "Of course. Shall we take a stroll? It's a lovely evening for it."

Rosalind consented grumpily, and they headed for the back gate.

"He's not what I was expecting," said Sara musingly, as she and Evvie watched the pair walk away.

"He's very pretty," said Evvie. "Is he more your type than middle-aged clergymen who look like you?"

Sara laughed. "Not by much. I'm pretty sure Rosalind did say he was a pilot. I *think* I heard her telling Daphne how many planes he'd shot down. Poor Rosalind."

"Poor Latham!"

"Yes, that goes without saying. Evgenia, I'm *so glad* Father told you the truth about me."

"It was a risk," said Evvie, who had spent some time thinking about this, "but I guess he had to take it—I'd already found out you weren't Fidelity, so either I could think you were insane, or … I suppose if I were an enemy agent or something, I would have *guessed* that if you had a false identity, you must be a spy, so he wouldn't have been telling me anything I couldn't work out for myself."

"I'm not a spy, Evvie," said Sara, looking a little alarmed. "Not an actual spy. Cousin Graham isn't a spy either, he's a civil servant, and I was just working for him unofficially. I *certainly* didn't lie to you because I thought you were an enemy agent."

After a moment they both laughed, somewhat sheepishly.

"Honestly, Evvie, I didn't even think you were untrustworthy, not once I'd talked to you—not ever, really. I went on lying to you because … well, because I was supposed to, I guess, but also because I didn't think you'd *believe* me if I told you the truth."

"Well … I might not have."

"If you could eventually forgive me, Evgenia, I'd like that so much."

"Of course! I do forgive you, right now!"

"I'm not sure I deserve that. I mean I'm quite sure I don't. But thank you."

"Fee—sorry, Sara—"

"Better not get used to calling me that, actually. I mean not around people."

"That's a good point. But *Fee*, why are you a … whatever you are, even if it's not a spy? Why is a sixteen-year-old Canadian girl working for the British government, even 'unofficially'?"

"Because I'm good at it." And she gave Evvie a little look, with one eyebrow quirked up, that was not Fidelity St. Clair at all, that was a whole new person. Evvie gasped.

"Okay, let me explain from the beginning. And, as a bonus, let me give you a *true* story about my family—not the soapy St. Clairs, but my actual family. You've heard a few true things about them already, mixed in with the lies. Graham Darby is my father's first cousin, but we didn't meet him or even know about him until 1938, because my father's family is a bit complex. His parents weren't married. His mother was totally cut off by her family for taking up with my grandfather—well, not for taking up with him, I guess, but for not eventually getting married to him. Anyway, they never saw her again, and the younger generation—my father's cousins—didn't even know she existed. Isn't that shocking? But it was the nineteenth century, and I guess they did things like that. My grandmother died a long time ago, when my father was still a little boy. But eight years ago my grandmother's younger sister died, survived by her two sons and daughter, and leaving a will that she had written decades ago and hadn't updated. This is important because the will mentioned her sister Adele, my grandmother, and that was the first her two sons and daughter ever heard of her. It's quite sad, really. Anyway, the legacy to Adele was just a token, a family Bible and some jewellery—a ring that had been somebody's wedding ring, and a little gold cross that had been in the family a long time. Actually it was a horribly spiteful gesture, because Adele never married and was a vehement atheist, and her sister knew that *very* well. But of course her children, who'd never heard of this Aunt Adele, didn't, and made a genuine effort to find her and deliver the legacy. Of course they learned that she had died, but also that—shockingly!—she'd had a son, that he'd ended up in an orphanage and then been adopted by some people—his father, actually, and his father's young wife.

"Anyway, it took the cousins two years to finally track him down in Canada, because it hadn't occurred to them that he would have kept his mother's surname. So they wrote and said they had this stuff to send him, if he wanted it, but that actually, they would be thrilled to meet him and heal this rift in the family that they hadn't even known about, and sort of hinted that if he wanted to come to England they would be happy to pay his way—you know, for all they knew he was living in abject poverty, since all they knew about him was that he was the illegitimate son of their disgraced aunt and had been adopted by some weird Canadians. So my father—being my father—wrote back, 'Knew about the rift but didn't know what was on the other side of it; would love to meet you of course; also have a large and picturesque family which I will bring with me; please recommend appropriate hotels.' We went for the whole summer, six years ago, and stayed with one of the cousins at his place in the country—they're all fabulously wealthy and were a bit embarrassed to find that we didn't think we *were* living in abject poverty. Actually at home we think we're rather grand because we have *two* servants—on account of my mother having a job—and a car, which mostly only my mother drives. Also my mother is quasi-famous. She's written two books, one about poetry and one *of* poetry. Anyway … gosh, I do wish you could meet my mother,

Evvie. I feel worse for telling you she was a socialite than for telling you my father was a soap magnate—at least the soap magnate story was funny, and didn't *devalue* him in the same way. Not that there's anything terrible about being a socialite—it's just that my mother works very hard to keep things in balance, you know, to be a good wife and mother and a first-rate scholar at the same time. I do wish you could meet her. Oh, did I tell you that I have three brothers, all younger than me, none of them called Calvin?"

"No, but I was beginning to be a bit suspicious of Calvin."

"You're so clever, Evvie. I don't know how I got any of this past you."

"What about Cousin George?"

"He's real. I don't think I said anything about him that wasn't true. He downplays the cousin angle, as I told you, because we're not blood relations at all. His parents and mine are best friends. It's all rather sickeningly quaint. But where was I? Oh, in 1938, when we came to visit our English cousins. Well, at that point, the eldest of the cousins, that's Graham, had just come back from his post in the Middle East to take up some quite important government job, and he had brought back all this stuff from Arabia: stone carvings and clay tablets and gold jewellery. It's quite an impressive collection. He wanted to loan some of his things to the British Museum, but he was having trouble with the curator, who didn't believe in the provenance—that's, you know, the details about what they were and where they were found and so on—and Graham was miffed at the idea of his treasures being catalogued with tags that said 'unknown origin' or 'supposedly something-or-other.' Anyway, he had them all in the basement of his townhouse, and he showed them to us.

"The pride of his collection was this ring. It's just a gold ring, with a red stone in it, carved in a kind of design, but very worn-looking, so you can hardly tell what the design is." She looked up at Evvie from under her lashes, her blue eyes very keen. "It looks like wax, the stone, a kind of flat red."

"Oh! But that sounds like ... "

"Something you've seen someone wearing around here?" Sara smiled a tight little smile. "Yes. But of course, it's a common type of ring. I think the stone is jasper. In any case, the story about this ring—"

"It was given to King Solomon by the Archangel Michael, to bind demons."

"I told you that already."

"Ye-es. Sort of. But go on."

"Well, I *started* to tell you this whole story, actually, when you told me about your vision of the angel, but I realized I couldn't have finished it without completely contradicting my soapy cover story, so I stopped before I quite got into it. I said I heard a voice when I put on the ring, but ... there was quite a bit more to it than that. Not everyone could hear the voice. Graham couldn't. He said if he'd known it really worked, he'd never have let us touch it—of course he had to say that after the fact, because our parents were there giving him a look that could have frozen a lake of fire."

"I think I saw that one earlier today," said Evvie, "when Archie told your father he wouldn't look up your name in the records."

"I'll bet. But my mother's actually much scarier than my father. He generally gets by on charm."

"But—what happened? Start at the beginning, can't you?"

"I was just about to. So Cousin Graham was telling us the story about King Solomon and the ring—it's out of an ... uh, an apocryphal—no, that's not even what I mean, not apocryphal, just completely fake and made-up, a thing called *The Testament of Solomon*. It's not even BC—my mother was quite scathing about it. Did I say that she's a Hellenist?"

"No, but I'm beginning to see why you couldn't properly tell this story before."

"Oh, it gets better. So Graham was telling the story of the ring, at the table after dinner, and he was quite a good storyteller, so he put the ring on, as he was talking about it, and waved his hand, and demonstrated how you would summon a demon by saying its name. 'Abezethibou!' he said." She gestured imperiously. "'By the power of King Solomon's ring, I summon thee!'"

Evvie shivered. "And then?"

"Well, then he went on with the story, and explained how Solomon made the demons help him build the Temple, and then he took the ring off to show us, and my brother Stephen tried it on. But he jerked it off right away and went white and said, 'Did you hear that?' but of course we hadn't. Cousin Graham thought he was just playing, but that's not really like Stephen—he's very serious. Father said, 'Hear what?' but by that time Stephen was embarrassed because Graham was laughing at him, and he wouldn't say. That was when I picked up the ring and put it on myself. I stuck it on my thumb because it was so big—even on my thumb it was very loose. And right away I heard it: this hissing voice. 'I am Abezethibou. What is thy will?' Cousin Graham had summoned him, you see, but couldn't hear him. And I saw why Stephen had torn the ring off, too. It was frightening—the voice was terrible, and I could feel the thing looking at me, even though I couldn't see it. He—it—said it again, sounding impatient: 'What is thy will?' And then he began suggesting things: *Do you want me to tear your enemies to shreds, do you want me to build you a great fortress, or seduce handsome men for you?*

"Of course I knew no one else could hear it, just me, and, I mean, that's the kind of thing you're always secretly prepared for, isn't it? And you wonder what you'd do? What I did was tell my parents. I said, 'There's a horrible voice, and it's asking me what I want. What should I do?' And my mother said, 'Trap it in something,' and my father—I said we were at the dinner table, didn't I?—my father grabbed the lid off the soup tureen, and my mother said, 'Tell it to get in there and stay there!' and I did. It whined a bit and tried to talk me out of it, but I was quite firm with it. And we heard a little splash in the leftover soup, and my father clapped the lid back on the tureen."

"And … then what?"

"Oh, he took it out to the garden and exorcised it—he let Stephen help, and they couldn't stop giggling afterward about Father saying, 'from whence you came' to the soup tureen instead of just 'where you came from.' He said the situation seemed to call for it. Meanwhile our mother was quite fierce with Cousin Graham and made him lock the ring up in his study. He put the soup tureen there too, because he didn't want his cook to accidentally put soup in it again—just in case. I missed most of this because just after Abezethibou went into the soup tureen, I got hit by a terrific migraine, with fireworks and everything, the worst one I'd ever had, and had to go lie down. And after that, I couldn't go into Cousin Graham's study without the same thing starting up. We figured it was some kind of reaction to the ring. Stephen didn't have the same reaction, but neither he nor the twins—who were very little—wanted to go in there or get too near the ring. We don't know exactly why it was that we could hear the voice and Cousin Graham couldn't, but we have a theory … we have a theory that it's hereditary, because my mother has from time to time been able to do things … not things like *this*, but things. And my grandfather on my mother's side is an honest-to-God faith healer. We didn't really pursue it, because it was all a bit unsettling.

"We came home after that summer, and then the war broke out the following year, and my father went to Italy as a chaplain with his old regiment. Meanwhile, Cousin Graham was promoted again to an even more important job that sounded so vague it *obviously* had something to do with Intelligence. We kept in touch with all the cousins—the business with the ring had actually been quite a minor incident in an otherwise lovely summer, and we were all still friends. Oh, and this," she drew the delicate gold chain out of the neck of her sweater and held out her tiny pendant for Evvie's inspection, "is the gold cross from the legacy. It's Elizabethan. Ironically, it's actually quite valuable, but of course now that we like these people so much, we wouldn't dream of selling it."

"It's beautiful."

"Isn't it? I like it and wear it all the time. But to return to the story. Last year Graham wrote us a very strange letter, practically in code, but what it seemed to say when we'd deciphered it was that Solomon's stupid ring had been stolen, and he was terribly afraid it might have fallen into enemy hands, and wanted me to help him retrieve it. I think he … actually thought I might be able to exert some powers from the other side of the Atlantic, but of course that was very silly. In any case, it was clear that he was dead serious and at his wits' end.

"So there were some wires back and forth, and even a couple of very expensive telephone calls, and Graham came up with a more sane-sounding plan of what he wanted me to do. He thought he knew who had taken the ring, roughly—he thought it had been one of his colleagues, and of course the main thing was to find out who, because that person might be some kind of mole or double agent, and could be very dangerous. It was at a pivotal point in the war, according to Graham. He remembered the bad reaction I'd had to being in the same room with the ring, and thought we could use that to figure out where it was. It sounds like it might have been dangerous, but it wasn't really, the way he had it planned. I had this cover story of being a reporter, and he was going to accompany me, and it should have been quite safe. I mean it *was* quite safe, actually. And … you must understand, Evvie, the crucial aspect of this part of the story is that I *so* wanted to do it. Not because of the mystical demon-summoning business—honestly that was embarrassing— but because it would mean a real opportunity to help the war effort. I was very, very clear with my parents that I wanted to do it, and why I wanted to do it. I don't think I threw a tantrum or anything, but what I want to explain is that I so *very* much wanted to come and help, and that is why they let me do it. My father was able to get leave to meet me, and come to England with me—it was all very exciting, travelling in the middle of the war like that.

"So we came to London, and then my father went back to Italy, and I was staying with Graham and his sister Eliza, and … I can't tell you what I did. But I can tell you that what I *actually* did had nothing to do with Graham's wretched ring. It wasn't that we didn't carry out his plan—we did. We went round to all his colleagues' houses, on one pretext or another, and there was just nothing. No headaches, no fireworks, nothing. So we started to wonder what that meant, you know, because it could have been any number of things. Maybe my allergy had worn off, or maybe the migraines that summer were a coincidence. Or maybe we hadn't got the right house—maybe it wasn't one of Graham's colleagues who'd taken the ring after all. We didn't know.

"Anyway, while this was going on, one of Graham's friends at the Foreign Office had some other work he needed done, and none of Graham's department really knew the truth about what I was doing, because I mean really—a magic demon-summoning ring that you think you may have accidentally let the Nazis steal? Obviously he hadn't been going around telling anybody that. But I had this security clearance, and I've got other skills besides … besides whatever the Solomon's ring skill is—did you notice that I'm quite good at staying in character and making up stories? Anyway, they had me do some … a little bit of ordinary spy stuff. *That's* the part I can't tell you about, except to say that it was quite a lot of fun, and I did a good job. It wasn't dangerous at all, so don't get any ideas about that. After the war is well and truly over, I suppose I shall be able to tell you all about it, and it'll seem like an anticlimax. But anyway … at the end of January Graham said he had a new lead, and I was to leave that night for Yorkshire, and he'd join me there the next day. He didn't say what we'd be doing—he didn't have time—but I assumed we were going after the ring again. And that was when I crashed at Newingthorpe, and ended up here."

"And then you started getting migraines again."

"Do you know, it took me a while to put two and two together about that, all the same? When I first got here, I was still taking painkillers, and they made me feel a little woozy, so I didn't quite notice the usual symptoms. And everything hurt, a bit, so the headaches didn't bother me at first. I did finally realize what was going on, that it must mean the ring was here somewhere. Then I saw who was going about boldly wearing it."

"Josephine Good."

"Exactly."

Evvie nodded. "Well, now I have a story to tell you. I should have told you earlier, only … only I wasn't really sure it was true. But I'm beginning to think it probably is."

*

"Yes, I see," said Sara, who was sitting curled up on the bench with a faraway, concentrating expression on her face that did not seem to belong to Fidelity St. Clair. "I had Ernest down as the thief, actually, as soon as I spotted the ring on Miss Good's finger, because he worked for the government, and I thought he was a likely person to have known Cousin Graham. Then when we found out about the gun, I got the idea Leo might have shot Graham, when he turned up in Yorkshire to meet me. So I saw Leo must have been involved—and that made sense of how Josephine got the ring, if she used to be a friend of his. Though I can't see how he would have let her keep it, if it was working so well for them."

"But you think it's true—his story? You think I really did … what he says I did?"

Sara frowned. "I think," she said slowly, "it's probably not a lie. But it leaves a lot unexplained, all the same. What did they do with the devil you supposedly summoned? How could they do anything with it, when you were the only one who could get the ring to work? I don't know—there's a lot about it that I don't quite buy. I mean … do Leo and Ernest *honestly* seem to you like men with a devil at their beck and call?" She crooked up an eyebrow.

Evvie snorted. "You're right. They should be flying about on a dragon's back or something, not driving that old boat of a car."

"Exactly. Would Faust have had to do his own murders, with an antique revolver, and have the police find the body—or not be able to divorce his wife and marry his mistress? It's just not credible." She uncurled herself suddenly and straightened her skirt. "Oops. Incoming."

Evvie looked up and saw Rosalind coming across the courtyard towards them. She looked upset.

"Hello, Rosalind," said Sara—or rather Fee—brightly. "Latham gone back to his base, has he?"

"What? Oh, yes." She flopped down onto the bench on the other side of Sara, knocking Sara's crutches over in the process. With a groan, she bent to retrieve them. "You'll have to put up with me for a bit. I had to get away from Daphne. She's being awful. And I know she won't come join us—she thinks the two of you are just ridiculous."

There was one of those *Rosalind, did you just say that?* pauses.

"Well, don't worry," said Sara cosily. "We think she's ridiculous too."

"What was she doing to be awful?" Evvie asked.

"Oh, just … *insinuating* things. About Latham. She met him just as he was leaving, and started flirting with him." Rosalind shrugged. "I don't mind that so much. You get used to it, with Lath. It was the things she started saying to me after. She doesn't know. Anyway, it's none of her business."

After a moment, Sara said lightly, "What isn't?"

"Whether Latham's … well, you know! I mean, it's probably all different in America, anyway."

"Um … ?"

"She thinks she's doing me some big favour by warning me," said Rosalind hotly, "as if I didn't already know! But we've known each other since we were kids—he couldn't have kept a thing like that secret from me."

Sara shot Evvie a wide-eyed, *oh–help* look. She turned back to Rosalind. "Is Latham … homosexual?"

"What do *you* know about it?" Rosalind snapped.

"Nothing! It was a question."

"Oh, I expect it's *obvious!*"

"It isn't obvious, Rosalind. But you did just kind of spell it out for us. And it's … maybe not the most far-fetched thing ever."

Rosalind slumped back on the bench and looked defeated.

"It was unkind of Daphne to make remarks like that," said Evvie after a moment. She felt out of her depth here, and was frankly waiting for Rosalind to say something like, *Oh, what would you know, you're a nun!*

"It was beastly," said Rosalind with feeling. "She thinks everyone has to be like her and Ernest, all falling all over each other with passion and sex and everything. But I don't see why you can't have a perfectly successful marriage if you just like each other enough. I just wish we didn't have to keep pretending to be madly in love! It's so stupid."

"Maybe," said Sara after a minute, "what you need is a new set of friends. You know, people who don't know the pretend version, where Latham's an ace fighter pilot, and you're head-over-heels, and all that. Then you wouldn't have to pretend all the time. You could—if you wanted to—you could start with us."

Chapter Eighteen

K+

Charlie had checked the service times on the noticeboard that said "Mass," and on Sunday he got up early with the intention of making it to the 8:30. Hal was awake already, and lay naked under the bedclothes, watching him dress. They had slept in Hal's bed.

Charlie turned to him to suggest that he should get moving, and Hal said, "I think it would be better if I did not come."

"What? Really? Why?"

"I don't remember how to sing, and I've never really known how to pray. I certainly can't receive Communion. I think it might be easier if I weren't there at all."

"You can just sit in a pew. I don't mind."

"I would rather not."

"That's okay."

"I can see that it upsets you."

"No! No, I'm not going to insist that you come to church with me. What kind of a thing would that be?" He took some time doing up the buttons on his shirt cuffs. "Hal—my love—when you say that you can't receive Communion ..."

"It is for humans. St. Paul makes that abundantly clear."

"Oh. Right."

"Did you think I meant something else?"

"Yeah, kind of. I mean, I haven't ... I don't know whether I should ..."

Hal looked at him questioningly.

Charlie sat back down on the bed and spoke rapidly: "St. Paul makes some other things pretty clear, too. If this'd been with anyone but you, I'd be sure it was sin—but it's you, and so I'm not sure. I guess I hoped you might tell me one way or the other."

"Charles," said Hal after a moment, "here is what I can tell you. When you returned to find me in that valley, you promised never to leave me. I made you the same promise. You have offered to provide for me and to bring me home with you to live in your house. I do not think we are lovers. I think we are married."

"We're not *married*—we're both men."

"We are not. But I am not sure it would change my judgment if we were. You will not have time to eat breakfast if you don't leave soon."

"I wasn't planning to—I usually fast." He bent down to tie his boots. "Married?" he repeated. "Do you really think … "

Hal laughed. "If you didn't intend it, then it didn't happen. I think that is the way it works."

"Can I retroactively decide that I *did* intend it, though?"

Hal knelt up and put his arms around Charlie from behind. For a moment he hugged him very tightly, his face pressed against Charlie's shoulder.

"Go to church," he said. "Ask God about it. And pray for me."

"Of course!"

*

Charlie walked to the church, St. Bede's, the squat little medieval place that he and Hal had passed more than once on their walks. He was early; he'd overestimated the amount of time it would take to walk here, because he'd thought he might be strolling at a leisurely pace with Hal, not striding with his hands in his pockets through the cold morning by himself. The grey stone of the church reminded him of the colour of Hal's eyes. The chilly interior smelled old and slightly dank, and was full of a maze of dark box pews, mostly empty before the early service. He slouched in the corner of one of them and wrapped his coat around himself. He studied the stonework, tried to work out which parts of the church dated to which period, flipped through the ancient hymnal, and wondered what colour the altar frontal was supposed to be. Finally he remembered Hal saying, "I've never really known how to pray," and it occurred to him that he, Charlie, *did* know how to pray, and ought to do it.

He found one of the hard, moth-eaten, needlepoint-covered cushions that served as kneelers, nudged it across the stone floor with the toe of his boot, and knelt on it. He was tall enough to rest his arms on the top of the box pew in this position. He buried his face in the crook of his arm and tried to quiet his thoughts.

The last time you tried to pray, God sent you Hal.

But he didn't think that was the right way to look at it. The last time he tried to pray, he had tried to listen for whatever he might need to hear, and he had heard Hal's call for help. It hadn't been what he wanted or expected—or at least it hadn't seemed to be—yet Hal was the answer to a prayer that he would never have dared to pray. Even now he could not quite bring himself to formulate it in the quiet of his mind.

Thank you, Lord, for letting me have my cake and eat it too.

He heard it as if in another voice, very familiar but not quite his own. In the privacy of the box pew he smiled to himself, gently amused that he would talk to himself—and to God—in that voice. And in the moment of stillness that followed, it came to him like a lightning strike that he had known the truth all along, since he was fifteen years old; he just hadn't tried hard enough to live up to it.

Other people were coming into the church now; he heard the clomp and shuffle of footsteps on the stones, the murmur of voices and opening and closing pew doors. He sat back on his pew and rubbed his eyes, and noticed there was someone standing in the aisle opposite his pew door, a step back, as if uncertain whether to move on or approach. There were still many empty pews in the place, so Charlie saw no need to invite a stranger to sit with him, but the man was in uniform, and Charlie looked up, wondering if it was someone he knew.

It was Father Underhill.

He smiled at Charlie, that masterpiece of a smile that always caught Charlie by surprise with its warmth of affection. He was in his chaplain's uniform, his hat in his gloved hands, the collar of his coat turned up against the cold.

"Hello, Charlie. I wondered if I might run into you here."

"Father!" Charlie jumped up and swung open the door to the pew. He hardly gave Father Underhill time to step inside before he hugged him, as naturally as if it were something he had done a hundred times before—when in fact it was something he had never done.

"How good it is to see you!" he said, releasing him and letting him sit down. "I was just thinking about you."

He dropped into his own corner again and looked at the older man, who had put down his hat and gloves and was unbuttoning his coat. He looked tired, and all of his forty-nine years—to Charlie, he looked surprisingly old. Charlie had not seen him since the start of the war. His hair was greyer, and he had lost weight, but it was weight that he'd put on in middle age; he was as trim now as he had been in his thirties. He had even acquired a light suntan, which looked glamorous with the grey hair.

A bell rang from the vestry, and the small congregation got to its feet as the service began. Charlie realized he had never sat in a pew beside Father Underhill, though he'd sat next to him in the sanctuary often enough. Father Underhill cared more about liturgy than almost anyone Charlie knew—cared enough, in fact, never to take it, or himself, too seriously. It was like the way you could tease someone you loved, Charlie thought. He would give you a friendly grin if you made a mistake, and might make faces or editorialize *sotto voce* about embarrassing lines in the hymns, and otherwise behave like a choirboy, but you never doubted his devotion.

In the cold little Yorkshire church with its box pews, Father Underhill behaved perfectly soberly. Of course it was a plain celebration, sparsely attended, so any nudging or whispering would have stood out. There wasn't much to laugh at, though Charlie was dying to ask Father Underhill what colour *he* thought the altar frontal was supposed to be. But he sensed it wasn't the time or the place. When the celebrant proposed an impromptu recessional, "Jesu, Lover of my Soul," Father Underhill stood up beside Charlie and sang quite seriously, in his fine, carrying voice. His accent, which sounded very English in Toronto, in Yorkshire sounded almost as transatlantic as Charlie's.

The service over, Father Underhill sat for a moment with his elbows on his knees and his head bowed—he'd given up on the awkward kneeler, which forced him practically to sit on his heels on the floor, since he wasn't as tall as Charlie.

Charlie leaned back in his corner of the pew and looked up at the medieval stained glass above the altar, images of saints filled with the light of the rising sun. St. Michael's wings were the same ambiguous colour as the frontal. Charlie wanted to laugh with joy.

Beside him, Father Underhill sat up, rubbing his face and pushing a hand through his hair.

"You no doubt have somewhere to be," he said.

"I'm headed back to the Feathers in the high street. Come with me. I'll buy you breakfast."

"You don't have to do that."

"No, but I want to do something. You look …" He was going to say *like a wreck*, but that wasn't quite right. Father Underhill was clean-shaven, his uniform fresh and spruce. He had smelled of aftershave when Charlie hugged him. "You look like you're trying to pull yourself together, and it's not quite working."

"No, it's working all right. You didn't see me yesterday." He got to his feet and opened the pew door. "I think I will feel better if I have breakfast, though. I'll just tell the vicar where I'm going—I'm staying at the vicarage, but I've not been a very entertaining guest, and I don't think he'll mind not having to breakfast with me. What an answer to a prayer you are this morning, Charlie."

"Really, Father?" Charlie followed him out of the pew.

"Absolutely. But tell me something." He gestured with his gloves towards the front of the church and lowered his voice. "What *on earth* colour do you think that is supposed to be?"

*

The sun was out now, the air beginning to warm. As they walked back to the Feathers, Father Underhill told Charlie the whole story.

He had been in Italy with his regiment when he received a telegram from his cousin in the Foreign Office, someone Charlie vaguely remembered having heard about. It said, "SARA INJURED IN YORKSHIRE. GOING THERE NOW. WILL UPDATE. GRAHAM." He had been spared the trouble of deserting, he said, only because his commanding officer had a daughter of his own and had been very willing to let him go. It had taken him ten days to get passage to England.

"It shouldn't have taken me that long," he said, "but it's hard to force people to take you places at gunpoint when you're a non-combatant and haven't got a gun."

No update from Graham in the Foreign Office had been waiting for him in London, and no one in the Foreign Office knew where Sara was, or what had happened to Graham after he left for Yorkshire. With no more information than that, he had spent the next three weeks searching Yorkshire for his daughter, and yesterday he had finally found her. She was alive.

Charlie felt weak with relief, but he had realized the story would have to end that way. There was no chance Father Underhill would even have been trying to pull himself together if he had just learned that Sara was dead.

It wouldn't have been fair to say that Sara was Father Underhill's favourite child, because Charlie was sure he was too good a father to have a favourite. But she was his firstborn, his only daughter, the only grandchild his own father had lived to see; she was special in a lot of ways. She was the child who most resembled Father Underhill physically—his sons were lanky, ash-blond, Viking-looking things—but she had inherited Dr. Underhill's intellect, and, Charlie had a suspicion, her spiritual gifts as well. What she had been doing in Yorkshire was a total mystery to Charlie, but he had a feeling he was supposed to know, so he did not ask.

"But you've found her now," he reiterated. "She's all right."

"She's very far from all right. She was in a plane crash, and she was badly injured. She lost her right leg above the knee. I don't know if that's the worst of it, either—she was in a wheelchair, and she looked … Oh, God help me. She's not dead, though, Charlie. She might have been dead, and she's not."

Charlie tried to process the idea of lovely, vibrant Sara Underhill reduced to a cripple for the rest of her life, and then to admit how much even that awful picture was preferable to the thought of there being no "rest of her life" at all, and he felt he had just the faintest inkling of what her father must be suffering.

He said, "So you don't kind of know whether you're coming or going, emotionally."

Father Underhill looked at him. "Well put."

He couldn't think of anything else to say, besides, "That must be awful," which was both obvious and beside the point, because really, what did her father's emotional turmoil matter compared to the terrible fact that she was crippled and the wonderful fact that she was alive? He decided to say nothing.

Father Underhill went on: "I wasn't able to speak to her, because she's still 'on assignment'—though whether that's because it's expected of her, which I can hardly believe, or because she's just clinging to the one thing that she can still do, which I could readily believe, I don't know. But it's fucking absurd, and I'm going to kill Graham Darby either way, when I find out where the hell he's gone to ground."

"'On assignment' doing what?"

"Working for the Foreign Office. Didn't Elsa tell you about that? We let our sixteen-year-old daughter go to work as a spy for the British government. Well, more or less. Actually she was staying with my cousins and the whole thing was unofficial, but they did have her helping with some genuine intelligence work, apparently."

"Yeah, Elsa did tell me." Just in so circumspect a way that he had not worked out that was what it meant. "Sara must have been over the moon about that."

He smiled wryly. "That's largely why we let her do it. Obviously I don't know exactly what she was doing. I don't even know what she was doing on a plane in Yorkshire. It was supposed to be a perfectly safe job, and Darby wasn't going to let her out of his sight. I'm going to kill him *with my bare hands.*"

"Father! I'll lend you my pistol, don't worry."

Father Underhill laughed, but only after he had given Charlie a look as though he might take him up on it.

"More importantly, though, Father—you said she's at Adderley Hall? But she's going by an assumed name, I guess—that's why you couldn't talk to her? What's the name?"

"Um …" For a moment he looked as though he couldn't remember; then he smiled faintly. "Fidelity St. Clair.'"

"Fidelity St. Clair," Charlie repeated, to fix it in his mind. "That's very Sara. Is there anything else I ought to know?"

"What?"

"Anything else I ought to know—about her cover story. You can't see her without blowing her cover, but there's no reason I couldn't be an old friend of the St. Clair family."

"They're American."

"Not a problem. Everybody around here always thinks I'm American myself. Look, if she's well enough, I'll suggest taking her out for a ride—I can get a car from the base, not a wretched jeep with no suspension—and we can meet you at the Feathers, or at St. Bede's. If she's not able to travel yet, I can at least find out more about what's going on and let you know."

"Oh, Charlie. That would be … Thank you."

"It's the least I can do. I'm just glad I can do it."

"Vera has kept me up to date, more or less, concerning you," said Father Underhill, after they had walked a little further in silence. "She told me you had been made squadron leader. It didn't surprise me—I've seen your capacity for command often enough in the sanctuary."

"You didn't think it was a good idea for me to enlist." He said it without bitterness; he didn't feel bitter about it any more, but he did want, finally, to talk about it.

Father Underhill didn't seem surprised by the change of direction. "I just wished you had talked to me first. I could have helped you find some other way to serve that didn't involve …"

"Risking my life?"

"Being in the military. I remembered what it was like, Charlie— how intense everyone's friendships were. I didn't think it would be a good situation for you."

"Oh." This explanation had never occurred to him, and he felt very sorry now for his former self for being so stupid.

"Maybe I was wrong."

"No, you were right."

Father Underhill sighed. "I had a feeling from your letters—especially when they stopped coming—that I might have been right. And I'm sorry. I suppose I should have told you what I was thinking right at the start, but … I realized that you also had the makings of a very good soldier, and you could be of great use. And clearly you have been."

"So you were right again. To nobody's surprise."

He shrugged, with the feigned arrogance that Charlie had always found so charming. "I don't do it on purpose."

"But—don't worry about me, Father."

"I'm inclined not to. You seem happy."

"I am. Something … something pretty incredible's happened to me."

"Oh? Tell me about it."

"When we get back to the Feathers. I'll—I'll introduce you to him."

Father Underhill looked at him appraisingly for a moment. Then he smiled. "I look forward to it. I'm happy for you, Charlie."

"Thank you, Father. That means a lot."

*

They crested the hill above the high street of Newingthorpe, and the sign of the Feathers was swinging in the breeze and caught a flash of sunlight. Charlie had to resist the temptation to run down the hill like a little boy.

In the bar, he pointed Father Underhill to the table by the window and said, "I'll be right back." He nearly collided with the landlady coming out of the kitchen.

"Morning, Mary! Hal down yet?"

"I haven't seen him yet, love. Goodness, tha's blithe this morning!"

"I've brought a friend for breakfast," said Charlie, already heading for the stairs. "Get him everything of the best, whatever he wants!"

Mary laughed and shook her head at him, and he took off up the stairs.

Hal was still in bed, dozing in the sunlight. Charlie leaned down and kissed him, sliding his cold hands in under the covers so that Hal gasped and twisted away.

"Get up," Charlie ordered, "and get dressed and come have breakfast with us."

Hal gathered the bedclothes more firmly around himself. "Who's 'us'?"

"Me and Father Underhill. He showed up at the church. His daughter's been injured and is at that hospital where I found you. But listen. You told me to pray for some guidance, and I did, and it helped. I remembered what I told you about love—even my kind of love, our kind—being maybe a vehicle for Grace, and I remembered I've known that, I've believed that, I've believed God had shown me that. I guess he reminded me of it this morning. I wanted to tell you that. Hope that was sufficiently incoherent. Now get up! We're downstairs at the usual table."

And he bounced up from the bed and was out the door again, afraid that if he stayed to see Hal get up to dress he'd be embarrassingly distracted.

He found Mary leaning against a chair-back at their table, flirting with Father Underhill in a much less motherly way than she flirted with Hal. Figured.

She left, patting her hair and looking flustered, to relay their orders to the cook.

"I'm sorry I stopped writing to you, Father," he said when she was gone. "I'm really sorry about that. It was stupid and thoughtless of me—I haven't any excuse."

"Don't let it worry you. I knew you were basically okay because Vera kept me informed. I didn't even have to ask—she just took it upon herself to give me regular bulletins about everyone. I think she sees it as her war work—keeping the lines of communication open. She's really a very good sister, you know. I don't always give her enough credit."

"I was just thinking that—I mean that she's a good friend. I didn't know she was writing to you about me. I owe her for that."

"Have you met her new man? Do you know anything about him?"

"Vaguely. He's a friend of a friend. I've never heard anything but good of him."

"That's comforting. Elsa had them to dinner, and said he seemed odd but pleasant, and devoted to Vera—which is about as much as one can ask, I suppose."

Hal arrived at the table at the same moment as their breakfast. Mary had brought toast for him along with the food that Charlie and Father Underhill had ordered, and she fussed about sorting out who had ordered what and explaining to Father Underhill the provenance of the jam, and the difficulty she had in procuring good bacon these days. When she was finished, and left, Charlie was finally able to say, "Father Underhill, this is Hal."

And Father Underhill, standing up to shake Hal's hand, said with his brilliant smile, "How d'you do, Hal? I'm Kit."

Hal beamed and said, "I have heard so much about you."

Father Underhill, in typical fashion, did not look embarrassed or say, "Nothing bad, I hope?" or any of the usual things.

"I have not yet had the pleasure of hearing much about you," he said, as they sat down to their breakfast.

"He can't tell you much," said Charlie, feeling suddenly that a discussion of Hal was too much to face before he had some toast and bacon inside him. "He's lost his memory. Hal isn't even his real name—but I had to have something to call him."

"Is that so? Did he give you the name, then?" Father Underhill asked Hal. "And did he tell you where he got it?"

"He did," said Hal, smiling as he spread jam on his toast.

Father Underhill laughed. "Well, you do look like your namesake. Charlie chose well."

Hal looked up at him. "He has been very kind to me."

"If I had to find someone to look after a friend in need," said Father Underhill, "Charlie would be at the very top of my list."

They couldn't talk about Hal, so they talked about Charlie instead. The conversation over breakfast consisted almost entirely of Father Underhill, at Hal's prompting, telling stories from St. John's, things Charlie wouldn't have thought he'd even remember. Flattering stories about Charlie being competent, and funny stories about catastrophes he had averted or coped with or cleaned up after. It was all very nicely judged: embarrassing for Charlie, but not unbearably so. Hal laughed and laughed.

"Shall I tell Father Underhill the story of how we met," said Charlie finally, "or would you like to?"

Hal stopped laughing. "Let's save it."

*

Late in the afternoon, his work done for the day, Charlie borrowed the wing commander's car and drove the couple of miles from the air base to the hospital. The crabby receptionist was not on duty when he entered, and he found his way unhindered to the library. It was deserted except for a couple of card-players, and a girl in a wheelchair reading by herself at the far end. It took Charlie a moment to recognize Sara.

She was wrapped in a fuzzy pink shawl and sat with her remaining leg tucked up under her, so it was not obvious that the other was missing. She looked frail and sick, but she had somehow acquired a boy's haircut that suited her bizarrely well.

She looked up and saw Charlie before he was halfway down the long room.

"Fidelity!" he said. He could see her expression melt into relief. He went on quickly, in case she should think it necessary to give him some kind of alias too: "It's Charlie Boult—do you remember me?"

"Charlie! Of course I remember you. How *perfectly splendid* to see you!"

Fidelity St. Clair, he realized, with a surprised respect, was not just a name; she was a persona, Sara Underhill with a twist, with the volume cranked up all the way. Of course, he hadn't seen her in several years, during which she had grown from a skinny little girl into a beautiful young woman, so it was possible that saying things like "How *perfectly splendid*" was just part of her adult personality. But he didn't think so.

"Your dad told me where you were," he explained. "I'm stationed at the Adderley airbase—if I'd known you were here, I'd have come ages ago."

"Oh, but I haven't been here for ages, only two weeks."

"Still. I'd have come before now." He took a seat beside her chair. "I like the haircut."

"Oh, you *would*. Could I pass myself off as a boy, do you think?"

"'Fraid not. You could've the last time I saw you, but your figure's become much less convincing."

She grinned at this backhanded compliment.

"How are you holding up?" he asked seriously.

"Oh, all right. You heard that I …" She fiddled with the hem of her skirt.

"Yeah. Are they going to get you a wooden leg?"

"Aluminium, but yes. Eventually. It's still too sore right now."

They sat in silence. He felt suddenly unequal to the task of cheering her up—but maybe that was just as well. She'd lost her *leg*. What could anyone really hope to say that would help?

"Your dad would like to hear from you," he said finally. Lowering his voice, he added, "I can … take him a message, or … if you're up to it, I can take you to meet him."

"I'll have to ask the Matron if it's all right," Sara whispered back. "I can't tell them he's my father, so I'll have to make up a story."

"Just say an old family friend wants to take you out for a drive."

She nodded. "Simple is best, right?" She looked up as a couple of girls came into the library from the nearer door. Sara was subtly replaced by Fidelity St. Clair once more. "Time to meet the gang."

Chapter Nineteen

FOR ANY TERROR BY NIGHT

"Popular, isn't she?" Rosalind remarked as she and Evvie came into the library to find Fidelity sitting with the tall, dark-haired RAF officer whose name Evvie had forgotten.

Evvie chose to ignore the comment. She was puzzled, though. Wasn't he involved somehow, in something? She remembered now: he had been in possession of Anderson's bag at some point before it turned up filled with bloody vestments.

"Charlie, these are my friends Evgenia and Rosalind," Fidelity was saying. "Evgenia, Rosalind, my old friend Charlie Boult. Charlie's known me all my life."

"And more," said Charlie. "I served her parents' wedding."

"Served what?" Rosalind asked, flopping into a chair opposite Fee.

"Cake," Fidelity supplied brightly. "Charlie's a baker on civvy street."

Charlie opened his mouth as if to contradict that, then appeared to change his mind, and settled for saying, "Well, when your parents were married, I was an *apprentice* baker—I was only seventeen."

"A mere child! Can you believe I'm *twenty* now, Charlie?"

"Wow. That is hard to believe."

Evvie could see Charlie considering how old this would make him, if he had been seventeen at least nine months before Fidelity was born, and not being too happy about it. He was clearly in the secret, somehow, but hadn't had a chance to work out with Sara all the details of her story.

They chatted vapidly for a while in this vein. Rosalind said that she was grateful for rationing, in a way, because she'd been trying to slim by avoiding sweets before the war, and it was so much easier now that you weren't *allowed* to overeat. A nurse came to fetch Fidelity for an appointment with Dr. Sheppard, and Rosalind left with them, self-importantly pushing Fidelity's chair. Evvie turned to look at Squadron Leader Boult, who sat back down in his chair after Rosalind and Fee left.

"They didn't brief you very well, did they?" she said. "I could see her feeding you details about her cover story."

He stared at her warily.

"You are from the Foreign Office, aren't you?" Evvie said, and then wondered if this had been terribly, dangerously stupid.

He shook his head. "No, just the RAF, as advertised. So … what happened to Graham Whatsisname?"

"What?"

They looked tensely at one another for a moment. Finally understanding dawned.

"Oh! I'm not a spy either," she said.

"Oh."

There was another awkward silence.

"Probably just as well," he said. "It doesn't seem like either of us would be very good at it."

She laughed, and so did he. But she realized she was still confused.

"So you really are an old friend of … Sara?"

"Yes."

"And you did bake her parents' wedding cake?"

"No, I'm not sure what that was about. I served their wedding—served as an acolyte, I mean, at the Mass."

"Oh, yes, but you see, Fidelity is a Baptist, that's why she stopped you saying that."

"Got it! I *wasn't* briefed very well. I ran into her father, and offered to come here to find out the lay of the land—he doesn't really know what's going on."

"Nobody really knows what's going on. She hasn't heard from Graham Darby since she got here."

"Darby! That was the name. Yeah, he's dropped off the face of the earth, apparently. That's why her dad had such a hard time finding her—"

"—and didn't know her cover story—"

"—and then, I'm guessing, burst in here in his chaplain's uniform, which didn't fit the cover story—"

"He was in civilian clothes, but with a clerical collar. And he made such a fuss that no one is likely to forget him."

"Yeah, that's him all over. So are you the only one Sara's confided in? I gather your friend Rosalind doesn't know."

"No," said Evvie, "she doesn't. It's just me."

Fidelity returned to the library without Rosalind, wheeling her chair by herself in what seemed a deliberate display of competence.

"Matron says I can go," she reported.

"You know, if you're supposed to be twenty, you needn't even have asked permission," said Charlie drily.

"I wasn't asking permission—I was asking to make sure they think it's a good idea. I am a patient, you know, I'm supposed to be under their supervision. Anyway, you're just sore because you talked your-self into a corner saying you were seventeen at my parents' wedding, so now you're nearly *forty*."

Charlie shrugged. "I don't look a day over thirty-five, though. Do people *believe* you when you tell them you're twenty?"

"Yes," said Evvie. "I did. I think everyone else does, too."

"It's all about how you say it," Sara explained. "You have to almost believe it yourself, to make it work."

Charlie got to his feet. "I have to get going, but I'll come back tomorrow afternoon. Around this time—or no, actually I can come earlier tomorrow. I'm on leave tomorrow." He gave a big stretch of satisfaction, and Evvie smiled, thinking he must have something planned for his day off that he looked forward to. "Shall we say three o'clock?"

"We'll be waiting. Oh—I want to bring Evvie, is that all right?"

"Sure thing. Unless …" He narrowed his eyes at her. "You're not making sure to have a chaperone so that *somebody* doesn't get the wrong idea?"

"What?" Sara gave him a mystified look.

"So you don't make somebody jealous, he means," said Evvie, who had got it.

"Jealous? Who?"

"*I* don't know," said Charlie. "But apparently they all think you're twenty around here, so …" He shrugged.

"Oh!" Sara finally got it, and began to blush immediately. "No! No, no, no! There's nobody like that, and I wouldn't, anyway! Wouldn't do that to you, I mean."

"No, I know. Calm down. I was one hundred per cent joking." He put a hand on the arm of the wheelchair and bent down to kiss her forehead, the bit that was accessible past the fringe of her man's haircut. "I'll see you tomorrow at three."

Evvie watched him walk away across the library. He moved with an unassuming grace that was beautiful in such a big man. His voice and his whole manner were like that too, Evvie thought: gentle, with an underlying hint of force effortlessly held in abeyance. Very attractive, in a complex way. So this was what Sara liked. She smiled to herself.

"I had a tremendous crush on him before he joined up and left for England," said Sara, as the library door closed behind him.

"Yes, dear. I was a nun, not a Martian."

Sara shot her a look. "I got over it," she said primly. "Intellectually, anyway. Not that it would have mattered."

"He does seem to be literally twice your age. Oh!" Evvie started up from her seat. "Sa—Fee! I've just remembered. The other place where I saw Charlie! He was in the lodge, just before Ernest said something had disappeared from a box. You don't suppose he knows anything about … about what's been going on?"

*

Evvie was woken that night by a soft tapping at her bedroom door.

"Who is it?" she called from her bed.

"Evvie? It's Rosalind. Can I come in?"

"Rosalind? Yes, of course."

The door inched open and Rosalind slipped inside. Evvie turned on the light beside her bed and sat up.

"Sorry to wake you," said Rosalind, standing awkwardly on the rug in her robe and slippers. "It's just—I thought I'd rather it were you than one of the nurses. I mean … we might have to tell them, but—I figured you'd know what to do."

Evvie tossed back her blankets and sat cross-legged on the bed. "Want to come sit down?" she suggested, foreseeing that she was in for a long story.

"Thanks." Rosalind came and perched on the edge of the bed. "They gave you a small bedroom, didn't they? Do all the staff have rooms like this?"

"The other staff sleep in the servants' quarters, so their rooms are even smaller. This was the night nurse's room, when there were children in the household. It's next door to the nursery."

"I see. I think I caught Daphne fooling around with one of the patients."

"What, just now?"

"Mm-hm."

"Oh. How—how unpleasant for you!"

Rosalind gave a surprised little laugh. "Thanks. I hadn't even thought about that—I mean, I hadn't thought of telling you for sympathy, you know. But it—it was unpleasant. It was a bit of a shock, actually."

"I expect it would be. You said … you *think*. Which part of it are you unsure of?"

"Um … oh. Good question. No, I'm sure of the whole thing, actually. I'm just not sure what to do about it. Here's the thing. I was going down to the kitchen to get myself a snack—I couldn't sleep, and I was hungry. Actually, I still am, because I never made it to the kitchen. It's sort of hard to get there from this wing of the house, and I'd never done it in the dark before, and I got turned around and went in the door to the great hall—I mean the ward—by accident. And when I came back out, in that sort of anteroom off the hall, someone was coming out another door—not the door to the office, but another door, I don't know what it leads to …"

Evvie pictured the anteroom and the arrangement of doors. "The supply closet. It's supposed to always be locked."

"Well, it's not locked now, because I saw Daphne coming out of it. There was moonlight coming in the window, so I could see her quite clearly, though she couldn't see me. She was doing up the buttons of her dress as she came out." Rosalind screwed up her face in an expression of distaste. "And I heard a man's voice from inside where she'd just come out of, trying to be quiet, you know, but calling after her, 'You can't leave me like this!' He sounded quite wretched, actually—not like he was just a jilted lover, but like he might really be in a jam. That was what gave me the idea it was one of the patients, and that …" She couldn't voice the rest of the thought.

"It definitely wasn't Ernest, though?"

"It definitely wasn't Ernest. He has quite a gravelly voice, and this sounded like a younger man."

"And she left him there?"

Rosalind nodded, lips pressed together. "And shut the door on him. I stayed where I was, and she went up the stairs, and I waited for her to get back to her room, and then I came straight here. I figured you'd know the best thing to do."

"Well, thanks," said Evvie, sliding off the bed and grabbing her robe. "I don't know that I do know the *best* thing to do, but I'll give it a shot."

"Are you going to go let him out?" said Rosalind, following her to the door. "I suppose I could have done that."

"It's okay. I can go in pretending I'm looking for painkillers for one of the men who's having a bad night, and act all surprised to find him there, and ask no questions. It'll be less embarrassing for him all round."

In fact, it didn't turn out quite like that. Evvie opened the supply-closet door, ready to utter a stagey little cry of surprise, only to find it replaced by a very genuine gasp of alarm. In the moonlight she could see Captain Carter sitting on the floor inside the door, head lolling back against the cupboard behind him, his pyjama shirt unbuttoned, an empty pill bottle in his hand. His one empty pyjama leg trailed across the floor like a limp flag.

He was still conscious, though he was very groggy. He must just have swallowed the pills; in fact, he had still got some of them in his mouth, and spat them obediently into the basin that Evvie held out for him. When she suggested he put his own finger down his throat rather than making her do it for him, he did it docilely enough.

"Oh, God," he moaned, wiping his mouth on his sleeve after the first round of vomiting. "She was right—I'm pathetic as well as disgusting. Haven't even the courage to kill myself properly."

"Nonsense," said Evvie. She pushed him gently back up against the cupboard and began doing up the buttons on his pyjama top. "You've the courage to go on living, which is *much* better. Okay— better have another go at throwing up, while I go get your crutches so you don't have to explain how you got in here. Then I'll get a nurse to look after you properly."

Carter leaned dutifully over the basin again. Evvie waited to see that he was more or less steady, then darted out of the supply closet, across the dark anteroom to the door of the ward. She glanced up at the stairs, half expecting to see Rosalind hovering—but she had apparently stayed upstairs. Just as well.

The night nurse was dozing at her station, as Evvie had assumed she would be—it explained how Carter and Daphne had got out of the ward in the first place. She found Carter's bed—fortunately she remembered where it was—gathered up his crutches soundlessly, and made it back out of the ward without detection. She found Captain Carter leaning back against the cupboard again, already looking rather better.

"Why are you doing this for me?" he asked, as she set the crutches down next to him.

"Because I know what happened, and I don't want you to feel embarrassed about it."

"Oh." He looked for a moment as if having her know what had happened—and she didn't, entirely, nor did she want to—was just about the worst thing he could imagine. She remembered him asking whether she had a sweetheart when she helped him down to the ward.

"Don't worry about me knowing," she said. "I was never a good bet. I have my heart set on becoming a nun, you see. I can't let myself get distracted by every pair of charming blue eyes I come across."

And just like that, she'd at last found the right thing to say to Captain Carter. He was flattered; he was awed. He goggled at her in amazement and started to blush at the same time. He had never looked more attractive.

Evvie smiled as she got up and went to fetch the nurse.

*

Rosalind was waiting for her outside her bedroom door. "What happened?" she whispered. "I heard a fuss. Is he all right?"

"I think so. The nurses are looking after him. He'd taken a bunch of pills."

"Oh, God! And I just left him there!"

"You didn't know."

Lady Rathburn's bedroom door opened. "Girls? What's going on?"

"Sorry to wake you, Lady Rathburn," said Evvie. "I'm afraid Captain Carter tried to kill himself. I found him in the supply closet when I went down to get myself a painkiller. I was having cramps," she added. This was actually true, though they hadn't been bad enough to keep her awake, and were quite gone now. "I think Carter will be all right. He was still conscious when I got there, and I think he threw up all the pills."

"How did he get into the supply closet?" asked Lady Rathburn, cinching in the belt of her dressing-gown.

"I don't know," said Evvie honestly. "The door was unlocked when I tried it."

"Did you know it was unlocked?" Lady Rathburn's voice was sharp. "How were you going to get in yourself?"

"I borrowed the key from the office," said Evvie, holding it up. She had gone to fetch it after leaving the nurse with Carter, partly to give colour to this story, and partly to check that it was still in its usual place, which it had been.

"Of course," said Lady Rathburn distractedly. "I'm sorry. I had better go down and see how the poor fellow is getting on. I really can't understand it—he seemed in good spirits lately."

Rosalind and Evvie were left alone in the corridor.

"Well," said Rosalind, "I guess there's nothing for it but to go to bed and try to sleep. Though after that, I'm not sure how I ever will."

Evvie thought to offer to lend her a book, but the one she had most recently finished and still had on her bedside table featured a gruesome murder made to look like a suicide, and she wasn't sure Rosalind would appreciate that. She said good-night instead, and watched Rosalind walk down to the far end of the corridor and disappear into her own room.

She heard the soft click of a door opening, and looked across the hall. Daphne was standing in her own darkened doorway, still in the long black-and-white dress she had been wearing at dinner. She had taken her hair down—or it had come down, anyway—and it fell messily around her shoulders. She was barefoot, and held her crumpled-up stockings in one hand.

"Did you hear much of what we were saying?" Evvie asked.

"Every word," said Daphne. She leaned one hip against the doorframe and ran the silk stockings delicately through her fingers. Evvie's eye was caught, in a dreamlike, unreal way, by a ring on her thumb, a strange, distinctive man's seal ring, the stone a flat red, like wax or blood.

"Well, you'll be glad to hear it looks like he'll be all right," Evvie heard herself say, sticking to what seemed a reasonable script, although Daphne's demeanour seemed chillingly unreasonable.

Daphne gave a little laugh. Evvie found herself reaching back for the knob of her own door and wanting to disappear through it. Instead she remained standing where she was.

Evvie went on: "He said a funny thing, you know, when I found him. He said, 'She was right—I am pathetic and disgusting.' But he wasn't talking about you, was he? You wouldn't have told him he was pathetic or disgusting—a wounded soldier whom you'd just seduced—you wouldn't have done that, would you?"

"And what did *you* tell him? Did you tell him he's heroic and lovely?" Daphne's voice was liquid with mockery. "No, not lovely—I don't suppose you told him he's lovely. He's not really your cup of tea, is he? You'd like someone with a face like *mine* much better, wouldn't you, Evgenia? How sickening."

"Daphne!" Evvie let go of the doorknob in her shock. "How can you behave like this? Your beauty is a gift from God—how can you use it like a weapon against other people? How can you hate yourself so much?"

Daphne had frozen in the doorway, stockings dangling from one fist. She glared wildly at Evvie for a moment before ducking back inside her room and slamming the door.

Evvie heard her last words echo in the stillness. In Greek.

Chapter Twenty

A PASTORAL PROBLEM

Charlie was late arriving back at the Feathers that evening, because the car he'd borrowed from the base got a flat tire on the return journey. It was dark by the time he got in, and Mary told him that Hal had already eaten, after waiting some time for him. He took a plate of leftovers from the kitchen and went up to Hal's room.

"It's me," he said, around a mouthful of bread, shouldering the door open without knocking.

Hal was lying on his bed in the dark. He started up at Charlie's entrance.

"Sorry to scare you," said Charlie.

"No, I—" Hal covered his confusion by reaching for the lamp. Its light showed the bed still made, himself fully dressed. He didn't look as though he had been sleeping. "I'm glad to see you."

"I'm glad to see you too, darling." He sat down on the bed beside Hal, putting his plate of food on the nearby chair. "I'm sorry I'm so late. Were you worried?"

"Yes, I suppose so."

He held out his arms, and Hal leaned into them. He still seemed tense, though, almost wary.

"I visited Sara at the hospital, and then got a flat tire on the way home, that's what took me so long." He stroked Hal's back and buried his face in his hair. "Did I tell you Sara's the one who named you? I mean the window you're based on."

"No, I didn't realize that."

"You'll have to meet her. She'll like you. Her dad does, I could tell."

"Could you?"

"Of course. Were you worried about that?"

Hal pulled gently out of Charlie's embrace. "Yes, quite. You should eat your dinner."

Charlie picked up his plate from the chair. "If you want to be left alone …"

"No. I don't like being alone."

"Good, because that was sort of a bluff."

Hal laughed shortly, and leaned back against the bed's head while Charlie dug into his dinner.

"I filched an extra piece of cake for you if you want it," he pointed out, between mouthfuls. "I know what you're like."

"I never refuse cake, it's true," said Hal, taking it from the side of the plate.

"So I'm officially on leave now. We could do something, if you wanted—go somewhere."

"What about your friend?"

"Who? Father Underhill?"

"Yes. Have you seen him again?"

"No, not yet. I was planning to go over this evening to tell him I'd seen Sara, but I don't know if it's too late. That reminds me—why'd you stop me telling Father Underhill the whole story about you this morning? You remember what I've told you about him—you know he won't have any trouble believing it."

"I am sure he won't."

Charlie set aside his empty plate, and turned on the bed to look at Hal properly in the lamplight. "What's eating you? It's something to do with Father Underhill, isn't it?"

"In a way." Hal met his gaze. He was sitting up straight, and looked very composed, which Charlie had learned could mean anything. "I think you will find, when you tell him the story of how you found me, that he gives it a different interpretation than you do. I think your priest may be much savvier than you are."

"No doubt. About what?"

"About me. It would not take much. You have been *quite remarkably* naïve."

"Excuse me?"

"You never asked me what I am," Hal said softly. "You didn't wait for me to explain, either—not that I would have. You came up with the idea of my being an angel all on your own."

"I didn't come up with it on my own! It was very obvious. What else would you be?"

"Oh, Charles. It is much more likely that I am a devil."

There was a stillness in which all the air seemed to have gone out of the room. In the lamplight, Hal's hair looked the colour of flame, his skin very white, his eyes dark and smoky. Charlie felt as if the world had slipped out of his hands and shattered on the floor, and he couldn't go back to the moment before he had let it fall. He was sitting awkwardly on the bed, twisted around to look at Hal, but he couldn't move. He heard noises from the bar downstairs: voices, laughter.

"Are you?" he said finally, feeling as if he hadn't spoken in years.

"I don't know," said Hal, his voice flat. "I can't remember."

Charlie turned finally, put his hands on his knees. "I see."

"You found me in a stone box," said Hal, very quietly. "I claim not to remember how I got there, but you shouldn't believe that. You shouldn't believe anything I say. I was summoned and imprisoned, Charles. My captors asked me to perform tasks for them—*they* certainly thought they knew what I was. You don't know my name or what I look like, beyond a form I created for the sole purpose of making you like me and help me." After a moment he added, "I think I hardly need mention the sex. Even you had your doubts about that." There was a mocking lightness in his tone now. Charlie heard him move behind him, get up from the bed. "I hoped that I might have been wrong, that you had some suspicion, had thought about it, weighed the probabilities even—but I didn't really believe that."

"No. It never crossed my mind." He looked back at Hal, who was standing behind the bed now, in shadow. "And you're telling me this now because … because you thought I was about to find out."

"Yes. I did not think the question would arise for some time. Oh, I knew it would eventually. I knew once we returned to Toronto, I would be faced with that man, and you would surely tell him about me. I planned to leave you before that happened."

"You planned to leave me."

"I planned to lie to you, to say something about Heaven—you would have been sad, but it would have been exactly what you expected. I thought perhaps, if I did that … I had unorthodox ideas about redemption." He sounded contemptuous. "Very stupid, no doubt."

"But you … how long have you been thinking this?"

"How long?" He shrugged. "Forever? I don't remember Heaven, I can't hear music, I don't know who I am. I have been thinking it all along. The very fact that I didn't tell you until now is a strong argument in favour of its being true."

Now that it was out in the open, Charlie could think of several times when Hal had probably been on the verge of telling him. He remembered how he had himself been the first one to use the word "angel," and Hal had commented on it. He remembered how Hal had resisted any suggestion that Charlie had been divinely led to aid him.

"No! You're telling me now—why would you do that if … I mean, it's ridiculous."

Hal was standing in the shadows with his arms folded, his hip propped against the edge of the windowsill. "It might be any number of things, Charles, but 'ridiculous' is not one of them."

"Shit, Hal—you really knew all along that this was a possibility? All the time we were … fucking, and I thought, 'This is okay, this has to be okay, *he's an angel*'? You were thinking, 'Well, I might be a devil'?"

Hal straightened up, took a step forward into the edge of the lamplight. He looked down at Charlie, who was still seated on the bed. There was a little smile tugging at the corners of his lips, of a kind Charlie had never seen there before.

"No," he said silkily. "That is not what I was ever thinking."

Charlie stared up at him. "You're being creepy on purpose to scare me away, because you really don't know what you are."

Something rapacious and very, very convincing flashed in Hal's eyes. "Oh!" he said, and the smile cracked open, horribly. "Would you like to think that?"

"You don't need to bother, actually." Charlie got up from the bed, his fists clenched to keep his hands from shaking. "We're done. We're not even friends any more. Not because you might be a devil—Christ, that's idiotic. You're not a devil—you're just kind of a shitty angel. You weren't honest with me, and I don't trust you, and we're through. You can seduce some other sucker into looking after you. Or—let's face it—you can look after yourself perfectly fine." As an afterthought he added, "You stay the fuck away from Father Underhill, though. He's been through enough."

*

There was a light in the front room of the St. Bede's vicarage, glowing behind the drawn curtains. Charlie paced the length of the fenced-in front yard. He blew his nose and dried his eyes with the corner of his handkerchief and tried to gather his thoughts. He wasn't sure of any of the things he had said to Hal. He didn't know Hal wasn't a devil; he didn't know that at all. The possibility had truly never occurred to him, but now that it had, it was terrifying. But he hadn't stopped loving Hal, either. He was angry, sure, but mostly he was aggrieved, hurt—and in a way that he knew he could get over. Hell, it felt like it could almost have been one of those things that happened to married people, where they could recover from some big explosion of grief and anger because there was so much at stake, could even come out of it feeling that their love was stronger than ever. If Hal really was an angel—if Hal was even just *human*—he could easily see that happening. He could see this looking, in retrospect, like a rocky bit at the beginning of the best thing in his whole life. If only it wasn't all a monstrous trap, if only the whole thing wasn't some kind of ghoulish illusion. If Hal wasn't a devil.

He looked up at the dark sky, remembering the thing he had been in the habit of saying to himself as his wheels left the runway. *No one could say I haven't lived an interesting life.*

Damn straight. And yet, set against all this dramatic metaphysical stuff was that simple, unexpected answer to his prayer in St. Bede's. It was just because it was so simple that he still felt a strong conviction that *that* came from God. But what, under the circumstances, did it mean?

He opened the vicarage gate and went up the walk to the door.

It was opened at his knock by the vicar himself, who was tall and middle-aged, with a round, red face. Charlie couldn't remember his name.

"How may I help you?" the vicar asked, his eyes crinkling up at the corners as he smiled.

"I've come to see Father Underhill. Is he in?"

He was, and he had appeared in the hall behind the vicar, in civilian clericals, a glass of something in one hand.

"Charlie! I was hoping you might call."

"Come in, then, come in," said the vicar, holding wide the door. "What will you have to drink?"

"I, um … I'm fine, thank you."

It must have been clear from his voice, and his face now that he was in the lamplit hall, that he wasn't really fine.

"I will be in my study," said the vicar tactfully. "The sitting-room is at your disposal." He gestured to the door Father Underhill had come out of, and took himself off down the hall.

Charlie was left standing in the entry with Father Underhill looking at him expectantly. With an effort, he recalled what would be uppermost in the priest's mind. "I've been to the hospital to see Sara," he said.

"Splendid," said Father Underhill. "You didn't come about that."

Charlie shook his head, feeling both defeated and relieved.

"Come in and sit down," Father Underhill suggested.

Charlie followed him into the sitting-room, which was a High-Church-flavoured, pipe-smoke-scented bachelor's cave of extraordinary untidiness.

"Reminds me a bit of Henley's place," Charlie remarked, as Father Underhill shifted a pile of newspapers from a chair near the fireplace.

"That," said Father Underhill, picking up a book from the mantel, "is not a coincidence. They're friends. That's how I knew to come here when I needed a place to stay in Yorkshire."

The book was Henley's *Hypostatic Union in the Writings of Saint Cyril of Alexandria*, and Father Underhill flipped open the cover to show Charlie that it was inscribed by the author.

"I never managed to finish that," Charlie admitted.

"Neither did I." He put the book back on the mantel and picked up his glass again. "I kept falling asleep. Elsa told me more or less what it was about. Even she thought it was pretty dry. I'll get you some of this Scotch—I think you'll like it."

He went to the sideboard while Charlie sank down in the chair he had emptied of newspapers. It was very odd to find himself in a room that could have been Henley's, talking to Father Underhill, here on the far side of the Atlantic. Especially so soon after having all the breath knocked out of him by Hal's revelation. It had the air of a dream.

He stared into the fire as a cold apprehension gripped him at the thought of dreams. He looked up to find Father Underhill standing in front of his chair, giving him a worried look. He held out the glass of Scotch, and Charlie accepted it.

"Talk," said Father Underhill. He leaned against the back of the chair opposite Charlie instead of sitting in it.

Charlie took a gulp of his drink and tried to pull himself together. "Listen—Father. Before I get—I mean, you're right, I didn't come about Sara, but I was going to, before I—before this other thing happened. I did see her, and she's all right, actually. She's recovering really well, her friend told me—the one you met, Evvie—and you were right that she was just keeping up her cover story because she didn't know what else to do. She'd no idea why she hadn't had word from your cousin, or why you hadn't shown up—she thought Darby would have told you her false identity, and you'd have to pretend to be a soap kingpin when you came to see her. She was pretty upset at the idea of you tearing across Europe and turning Yorkshire upside down looking for her."

"Oh, for—nobody needed to tell her that happened! It wasn't her fault."

"I don't know that anybody did tell her. I didn't. But it's not hard to work out what you would have done."

Father Underhill sighed and drank the last of his Scotch. "Still. It's not the point."

"Well, she's in good shape, all things considered. I said I'd come back to pick her up tomorrow and bring her to see you."

"But that was before 'this other thing' that happened?"

"Oh, that doesn't change anything. I'll still be able to do that. I've got three days' leave and … nothing much to do with it now."

Father Underhill came around and sat in the chair, putting his empty glass on the hearth, next to a teacup and an overflowing ashtray.

"You know," he said, leaning back in his chair, "I really did like him. But I wondered … well, whether it might be a bad sign that he wasn't at church with you."

Charlie dropped his head into his free hand. "There's two possible reasons—and you're right, neither of them is good. It was either because he couldn't have come in the door, or because he thinks he *might* not be able to, and doesn't want to know for sure." He took another gulp of Scotch, numbly noticing that it really was very pleasant. "I'll explain."

"Mm. It sounds like you'd better."

He told the story of the sarcophagus in the ugly Victorian outbuilding, of escaping with Hal in the stolen car and the stolen airplane, and of what Hal had just told him. He skated over the part in the middle, but he didn't think Father Underhill was fooled.

"I must admit that's not *quite* what I was expecting," Father Underhill said when he was finished.

"But you can see that he's right, can't you? He's more likely to be a devil than an angel, and I've been incredibly stupid."

"Did he say you'd been stupid?"

"No, he said 'naïve.'"

"I see. Because I agree that he's most likely a devil, but I don't think you've been stupid. He looked like an angel."

"He didn't really behave like an angel," said Charlie quietly.

"No. Well."

"I think I was so excited by the idea that something like that was happening to me—you know, something out of the ordinary, something …"

Father Underhill nodded. "I know."

"I think it blinded me to what I should've seen. That there's no reason an angel would have been trapped in a fucking sarcophagus."

"Yes, it is certainly the sort of thing one associates more readily with devils. There's also the fact that … well, this is information that you weren't to know, Charlie, but do you remember when we visited my cousins in Warwickshire in '38?"

"Yes. Sara told me some story about a … magic ring and a devil in a soup tureen—I thought she was making it up. That was in the days when she …"

"Had a crush on you and spent a lot of time trying to impress you?"

"I didn't realize you'd noticed that."

"Of course I had."

Of course he had. "You think there's some kind of connection? With the ring? Or the soup tureen."

"The ring. It was stolen in April of last year. Graham wanted Sara to help him look for it, as she seems to have some kind of affinity with it. Or disaffinity—it gives her headaches. That's what she came here for."

"Oh, God. I've made a real fool of myself."

"You've been—it would seem—taken in by the Prince of Lies. It happens. It happens *all the time*. And for what it's worth, Charlie— which, though, is emphatically not a lot—I meant it when I said liked Hal. I thought he seemed a thoroughly decent chap."

Charlie managed a laugh. "Thanks. The thing is, Father … at the end he did the right thing. He warned me off. First he just laid it out for me, and said, you know, 'You shouldn't actually believe anything I say because you don't know what I am.' Then he realized he was still acting like he cared, and that wasn't really getting the message across, so he put on a little show of not caring—which *almost* worked, because it started to make me mad. But I called his bluff. I said you're just doing this to try to scare me off. All he would have had to do to reel me in at that point was say, 'You've got me, Charles—that's what I was doing.' But he didn't. He cranked up his devil impersonation—he practically grew horns. And I shouted a bunch of stuff and took off. But I still don't believe it. I don't believe he's a devil. He's right—he's done enough shitty unangelic things, starting with letting me believe what I wanted to believe, that he can't be pure goodness or anything like that. But does that neces- sarily mean he's the opposite? Can he be an angel who just made some bad choices? Does that even make sense?"

Father Underhill was leaning back in his chair, chin resting on the fingers of one hand. Charlie remembered telling Hal how he had thought, *I'm just a fucking pastoral problem.* He was really excelling himself tonight on that front. *The poor man comes to Yorkshire frantic about his missing daughter, and before he has a chance to catch his breath, you burst in to tell him you think you may have been having an affair with a devil.* Then he realized that the expression on Father Underhill's face was just thoughtful.

"It makes about as much sense as anything, I suppose. I'm not sure what Dionysius the Whatchamacallit would have to say about it—Father Burgess could probably tell us, *in detail*—but I'm not sure that's relevant, either."

"But do you think … No. I'm sorry. It's not fair."

"Of course it's fair." He leaned forward in his chair, elbows on his knees, blue eyes looking straight at Charlie. "Here's what I think. I've known you a long time, Charlie, and I think you are a moral man, and that you have good instincts about people." He stood up, picking up his glass from the hearth and reaching for Charlie's, which was empty by this time. "I don't think you should go back there tonight, though. If you're right, he's probably left—but if he's still there, it's either because you're wrong, or because he hadn't the courage to go through with his plan of properly jilting you. Either way, better if you're not there. I'll ask Father Burgess if he can accommodate another guest for the night."

"Thank you, Father. I don't know what I'd do without you. I …" He was teetering on the edge of some kind of embarrassing declaration—tears, maybe, something awful. He didn't know how to stop it …

"Thank *you*," said Father Underhill, with one of his classic smiles. "This makes me feel like I'm doing my job. Which, as you know, I enjoy."

*

"So you met a devil when you were a teenager?" Hal had said one evening, while he was still bedridden, lying there languorously under the covers, Charlie sitting on his chair by the bed. "What was that like?"

"Terrifying! It broke down the door of the church in the middle of the service. At first it didn't look like anything—just kind of a shape, like a thing all wrapped in cloth. Then later it took a form … a naked woman, who looked like Dr. Underhill—Miss Nordqvist, I mean, as she was then. I was close enough to have hit it with the thurible. I could have given it a solid whack. Except of course it looked like a girl, and you don't hit girls, you definitely don't hit girls with thuribles. Maybe in another minute I'd have been able to work up the courage to do it—I knew it wasn't really a human woman, but still … "

"So it looked perfectly human, then?"

"Oh, yeah. To me, anyway. I know some people can see through the disguise—sense something off, you know—but I don't think I'm one of them. I expect you have to be an awful lot saintlier than me."

Hal had changed the subject after that, and the evening had ended with Charlie showing Hal how to play solitaire, something that—as Charlie reflected later, in his own bed—Hal could certainly have figured out on his own, but had for some reason preferred to let Charlie explain.

For some reason. Because he had been falling in love with Charlie, and liked to listen to him talk. Liked to lie there, looking perfectly human, and watch Charlie embarrass himself explaining a card game to a being as old as the world. Knew that every moment Charlie spent in his company, no matter what the pretext, sunk his heart a little deeper into the abyss of his love.

But Father Underhill had liked Hal. Not just thought he was human, but liked him. Surely that had to count for something? Charlie didn't think Father Underhill had ever liked that awful thing that had disguised itself as Elsa twenty years ago.

He surprised himself by sleeping for a few hours that night. When he came downstairs in the morning, he found his host in the dining room, breakfasting by himself on food obviously prepared by a housekeeper or cook or whatever they called it around here.

"Father Underhill has gone out for a walk, in spite of the menace of rain," the vicar explained. He rose and moved some clutter from the table to clear another place. "Do join me. Charlie, isn't it? I hope you feel that the world looks somewhat brighter in the morning—as I so often find. Though," he added quickly, holding up a hand, "you should feel no obligation to answer that. I am merely wittering on like the tedious old bachelor that I am. Now then—would you care for some kippers?"

His plate filled with food, Charlie sat down and agreed in a general way that things did always look better in the morning, and Father Burgess beamed pleasantly at him.

"I understand from Father Underhill that you and I have a mutual friend in Father Tom Henley."

Charlie looked down at his plate and realized that he wasn't hungry. "That's right. He and I were acolytes together for years at St. John's. He went off to get ordained and then teach at the university, and I stuck around and took over running the guild."

"Ah, I see! I understand now why Father Underhill spoke so highly of you. You must have made yourself indispensable."

"And how did you and Tom meet?" Charlie tried to change the subject, embarrassed. He wasn't terribly keen on talking about church at all, actually, but he had a feeling that Father Burgess didn't talk about much else.

"Ah, well, I should perhaps more properly have described myself as an admirer—I have corresponded with Father Henley regularly since I read his excellent book, but we have not yet had the opportunity to meet. As a matter of fact, I had no idea he was so young—I gather he is your contemporary?"

"Roughly. I think he's a couple of years older."

"Yes, you see, *I* thought that he was a contemporary of Father Underhill—it led to a most amusing misunderstanding the other night. I was simply flabbergasted when Father Underhill spoke of Father Henley being formerly among the young servers in his parish—though to tell the truth, I had also rather underestimated Father Underhill's age." He gave a laugh which was almost a giggle. "He turns out to be a year my senior, in fact! I would never have guessed it. I must say that he has aged remarkably *gracefully*."

In fact, thought Charlie, you think he's hot stuff. Why can't we just admit that and have a good laugh about it instead of giggling coyly like this? Not that he, Charlie, was giggling. He poked glumly at a kipper. Who was he to criticize Father Burgess, anyway? As far as he could tell, the vicar was doing just fine with his life of self-denial—if that's what it was. Charlie was the one who couldn't hack it.

"There's something I've been wondering," said Charlie, forcing himself to swallow a mouthful of fish. "It's a theological question. About angels. Do they—I mean, they do have free will, don't they? As far as we know?"

Father Burgess looked up from his breakfast in mild surprise. Charlie could see him hesitating between scholarly and pastoral modes, trying to decide which was required here. Finally he settled on a compromise.

"Theologians have generally agreed that they do, yes. They must, in order for some of them to have chosen to turn from God. But being passionless and in eternity, you see, their decision once made is irrevocable. Aquinas addresses the question quite definitively. As a matter of fact, I think I have that volume around here somewhere, as I was referring to it only the other day. Let me see." He got up, a half-eaten slice of toast in one hand, and began rummaging among the books on his sideboard.

"But what about when they leave eternity? When they visit earth?" That made it sound like he was talking about space aliens in a pulp novel.

Father Burgess paused at the sideboard and absent-mindedly

took another bite of his toast. He seemed to decide that they were venturing into the territory of imaginative fiction, and a different kind of answer was warranted.

"I have always imagined," he said thoughtfully, almost dreamily, "that an angel appearing in the stream of time is rather like a man leaning in at an open window. You know, he can talk to the occupants of the room, perhaps even touch them, but his feet are still planted firmly in the outside world—that is, in eternity. That is how I see it." He looked slightly embarrassed. "Of course, that is necessarily pure conjecture. For a more authoritative view, you might read … let me see … "

"Don't worry about it," said Charlie. "It was just something that occurred to me—it's not important."

"Ah," said Father Burgess, looking unconvinced. He cast one more glance at the books on the sideboard before he sat down again with the remnants of his toast. "I don't know what's become of that volume of the *Summa*. But it must be somewhere—if you should change your mind and want to take a look, I'll happily hunt it up for you."

Father Underhill returned, eventually, in his uniform and greatcoat, but bareheaded, his grey hair glamorously windswept. He came through the French doors from the garden while Charlie was still trying to finish his breakfast, and Father Burgess was on his second cup of tea and well into a long monologue about Cyril of Alexandria.

"I see you didn't get rained on after all!"

"No, it was beautiful," said Father Underhill, shrugging off his coat and looking around for a reasonable place to put it. There wasn't one. He slung it across a chair filled with boxes of candles. "I posted a couple of letters and then walked along the sea cliffs. They're magnificent. I could imagine coming back here after the war for a holiday with my family. Do you get much of that sort of thing, in peacetime?"

Charlie smiled privately at this (to him) transparent hijacking of the conversation. Father Underhill would have been able to get the lay of the land pretty effectively through the dining-room doors before he came in, and was acting accordingly. It was very typical.

"Holiday-makers?" said Father Burgess with a hint of distaste. "No, not really—we're too much out of the way. I'm afraid your wife would find it dull. Not many places to shop, you know."

"Nah, that bookstore in the high street is great," Charlie cut in casually, setting down his fork. "Big Classics section—they had Elsa's translation of Hesiod, I checked." He pushed back his chair from the table. "His wife's a university professor," he tossed in Father Burgess's direction. "Excuse me."

On his way out of the dining room he caught Father Underhill giving him a quizzical look, as if he couldn't decide whether he was pleased Charlie had done that, or annoyed not to have been able to do it himself. Charlie knew the look was one of his elaborate fakes; he did love bragging about his brilliant wife, especially to the unsuspecting, but he had *plenty* of opportunities to do it, and liked it even better when other people did it for him.

Once out in the hall, Charlie realized he should have stayed where he was. Listening to Father Burgess talk incomprehensibly about the Holy Spirit or say vague silly things about women— or anything, really—was preferably to being alone with his own thoughts. They weren't even properly thoughts at this point, just disconnected shreds of emotional nonsense tumbling around in his mind. Was I betrayed, or did I just have a lucky escape? Is this Providence again, or damnation? (Those aren't opposites, Charles.) And sensory details about Hal stirred into the whole mess: the cool, smooth tips of his fingers, not as soft as you'd expect them to be; the way that each hank of his hair twisted into its own specific coppery whorl; the very human, but very charming noise that he made when he came. His beautiful voice, which—apart from the wings—had always struck Charlie as the only really preternatural thing about him. Though when he came to consider it, it was probably preternatural—and beautiful—in the wrong way. Who had ever heard of an angel being a baritone, anyway?

He wondered whether Father Burgess's metaphor of a man leaning in a window was right. And if it was, what did that mean about Hal? By his own account, he couldn't feel the ground under his feet, which must mean that he had somehow been pulled too far inside the room and lost his balance, and wasn't really standing outside any more at all. And that did, undeniably, open the door to the possibility that the eternity he had been standing in all along hadn't been Heaven.

"Do you need marching orders?" Father Underhill had come out of the dining room, his coat slung over his shoulder, and was closing the door behind him. "Or is that the wrong metaphor for a pilot? You look as if you need someone to tell you what to do, is what I meant."

"Oh. Yeah, that might help. I didn't get much sleep—I was afraid to. I, uh, didn't explain that part. He can get into my dreams."

Interesting you didn't mention that, said Father Underhill's expression. Aloud, he said neutrally, "He can, can he?"

"Yes, but—angels do that. In the Bible."

"So they do."

Charlie waited a moment for Father Underhill to decide to walk back from his statement of the previous night about his being a good judge of character. Modify it maybe to something more like, *I don't think you should be allowed out.*

Instead what he said, thoughtfully, unslinging his coat from his shoulder and beginning to put it back on, was, "They can be quite frightening, too. Or so we're led to believe."

"Are you going out again?"

"Yes. I'm coming to the inn with you so you can settle your bill, and we can see whether he's beat his retreat—which, if he hasn't by this time, I'll find suspicious."

"You don't have to do that, Father."

"You know, I'm quite sure I don't," said Father Underhill, smiling. "All the same, I will."

Chapter Twenty-One

A KIND OF ELECTRICITY

At three o'clock on Monday, Evvie was waiting alone in the lobby for Squadron Leader Boult. Archie, his feet up on the reception desk, kept asking why she couldn't mind the desk for him, since she was hanging about the lobby anyway. Evvie peered out through the small panes of the window by the door, which were streaked with raindrops.

"I'm waiting for a friend, Archie," she said. "We're going for a drive."

"In this weather?" Archie snorted. "Must be quite a 'friend'!"

Evvie wished Father Underhill were coming with Charlie and could give Archie a shake.

A closed car, painted military green, pulled up in the rain on the curving drive, and Evvie saw Charlie emerge from the driver's side and run up the steps of the terrace. She hauled open the front door for him.

"Fee's upstairs," she told him as he took off his cap and turned down the collar of his coat. "We'll need to go get her. She had a fall this morning, walking with her crutches—she's all right, but the nurses are fussing and threatening not to let her go out. The weather's not helping matters."

"We have to spirit her away, you mean?" he said, looking doubtfully across the lobby at Archie, who was making it plain that he had heard all this.

"No, I wasn't thinking that. We just have to make it clear that we're going to look after her, and that we'll be ever so disappointed if she can't come out with us."

"Right. We can do that."

"Where did you park?" Archie asked, swinging his feet down to the floor as they passed the reception desk.

Charlie looked at him. "Directly in front of the door." He pointed. "It's raining. We're picking up our friend and her wheelchair." He stared at Archie a moment longer, daring him to object.

"Fine," said Archie, shrugging.

Evvie led the way through the service passage towards the north range of the house.

"Are you all right?" she asked, when they were alone in the passage. She'd noticed as soon as he came in that he looked haggard and pale, as if he hadn't slept.

"I'm not sure," he said. "Thanks for asking, though."

She stopped walking. "Can I ask you something else?"

"Shoot."

She looked up at him; at close quarters in the service passage, his height was intimidating. But she wanted to get this out of the way before they collected Sara. If there was nothing in it, she didn't want to get her friend's hopes up.

"Do you remember that day when I found you sitting in the lodge?"

"That's what you call it? That funny little overbuilt Victorian outbuilding by the old front gate of the house?"

"I … guess so. I thought it was medieval."

"Nah. Victorian imitation medieval. That's neither here nor there," he admitted. "Yes. I do remember that day. You asked me if I was praying."

"That's right, I did."

"Made me think I should have been, actually."

"Did I? That's good." She didn't know how to work around to asking her actual question.

"What did you want to know? About that day."

"Whether you saw a box, in the lodge. I don't know exactly what kind it was, but … "

He was already nodding. "Alabaster, with carvings. A kind of sarcophagus. Yes, I saw that."

"Was it open?"

"Not until I opened it."

"Oh."

There was a long silence before he said, "So you know something about that?"

"I … don't know. I might."

"For instance, what was inside of it?"

"Yes. I mean maybe." It seemed the only explanation that fit together Leo's story of the demon-summoning, Ernest's remarks about something dangerous in a box, and Leo's panic about it getting out.

There was an even longer silence. "A devil?" he said finally, sounding very tired.

"Yes."

"Right."

She suddenly found his weary calm unnerving, and wanted to get out of the narrow passage. She wasn't afraid of him, exactly, but of something connected with him.

"We should go get Sara," she said. "She knows about this too."

He nodded. "I know. Everybody seems to have known about it except me."

*

They put on a show of eager competence for the nurses, bundled Sara up against the rain, and brought her downstairs in her wheelchair and out to the car.

"I've two new things to report," said Evvie, when she and Sara were seated in the back of the car, and Charlie had finished stowing the wheelchair and swung back into the driver's seat. "Daphne has the ring now, and Charlie … knows about the box in the lodge."

"I see," said Sara, furrowing her brow. "Well, I suppose Daphne having the ring makes some sense, since she's Ernest's floozy."

"His what?"

Sara rolled her eyes. "Paramour, if you prefer. Lady-friend. Mistress. But explain about this box."

"I think it's where Leo and Ernest put the devil that … that Leo says I summoned."

"They did," said Charlie. He had started the car and swung it around the curving drive, windshield wipers squeaking against the rain.

"What?" said Sara. "How do you know?"

"Because I found the box later—two weeks ago—and he was inside."

"And you … know that because … "

"I opened it and let him out."

"Oh," said Sara, wide-eyed. "I see."

"It's worse than that. I didn't just let him out. I was completely taken in by him. I thought he was an angel."

"An angel?" said Evvie in disbelief.

"A beaten-up angel with broken wings and … a lot of other injuries, but yeah, an angel." Charlie shrugged wearily. "He was very convincing, I thought."

Evvie remembered the beautiful young man who had stood by her bed, and how sure she had been of what he was. She looked out at the grey rain and felt cold, although the interior of the car was cozily warm.

"What happened to it?" Sara asked.

"It?" Charlie repeated.

"The devil. Where is it now?"

"I don't know, exactly. He's checked out of the inn. But I can look for him."

"No, don't do that!" Sara cried. "Don't go looking for a devil by yourself! Charlie, promise me you won't."

Charlie said nothing.

*

The rain had trailed off into a half-hearted drizzle by the time they pulled up outside the vicarage of St. Bede's in Newingthorpe. Charlie got Sara's wheelchair out of the boot, scooped her gently out of the back seat, and put her in it. He opened the gate and had just begun to negotiate the cobbles of the path when the door of the house opened and Father Underhill appeared.

He ran down the rain-slick path and dropped to his knees on the stones and grasped the arms of the wheelchair, and the first thing he said was, "Darling, I am so proud of you. So proud."

Evvie wanted to cheer for him again. She actually bounced a little where she stood—no one was looking at her.

"I'm so sorry I—" Sara started.

"I don't even want to hear it," said Father Underhill. "It took me a month to find you, and I wasn't there when you were going through this terrible ordeal. You think *you're* sorry?"

She wriggled out of the wheelchair into his arms. He squeezed her tightly, and she curled up into a ball in his embrace, like a little girl. By this time they were both crying.

"It's okay," she snuffled against his shoulder after a moment. "I'm okay, even if I'm not literally all in one piece, and I'm *so* glad you decided you couldn't bear not to see me after all, I don't know *what* I would have done if you'd been completely stoic about it."

"When was I ever completely stoic about anything?" He wiped his eyes. "I like your haircut," he said, mussing it affectionately. "Was it an eccentric whim, or did you have to spend some time masquerading as a boy, or … ?"

"It caught fire. They gave me a terrible haircut at the first hospital, just to get rid of the charred bits, and then some nurses at Adderley were threatening to 'make it look nice' for me, so I went to the men's barber and got him to do this."

"That's my girl," he said tenderly.

He picked her up and carried her inside the vicarage as easily as Charlie had carried her to the car, though he was not nearly such a big man.

*

"I'm not sure," said Father Underhill, "that I see the wisdom in your going back there."

He was seated on the hearth rug in the vicar's chaotic drawing room, as Evvie and Charlie were occupying the two chairs, and Sara the half of the couch that wasn't covered in vestments. They had been drinking tea, provided by the vicar's housekeeper, who had been flitting in and out (the vicar was out visiting parishioners), while Sara told the whole story of what happened to her, from leaving London on her mission to Yorkshire to meeting Evvie at Adderley. Her father had taken it remarkably well, like one soldier listening to another recount his war stories. That must have been hard for him, Evvie thought. She remembered how her stepfather had reacted when Aphrodite had got into a minor riding accident and broken her wrist. He had rampaged around the house shouting at everyone as if they were all at fault, and in his anguish completely forgotten to praise Aphrodite, who was twelve at the time, for being brave and not crying. Of course, he hadn't just come from serving as a chaplain in a war zone.

It was only when Sara began talking about going back to Adderley that Father Underhill started to behave more like an ordinary father.

"I have to go back, Father. I have a mission to complete."

"Do you, darling? Or were you going to help Cousin Graham

with something that he never fully explained to you before he disappeared?"

"Well … yes, but—he did disappear, and I think he might quite likely be dead. So it's my mission now."

Father Underhill looked up at his daughter from where he sat with his hands clasped around one knee on the hearth. After a moment he rocked up onto his feet and shoved aside the pile of vestments on the couch to sit down beside her. Evvie saw with surprise that Sara looked like she was about to start crying again.

"How about you stay here," said Father Underhill, putting an arm around her shoulders.

"I think maybe I will," said Sara in a small voice. "Evgenia, would you mind very much?"

"I'm sure we can find room for Evgenia to stay as well."

"Thank you, Father," said Evvie, "but I do have to go back. It is my job. But I'm not afraid."

"No." He smiled at her. "No, I didn't think you were afraid. But will you think less of me if I admit I'm a little afraid on your behalf?"

"No, Father. I understand." She looked across at Sara. "I'm worried about Rosalind, actually. Daphne was being … more than usually nasty, last night, and I don't want her to have to deal with that alone."

"That's heroic of you," said Sara seriously.

*

After dinner at the vicarage, their goodbyes said for the time being, and a meeting arranged for the following day, Charlie and Evvie got back into the military-green car, which he had to return to the Adderley airbase. The rain had finally ended altogether, though by now the sun was dropping behind the hills, and the sky was a grubby-looking pink. Evvie sat in the front passenger seat, hands clasped in her lap, as the car pulled away from the vicarage gate. She realized, though she was ashamed of it, that she still found

Squadron Leader Boult intimidating, and she had no idea what to talk to him about for the hour's drive to Adderley. But she couldn't just sit there in silence.

"So," she began, just as he too was drawing breath to speak. "Oh. I'm sorry. What were you about to say?"

"I'm … not entirely sure," he admitted. "You?"

"Oh … the same, really."

He shot her a wry smile. She was struck again by how different he looked from the previous day. Then she had taken away the impression of someone confident, strong in more than body, comfortable in his own skin. Today all that was gone. He worried her today more than he had yesterday, she realized, because he had that same vulnerability about him as the wounded soldiers at Adderley who were so awkwardly apt to latch onto a sympathetic pretty girl. Not that he had ever been the least bit flirtatious with her.

"You've known the Underhills a long time, then," she said.

"Ages, yes." He settled back in his seat, strong brown hands relaxing on the steering wheel. "They're some of my favourite people in the world. If you want to hear stories about Sara as a little girl, I'm your man."

"That does sound like one of the more cheerful things we could talk about," she said.

"That's true." He was silent for a moment. "Tell me something first. I just remembered—you don't know anything about a place near here called Zion, do you?"

"Dr. Good's place?"

"That's the one."

"I haven't ever been there. I've met Dr. Good. He used to give talks at the hospital. He seems nice enough." A bit soft, in fact, had been her opinion—especially when he tried to talk about sin. "His sister …"

"Yes?"

"She comes—used to come—to Adderley Hall all the time, with

tracts. We had to tell her—that is, Lady Rathburn instructed me to tell her to stop coming."

"Any idea why?"

"Oh yes. I told Lady Rathburn what she'd said to Fee. To Sara, I mean." And she explained about Miss Good's remarks, and Reardon's suicide attempt. It didn't seem to surprise Charlie particularly.

"I saw their tract about suicide, at Zion. It was ... unsettling. Think I'd've found it encouraging if I'd been considering suicide. In the wrong way."

Evvie shuddered. "She's a friend of Leo's, and it seems he gave her Solomon's ring, for safekeeping maybe. I certainly saw her wearing it. But now Daphne has it."

"Huh. So if they were in this ring-stealing and devil-summoning business together, then it's not beyond the bounds of possibility that they might have intended to take the ... the thing they'd summoned to Zion at some point."

"You're thinking that's where it might be now?"

"No. He didn't seem to like that place. I was thinking that it sounds as if he might have been telling the truth, though, about the Zion connection. Which ... would be odd."

She wasn't quite sure what he was talking about now, but didn't want to ask. He changed the subject back to Sara's childhood, and they drove on talking companionably about their friend, as the sky grew darker overhead.

He seemed to know that Sara had been in love with him. He seemed apologetic about it, which made Evvie like him. She ended up telling him about Patmos, though not about her vision (she thought angels might be a topic best avoided).

"That's splendid," he said sincerely, as if she were an old friend, or his sister, and had just told him she was engaged to be married. "And you're going to go back there?"

"Well, I hope so. God willing."

"Sara'll miss you."

"I'll miss her too."

They drew up in the curved drive in front of Adderley's austere white facade. To Evvie it looked strangely unwelcoming.

"I'll come in with you," said Charlie, closing her door behind her. "Avert suspicion. Make it clear that we're not out here kissing goodbye."

"Thanks," said Evvie, starting up the steps. She liked the frank way he said it.

There were two policemen in the lobby, the same ones who had come with Leo's car and the bag of bloodstained vestments, and before that, about the murdered man off Horrey Head. They were talking with Lady Rathburn. Archie came out from behind the desk to meet the new arrivals as they came through the door.

"There's been another murder!" he announced in a stage whisper.

"Where?" Charlie asked. "Here?"

Archie gestured vaguely. "Somewhere on the grounds. They haven't said exactly where. It's Josie Good. She was found dead this afternoon."

Chapter Twenty-Two

VEHICLE OF GRACE

Charlie left the house, but stood for some time leaning against the hood of his car outside. It wasn't that he expected Evvie to change her mind and come running out asking to be taken back to the St. Bede's vicarage. She was obviously much too courageous and determined for that. But there was always the chance something more alarming would happen to disturb even her resolve. Besides, he didn't want to leave without more information.

Eventually the two policemen emerged, came down the steps from the terrace, and retrieved their bicycles. Charlie intercepted them. He recognized the sergeant and inspector who had come to the base two weeks earlier. They remembered him as well.

"Did you get anywhere with that other murder?" he asked.

The inspector was ready enough to tell him about it. "We managed to identify the victim. A tip from one of the patients here put us on the right track, as matter of fact, and we've just had confirmation this afternoon. He was a senior Foreign Office secretary by the name of Darby."

So that was what had happened to him, then.

"And is this second murder connected, do you think?"

"Connected?" said the inspector musingly.

"We don't know that it's a murder," said the sergeant repressively.

"It's a suspicious death," said the inspector. "*Jolly* suspicious, too."

"It was a woman?" Charlie prompted.

The inspector nodded, while his subordinate frowned at him. "A local woman, Josephine Good."

"I've met her. Had she been reported missing?"

"Aye. Her brother reported it, only yesterday—said he hadn't seen her since Saturday morning. And she was found this afternoon in a field near the manor by a couple of childer. She must have been killed elsewhere and dropped there after, though."

Charlie opened his mouth to ask how she had been killed, but the inspector went on unasked:

"She was smashed to death. Crushed. Looked like a house fell on her."

It was all he'd needed to hear—what he'd been fearing to hear, though he hadn't realized it. He knew Hal had done it.

*

He returned to the base, not sure what the point of this was, but not knowing where else to go. Sleep, of course, was out of the question. At this point he didn't know what he feared more: that he might meet Hal in a dream, or that he might not, now or ever. And if he did meet him, how would he know whether it was the real Hal or only an ordinary dream? What would he say to him? Would the dreaming Charlie be ready to forgive him? The waking Charlie sometimes almost was, but he didn't trust himself when he felt that way. A devil, he reminded himself sternly: not just a man who treated you shabbily, but an actual devil. Potentially.

Almost certainly. The story he had heard from Evvie and the Underhills seemed to leave little room for alternate interpretations.

And potentially—almost certainly—this devil had killed a woman just for "having designs" on Charlie. Whatever that meant. He remembered the strange look Hal had given Miss Good, the out-of-character, take-charge way he had pushed Charlie back against the wall to kiss him. He hadn't been turned on—Charlie had been, instantly, in spite of the stupid situation, but he remembered Hal's slim body pressed up against him, and he hadn't been. He'd just done it as a thing to do. It was disquietingly easy to imagine

Hal coming upon Miss Good again, after he'd left Charlie, and tightening his white fingers around her throat in the same spirit. As a thing to do.

But that was unfair, some perverse part of him protested. Just because you don't understand *why* he behaved like that in the alley doesn't mean he didn't have a reason.

If Miss Good had only been strangled or stabbed, he wouldn't have been so sure. But killed in exactly the way that she had *almost* died seven months earlier? And she had been involved, somehow, in the exploit with the demon-summoning ring that had happened around the same time. She had in fact been the possessor of the ring for a while. She had posed a threat to Hal.

"Sir? I thought you were on leave!"

Lost in thought, he had almost run into Flight Lieutenant Benson, who looked startled to see him.

"I was—am, I mean. Just realized I forgot something." He forced a smile and headed for his office. He wasn't going to be able to spend the night here, sleep or no sleep. It would look too strange.

He slumped in his desk chair, flicking on the light and shuffling papers to make it look like he was doing something.

Think rationally about this, Charles. (And don't let your subconscious call you "Charles.") *What do you know that he can do? He looks wispy, but in fact he's implausibly strong. How strong exactly, you don't know, but strong enough to take you*—that had been proven, in real life as well as in the dreams.

The dreams, too—he could do that to Charlie, but could he do it to anyone? Could he do it to you while you were awake?

Charlie remembered how he had felt about the dreams, when he had thought them the product of his own subconscious. He had been horrified, disgusted with himself; but all that had melted away when he realized Hal had actually been there. The past had been rewritten—or not rewritten, exactly, because it hadn't needed to be. He'd just been able to look back on the scenes from his dreams without the lens of self-loathing interposed. It was all right; he hadn't done wrong. Hal was an angel.

Think rationally. He's strong, can get inside people's heads, can fly, turn invisible … What exactly is the point of thinking rationally, in the face of all that? But where's he gone, that's the question, and what'll he do next?

The door of his office had popped open, and he stood up to close it, then realized that someone was peeping in.

"Come," he said, beckoning.

Latham eased himself in the barely-open door and shut it behind him. He shoved his hands in his pockets.

"I wondered if you were all right," he said.

Charlie looked at him. On an impartially aesthetic level, Latham might have been more than a match for Hal. Hal was striking, unusual-looking; Latham was just extraordinarily, effeminately lovely. He was shorter than Hal, looked slightly older, and lacked that strange, awkward gracefulness. He was neat and light on his feet, probably a good dancer, definitely skilled with his hands. His emotions showed on his face like water soaking through thin cloth.

"I'm fine," said Charlie

"Ah. Thought you were on leave. Wondered if anything was wrong."

"Yes." Charlie smiled wearily. "I am, and there is. A woman's been found murdered. I just heard about it, down at the hospital."

"Murdered … you mean by a spy or something?"

"No, they don't think that. Just mysterious circumstances. I said I'd check who was off the base around the time they think it happened." This was true, though it was just something he'd said at random to the police, and wasn't what he had been doing. The less garrulous officer had told him they would look into all that in due course, thank you very much.

"I see," said Latham. "So you're going out again. Not staying."

"I … I don't know. Hadn't decided. I'm … tired."

He felt trapped. He couldn't stay at the base now, couldn't return to the Feathers, where Mary would ask a thousand questions, or to the vicarage, where Sara would be in the bed he'd occupied last night, and everyone would probably be asleep. A few minutes ago he'd imagined he might spend the night scouring the moors where the imprudent policemen had indicated Miss Good's body had been found, looking for a tall, red-haired figure. But if he found him, it would only be because Hal wanted him to, had hung about waiting to be found—and what then?

And that perverse voice pointed out that if he went looking for Hal now, it would be the final admission that he believed Hal really was a devil.

He leaned against the side of his desk. He felt the need to say something to Latham, who remained standing there looking limpidly sympathetic and sad. He imagined himself seizing the younger man by the shoulders and crying, "Save yourself! Marry Rosalind and bury your desires as deep as you can, and never act on them—it's the only way you can hope to avoid damnation." Only he'd been prevented, by what he'd heard or glimpsed or felt in St. Bede's on Sunday morning, from really believing that. And it occurred to him that maybe he had the capacity to be a vehicle of Grace in Latham's life. Maybe advising him was exactly what he needed to do. But what was the right course for Latham? Surely denying his nature and going ahead with a marriage founded on a lie and a delusion wasn't it.

"I feel bad about what happened with us, Latham. How it ended."

"There's somebody else now, isn't there?" said Latham. He didn't sound bitter. He went on without waiting for Charlie to answer, "It would stand to reason. You're a magnificent lover."

Charlie startled himself by laughing aloud. "You've no basis for comparison whatsoever!" And frankly, not that much evidence. They had only twice progressed further than kissing, and neither time had done anything particularly elaborate.

But Charlie himself hadn't been anything like as experienced as he had imagined. In a couple of nights and one afternoon with Hal, he'd learned more about sex than in all the nearly thirty-five years preceding; he'd done things he'd only ever heard vaguely described and fantasized about before. He didn't think Latham had experienced him as a particularly adventurous lover—but Hal had.

"And a damned fine fellow all around," Latham persisted. "I don't mind saying it. Everybody thinks you've got a girl in Newingthorpe that you're being very coy about—only I know better. And if you think I don't regret losing you because I was such an ass about Rosalind—well, you're wrong, that's all. I know there's somebody else because you've stopped even being tempted with me, haven't you?"

"I stopped being tempted after you told me about your fiancée. Not of my own will. By the Grace of God."

"By the what of who? Wait, was I wrong? Did you get saved or something? Is that what happened?"

"No, I did meet somebody else. I've always been religious. How did you miss that?"

"I dunno. You just don't seem the type. How religious?"

"Church every Sunday, Grace before meals, wearing a crucifix … I really don't know how you missed it, Latham."

"So what's this all about?" Latham asked warily.

"I'm trying to make amends, that's all. I think you're in turmoil and it's my fault."

"I'm the one who came on to you."

That made Charlie laugh again. "I gave you a lot of encouragement. Don't say 'When?' I get that you're not observant. But I abandoned you in a self-righteous huff when I found out you were engaged, and I never really told you why."

"I know why! I didn't at first, and when I figured it out, I kicked myself for being such a fool. You thought we were going to stay together, and when you found out I meant to get married, you realized

I didn't think it. But it was just that I hadn't thought that far ahead. You wanted to be with me for good. I can't believe I gave that up."

Charlie did not immediately reply. It was tempting to let Latham's rather romantic picture stand. It was flattering to Charlie, and might even have been salutary for Latham; imagining this seemed to have inspired some helpful self-reflection.

"I didn't think that, Latham," Charlie said finally. "I have a career and friends in Canada, and I intend to go back there. You've a family and everything here that I wouldn't expect you to leave. I … don't think we were particularly well matched, except physically, and I didn't think we'd be together for long. But I made the decision a long time ago to live my life in a certain way: not to pretend to be other than what I am. Getting married, promising before God to love and cherish a woman I couldn't feel anything for except some kind of Platonic friendship—that would be a pretence. I made up my mind when I was younger than you that I wasn't ever going to do that. I also try to be honest with the people I care about."

"Oh." Latham thought about that for a bit, then worked it out. "So you lost respect for me."

"Yeah."

"Oh." After a moment, looking embarrassed, he said, "I thought it was … I thought I broke your heart."

"Not really."

"Oh. So is he better-looking than me?" He sounded hopeful.

"No," said Charlie promptly. "He's lovely, but he's not better-looking than you. And he's beside the point."

"What is the point?"

"You and your fiancée, and what you're going to do about your engagement. I want to help you make the right decision. I'm older and—well, maybe not wiser, but at least I've spent more time thinking about what it means to be gay than you have. But I'm not you, and what's right for me isn't necessarily what's right for you. For a start, I don't have a family to worry about, and you do. But tell me about Rosalind."

"Tell you about *Rosalind?*" Latham repeated, as if Charlie had asked to be told the easiest way to learn Chinese.

"Tell me about Rosalind. Do you have anything better to do?"

"Well, I don't know," said Latham petulantly. "I came here thinking, hoping, maybe your new man had kicked you out, and I might get a second chance. I don't want to talk to you about my fiancée."

He pulled open the office door and stalked out.

Charlie stood leaning against his desk for a few minutes, feeling useless and defeated.

All very well for you to take that line about marriage. You swore never to leave Hal—and you did.

Finally he left the building, locking his office behind him. He took the closed car again because it was too cold to sleep in the jeep, drove aimlessly south for a while, and finally pulled off onto a track behind a stone wall. As he tipped the seat back, he thought of the last time he had slept in a car. He looked into the back seat, remembering Hal sitting there that morning, in the other car, with the red cope over his knees, his long hair untidy, holding up his hand like an angel in a painting. He reached back for a moment, into the empty space between the seats, and knew he would have given anything to feel his fingers brush against Hal's in the dark.

*

He was in Mr. Oates's shop, just the way it had been twenty years ago, when he used to stock shelves. A big crate of blueberries had arrived, tiny berries heaped in cardboard baskets, sweet-smelling and mottled like precious stones. It made him happy just to look at them. And he was just looking at them, although the phone was ringing, seemed like it had been ringing for some time. He rushed over to the counter, banged back the folding section, and dove behind it, lest Mr.

Oates come out and give him that 'I'm-disappointed-in-you-Charlie' look. Dimly aware that the reason he hadn't received that look in a while was because Mr. Oates had been dead for nearly ten years.

"Hello?" His teenage voice: deep already, but still rough, intentionally quiet. Slightly out of breath now.

"You didn't leave me, Charles." He sounded distant, but only in space. Charlie's whole body thrilled at the sound. Like a deep bell, like a perfectly-running engine. "I drove you away. It's not the same thing."

He woke, stiff and cold in the driver's seat of the car, tipped back as far as it would go. It was morning.

*

He drove back to the base with the intention of finding Latham and apologizing, but Latham surprised him by meeting him at the entrance of the officers' barracks with an apology of his own.

"Sorry I stormed out on you last night. Ungrateful of me. You were trying to be a good influence and all that."

"I botched it myself. My fault entirely—no need for you to apologize."

Latham looked genuinely surprised and gratified, but then Charlie didn't know what to say next.

"I care about you, Latham. And you've got to understand, that's not been normal for me. Most of the men I've been with, I haven't given a damn about. I wanted it that way—it made sense to me somehow. I'm telling you this because I don't want you to end up like that, fooling yourself like that. It's just a miserable way to live."

And the irony of it was that it was Hal who had made him see that.

"I get it," said Latham, and Charlie thought it sounded like maybe he did. "Thanks."

"How'd you like to join me in a mission of mercy?" The idea had just occurred to him. "You haven't got any work to do around here this morning, have you?"

"There is *nothing* going on here this morning—it feels as if the war's already won around here. If you give me leave, I'm at your disposal."

"Well, wait till you hear what it is—it'll be hard work."

He explained about the half-collapsed roof of the Zion Retreat Centre, and how he had promised Dr. Good to find volunteers to help repair it.

"Count me in," said Latham cheerfully. "And I know where you can find some other chaps who might be willing to pitch in."

They took a jeep, leaving the car that Charlie had borrowed the previous day, and headed down to Adderley Hall. The "other chaps" that Latham knew were apparently Ernest and Leo, the men that Charlie had been introduced to in Evvie's story about using King Solomon's ring. Charlie was morbidly interested in meeting them. He could check on Evvie at the same time.

On the drive down, Latham seemed thoughtful. "If you care about me," he began finally, then trailed off. "There's still no second chance for us?"

"No," Charlie said firmly. "I'm sorry."

You're pretty, Latham, and you're loyal, but you're also a bit dim. And I've been finding *intelligence* a big turn-on lately.

The thought of never being able to tell Hal that one made him want to cry.

At the hospital, Latham went to round up Ernest and Leo, while Charlie looked for Evvie. He found her alone in the office. She looked as bad as he must have looked yesterday. Her big dark eyes were ringed with shadows like bruises.

"What happened last night?" he asked immediately, closing the office door behind him.

"Actually, nothing." She got up from her desk, looking grateful for the opportunity to stop pretending to work. "It's what almost happened. Mr. Anderson got up onto the roof and nearly threw himself off."

"Anderson? Oh, God. He seemed so … I wouldn't have expected that of him." He'd visited again the previous week, on his way back to Newingthorpe one evening, and Anderson had seemed to be doing well. "How did he get up onto the roof?"

"He had help, obviously. He's not saying who." After a moment she added, "I know why. It's because he's trying to be a gentleman."

"Oh, no. You mean he … was up there with a woman?"

She nodded. "I went looking there for him—I was the one who found him—because I'd seen … her … coming down the stairs from the roof."

Trying to be a gentleman himself, he didn't ask who she was talking about. "Anderson has a fiancée, doesn't he? I remember he showed me a picture of her."

"Yes, but she hasn't come to visit, and he's worried she's going to have second thoughts now that he's crippled." She rubbed her eyes. "He told me all about it, after we got him down from the roof. And I do mean *all* about it. Details—I really didn't need to hear. I think he'll regret that, today. I'm going to make myself scarce. Sara phoned from Newingthorpe, and I've asked Lady Rathburn for the day off. They're going to borrow the vicar's car and come pick me up."

"I'm glad to hear it! I'll be out that way myself." He explained about his mission to Zion to fix the roof. "This thing with Anderson—did you know it was going to happen? Is that why you wanted to come back here last night?"

She looked up at him, her expression solemn. "I didn't *know*, not to say … not like precognition. I was afraid of it, though. It's Daphne. She's had some sort of fight with Ernest—her lover—and she's going around seducing everyone. She even had a crack at me the other night. She makes it all seem so *sordid*." She paused, as if listening to her own words, wondering what she meant. She shook her head, frowning. "I feel as if it's expected of me, to loathe it and think it's all disgusting. But I don't. And that's why I'm offended when people use it as … as a weapon against each other. I have no idea why I'm telling you all this—I didn't get much sleep last night, and I expect I am not making any sense."

"No, no—I get it, actually. You're called to celibacy, but that doesn't mean you think sex is a bad thing."

"Thank you. You're very understanding." She smiled warmly up at him. "I'm glad I stopped being afraid of you."

He smiled. "Me too!"

He reached out and brushed a strand of her curly hair back from her face, and she surprised him by stepping in and giving him a brief, friendly little hug.

*

Latham came down to the lobby holding hands with Rosalind, who was the dark-haired girl Charlie had met before with Sara. *Well, this is going to be weird*, Charlie thought. They were followed by the tall blonde whom Charlie had pretended to stare at when he first came to Adderley two weeks ago, and two men about Charlie's age: one light-haired and rather predictably good-looking, the other dark and interestingly ugly.

"The girls are going to come too," Latham announced.

"Great," said Charlie, looking doubtfully at the blonde girl's white frock. Rosalind at least was wearing trousers and sturdy shoes. "But we've only room in the jeep for five."

"It's all right," said Rosalind. "We've already worked that out. Ernest's going to come on his motorcycle, and Daph will ride in the sidecar."

So the blonde girl was Daphne. Well, if she was riding in Ernest's sidecar, maybe that meant they had made up their fight.

Chapter Twenty-Three

GINGERBREAD AND ONTOLOGY

I t was not long after Charlie left that Father Underhill and Sara arrived. Evvie was waiting for them on the terrace. They pulled up in a small, neat, open car that looked like it could probably go much faster than Father Underhill was driving it. A new side of the vicar of St. Bede's, Evvie thought in amusement; she had gained a specific impression of him from his messy house and his conversation over dinner the other night, which didn't quite accord with that car.

"I hope you can cram yourself into the back seat," said Father Underhill. "We had considerable difficulty fitting the wheelchair into the boot. I'm afraid this is rather a ridiculous car."

"It looks like it would be fun to drive," said Evvie, squeezing into the back seat, which did seem like an afterthought in the design of the car.

"If you like driving," said Sara. "It's wasted on my father."

"Entirely wasted," Father Underhill agreed. "Are you all right back there?"

"Quite all right, thanks!"

"We thought instead of going all the way back to Newingthorpe," said Sara, "we'd drive to a village called Towton Hoe that Father Burgess told us is picturesque. Are you agreeable? He's drawn us a map, you see." She flourished it. "I'm in charge of navigation."

They drove off into the fine morning, following the vicar's hand-drawn map in the vicar's stylish little car, and Evvie was able for a short while to put Daphne and Anderson and everything connected with Adderley Hall blessedly out of her mind and enjoy the company of her friends.

*

"If you were a devil wandering the Yorkshire countryside, where would you go?" Sara asked thoughtfully.

"I'm not sure that's a question I can answer," said Evvie, pouring out a cup of tea for herself, after having filled one for Sara.

They were in a tea room in Towton Hoe, which had proved to be a sleepy, grey-stone place with a steep main street running up a hill, on which Father Underhill had been unwilling to park the car. Sara hadn't wanted to be pushed up the street in her wheelchair either, so he had dropped the two girls at the tea room and gone to find parking on level ground. He was taking a long time. Evvie had filled Sara in on the events of the previous night, and Sara had moved on to discussing how they might go about tracking down what she referred to—unfairly, Evvie thought—as "Charlie's devil."

"I suppose the first thing any self-respecting devil would do under the circumstances," said Sara, "is change its shape. I mean, it must know it's been made."

"Been what?"

"Made. Rumbled. Found out. Charlie'd worked out what it was."

"Had he? Before he talked to us, I mean."

Sara frowned. "Yes, you're right—I'm not too clear on that, either. It's all rather surprising, you know. Charlie's such a sensible person, normally. I wouldn't have expected him to make a mistake like that."

"Like mistaking a devil for an angel, you mean?"

"Like opening the box in the first place, is what I was thinking. When there was a devil inside of it? I just thought … he seemed to have more intuition than that."

"Yes. You're not exactly impartial where Charlie's concerned, though, are you?" She couldn't resist.

"Aha. I knew I would regret telling you that. That's all in the past, Evgenia, I assure you. I like and respect him very much, but I'm quite clear-headed about it. I'm surprised, that's all, to think he'd do such a … such an obviously silly thing."

Evvie nodded. It did seem at odds with Squadron Leader Boult's character, as far as she had been able to discern it, in the short time she'd known him. And she wasn't really one to talk about being impartial. She remembered with a touch of embarrassment how she had impulsively hugged him at Adderley that morning. She liked him, too, and he had really looked as if he needed a hug.

"At least now we've solved the mystery of the blood-stained vestments," she said. And the little red feather—not an angel's feather after all.

"Evgenia," said Sara suddenly, looking intently out the window, "I know you're not interested in men, but there's a specimen standing outside this shop you really should see. He looks exactly like a stained-glass window in my father's church."

Evvie turned and looked.

*

In her memory, she looked out the window at the purple and grey of sunset and clouds pouring down to meet the purple and grey of the Yorkshire hills. She was closing blackout curtains, moving through the old part of the house, where the floors were uneven and the wood panelling was dark. Out one window she saw Jeremiah Good marching toward the stables with his hand grasping his sister's arm. They had been visiting at the hospital, and as usual, Miss Good had embarrassed her brother somehow, and he was insisting they return home. It was a familiar scene, but Evvie remembered now that it would be the last of its kind. That was the same night the Goods' house was hit by a stray bomb, and Josephine was nearly killed.

Evvie reached the back of the north range, and looked out onto the park. Lights were glowing in the windows of the lodge. She let herself out the door in the back gate and crunched down the drive, intending to remind whoever was out there not to break the blackout.

When she reached the door, she could hear voices from inside but could not make out the words. She pushed the door open and stepped confidently in. But she stopped just inside the door, astonished. The air was thick with some kind of oily, clinging fog, and in the corners of the room she glimpsed indistinct shapes moving, like crowds of milling people.

Ernest was sprawled in one of the wicker chairs, twisting a heavy, old-fashioned seal ring on the ring finger of his left hand. Evvie had never noticed him wearing jewellery before. Leo stood in the middle of the room, hands pushed into his disordered hair, looking wild. He started at Evvie's appearance, staring at her as if for a moment he couldn't remember who she was. Ernest went on sprawling and twisting his ring, a little smile on his lips, as if he were listening to some amusing story.

"What do you want? What are you doing here?" Leo demanded.

Behind him, a wooden crate stood open, and a piece of carved stone, ancient-looking, was propped next to it.

"You're breaking the blackout with your lamp, Mr. Rathburn," said Evvie as neutrally as she could manage.

"Damn the blackout to Hell," Leo muttered fretfully.

There was a strange shivering through the corners of the room.

"Evvie," said Ernest suddenly, "can you see them?" He sounded drunk.

"What are they?" she asked, although she didn't really need to. She knew well enough. "How—how did they get here?"

Ernest held up his left hand lazily. The lamplight glinted on the gold of the ring, but the stone was flat and unreflective, a solid red like wax or blood.

"She can see them?" said Leo jumpily. "She can see them! Ernest, give her the ring—maybe she can make them get in the box!"

Ernest cut him off with a gesture, still looking at Evvie. "You want to know what we're doing?"

Leo made an impatient noise, but Ernest went on with the story, explaining about King Solomon and the archangel Michael and demons vanquished and forced to help build the Temple in Jerusalem.

"Think what a man with that kind of power could accomplish in this modern world," he said huskily. "I looked into it after Darby told me all this one night when he'd been drinking. It's all there in the *Testament of Solomon*—the names of the demons, their weaknesses, everything. All you'd need to make it work would be the ring."

Evvie eyed his left hand and knew what he was going to say next. If it hadn't been for the shifting shapes in the corners of the room, she would have been prepared to dismiss it easily.

But Leo had lost patience, and before Ernest could complete his story, he dove at him and wrestled the ring off his finger. Ernest put up surprisingly little resistance.

"Here, Evvie," said Leo, advancing on her. "Here, put this on and have a chat with these fellows, see if you can't persuade them to get into our nice cozy sarcophagus, what?"

"No, thank you," said Evvie, backing toward the door. "I had better—"

She gasped as Leo surged forward and caught her wrist. She squeezed her hand into a fist and tried to tug herself loose. Behind Leo, Ernest was leaning forward in his chair, coughing or retching. Leo's fingers dug painfully into her arm.

"Open your hand," he growled.

"Do as he says," croaked Ernest. "For the love of—" He made a choking sound. "Get it over with!"

Suddenly afraid Leo was really going to hurt her, Evvie unclenched her fist, and Leo crammed the ring onto her thumb, painfully hard.

Nothing outwardly changed in the room, but she felt the attention of a hundred *somethings* suddenly focussed eagerly on her.

They shifted malevolently in the corners of the room. Then the voices began, clamouring and hissing avidly over one another: *I am Klothod, I am Rabdos, I am Asmodeus, I am Enipsigos, Metathiax, Atrax, Obizuth—What is your will? What is your will? What is your will? Your will? Your will! Your will!*

Sara had encountered a single demon, and it had presented her with a horrible catalogue of possible favours. When it happened to Evvie, there was a crowd of them, milling and clambering over one another in the small room, awaiting orders from the men who had summoned them but hadn't been able to hear their voices. The whispered offers poured over Evvie: ways of killing people, seducing people, stealing from people; riches they might fetch her, places they might take her, knowledge they could supply; a tumble of horrible images and beautiful ones, in frantic succession, suffocating her.

Evgenia? This was another voice, wholly different but familiar, sounding as one might on spotting a friend unexpectedly in a crowd in a strange city. *Evgenia!* Now alive with concern. *Speak, and I will come to you.*

"Help!" she called out to him in Greek. Βοήθεια! Not a demon's name, as Leo had imagined, but a cry for help, addressed to her angel.

And he came. He had not troubled, this time, to put on human form. He was a tall twist of flame, with a suggestion of lilies. But it was still like seeing an old friend.

"It's you!" Evvie cried in delight.

Of course it is I.

The shadows in the room had lost interest in Evvie. They were shrinking back against the walls with an agitated chittering, mashing each other down in their efforts to get away from the new presence.

"Now *that's* more like it!" Leo crowed.

Ernest was hiding his face in his clutching arms.

"You can see him," said Evvie in surprise, glancing between them.

Leo grabbed her sleeve excitedly. "Tell it to go in the sarcophagus!"

"What?" said Evvie, almost laughing. "I'll do no such thing!"

"I want it! I'll have it. I've never seen anything so … " He was panting in his excitement, his eyes feverishly bright.

He had seized her hand and snatched the ring before she could stop him. Then he was gripped by the throat and borne up, off his feet, gasping and kicking. Evvie's angel had half-materialized in front of him, still flame, but flame in the shape of a man, with a definite expression of annoyance on his face.

Leo clenched his right hand around the ring, scrabbling with his left at the angel's bright fingers.

"Get—go—ggh—" he tried.

"Summon another one!" This was Ernest, looking up finally from where he crouched in his chair. "Quick!"

The angel was looking down at Evvie, calmly, as if he might be about to ask her opinion of the situation. Leo kicked and squirmed in his grasp.

"Summon another one that outranks it!" Ernest shouted.

"Be—el—ze—bul!" Leo choked out.

*

The young man stood in the street with his hands in the pockets of his coat, looking at the tea-room menu listlessly, as if for something to do rather than because he planned to come in. He had bright red hair, and the morning sun was behind him, lighting him up as if he had a halo.

Evvie got up from her seat and rapped on the window to get his attention. He looked up and took a step back, as if expecting her to be shooing him away. She saw that he was unshaven, his clothing rumpled as if he might have been sleeping out of doors. His eyes were grey and sad.

She beckoned to him. "Come in! Come in!"

"E-Evvie?" she heard Sara say uncertainly behind her.

The young man smiled tentatively, looking around him to make sure she was really gesturing at him, and finally turned toward the tea-room door.

"Don't worry," said Evvie, sitting back down.

"Not worried," said Sara. "Just, you know, checking that you haven't gone mad."

Evvie smiled across the table at her friend. "Of course not," she said. "You recognized him too."

He had come through the door and arrived at their table. He had put his hands back in his pockets, and looked uncertain. He also looked very young, not much older than Evvie.

"I'll get you a chair," she said, hopping up again.

"My friend seems to want you to join us for tea," Sara said. "I don't suppose you're called Hal?"

"I am," he said. "Though it is not my real name."

Evvie pulled out a chair from an empty table and brought it over. The red-haired young man and Sara were looking at one another as if they both wondered which of them was going to remark on the fact that she had guessed his name. Neither of them did. Then he noticed that Evvie had fetched him a chair, and he reacted with embarrassed surprise.

"Oh! Pardon me. Thank you." He took it from her, and waited for her to sit down before drawing it up to the table and joining them.

"I'm called Fee," said Sara, "and she's called Evvie. Those aren't our real names either."

"Evvie is just short for Evgenia, and that is my real name. But you knew that."

He looked at her searchingly. "Did I? Have we met, Evgenia?" She would have known that voice anywhere. He spoke to her in Greek.

"Yes," she said eagerly. "Twice. This is the third time."

"Forgive me," he said. "I have lost my memory. I almost remember you, but not quite." He leaned back in his chair and looked at

Sara. "I am sorry," he said in English. "I was speaking the wrong language, wasn't I?"

"Well, um … if you wanted me to be able to contribute much to the conversation, then yes."

"She can only order coffee and recite the beginning of the *Iliad*," said Evvie.

"Speaking of ordering things," said Sara, after making a face at Evvie, "shall we flag down a waitress for you, Hal, so you can join us in tea and cakes?"

"I don't have any money," he admitted.

"We'll treat you," said Sara promptly. "It's not every day we meet an old friend of Evvie's who looks like a stained-glass window."

He laughed, a gorgeous, musical sound that Evvie remembered so well.

"Oh! It's so good to see you again. You've—you said you've lost your memory, and I had too, but seeing you now has brought everything back."

"Has it?" His gaze seemed fleetingly hopeful. "You must tell me what you remember."

They were interrupted by the waitress bringing an extra teacup for Hal. Evvie filled it, and on Sara's prompting he ordered gingerbread. As the waitress moved away, the tea-room door opened, and Father Underhill came in.

He paused for a moment to take in the scene at the table. Evvie saw how it must look from his point of view—a strange, scruffy young man sitting with his daughter and her friend—and wasn't surprised when his expression became unfriendly.

She *was* surprised when he strode over to the table, yanked Hal's chair out from under him, seized him by the front of his shirt as he fell backward, and twisted his arm behind his back in order to force him across the room and out the door. Hal himself was too surprised to offer more than a gasp of protest. The other patrons in the tea room stared in shock.

"Don't you dare go near my daughter again." He barely raised his voice, but such a profound silence had fallen over the tea room that everyone heard it.

He returned to the table, picked up Hal's fallen chair, set it back on its feet, and sat down composedly, taking off his gloves and stowing them neatly in his officer's cap. He picked up a menu from the table.

"Sorry about that," he said, looking at the menu.

"Have you *gone insane?*" Sara demanded.

"No, I don't think so. Should I get scones or cake?"

Sara leaned back in her wheelchair and folded her arms. She looked furious. "You could just tell the waitress to bring you the gingerbread that Hal ordered before you *threw him out into the street.*"

"Sara? Not in front of your friend, all right?"

"You hauled him out of his chair and marched him out the door in front of everybody in the tea room!"

"Yes, and we can discuss that later. Not right now."

Evvie decided to go out on a limb. "We both thought he was an angel, Father," she said, as quietly as she could manage.

"Um …" said Sara. This was clearly news to her.

"I thought he was an angel," Evvie amended. "I *know* he is an angel."

Father Underhill was looking up at her. "There's a lot of that going around."

"Didn't you recognize him, Father?" said Sara.

"I did indeed," he said crisply. "We have met."

"No, I mean from the window, at home. He's got short hair and no wings, but he's Hal. My Hal."

"He *looks* like your Hal—that doesn't prove he's an angel."

"But Evvie recognized him."

"Did you?"

"From—from a vision that I had once, Father. And … from one other occasion."

"And he looked to you like an angel?"

She nodded.

"The thing is, Evgenia—and I'm sure you know this, from many lives of the saints and so on—that devils can disguise themselves as … as what we expect angels to look like."

"You think he is a devil?"

"Mm-hm. On the whole, I do."

"So that's … that's why you threw him out of the tea room?"

He shrugged. "It seemed like the thing to do."

They looked at one another and all three began to laugh at the same time. They were still giggling when the waitress came up to the table, clutching a plate, to say timidly, "Did someone at this table … order … gingerbread?"

*

The thing that had appeared in the lodge at Leo's final, choking summons was like a fissure in the substance of the world: a yawning, cold darkness. Little gibbering noises came from the shrunken remains of the oily clouds in the corners. Hal spun around, casting Leo away and becoming wholly material in the same motion, bright wings unfurling in the cold air of the stone room. He wore flame-hued armour, like an icon of St. Michael, and he drew his sword as the black fissure folded in on itself to become a solid shape, towering over him, too tall really to be inside the low-ceilinged lodge.

Sword rang against sword, and Evvie watched her angel hold his own against the prince of Hell.

"What's happening?" Leo demanded, grabbing Evvie's arm as he tried to follow the progress of a combat he could not properly see. "Who's winning?"

"The one who will always win," she snapped back, wrenching herself away from him.

Even as she spoke, the cloudy onlookers began to advance into the room, drawing towards the fight with wary, darting motions. They too were beginning to take on more definite shapes.

First one of them nipped at the angel's heel, and he kicked it easily away. But the next one leapt in immediately to snap at his sword hand, and that distracted him enough to allow his enemy to land a solid blow against his gold breastplate. He staggered and caught himself, but two more of the little devils, emboldened now, jumped up and latched onto one of his wings. He gasped—a strangely human sound—as he flung his sword up, clumsily defending himself as he tried to shake them off.

Evvie turned to Leo, who was standing slack-jawed, squinting at who-knew-what. The ring was still in his right hand, but held loosely now. She reached across his body for it, but she was too slow; he clenched his fist and batted her out of the way. The creatures clinging to Hal's wing had been joined by two more, and succeeded in tearing off a whole section of feathers. Evvie heard the angel cry out in pain a moment before the hilt of the black sword came up and clouted him on the side of the head. He fell.

She was on the floor, on top of Leo, and it must be because she had knocked him down. She was grabbing his fist to bang it against the flagstones to make him release the ring. Slithering, oily shapes were dropping down now in droves on the angel's fallen form. The black fissure reared above them, remote and impassive, leaving the rest of the job to the scavengers.

Ernest hauled her off of Leo, and the two of them pinned her to the floor. It wasn't easy—both men were panting with exertion and seemed disoriented, and Leo's nose was bleeding. And Evvie was determined to get the ring and call off the creatures savaging her angel.

"Get them to stop her, damn it!" Ernest thumped Evvie back onto the floor and leaned all his weight on her shoulders to keep her there.

"You mean kill her?"

"Of course I don't mean kill her!" Ernest sounded alarmed. "Get them to make her forget all this. Do it the way Solomon did it—we know it works, now, anyway. Call one of them, and ask it which of its brothers can change memories. Damn it, Leo—look, give me the ring and I'll do it."

*

"I'd be the first to admit that I could be wrong," said Father Underhill, carving off a forkful of gingerbread. "I'd be happy to be wrong. But if I am, he is too."

"You mean he thinks he's a devil?" said Sara. "That's a different story entirely. Though I must say, if that's what he looked like, I don't blame Charlie for thinking he was an angel."

"Of course not," said her father.

"He has lost his memory," said Evvie. "He doesn't know what he is. But I do. I met him before, when he knew what he was and was doing his job. He's an angel of the Lord."

Father Underhill set down his fork and looked at her.

"He appeared to me in a vision," Evvie went on, "and told me to go to Patmos. The second time we met, he came to my aid when Leo was trying to make me control the devils he and Ernest had summoned. They stole my memory of that night, but it's come back. It wasn't another devil that I summoned—it was Hal. Well, he came as a favour to me. And he faced down Beelzebub, or someone like that, and would have beaten him if he hadn't also had all the little devils to contend with. If he was in that sarcophagus in the lodge, it was because Ernest and Leo ordered the little devils to put him there after they … after they'd finished with him."

Father Underhill pushed back his chair and stood up.

"He can't have gone far," he said. "It's not as if he has wings. But perhaps it would be better not to create another scene." He pulled out his wallet and counted out money. "I'll settle up, and we'll go after him."

"I am rather dying to get out of here," said Sara.

Outside in the steep street, Father Underhill braced Sara's chair with one knee while looking along the house fronts for Hal's distinctive figure. He was sitting in a doorway a few houses uphill from them. He stayed put as they approached, watching them warily.

They reached the doorway, and Father Underhill wedged the wheelchair securely against the stoop to prevent it rolling down the hill. Hal had got to his feet, but remained backed into the doorway.

"You have spoken to Charles, I take it," he said, looking at Father Underhill.

"Yes. I'm sorry for what may have been an overreaction. I don't know what you are, and the possibility of your being a devil, drinking tea with my daughter—"

"I quite understand. I would think less of you if you had not done it." His gaze flicked towards Sara, and he smiled slightly.

"Well," said Father Underhill, "that's either good of you, or … not."

"Yes. I think that kind of uncertainty is likely to dog all of our attempts to communicate, don't you?"

"Indeed. I suppose that is why you decided to cut your ties with Charlie."

"Well … it either is or it isn't."

"Here we go round the mulberry bush, in effect." Father Underhill folded his arms. "Let's just accept the premise that you don't know whether you're good or bad. What that would make you, basically, is human."

"I am not that. I will show you."

What he did, or tried to do, Evvie could not at first guess. But the effect on Sara's father was instant and startling. He took a step toward Hal, right hand raised as if to strike him. He stopped himself just short. "Don't," he bit out. He dropped his hand, stepped back. "Don't try that again. I realize you're immortal, but I'd have a go at killing you, and it wouldn't do either of us any good."

Hal had shrunk back against the door, looking alarmed. "I am so sorry. I didn't realize someone had been in there before. I would never had done that. I'm so sorry."

"Not to worry."

"I'm tired of hurting people," Hal muttered unhappily.

"It's all right. You weren't to know. And I take your point—but I didn't mean literally human. I meant spiritually. All any of us can do is hope that we're good—that with God's help we can be good. Isn't that more or less the situation you're in?"

"I'm not at all sure that I can avail myself of God's help. I am not sure it's … accessible to me."

"Also quite a human thing to feel, I'm afraid."

"Is it?" Hal seemed genuinely astonished. "But it is never true for you!"

"No, but we are very prone to forget that."

Hal nodded, straightened up, and ran a hand through his hair. He looked Father Underhill in the eye. "What do I seem like to you—honestly?" he asked.

"Honestly? A troubled young man. A very *brilliant* troubled young man, with tremendous potential."

The angel laughed.

"Come with us," said Father Underhill. "I've just thought of something."

*

The church was small and grey like the rest of the village, standing flush with the street, and behind it was a lumpy green churchyard full of ancient headstones, surrounded by a mossy wall. The street door stood open onto a dim interior. Sara steered her wheelchair inside, and Evvie followed her. The door let them in on the side at the back, behind the rows of pews, facing a stained glass window of a saint whose coloured light fell on the font with its carved wooden cover. It was cold, like the inside of a house that has been shut up over the winter.

"Well?" said Sara, turning her chair.

Hal had followed them in, and stood looking around the interior of the church.

"I owe you an apology," said Father Underhill.

"No," said Hal. "I should have come here before. I didn't think of it at first, and then … I was afraid."

"So we're all agreed now that he isn't a devil?" said Sara.

"Yes," said Father Underhill. "He couldn't have walked in here so easily if he were."

"You should have told me you were worried about that," said Evvie shyly to Hal. "I could have reassured you. I do remember you. In fact, I think I am to blame for what happened to you. You were coming to my aid when you were attacked."

"That does not make you to blame! I should have been better able to defend myself."

"Well, you were very badly outnumbered, and they summoned a … quite a senior devil to take you on."

"I see. Then I should have called for assistance myself, don't you think?"

"I did try to help."

He smiled. "I didn't mean you. But thank you." He looked at Father Underhill. "I don't suppose you know where Charles is now?"

"Oh!" said Evvie. "I do."

Chapter Twenty-Four

FREE WILL

D r. Good was pitifully grateful to see Charlie and his crew arrive. He was not, as Charlie had expected, sitting around his farm house in a state of desperate despondency. Instead, he seemed like a man galvanized into action. The piles of books were gone from the lobby, the old sign had been put back up, and when the men arrived, Dr. Good said he had just got off the phone from ordering a shipment of shingles for the roof. Timber and other supplies had already been delivered.

"I can't believe I have left it so long," he kept saying. "I don't know what I was thinking."

A big "Closed for Repairs" sign hung on the front gate.

"Oh, Mr. Boult!" said Dr. Good. "That reminds me! I met a man at the lumberyard who told me that he has received a grant of money for the rebuilding of bomb-damaged churches in Kent. I immediately thought of you, as you had told me of your specialty in church restoration. I mentioned your name, and the man seemed interested in meeting you. I made sure to procure his card—here it is—so that you might contact him. I hope I did not do amiss?"

"No! Golly. I … thank you! That's awfully kind of you. I'll get in touch for sure."

He stood looking at the card, picturing a whole new future spooling out ahead of him. He slipped it into his pocket.

Charlie explained the plans for the repairs, and they got to work. Latham, who had a talent for working with his hands and was a skilled mechanic, was the most useful, as Charlie had known he would be. Ernest and Rosalind were both good at following instructions. Leo Rathburn was clumsy and distracted; Rosalind explained in an undertone that he had been friends with Josephine Good, and was suspected of being involved in her death. Charlie was reminded uncomfortably of his conviction that he knew very well who had killed Miss Good. Only, of course, he didn't.

The first task in working on the farm house was to build scaffolding around the destroyed section. The young men and Rosalind got to work on this while Daphne traipsed moodily about the yard, seemingly doing her best to distract Ernest and make him drop things. Charlie wanted to order her inside, or at least make her sit down somewhere at a safe distance. If she hadn't been so pretty, he would have done it. But he was hampered by the suspicion that a normal man would have been incapable of getting angry with someone who looked like Daphne.

She was flirting, in a desultory way, with all the men there, except, for some reason, Charlie himself. But she seemed to have taken a special interest in Latham. He was putting together sections of scaffolding on the ground, a task that couldn't be entrusted to any of the others, and Charlie was annoyed to see her trying to distract him from it. Rosalind was looking daggers at both of them, Ernest just looked anguished, and Latham was too ludicrously chivalrous—or maybe just too oblivious—to brush her off. Charlie climbed down from the roof.

Some of the things he'd been thinking were ridiculous. Men got angry at beautiful women all the time, beat them and murdered them even. And he wasn't proposing to go that far.

"Can I talk to you for a moment?" He interrupted her mid-sentence.

She turned her big blue eyes on him in surprise. Latham went back to his task, mouthing "Thank you," behind Daphne's back.

"We have a lot of work to do here, Miss Montague," said Charlie. "I don't expect you to help, but right now, you're getting in the way, and I need you not to do that. Okay?"

Daphne looked at him curiously, her head tipped to one side, in a gesture that he recognized from somewhere, though he'd certainly never seen her do it before. He'd never even had a conversation with this woman. But she was staring at him now, her eyes wide and dazzlingly blue, and he felt as if at any moment she would throw him open like a book, and flip expertly through to the right section, the one she knew well how to find …

He wanted to take a step back, but he stood his ground.

"I see what it is," she cooed, in a soft, almost motherly voice that sorted oddly with her femme-fatale exterior. "You're jealous, aren't you?"

"Jealous?" Charlie repeated, forcing a confident smile that did not at all reflect how he felt. "I'm not the one who needs to be jealous."

"Where's your red-haired friend? I haven't seen him around."

Charlie stared. "Didn't know you knew him."

As he climbed back up to the roof, his mind raced. She knew all about him—a woman he'd never spoken to before—and she'd done the same thing as Miss Good, who had just been killed. What did it mean?

Sitting astride the intact section of roof, keeping a sharp eye on Daphne below, because he was now convinced she was up to no good, he remembered what the police officer had said about how Josephine Good met her end. *It looked like a house fell on her.* He looked down at the fallen section of the farm house, the rubble still lying on the ground. When he'd heard that, he'd thought it had been a cruel joke on Hal's part, killing her that way after the woman had survived the fall of the actual farm house. But now a different possibility occurred to him. In spite of the warm sun baking the rooftop, he felt as if a cold wind had snuck down the collar of his shirt.

Daphne was wandering about the yard, her bright red shawl tossed loosely around her shoulders. He could see her cascade of blonde curls bouncing as she walked. She paused in the far corner near the stone wall, and looked straight up at Charlie. For a moment she held his gaze, and he felt a stirring of unaccustomed vertigo.

What if Hal hadn't killed Miss Good? What if the falling house had killed her last July, and something had been keeping her alive—not even keeping her alive, but using her body—in the meantime, only to abandon it on Saturday for a new host?

She'd been avoiding him not only because she knew he was gay—she'd seen him kissing another man in an alley—but because she'd been warned off. *She has designs on you*, Hal had said. *I want her to know that they will fail because you are mine.*

Why not just tell me right then what she was? Because he'd looked at her and recognized himself?

But he wasn't the same thing—that was clear. His body hadn't belonged to anyone else; he'd made it wholesale out of something in Charlie's memory. If something had been using Miss Good, and now Daphne, it was something from quite the opposite end of the spectrum. He couldn't see yet how this fit together with Evvie's story of summoning a demon in the Victorian lodge, but he had a feeling he was onto something, all the same.

Below him, Daphne's blue eyes gaped like pools, beckoning, daring him to jump, whispering something about shame, ending it all because of the shame … He wasn't listening. Beyond her, on the other side of the stone wall, in the street, he'd seen a party pulling up in a sporty little open car. The driver was Father Underhill, and Sara and Evgenia were together in the back seat. And in the front, beside Father Underhill, opening the door now and jumping down to help with Sara's wheelchair, was Hal.

They were all smiling and laughing about something, Father Underhill turning to talk to the girls in the back, Hal pausing in opening the trunk to share in the joke. Charlie felt as jealous as he had that first morning in the pub, that someone was talking and laughing with Hal, and it was not him. But mostly what he felt was an overwhelming joy.

"Leo!" He heard Daphne's voice from below. "Oh, Leo!"

Charlie looked for Leo, and saw him clambering awkwardly up onto the top of the half-assembled scaffolding. The man was still wearing his jacket and tie, and looked like an ass, and he was climbing from a clearly unstable bit of scaffolding onto a precarious, unsupported piece of roof. Charlie held his breath. It was one of those situations where it was best not to berate the idiot until he was finished with his idiocy. If he got quickly up onto the roof, he'd likely be fine, but if he hesitated—

"Leo!" Daphne called again.

Leo paused and looked down. "What?" he demanded angrily.

A whole section of roof that had been hanging unsupported for months shuddered and split from the rest. The frame under Charlie groaned and sagged to one side. Leo caught one of the uprights of the unstable scaffolding and swayed poised there, unable to move in either direction.

"Be careful!" Daphne called.

"Be careful?" Rosalind shrieked. "That's your fault, Daphne! You just distracted him! That's your fault!"

Charlie swung his leg over the roof beam and let himself down the side towards Leo. The roof gave a sickening lurch under him, and he froze. Looking down over his shoulder, he could see Leo clinging white-knuckled to the swaying scaffolding as the beam holding up his section of roof sheared slowly away beneath him. And past Leo he could see the road, the car parked on the other side of the stone wall, its occupants looking up with horror. And Hal, springing from the running board to the hood of the car and across to the stone wall, wings unfurling, Lenten purple in the strong sunlight. Three great wing-beats carried him through the air between the wall and the rooftop, and he caught Leo by the front of his shirt as the shingles and beams slid away beneath him to clatter to the ground. Charlie scrambled back up to a solid perch on the roof beam. The purple wings passed over him in an elegant arc as Hal swept Leo out of harm's way, and finally saw the face of the man he had rescued.

"You," Hal said, eyes widening in recognition. And he dropped him.

Chapter Twenty-Five

JUST YOUR BASIC GOOD-VERSUS-EVIL

Evvie felt the wind of the angel's wings like a blow as he vaulted over the car into the air. She saw him seize Leo by the front of his shirt, plucking him effortlessly off the falling section of roof, before he wheeled in the air and opened his hand, and Leo fell. He flailed his arms on the descent, and his tie flapped. His body disappeared behind the wreckage of the farm house, but she heard the thud of his landing. Her eyes had gone back up to the angel, who had alighted briefly on the roof, his purple wings still spread. Looking into his face, she saw just the faintest trace of shock. He had not punished Leo, though Leo might have deserved what he got; he had murdered him.

He turned, and as he sprang again into the sky, she heard Charlie call his name, saw him reach out his hands towards him. The angel dodged away and took flight.

Father Underhill opened the gate by the car and ran for the back of the house. Evvie stood between the gate and the car, where Sara was still seated. She was aware of Dr. Good shouting, Rosalind wailing, and Daphne for some reason walking towards her across the lawn. But she stood still staring after the speck in the bright sky that the angel had become.

Daphne walked through the gate and brushed past her. Father Underhill came out from behind the rubble where Leo had fallen, to meet Ernest and Dr. Good. He shook his head. Ernest let out a moan that sounded like a curse, and pushed past the priest to see for himself.

If Hal hadn't intervened, Evvie thought, Leo would surely have fallen, and surely have died. Did that make any difference? You could be the instrument of God's wrath and a murderer at the same time. Scriptural passages about Assyrians tumbled half-remembered in her mind.

Behind her she heard a car door slam, and Sara's voice: "Daphne? What are you doing?" She spun around just as the car's engine roared to life, with Daphne behind the wheel.

The ignition key had been on the front seat. They had been joking about letting Evvie drive home, and Father Underhill had laughingly passed her the key, which she had tossed back, and it had landed on the seat just a moment before everyone's attention had been drawn to the man about to fall from the roof.

"Daphne!" she cried. And then she threw herself back through the open gate as Daphne floored the accelerator, aiming the car straight at her. She picked herself up from the grass in time to see the vicar's little car speeding away down the country lane, with Sara leaning forward to grasp the front seat and expostulate with the driver. The world seemed to sway around her, and she sat down again abruptly.

Father Underhill was kneeling in the grass beside her.

"Are you all right, Evgenia?"

"I threw the key on the seat, Father—I'm so sorry!"

"That's not important. I shouldn't have left it there."

She still felt shaky. She had caught a glimpse of Daphne's face as the car bore down on her, and it had been frighteningly blank.

"Do you know what happened?" he asked calmly.

"Daphne got in the car and tried to run her down!" came Rosalind's voice. She had arrived at Evvie's side. "I saw the whole thing. Then she drove off. She's been acting *very* strangely for a while. Hello, padre, I don't think we've been introduced—I'm Rosalind Lake, and I'm—"

"Thank you, Miss Lake. Do you have any idea why your friend would have taken the car just now?"

"She's my cousin, padre, and as I said, she's been behaving very oddly, why only the other day—"

"She's possessed."This was Charlie Boult, out of breath, running up from where he had just climbed down from the roof. "Come on, I'll explain on the road. My jeep's parked around the front."

Father Underhill got to his feet, and reached down a hand for Evvie. She grasped his hand and let herself be hauled to her feet and hustled along towards Charlie's jeep.

Rosalind came scurrying after them, and by the time they reached the jeep, Latham had attached himself to the group too. They crammed themselves into the back seat on either side of Evvie as Charlie was starting the engine. Father Underhill glanced back as if he would have liked to tell them to get out, but didn't want to waste the time it would have taken. Evvie knew he wanted her along for some reason, that there was something he thought she would be able to do. She hoped he wasn't wrong.

"You see, as I was saying, padre," Rosalind went on, having caught her breath after running to keep up, "she began acting strangely on the weekend, when—"

"She drove north past the house, didn't she?" Charlie interrupted her, steering the jeep down the drive.

"She went that way," said Evvie, and she pointed, not confident she knew which direction was north.

Charlie swung the jeep out of the Zion drive and into the lane. Evvie hung onto the underside of the seat while Rosalind and Latham careened around on either side of her. Rosalind was still trying to talk to Father Underhill.

"Do you think she's headed for York, padre? I think she might be, because this is the right direction for it, isn't it? It's too bad the road signs are all gone, that'll make it much harder to follow them. Do you know, I think she tried to talk one of the patients into killing himself the other day?"

"Ros, for God's sake, shut up!" Latham cried. "Nobody wants to hear it right now."

But Rosalind had succeeded in getting Father Underhill's attention. "What do you mean?" he asked, turning in his seat to look back at her. As he did so, the jeep made a tremendous lurch around a sharp turn in the road, and he had to hang onto his seat to avoid being thrown out. "Charlie! Kindly remember this vehicle doesn't have wings!"

"Sorry, Father!"

"Miss Lake, what were you saying?"

"Um ... well, it was just ..." Rosalind became unexpectedly bashful.

"You told me about it," Latham cut in. "It was nothing. Ros saw her talking to Anderson the same afternoon that he tried to pitch himself off the roof, that's all. Just a coincidence."

"No," said Evvie, "that's not all." As soon as Charlie said the word "possessed," it had all fallen together in her mind. She knew she'd seen the same thing he had. "She seduced Captain Carter, told him he was disgusting, and shut him in the supply closet with all the medication, and he'd swallowed a big handful of pills when I found him. Then she took Anderson up on the roof, treated him the same way, and left him there. And it's the same thing Miss Good was doing, more or less. She was muttering things about suicide to Reardon just before he went off his head and started waving a pistol. That was when she was wearing King Solomon's ring, but now Daphne has it."

"That makes sense," said Charlie. "I think Miss Good was possessed by the same devil that's got Daphne now."

"Oh, my God!" Latham wailed. "Sir, have you gone insane? Padre, should he be behind the wheel of a car when he's gone insane?"

"He hasn't gone insane, soldier. Be quiet. Charlie, I do think an explanation would be in order, if you can talk and continue to drive safely—I assume you're driving safely."

"Absolutely, Father."

"I don't know what your problem is, Latham," Rosalind was saying. "Didn't you see the angel?"

"The what?"

"What do you think happened to Leo?"

"He fell off the roof! I didn't see it happen, I just heard the shouting and stuff falling, and I came around the house and he was lying there with his head smashed—sorry, Ros, but he was. Don't try to tell me there were angels and devils involved in that!"

"The angel threw him off the roof! I can't believe you didn't see that. Leo *was* a bit of a rotter—I'm sure he did something to deserve it. I don't know how the devils enter into it, but—"

"It was the devil who tried to kill Leo in the first place," said Charlie. "You spotted that yourself. It was Daphne calling to him that would have made him fall. Hal saved him—and then thought better of it."

"Hal?" Rosalind and Latham repeated.

"The angel," said Evvie. "His name is Hal."

"Short for Henry?" said Latham, sounding hysterical.

"I don't think so," said Evvie. "Shh."

"Perhaps if we let Squadron Leader Boult explain," Father Underhill suggested tersely.

"It's not much of an explanation," said Charlie. "Evvie's worked it out too. It's just that I think Miss Good really was killed last summer when the farm house was hit by a stray bomb, and one of the devils that Ernest and Leo summoned was using her body. Everyone said she'd had an amazing conversion and suddenly started helping her brother run the retreat centre and distributing tracts at the hospital. But the retreat centre was going bankrupt printing books and putting up new signs, while the building was falling down around their ears, and the tracts she was distributing at Adderley were convincing men to kill themselves. Miss Good wasn't the, uh, good influence everybody was fooled into thinking she was. The first time I met her, she weaselled all kinds of personal information out of me and tried to make me feel bitter about everyone I know—and that was in half an hour over coffee and a sandwich. I can only imagine what she could have done to a man who was stuck in a hospital bed.

"But none of that was really Miss Good's fault. Miss Good was dead. And when the devil was done with her body, he left it lying in that field, looking like a house fell on it—because it had."

"And then he moved on to Daphne?" said Rosalind. "Does that mean that Daph's … dead?"

"I don't know," Charlie admitted. "I don't know for sure that it's the same devil, only that something about her seemed the same to me. And it would make sense."

"No, it wouldn't," Latham muttered despairingly. "None of this makes sense."

"Cheer up, Lath," said Rosalind. "It's just your basic good-versus-evil, angels and devils—it's not that complicated."

"I think I know why the devil switched to Daphne when he did," said Charlie. "I think it was because he got made as Miss Good. Hal did something strange that would make much more sense if he'd started to suspect what Miss Good really was. He should've told me what he was thinking, but … well, there's a lot he should've told me, and definitely a few things he shouldn't have done. He's not what you'd call a top-notch angel."

"Is he … " Rosalind started. "Is he your … guardian angel?"

Evvie was about to say that no, he was *hers*.

"He was my lover," said Charlie. "I think we're probably through now."

"Oh, my God," moaned Latham.

"All due respect to your mediocre angel," said Father Underhill, "but I think it was Evgenia who made the fiend abandon Miss Good."

"Really?" said Charlie. He glanced back at Evvie with a look of respect. "How do you figure?"

"She ordered her out of Adderley—didn't you, Evgenia?" Father Underhill looked back at her too.

"Yes, Father." She felt suddenly frightened. That wasn't why he'd brought her along, was it? He didn't think that she could do anything now? Not now, not after her angel had proven himself to be a fraud.

"But why do we suppose Daphne's taken Sara now?" asked Charlie.

"Who's Sara?" Rosalind and Latham chorused.

*

Daphne was not, as Rosalind had speculated, going to York. She was driving over a bleak stretch of moor; they could see the little car speeding along the grey streak of road. Evvie had been right to think it could go fast.

The roar of an engine behind them made her look back, and she saw Ernest on his motorbike, the sidecar empty, gaining on them. Racing after the woman he loved, who might already be long gone. Her heart ached for him.

"She's driving to the coast," said Charlie, breaking the loud monotony of engine noise and wind. They could all see that he was right; ahead of them, the brown and green of the moor rose gently and then dropped away towards a glittering line of sea just visible now on the horizon. Their quarry had crested the hill and disappeared from sight.

"Well, I don't understand that," said Rosalind. "What can she possibly be doing?"

"I still don't understand why Fidelity was—I mean why Sara was calling herself Fidelity," said Latham.

"It's classified, Lath, you dope!"

"Shh!" said Evvie. She had a feeling she knew, as Charlie and Father Underhill knew, what Daphne was doing. They were just north of Newingthorpe; the coast here was not gentle beaches but dramatic white chalk cliffs towering above the tides.

Ernest overtook them on his bike when the jeep was slowed by a number of sheep meandering across the road. The sheep scampered and fled as Ernest drove recklessly in among them and ploughed onward, going downhill now. Daphne's car was in sight again, though far in the distance. They saw when she stopped, saw the little figure of Daphne, in her bright red shawl, getting out, hauling Sara's wheelchair out of the boot. Sara remaining firmly in the car. An argument, the car door hauled open. Sara in the wheelchair now, the two headed for the cliff's edge.

"She won't want to push her over," Charlie said grimly. "She'll want Sara to do it herself."

She'll never do it, Evvie thought. But then she thought of Reardon and Anderson and MacGregor and Carter, and of how hard it would be to face life as a pretty girl with a missing leg. She thought of how much Sara would hate to be reduced to a damsel in distress like this, with all of them rushing to rescue her. How tempting to escape the whole thing, just by rolling gently over the edge …

Ahead of them, Ernest slewed his motorcycle around and jumped off, leaving the machine to skid across the road, blocking the way.

He'd chosen a good spot; there was a ditch on one side of the road, marshy ground on the other. Charlie slammed the jeep to a halt, cursing under his breath.

"What are you playing at?" he shouted, standing up in the front of the jeep. "Get that thing out of the way!"

Father Underhill was already down from the jeep, had jumped across the ditch, and was running down towards the cliff.

"Stay back!" Ernest yelled at him. "Stay away from her!"

Evvie had barely registered that he had something in his hand before he had fired the first shot, and she saw that it was a gun. Rosalind was screaming; actually, both Rosalind and Latham were screaming. Evvie had to scramble over one of them—she wasn't sure which, as they were both trying to clutch at one another—to get out of the jeep. Ernest fired again, and a third time, but the third shot was directed at Charlie, who was out of the jeep and running towards him. The bullet shattered the jeep's windscreen, and Charlie tackled Ernest to the ground. Evvie had slipped and fallen into the ditch, which was full of muddy water at the bottom.

She scrambled up the other side, wiping her hands on her skirt. Ernest's gun went off again, and she heard the air going out of one of the jeep's tires. She began to run down the rough hillside after Father Underhill. He had thought she could do something. She didn't know what it was.

He hadn't stopped running, even for an instant, when Ernest shot at him. He had reached the two women at the cliff's edge now, and Evvie, coming down the slope, had a clear view of what happened when he arrived.

Sara chose her moment perfectly. Her father was within a few seconds of reaching them when she dug her heel into the turf and shoved the wheelchair back, knocking Daphne to the ground. Sara reached for her father, and he grabbed her, and swung her up out of the chair as Daphne kicked it. The wheelchair rolled the foot or so to the edge of the cliff, toppled, and then stuck, tipped crazily to one side, and hung there, silhouetted against the sparkling water.

Daphne gathered herself up and rose from the ground, leaving behind her red shawl, which the wind caught and rolled away up the slope.

Evvie was still running towards the group by the cliff's edge, faster now because of the incline. She saw Daphne step back, past the poised wheelchair, and spread her arms like a diver. She knew what it must mean.

So did Father Underhill. He caught Daphne's wrist as she dropped backward, and for a horrible moment he was supporting almost all her weight, still holding onto his daughter, who couldn't let go because of the wheelchair that was in the way.

Daphne was still alive, and the thing possessing her was trying to kill her. *This is what he thought I could do!* Evvie's heart cried.

"Help!" he shouted. Daphne was not just hanging from his grasp; she was pulling on him, her heels poised on the edge of the cliff, with a strength that looked more than the human Daphne had ever possessed.

Evvie reached them, and realized she still had no idea what to do.

"Take Sara," he ordered.

Of course. That made sense. Much more practical than her trying to take on the thing possessing Daphne. She ducked under his arm and got her arms around Sara's doll-like little body, and Sara hugged her back just as hard as she had been hugging her father. He extricated himself neatly, even managed a cheerful-sounding, "Thank you, Evgenia!" before grabbing Daphne with his free hand. With Sara out of danger, he had the situation under control.

Evvie overbalanced and sat down hard in the grass, still hugging Sara.

"Are you all right?" she asked.

"Mm-hm!" Sara's reply came out from where she had buried her face in Evvie's sweater. She looked up. "Unscathed," she said brightly.

Father Underhill had pulled Daphne towards him and caught her by the waist, so that for a moment they looked for all the world like a pair of dancers on the edge of the cliff. She tried to pull back, with a little snarl, then when she couldn't break his hold, she wriggled lasciviously, trying to wrap her leg around his thigh, but he held her just far enough away from him that she couldn't manage it. She went limp, head flung back, trying again to drag him towards her and over the edge.

"Daphne!" he said sharply. "This is just silly. Stop it."

And that was what got through to Daphne. Not the devil possessing Daphne, but the real Daphne; she couldn't stand being called silly. She jerked her head up, looking at Father Underhill with outrage.

"In the name of the Father and of the Son and of the Holy Spirit—*get out*," he said, giving her a little shake. She convulsed slightly, as if she was about to be sick, and an oily cloud separated from her and hung in the air over the water as she let herself be pulled up finally onto solid ground.

She stumbled forward, putting up her arms in a wilting gesture, confident of being caught by Father Underhill. He didn't catch her; he stepped aside, clapping her casually on the back in the kind of *you'll-be-all-right* gesture he might have used with one of the men in his regiment. She caught herself, wholly startled and confused—but she didn't fall down.

She tugged at the thumb of one hand, and something gold flashed down into the grass. Behind her, the cloud was dense and dark against the glitter of the sea, but it was fissuring now into squirming pieces. It was not *one* of the little devils that Leo and Ernest had summoned and that had fallen upon Hal. It was all of them.

Evvie let go of Sara to reach for the ring, and then stood, planting herself firmly between the cloud of wriggling, oily things and her friend, as she slid Solomon's ring onto her thumb.

She heard a chorus of giggles.

You again! The voices spoke in unison now, not competing with one another as they had before. *We remember you!*

*

She was in the Cave of the Apocalypse on Patmos, as in her vision. Of course, because this *was* her vision. But in the place where the angel had sat, there was no one. Her angel was a murderer and a homosexual. The vision was ruined forever. As Evvie looked around, she realized that the cave had been desecrated. The lamps hung broken and askew, the iconostasis had been smashed and defaced, and rude words were scrawled over the walls in English and Greek. Over in the corner where St. John used to sleep, a couple lay on the stone floor, twined round each other and kissing hungrily. It was all somehow her fault; she had brought sin and shame into this holy place and destroyed it. She didn't deserve to live.

She looked up at the ceiling and found it roiling and dripping with an oily darkness.

"No!" she screamed. "No!"

She knew what it meant. They had found their way into her vision, polluting and corrupting. She was possessed.

"I can't be!" she shouted. "I'm a Bride of Christ! I'm off limits!"

She fell on the floor, her head on her clasped hands on the end of the bench. She remembered him sitting there, leaning down with his forearms on his knees to talk to her as she sat where she was now.

"And I fell at his feet to worship him," St. John had written of one of the angels who appeared to him. "And he said unto me, See thou do it not: I am thy fellowservant, and of thy brethren that have the testimony of Jesus …"

And she, sitting at her angel's feet, had got the idea that she could be like him. His fellowservant. But he was not as she had imagined. He had killed a man in anger, and lain down with another man in lust. The heavenly messenger sent to her had not even been able to live up to fairly basic human standards. Did that mean that she couldn't either? Maybe the life that she had imagined she was called to was illusory after all.

Or maybe it meant something else. She had summoned Hal, and he had come to her aid, and been maimed and imprisoned, lost his name and his memory and his otherworldly purity, and it was all her fault.

She looked up, reaching a hand to brush back her hair from her face, and realized that for some reason her hair hadn't fallen in her face. A shadow fell across the floor, crisp in the bright sunlight spilling through from the door. She turned and for a moment could only make out the dark outline of a tall figure in the doorway, wings half-folded behind him. She blinked, and as her eyes adjusted to the light, she saw that they were not wings but the hanging sleeves of his surplice. It was Charlie Boult, vested as an acolyte, standing in the sunlight and stooping to look inside the cave.

"Do you need a hand in there?" he asked.

"What are you doing here?" Had she wronged him in some way, or was his appearance in her vision the work of Grace?

He appeared to think about his answer. "I … kind of want revenge?"

"On me?"

"On you? No!"

"Yes!" It made sense. "I'm the one who destroyed Hal."

"Destroyed him? How do you figure that?"

"If he hadn't come to rescue me—if I hadn't let Leo put the ring on my hand, or if I'd only been able to get it back from him afterward … But they tore Hal apart and shut him in a coffin, and … " And what? *He was reduced to making love to you?* "He wasn't a devil."

"I know."

"Leo thought he was a devil because he couldn't tell the difference. All Leo knew was that he wanted him. He was an angel. He was a terrific angel, Charlie—you should have seen him when he took on the prince of Hell."

"What! How?"

"With a sword. And if it had been a fair fight, he would have won, I am certain of it."

"Well, sure," said Charlie, with a kind of half-suppressed smile.

"It was all the little devils ganging up on him that were his undoing."

"All the little devils, huh?"

Evvie tried to remember now why she had felt so guilty a moment before. She looked at Charlie, standing there in his acolyte's vestments, with his arms folded, looking proud of his lover and wanting revenge on the creatures that had hurt him. Because of course that was what he had meant; he had come to help her deal with the devils who were polluting her vision, because they were also the ones who had ganged up on Hal.

She got to her feet, gathering the fabric of her skirt in one hand. She looked down at her white novice's cassock, clean and crisp, falling down to the floor. Reaching up, she touched her veil, feeling it snugly in place. She looked at her hands. Solomon's ring was not on her thumb; it was back in the real world, to which she needed to return.

She cast her eyes around the interior of the cave again. Everything roiled with the same oily contagion, because everything was *made* from it. The lamps were not silver but made out of tin cans; the icons were crude, misshapen scribbles, like the work of a malevolent child. The couple writhing on St. John's bed were lizards in human clothes. It was all fake, a crude imitation of her vision. She was not possessed; she was the one in charge here.

The cave shuddered around her, the details dissolving. Now the iconostasis looked like nothing but a bunch of old boards, the lizards had lost their clothing and seemed to be fighting rather than making love. Great gobs of syrupy darkness dripped from the ceiling.

"How did you do that?" Charlie asked in awe.

Evvie just laughed.

When the lizards had melted into an indistinct lump, and the iconostasis had burst and rattled to the ground in fragments, the remainder of the oily cloud had gathered itself again in the middle of the cave, and began hardening into human shape—or not exactly human shape.

His wings were grey and speckled, like an owl's; folded back and up behind him, they brushed the ceiling of the cave, and he moved them restlessly. His hair was long, falling around his shoulders in bright red curls. He was vested in black, the gold embroidery exquisite, unlike anything she had ever seen. The urge to step forward and examine the stitching on the black phelonion was almost unbearable.

Her head snapped up and she looked at Charlie. He had taken

a step in from the door, as entranced by the figure as she had been a moment ago, though in a different way.

"The vestments are wrong," she said sharply.

His eyes flicked vaguely in her direction. "Wh—what?"

"He's vested incorrectly—as a priest, not as a deacon. It's the wrong … the wrong metaphor. He shouldn't be wearing the phe-lonion—the—the chasuble."

"Oh! No, that is wrong." He shook himself slightly, as if waking himself up. "You know what they say: God is in the detail."

She hadn't heard them say that before, but it fit the situation. To distract them both, she went on talking: "The epitrachelion, too—you would call that his stole—that is only for priests. A deacon would wear a different style, one that goes over his shoulder."

"No kidding? The wings aren't right either," said Charlie. "Those long feathers—what do you call them? Ailerons?"

"I don't know," she admitted.

"They should be longer—bigger altogether. Otherwise there's no way he could, uh, control his roll properly." He demonstrated by swaying his hand in the air, and she realized he was using airplane terminology. The fake Hal didn't seem to get the joke. "And of course the colour of the wings should match the vestments."

"Obviously," she said. "Not just flat black, though—there should be a bit of iridescence—"

"Matching those flowers on the front of his—what did you call it?"

"Well, it should be a sticharion—"

"A dalmatic?"

"Exactly. And of course those flowers should be lilies, too."

"Right. No, it's a poor effort overall. Actually the most telling thing is the fact that he hasn't started to laugh at us yet." He reached out his hand for hers, and she grabbed it. "Shall we?"

They ran together out the door, and were back on the hillside in Yorkshire. She let go of Charlie's hand to cup her own around the ring with its flat red stone.

"Go back from whence you came!" she shouted. "All of you! Never trouble us again!"

Chapter Twenty-Six

THE ROAD TO ZION

Under the circumstances, the mundane process of sorting out who would ride back with whom seemed surreal. It was Father Underhill who remained adamant that they all needed to return to Zion to await the arrival of the police. Charlie, for his part, felt as though he had to keep moving or he would sink under some inescapable weight.

"I still don't *quite* understand what happened," said Rosalind, as if she thought she were the only one who hadn't got a particularly difficult joke.

"Angels and devils," murmured Latham, sounding a bit drunk.

"Just devils," said Charlie. "Definitely just devils, this time."

Rosalind and Latham had come down from the road last of all; Charlie hadn't noticed when they'd arrived, but they had probably witnessed the whole scene, if they had been looking. They were holding hands.

Ernest, who had calmed down after Charlie punched him soundly in the jaw and confiscated his gun, was already walking slowly back up the slope towards his motorcycle, his arm around Daphne's shoulders.

"Do you think it's safe to let them go off on their own?" Charlie asked, finding Father Underhill at his side, with Sara in her wheel-chair.

Father Underhill was looking after the retreating couple as if he wouldn't have minded if they did, and never came back. But he sighed and said, "I think they're both genuinely remorseful. And he said something about owing us an explanation. Which, if he has one, he certainly does."

Daphne had at first tried to pretend that she didn't remember anything that had happened while she was possessed. She'd given herself away by finally not being able to resist thanking Father Underhill for saving her. He just looked at her until she admitted that this was not the only thing she remembered, and began a fumbling attempt at an apology.

"What should we do with this, Father?" Evvie was holding out the ring with the red stone, cupped in the palm of her hand.

Father Underhill took it from her. "We'll return it to my cousins, Graham's next of kin."

"Is that safe?" asked Sara.

"Safe enough, I think. If you don't know the names of any devils, it's just a ring." He dropped it into his jacket pocket.

"You're not shot, are you, by the way?" said Charlie.

"Shot?"

"You don't look it, but I wouldn't put it past you to get shot and just carry on."

He didn't deny that it was a possibility. "I haven't been, though. When was anybody shooting?"

"Ernest. Fired at you twice."

"Did he? I honestly didn't notice." He started to turn away, stopped, looked back at Charlie. "Can I assume that the reason he didn't go on shooting at me is because you stopped him?"

"Uh … yeah. That's what happened."

"Thank you, Charlie."

"My pleasure."

It occurred to him that there had been a time—not too long ago—when the thought of saving Father Underhill's life and having him *not even notice* would have been almost unbearable. But that time was past. He wondered exactly how that had happened.

In fact, it appeared that Ernest was a terrible shot, and the only thing that had taken a bullet was the jeep. The windscreen was shattered, and the front tire was flat. Charlie told Latham to help change it for the spare. Having a practical task to do snapped Latham out of his daze somewhat.

"What did you do?" he asked. "You and that Greek girl."

"What did it look like we did?"

Rosalind, cleaning up broken glass in the front of the jeep, said, "It looked like Evvie put on Daphne's ring and spoke to that … that *thing*, and then you took her hand."

"That's what we did."

"And then the *thing* disappeared."

"I guess so," said Charlie. "I mean, yeah. That's what happened."

Evvie appeared beside the jeep, where Charlie was kneeling to deal with the tire. "We're going to set off—is that all right? Father Underhill thinks we shouldn't give Ernest and Daphne too much of a head start."

"Good idea," he said.

He looked up at Evvie. Her face seemed full of things she didn't know quite how to say. He could understand that. He had a ridiculous feeling, as if they were two people with a mutual friend awkwardly trying to assess where each of them stood with him. (Are *you* still angry with him? Can you and I still be friends if you hate him now and I don't? Or vice versa.) And then something drew him up short. In all the flurry of strangeness that had just occurred, possibly the strangest thing was what he had done, without even thinking about it. But she didn't necessarily know that he had done it.

He got to his feet, wiping his hands on his handkerchief, and with an effort smiled down at her. "You looked adorable in your habit."

For a moment she just beamed with self-conscious pleasure. Then her eyes widened. "How did you do that?" she whispered.

"I have no idea." He paused, then corrected himself. "I have some idea. But it doesn't make much sense." He shrugged. "It must be something I picked up somewhere."

*

The police had arrived by the time Charlie pulled the jeep up outside Zion's front gate. The door of the farm house stood open, and Ernest's motorcycle was parked on the lawn. Charlie dragged himself wearily up the path and inside, Latham and Rosalind following, hand-in-hand again. Inside, the inspector and sergeant whose names Charlie thought he should remember by now were in the library with everyone else who had already returned.

"It is quite clear to me that I must abandon this house now," Dr. Good was saying. "It has already claimed its second victim."

"Second victim?" said the sergeant suspiciously. "What do you mean?"

"My sister Josephine, you know. Last July. Though—" he looked momentarily startled, as if wondering why he had said that. "Of course, she survived ... "

Charlie propped his shoulder against a window-frame and leaned there, listening to find out what story they were all telling about Leo's death. He had fallen, of course, a terrible accident, though Daphne claimed full responsibility for having called out and distracted him, even seemed quite sorry about it. Charlie watched Ernest hovering tensely by her side, and wondered how you could forgive someone, love someone, after a thing like this happened. Then he wondered why he was asking himself that question.

Nobody mentioned seeing an angel, and Charlie knew he wouldn't either.

"You know, it's interesting he should turn up dead just now," said the inspector. His subordinate looked at him wearily. "We were coming this very morning to arrest him for the murder of one Graham Darby, whose body was found off Horrey Head two weeks ago. We had our eye on Mr. Rathburn for some time, you see, owing to one or two suspicious circumstances, but when Mr. Darby's housekeeper discovered papers recording his own suspicions of Rathburn, dated shortly before it seems Darby left to travel to Yorkshire, well, then we felt we had enough evidence to bring Rathburn in for questioning. And this morning a witness appeared as well. It seems Mr. Rathburn was seen by a fisherman, hauling something out to Horrey Head on the first of February. So you see, we were very close to being able to make an arrest."

"So that's what happened," said Ernest. "I wondered why he stopped worrying about Darby. At first he fretted about Darby being able to connect him with the robbery at his townhouse, but he'd been quiet about that lately. I suppose it was because he'd shot Darby. That would explain it."

"Sir?" said the sergeant sternly.

Ernest unwrapped his arm from around Daphne's waist in order to take a small step away from her. "You know he was a whatdoyoucall—a fence? He dealt in stolen artifacts."

"We believe him to have been dealing in black-market petrol," said the sergeant.

"Oh, he might have been doing that, too," said Ernest with a shrug. "I honestly don't know anything about that. But his antiques business had been crooked since before the war. I don't think he did it for the money, so much as the thrill of having things pass through his hands that properly belonged in museums—he liked the power of it. That's why … that's why he was the first one I turned to when I wanted to take that ring from Graham Darby's house."

Charlie was watching Daphne, waiting for her to move towards Ernest, touch him to show her solidarity—since it was clear that he'd stepped away from her only to avoid implicating her in what he was about to say. She didn't do it. Something about this struck Charlie as incredibly sad.

"Darby had shown me the ring one night when he'd been drinking, and told me some tale about King Solomon, and how his young niece or somebody had been able to make the ring work. And I thought, what a man could do in this world with a tame devil or two! I thought Darby was a fool and a coward not to be trying to use the thing himself, for the sake of the war effort."

"Beg pardon, sir," the sergeant interrupted. "A tame …"

"I know, I know," said Ernest, who didn't appear to have heard him. "I'd cracked up and lost perspective, I see that now. It was after—after Daphne was nearly killed in the Blitz. She wasn't hurt—it was just a very near thing, that was all. It was the thought of losing her that sent me over the edge. And then being told to take a leave, not to keep working—I mean, that was the last straw! I *wanted* to keep on, taking a rest was the *last* thing I wanted. So when I heard about this supernatural business of Darby's, of course I went after it like a shot. And it sounded decent, as these things go—not the least whiff of Faust or selling souls or anything about it. I thought it'd be all right.

"I recruited Leo, as I said, by telling him what a fabulous collection Darby had, and he hired someone to do the actual burglary for us—he's not literally a thief himself, just a fence or whatever you call it. I said I only wanted the ring, and he could take what he wanted of the rest, but when he heard the story about the ring, he wanted to help me try it out. So that's what we were doing when Evvie wandered in."

"Yes," said Father Underhill, glancing at the police officers, "we know this part."

"Oh, did she remember it after all? That was my idea, getting her to forget." He didn't seem able to look at Evvie. "I thought it might be the most merciful option. I wasn't interested in murdering people, or … that kind of thing. To be honest, after that first night, I didn't want any more to do with any of it. I was the one who talked Leo into giving the ring to Josie Good for safekeeping, since she seemed so keen to have it. I said we weren't going to use it any more, it was too dangerous. And he was fixated on what he could do to that one he'd got trapped in his ghastly Etruscan sarcophagus. The … thing that Evvie had summoned. Leo was so sure it was a devil, but I don't know. I don't know what was wrong with Leo. In the end, I'm not surprised that angel killed him."

Both policemen were now looking at Ernest with very worried expressions. Father Underhill sighed.

*

Charlie remembered the glimpse he had got of Hal's injuries, through the gashes in the front of his alb: the skin gaping open around a raw, red cavern where vital organs should have been. He felt like that now. Ripped open. Hollowed out.

"He's out there somewhere," he said to Father Underhill, "regretting that. Tying himself into knots with guilt over it. I know he is. And I can't get to him to talk sense into him. Of course it wasn't right, what he did, but it was pretty damn understandable—I don't know anyone who wouldn't have dropped that son of a bitch in the same situation." *Except maybe you*, he thought, looking at the priest.

But Father Underhill just nodded. "Mind you, one might say he would be justified in holding himself to a higher standard."

"No, he wouldn't! Not when all he had to work with was a human body with no memory."

"Yes, fair enough. Where might he have gone?"

"I have no idea. It's as if I didn't know him, because there was so little to know. He has no past, no … no place in the world. He's just—he was just himself, here, in the present." *Filling up my life with light and warmth, needing me, letting me care for him.*

And I believed him when he said he might be a devil.

"I wonder," said Father Underhill, "if perhaps it's not a matter of looking for him, so much as being where he can find you, when he thinks to look himself. And if perhaps … 'where he can find you' doesn't necessarily mean a place." He winced. "Could I be more vague and cryptic, I wonder?"

"It's okay," Charlie forced out around the tightness in his throat. "I understand."

He didn't, though. It was taking all his energy just then to keep from breaking down. He didn't even know why he was trying so hard; it wouldn't have been the first time Father Underhill had seen him cry.

"Maybe this is what I mean," said Father Underhill, clearly not believing him. "You found Hal the first time because you tried to pray, right?"

"Yeah," said Charlie wearily. "I get it. 'Don't lose your faith over this.' I won't. I don't think I will."

From the look on Father Underhill's face, he still hadn't understood him.

"Charlie … feel whatever you feel. There's no point in trying to be dishonest with yourself, much less with God. Just don't cut yourself off."

"From …"

"Love." He said it as though it should have been obvious.

"Oh. No. Okay."

"And by 'love' I mean God. I mean … your mixed-up angel. I mean me." He was silent for a moment. "Right?"

"Right," said Charlie, and by this time he had started to cry.

Chapter Twenty-Seven

FROM WHENCE THEY CAME

"Was it very awful?" Evvie asked Sara, in the back seat of Father Burgess's car again. "With Daphne?"

Sara shrugged. "Not *very* awful, no."

"What did she do?"

"Oh, you know. Tried to talk me into killing myself. The usual. I'd have flung myself out of the car right away—before she started driving, I mean—only I could barely see from the migraine fireworks going off in my eyes. Somehow I knew from the start what was going on. I don't think it's the ring I'm allergic to at all—I think it's the devils themselves. Droll, isn't it? Allergic to evil. It probably wasn't the ring that bothered me in Cousin Graham's house, but the soup tureen. Speaking of which, how is it that they were only able to possess Miss Good after she was dead, but Daphne was possessed alive? Do we know why that is?"

"Are you talking to me?" said her father.

"I hope so," said Evvie.

"Well, I don't know. They don't actually cover this stuff in seminary." He drummed his fingers on the steering wheel thoughtfully. "We might suppose the spirits had gained in strength in the interim, or that they had grown desperate—but I'm afraid Daphne must also have made herself easy to possess."

"She wasn't … drastically different, possessed," said Sara. "That's an awful thing to say."

"I know what you mean, though," said Evvie. "And Leo, who was the most responsible, in a way—he was never possessed at all. He just … did what he did because he wanted to."

"When I was in the car with Daphne," Sara said, "I just kept talking, the entire time—that was my strategy, just to keep talking until the rest of you caught up with me. I knew you would. The thing is, Daphne—I mean Thingigummy, Legion—still thought of me as Fee St. Clair. And it wasn't actually too difficult to come up with reasons why Fee wouldn't want to kill herself. Her brother Calvin would have been heartbroken, you know, and his fiancée Mindy, my soon-to-be sister-in-law—I don't believe I ever told you about Mindy, Evgenia. A major player in Fee's life, Mindy, as it turns out. Very pretty, too, in spite of her glass eye."

"Glass eye?"

"Yes, I had to give her a glass eye, to counter some remark about wooden legs. Poor Mindy. But she's very practical, in some ways, very no-nonsense, almost ruthless—I think she does it on purpose, to kind of put a curb on her mystical tendencies. You see, the secret to making your cover story convincing is to use bits of real life mixed in among the make-believe. That way it's easier to … to inhabit it—it feels more real to you."

"I see." Evvie smiled, understanding that the bit of real life mixed in with the make-believe of glass-eyed Mindy was her, her own ruthlessness and her mystical tendencies. "That makes sense."

"I don't mean to sound prideful, but I didn't feel nearly at the end of my resources when you and Father got to me. What I mean to say is, you were very quick. I'm awfully lucky."

Evvie leaned across the cramped back seat to hug her. "I'm so glad you're safe."

"Evgenia," said Father Underhill, "when the war is over, can we take you home?"

"To London, you mean?"

"No," said Sara. "We mean Patmos. Father and I talked about it last night. I remember you said it was getting back there that was the main difficulty, and that you don't need your mom and stepdad's permission."

"Though we'll go by way of Oxford, of course," said Father Underhill, with a look of mock severity for his daughter. "So that you may take your leave."

"Obviously," said Sara, rolling her eyes, "because she's a dutiful daughter."

Evvie thought about that: going back to Patmos now, not hanging around in England while her mother and stepfather tried to talk her out of it again. She thought about the delight of travelling for weeks more with Sara and her father, showing them Patmos and the places she had called home. What would it be like there, after the years of war? Would the worldly beauty of the place remain? Should she care about that? She knew that she did, but she didn't know what that meant.

"I don't know how to thank you," she said finally.

It didn't seem to escape either of them that this was not exactly a "Yes."

*

They ended up back at the Feathers in Newingthorpe that night. Father Underhill, Sara, Charlie, and Evvie sat around a table by the front window. The landlady seemed to know Charlie, and asked anxiously after someone named Henry.

"I don't really know," said Charlie, looking very tired. "He had to take off."

Their meal was eaten mostly in weary silence. Even Sara was quiet, worn out by the events of the day and looking ready to fall asleep in her chair. Evvie sat across the table from Charlie, and she looked at him from time to time, when he was not looking at her, and thought about what had happened between them. He had walked into her vision. He had taken care to let her know that he had been really there, and she was glad he had. But she couldn't help wondering about it: not why it had happened, but what she should do now, since it had. She felt she owed him something, and had no idea how to repay it.

She wondered if he thought she felt superior to him, because her love for the world didn't include the same kind of desire that he felt—didn't include anything like it. But she didn't feel superior to him at all, and she wished she knew how to tell him that. Then she wondered whether she was jealous of him.

For a moment it seemed like an absurd thought, and then, as she looked at it longer—while literally, she was staring at a carrot on her plate—it made perfect sense. She remembered Sara saying, "I expect you'll have noticed I'm very possessive." Evvie had said she was the same way, and she was. She was jealous of Charlie because her angel had been his, too, had shared something with him that she would never share with anyone, that didn't even make very much sense to her.

She knew she needed to try to say something to him. Not *that*, exactly, but something. Because having been recognized, the feeling of jealousy dissolved into something much nicer: a kind of amusement with herself for being a girl who could feel possessive about an angel. She wondered if having walked out with an angel and then broken with him because he'd been keeping secrets—whether that might feel at all similar.

She found her moment to speak to him when he got up to go out and start the car. She followed him out the door, and he looked back as if he knew she had something to say.

"You reached for him," Evvie said. "When he was on the roof. After he dropped Leo."

"Yeah, I did, didn't I?" He looked at the ground and left it at that.

"I wondered why."

"Yeah … me too. I guess it must have been weakness. Right?"

"Weakness?" she repeated. "Are you sure it wasn't love?"

He looked at her. "Love again, huh? Well. Could be. That is how I think of it."

She wanted suddenly to be a prophetic voice telling him that it was the only way to think of it, but she was aware that she was just a girl, much younger than he, and there was no reason for him to think she knew anything about it. There was no reason for *her* to think it. She pictured a future when she was old and wise and could command authority when she spoke to men like him, when she could be that prophetic, compassionate voice. It wasn't a vision, just an image she conjured up before her mind's eye, but she knew as she saw it that the path to that day lay through the monastery doors.

Coming back to the present, she said, more uncertainly than she would have liked: "Well—that means something, doesn't it?"

He smiled. "Maybe." And after a moment he added, "Thanks. If you should see him again, tell him I'm sorry? Not sorry that I forgave him. Sorry I didn't do it sooner."

"I expect he knows."

*

Evvie left England in early June, with Sara and her father. Sara was walking with her prosthetic leg by then, though she still needed a stick to lean on. She had kept her boy's haircut. Evvie's mother and stepfather had both liked her, in their different ways, when she came to stay with them in Oxford, though Aphrodite and Hero hadn't known quite what to make of her. Now she stood at the rail in stylish trousers and a light cardigan, as the ship made its slow turn out of the harbour, and they waved to Evvie's family on the dock.

They had made their good-byes in Yorkshire weeks before. Charlie Boult was still with his squadron, but after he was demobilized he planned to stay in England and join a team restoring bomb-damaged churches.

"Well, that makes more sense," Rosalind had said, when it was explained to her that Charlie was really an architect in civilian life.

"I never understood how a baker got an officer's commission, even if he is Canadian."

Rosalind and Latham had set a date for their wedding, and Ernest had filed for a divorce. Nobody else was sure that either of those things was for the best, but for now, all four of them seemed happy.

Other people were happy too. Anderson had gone home to his fiancée, and Captain Carter had proposed to a girl who worked in the tea room in Towton Hoe, and she had accepted. Lord Rathburn had returned home from London, and a funeral had finally been held in Warwickshire for Graham Darby. Sara and her father had attended. King Solomon's ring had been returned, along with the other stolen artifacts, to rejoin the collection that Darby had willed to the British Museum, where it would be put in storage because of its uncertain provenance. "Safest place for it," Father Underhill had said. "Probably."

He joined them at the rail; he had been helping a family of fellow passengers with their luggage. The ship's trajectory had all but stolen the view of the watchers on the dock.

"Hal was short for something," said Sara, out of the blue. "When I was little, I mean."

"Henry?" her father suggested, leaning on the rail and taking the sudden introduction of the topic in stride. They had not spoken of the angel in a long time.

"No … something else. A made-up name."

"Oh, yes," he said. "I think I remember that. I seem to recall saying, 'You could call him Hal for short.' I can't remember what the name was, though."

"I can't remember, either. I just wonder …"

"Mm?"

"I wonder if it was made up after all. I wonder if it isn't his real name."

He didn't say anything for a while. Evvie looked out at the widening harbour. Just when she had begun to think of something else, and was about to change the subject, Father Underhill said to his daughter, "When we get home, you should ask your mother."

EPILOGUE

I watched him from across the nave of the cathedral. He was sitting by the base of a column, making a careful sketch of some part of a stained-glass window. From where I stood, I could not see what he drew, but I watched him glance up towards the window as he worked. There was an angel in the window, but it did not look like me, and I thought it more likely that he was sketching the shape of the tracery or some other architectural detail. I was aware of every movement of his body: the small motions of his hand and wrist across the sketchbook's page, the tilt of his head, the shifting of shoulders and spine as he rearranged his posture on the stone floor. I found the specificity of him beautiful, as I had ever since I began to love him.

My intention in that moment was to watch him only for a short time, to assure myself that he was not unhappy—not too unhappy—and then to leave without speaking to him. I thought it was something I might do from time to time, an idea I think I had assembled from hints in the novels loaned to me by the landlady of the Feathers. In one of them, a mother had assured her young son that his guardian angel watched over him always. In another, a high-minded man had made a great production of separating himself from the woman he loved for her own good. This was supposed to indicate his reformed character, but in truth he had had a good deal less to reproach himself with, in his prior conduct towards the woman, and his behaviour in the world in general, than I had.

As I watched Charles sketch, I realized that my idea was a stupid one, in the same way that those novels were stupid. I couldn't see Charles in the role of either the young boy of the one book or the heroine of the other. And that was telling. I could watch him from a distance in self-denying love, and maybe that would better for him than any alternative. But maybe it wouldn't. What I couldn't do was pretend that I knew.

I crossed the nave to him. I leaned one shoulder against the column, letting my shadow fall across the page where he had, as I'd guessed, been sketching the cathedral's stonework. He looked up.

ACKNOWLEDGEMENTS

I want to thank everyone who enthusiastically greeted the release of *From All False Doctrine*, my first published novel, by coming out to the launch, by making the significant investment of time necessary to read all 500+ pages, and especially by telling me what you thought of it. I have a whole stockpile of comments to cherish, such as, "Your prose is worthy of the ideas you express," and "The ending felt like being punched in the stomach … in a good way," and "I'm in love with Elsa and Kit!!"

In launching my first book I was blessed with the support of two wonderful Anglo-Catholic parishes: my beloved St. Thomas's, and my new home-away-from-home of St. Bartholomew's, Regent Park. I want to thank everyone in both places (and elsewhere) who has asked, in the course of the last year, "How's your writing going?" or "When will the next book be out?" I love these questions even when I don't know exactly how to answer them.

As always, I am deeply indebted to my dear friends Alexandra and Victoria, who read early drafts of *Neither Have I Wings*, made brilliant suggestions, and kept me going through the tricky parts. I don't seem able to kill my characters without being told to do so by my friends; this time it was Alexandra who effectively sealed Leo's fate with her advice.

Thanks once again to Pat Kennedy for her gracious editorial assistance, and for encouraging me to go back to the drawing-board at a point when I thought I was nearly finished. Thanks to Fr. Walter Hannam for all his encouragement and for suggesting the title of Henley's under-appreciated book. The real title, I mean, not any of Charlie's variations. Thanks to Jim MacMillan for helping me to avoid some egregious factual errors; any egregious factual errors that remain are *my fault entirely*.

Finally, as always, abundant, overflowing thanks to my family for all the ways they have encouraged and supported me, and to my husband, Mike, the best possible partner.

ABOUT THE AUTHOR

Alice Degan is an academic, novelist, and Anglo-Catholic living in Toronto with her divinity-student husband. She studies and teaches medieval literature, and writes fantasy and something she likes to call metaphysical romance.

You can follow her and sign up to her newsletter to hear about new releases at: **www.alicedegan.com**.